Praise for Banana Bay

Banana Bay was a Local Best-Seller in Boston in 2004

"Banana Bay is a great read with an unrelenting pace. Cindy Cody brings the country of Panamá to life with her elegant prose and insightful commentary. Move over Spenser, Carlotta and Brady—Matti Maitlan is in town."
—Al Blanchard, past President NE Chapter of Mystery Writers of America

"In Cindy Cody's *Banana Bay*, readers are introduced to Matti Maitlin, an investigator for a Boston-based insurance company whose current case assignment finds her in the tropical paradise of Panamá. She must venture far into the depths of the jungle to find the shocking truth, but getting out won't be so easy in this action and suspense-filled mystery."
—Midwest Book Review

"You want to feel really good without opening the Jameson…two words: Cindy Cody. Her novels are the best feel good factor in the business…terrific narrative combined with gripping style."
—Ken Bruen, best-selling author, Edgar nominee for *Priest*.

"This book is full of adventure and suspense, thoughtful insight and romance. The dialogue flows naturally between the characters and the plot is a well thought out web of twists and turns. A delightful read you won't want to put down!"
—Book Review.com

"Cindy Cody's *Banana Bay* is a refreshing novel that takes you to the heart of Panamá. You won't be disappointed as you travel with Matti Maitlin into the heart of this lush country. Cody is a gifted writer."
—Lorna Schultz Nicholson, best-selling author

Banana Bay

CINDY CODY

BANANA BAY
A NOVEL

2008

Banana Bay

ACKNOWLEDGEMENTS

Though this is a work of fiction, I cannot invent the support I had in its creation. Thanks go to:

Lucho Nuques, *bananero supremo*, who took time from his busy schedule to give me an in-depth knowledge of the banana business from its earliest days. Lucho's gregarious, big-hearted nature inspired me to keep making all those research trips to Changuinola. Thank you, Lucho, for being so generous in time and spirit.

Laurie Kelliher is not only my best friend and my muse for Matti, but the series' most unflagging supporter. Thank you, Laurie, for reading my words again and again, and for your enduring support and friendship.

Neil McCluskey, Ph.D, my first agent, was one of my earliest champions. Thank you, Neil, for believing in me, and for encouraging me to "write the next one" while I was waiting for my career as a published novelist to begin.

In the gone, but not forgotten category, love and credit go to my father, Harry Ellis, whose love of words and reading obviously rubbed off. My dad—no shrinking violet about making a point—bought a hundred dollar dictionary in the early sixties and propped it open on a stand in the living room.

"Look it up!" he liked to say, between sips of his martini while reading the latest Isaac Asimov. In perfect synchronistic counterpoint, my mother's nurturing love and voluminous reading to me also had a tremendous impact, as did all those weekly trips to the library. Thanks, mum, for teaching me that reading can be so much fun, and that being cozy with a good book is one of life's great pleasures.

Paul Cody, my soul mate and husband for the past thirty years has been a constant believer in my ability whose support has never faltered. Paul's love and devotion are like sun and water to the seed of my creativity; our marriage has been one, great, loving, ever-changing adventure. Thank you, Paul, for traveling through this life with me. You truly are a prince.

For Janet and Vicky, constant lights. And for Paul, my oldest flame.

Row, row, row your boat
Gently down the stream
Merrily, merrily, merrily, merrily
Life is but a dream.

Children's chain song, anonymous

CHAPTER 1
Boston, Massachusetts

Matti looked at the Megabucks sign scrawled in purple magic marker taped to the wall at the Watta Week Mini Mart: "130 **MILLION BANANAS THIS WEEK!**" and felt herself slide into a netherworld between dreaming and reality.

Was the owner of the banana plantation in Panamá kidnapped, or was he lying senseless under a banana tree? Did he have amnesia, or did he run away with the Frutas Tropicales poster girl?

"Wanna bag for the coffees?" the cashier asked. He was new and had a disturbing resemblance to her ex-husband.

"Umm. Okay…but just for one of them." Early morning indecisiveness too—she was really on a roll now. Her caseload was already loaded with the exotic and nefarious and the stress could make her heart thrum. *Insurance Investigator Has Meltdown at Mini Mart Before Morning Coffee.*

But worse than ending up in a padded room, Matti thought, was that Sam might finally decide she belonged inside, chained to a desk.

She hip checked her way out the door while two men in a phone company truck watched her. Why hadn't she put both coffees in the bag, for God's sake? Now she had to put them both on the hood of the car, and look for the keys in the bowels of her bag.

"Hey honey!" the driver of the truck called out. "Need a hand?" They both started clapping.

She gave them a withering look, and couldn't get the clicker to work. *Dead battery?* She began sorting through the keys looking for the one which would open the door.

The men were enjoying themselves now. But what they saw: a well-endowed blonde in a summer suit and heels, wasn't the whole package. They couldn't see behind the sunglasses that her eyes had just turned a more vivid shade of green. Or know that because of a delay at the gynecologist's office, she was already late for a committee review about a missing banana baron. Neither knew that beneath the suit she had shoulders that looked more like Tom Brady's than Michelle Pfieffer's, or that she swam ten miles a week and had a short fuse, compliments of her Irish father.

Maybe it was her aura—or the set of her jaw—but when she looked up again, they'd backed up and gone.

***

She arrived at Atlas before ten. The traffic had been murderous, as usual, even post- Big Dig, thanks to the fact that the Southeast Expressway, all the way to Rockland was still obsolete. She headed up 3A from Hull to Neponset Circle to avoid the nightmare, wishing she'd taken the commuter boat from Hingham to Rowe's Wharf, instead.

Fortunately, she was among the lucky few whose company provided paid, secure parking just a short walk from its offices. She turned into the familiar narrow lot wedged between two towering office buildings, jumped out, and threw Chili Wong her keys like she always did when she was in a hurry.

"Hey, Miss Matti," he said, grinning at her. Sam, president of Atlas, and a detail man, had bought him a navy uniform to wear, and the epaulets slumped off his skinny shoulders while the matching peaked cap was pulled so low over his eyes he had to tilt his head back to see anything. Chili, an Italian-Chinese, had worked for Atlas longer than she had, and they could nearly read each other's minds.

"Okay you late. So what? Big meeting today?"

"Committee review."

"Uh-oh. Mr. Sam don't like to start meetings late."

"Thanks for reminding me." She raced down the sidewalk as a warm September wind whipped around her knees, then sped through the marble foyer of 75 State—a short-cut—and into the nearby lobby of Atlas's own older building at 52 State. The eight stories of prime Boston real estate were another legacy from Sam Adamson's grandmother, Katherine. The company used the four top floors itself. The lower four were rented to a re-insurance company; on the street level high-rent retail space was occupied by Hair by Luis, The Gap, the Edelweiss Café, and a Bertucci's restaurant.

She got out on seven, and walked briskly to her office, a perfectly turned out executive woman. Who'd guess she'd had an early morning exam with Dr. Smart?

Ashley wasn't at her desk. Matti left the bag with the other coffee on her PA's blotter and went into her office, swung herself into a chair and simultaneously picked up the phone, the adrenaline thrumming now. "I'm late," she said into the receiver. And then: "Oh good. No one told me that. Eleven is perfect."

She inhaled deeply, vowing she'd cut down on the caffeine. Really. She was going to order decaf next time. Or half decaf.

"Thanks for the coffee," Ashley said, leaning in through the door. She had a very big smile on her face, Matti thought.

"De nada."

"I heard an espresso cart is coming to the building, courtesy of Sam the Man. Our very own mainline caffeine."

"Great," Matti said, thinking of how luscious coffee was the way they made it in Europe; decaf was as much of a non-starter in those countries as non-alcoholic beer.

She picked up the Frutas Tropicales file, and felt herself calming down. She was comfortable sitting at this desk in this office with these familiar monsters: claimants, lawyers, litigants, and files thicker than the Sunday Globe.

She was prepared for the committee review but liked to have a few minutes before hand to go over the facts one last time.

"Call the attorney on the banana case again, Ashley? See when he's free."

She adjusted her large glasses framed today in granite-simulated flecks of gray, blue and mauve, and began preparing her preparatory remarks when she looked up and saw the claims manager heading her way.

"Shit," she said under her breath, and tried to smile as he strode through her door without knocking.

"Good morning, Matilda," he said. He had on another one of his Hermès ties today, and a cashmere jacket that would have set her back a mortgage payment.

"Good morning, Richard."

"Everything okay?"

"Fine, just fine." In contrast, Richard didn't look fine at all. Positively twitchy, her British friends would say. Matti judged a lot about Richard by how much he patted and preened himself. If he began pulling his mustache, she'd discovered, it was a particularly bad sign.

"I heard the committee review was rescheduled."

"Yes." What the *hell* did he want? She sipped her coffee and waited.

"Listen," he blurted, "You're prepared on this banana case?"

"As prepared as I can be, given what I've got so far."

"Right. Well, let me know if there's anything you need from me. Talked to the attorney yet?"

"No. I've just asked Ashley to set up a conference call."

"Good. Good," Richard said. He couldn't leave his hair alone. "Look," he said. "Would you like to come for dinner on Saturday?"

"Well...sure," Matti said. The shock of the invitation, and the timing, had caught her off guard. In the several years they'd worked together Matti had never been to Richard's home or socialized with him outside of the office. Theirs was strictly an office relationship: a claims manager and claims investigator for an international insurance company working to save the company's premium dollars whenever possible. Matti traveled frequently while Richard was mostly Boston-bound. They didn't do lunch or drinks.

Matti's memory flashed to a picture of Richard's wife from the last office Christmas party. She was a wound-up little blonde, very petite and perky who laughed with her head thrown back.

"What time?"

"Sevenish? There'll be about a dozen of us. My wife thought we'd have lamb." He looked at her uncertainly.

"Lamb sounds great." Again she waited. For all his apparent temerity, Richard could be incredibly blunt. His management style was to throw you a quick hard pass then sit back and see if you caught it.

"So. Will you go to Panamá?"

"Too soon to tell."

"The attorney will probably force the issue, so be prepared. The family will want a quick settlement. They've hired a corporate referral from Miami and he's the high-priced spread. Just keep me informed, okay? We wouldn't want to upset the apple cart with Frutas Tropicales." He snorted out a laugh, and Matti gave him a tight smile. What a dork!

"I'll keep you clued in," she said. They both knew she had a large degree of autonomy in her position as one of the company's only three investigators. She'd been offered Richard's job before he'd been hired, and turned it down.

"Good," he said, his face was still flushed from laughing. Matti thought of the word suave, but the way her father used to pronounce it as a joke about certain people: "swave."

"See you in a few minutes in the conference room," he said, brushing invisible lint from his sleeve. "I'll confirm with Carol Ann that you'll be coming on Saturday."

"I look forward to it," Matti said. *Like a bikini wax.*

CHAPTER 2

The conference room was monitored by video loop during all meetings, a long-ago requisite of William Porter Adamson, founder and former president of Atlas International. Willy P, as he was fondly known, was officially retired, but could still be seen jogging through reception and up the stairs to his former office to occasionally visit his son, Sam, president for the last five years.

"Just checking in," he'd say smiling and waving at everyone as he avoided the elevator, and bounded up the stairs in white running shoes.

The conference room he'd inaugurated hadn't changed since his departure. It was an innocuous-looking cream room with a long oak table, seventeen adjustable kid leather chairs, and a large oil portrait of Willy P's mother, Katherine, a former stenographer who'd re-started Atlas in the early forties after her former boss—unable to meet his obligations—closed it in 1939.

When everyone had been seated, Sam, Katherine's forty-five-year-old grandson, pushed the button to activate the system and began. "Good morning everybody. We have five cases for committee review this morning, so let's get started. Emeline, will you start?"

A tall elegant woman with flame red hair and pale skin addressed the group in French-accented English. "Thank you, Samuel. Yes. We have the case still pending of the Formula

One driver, Franz Meyers. It appears he has indeed had permanent damage to the spinal column and partial damage to his liver. He'll never drive again, and never walk unless a means is found to repair catastrophic nerve damage." She paused, letting everyone digest this fact. "I have all the doctors' and surgeons' reports now on file from Germany and they all concur. I suggest we lump sum it for permanent disability. It has cost the company to date $834,590 for hospital bills and paraplegic equipment, and he is coming up to his medical ceiling of one million dollars. We need to establish what his permanent disability is worth. The careers of these drivers are, of course, short-lived."

"How old is he?" the analyst Bruce wanted to know.

"Twenty-eight."

"Average career span of a race-car driver?" Everyone looked at Susan, the actuarial expert.

"Six years, though Mansel pushed it up. We can safely argue a top end of six."

"Well then," Richard doodled on a paper in front of him. "Six years, at a base salary of $250,000 plus sponsorships of up to $100,000 is the agreed cap?"

"Yes" Emeline confirmed.

"And then there's the rest of his life," Richard added.

"With payouts reduced to present value, which is?" Sam asked, looking through his papers.

"A million max on med, with permanent and partial disability also of one million."

Everyone turned and looked at the company's legal counsel, a swarthy-complected man with a thin layer of hair and shirt cuffs monogrammed BH. Brandon Howard wore an oversized onyx-and-diamond ring on the pinkie finger of a hand that was nearly always drumming a hard surface. Everyone was captivated by this gesture, even those who'd been watching it for years.

"Well," he said doing a final thump. "We can argue that the lump sum we pay him will *yield* him one million, but his attorney probably won't find this acceptable. Superman only got a million, and we know from all the media on him that this was a drop in the bucket to cover this kind of bodily injury. I'll start with three quarters of a mil, but I don't think I have much of a chance of getting this accepted. The kid is completely disabled."

"We'll settle this out of court," Sam said. It was a statement of fact. "This is a high-profile case involving a young German race car driver who's been tragically cut down at the height of his career. I can see the headlines now. Every day we don't settle is another day we risk negative exposure in the international press."

Everyone nodded, Emeline more vigorously than the others. As manager of Atlas's London office, she handled many high-visibility cases and didn't want the payout bungled. She could then have public relations write up a press release saying how quickly and willingly Atlas had paid out, giving the impression that the company was more philanthropic than corporate. Even tragedies like this which were ostensibly a loss to the company could be converted into an asset. As a result of a quick payout on the Meyers case, several race car drivers could be relied upon to begin paying Atlas the hefty premiums it demanded for this kind of coverage.

"I'll make our offer to the claimant's counsel this morning which will be afternoon in Germany," he paused, "after the wine, Wiener schnitzel, and whipped cream torte." Everyone around the table smiled. Brandon, a Jew of German descent, had a passion for northern European food.

"Right. Let's move on," Sam said. He had an MBA from Harvard and his management style was brisk and precise. A fit and well-built six feet, he wore half glasses for reading, and his tie was slightly loose at the collar. His jacket was permanently attached to the chair behind him.

They moved through three more cases in rapid succession. The Italian opera singer who'd lost his voice and therefore had to cancel four sold-out concerts. The theft of a 92' Cheoy Lee motor yacht in the Bahamas, which was headed in all likelihood to South America or possibly Africa. European insurers had collaborated to establish a maritime network with agents in every port from Skye to Sardinia which was quickly becoming worldwide. A well-informed crook would avoid the Straits of Gibraltar like a tidal wave. In these days of computer communication, the yacht had more than an eight-five percent chance of being recovered. The company would then salvage it and resell it to recoup a percentage from the total loss paid out. Perhaps the original owner would bid on it through a straw; perhaps the insured had set up the scam from the beginning. It was Matti's job to unravel the story, find out the truth, then pay or deny the claim.

Sam moved quickly along to Matti's case: Ramón Cardozo, missing banana baron.

"Matti?" Sam asked. "What updates have you got?"

"I'll be speaking with the insured's counsel soon, but the information I have is as follows. We're carrying a life insurance policy with a kidnapping and ransom or K&R endorsement worth a potential two million dollars on Ramón Cardozo, majority shareholder and president of Frutas Tropicales S.A., a privately-held company."

"Frutas Tropicales is one of the largest independent banana producers in Central America, and an APC, Atlas Preferred

Client, with premium billings of over $10,000 monthly. The policy stipulates payout within one year in the case of a missing person believed dead of one million. Kidnap/ransom scenarios are also covered. In this case a ransom demand of up to two million is the limit of our liability; death by natural causes is a million, accidental death two. Mr. Cardozo has been missing for three weeks, and the family is pressing for early payout through their attorney citing accidental death. The attorney is trying to make the case for a kidnapping/murder scenario, though there's no note, no ransom demand, and no body.

"The policy has been in force for three and a half years, and all premiums have been paid up to date. I believe that early action on this could work in our favor. Mr. Cardozo's personal and corporate coverages through Atlas make him an important client, and I believe a personal visit will work in our favor." Matti consulted her notes. "If I go to Panamá, I'll be able to verify evidence that could evaporate in six months' time. If the insured suddenly returns after a bout of amnesia, we're heroes because we showed up. If a kidnapping *has* taken place, we need to try and establish what happened. " She looked around the table. "In spite of the lack of evidence, the family insists this is what happened, and they're demanding payment under the terms of the policy."

Brandon Howard began drumming. "No witnesses? You mean he was kidnapped three weeks ago, and no one saw it happen? I don't like the fact that there's no ransom note, and even less that there's no body. Hell, even Robert Maxwell popped to the surface eventually."

"That's just one aspect of the case that's disturbing. Platanillo is apparently a small town where Sr. Cardozo, or Papi, as they call him, is an extremely visible man. Frutas Tropicales drives the whole economy of the area according to the agent.

On the morning of August 22nd, the insured rose, shaved, worked out on his rowing machine, and ate a light breakfast according to a statement from the insured's wife."

"Bananas?" Bruce asked, and everyone laughed.

Matti smiled. "I couldn't say, Bruce. Maybe he only had the Rice Krispies. In any case, he drove himself to work as he did every morning and everyone interviewed says he was in good spirits and there was nothing out of the ordinary. At one p.m. or thereabouts, he left for lunch which he generally ate at a local restaurant with his son. He never showed up there or at home. No one ever saw him again."

"And now they want their moola," Brandon interjected.

"You've got it," Matti answered. "There's no proof of what happened, but the family is assuming he's dead, and not by natural causes, which makes it accidental death—a double indemnity situation for us. Their lawyer pressed this point home in his letter to us last week: Papi Cardozo is dead by misadventure. The problem is, as I've stated already, they've got no evidence to back up the claim. If Mr. Cardozo had a heart attack and died of natural causes, it wouldn't be a double payout under the terms of the policy."

Brandon nodded vigorously at this. "Anything missing? Suitcase, clothes, money?"

"According to the lawyer, no, but I still haven't seen a police report," Matti said. "And if it *is* a kidnapping or a scam of some type, we can't forget that the family could be in a position to substantially influence the police report. Platanillo was built around the Cardozo company in the early 1960's according to background information provided by a Miami agent who's managing this policy. Frutas Tropicales *is* Platanillo."

"The Panamá version of All *in the Family?*" Bruce loved to clown, and Matti was surprised when Richard reacted.

"I doubt it," he said indignantly, and everyone turned his way. "It just so happens, I know Ramon Cardozo, Jr., the insured's son. Ramón, *hijo*. He's an old school friend of mine, and I know his family. They certainly don't seem like scammers to me." He pressed on. "They're extremely wealthy people who simply want justice done. They've lost their father and Doña Violeta has lost her husband." He began looking around the table for support and found everyone gaping at him.

Sam broke the silence in a dead calm voice. "Richard, it sounds to me as if you have a personal interest in this case. You seem to know quite a lot, in fact, about the family's feelings on the whole subject."

Matti winced inwardly to see the blush start at Richard's collar, and rise to his face like destiny fulfilling itself.

"Well," Richard stammered, "well, yes. As I said, I'm an old school friend of Ramón's. As claims manager, it's only natural that I try and resolve..."

"Ahem," Brandon took the floor again looking at Richard as though he were the school principal and Richard a misbehaving student sent to his office for discipline. "Conflict of interest," he declared, wagging his finger back and forth.

"Don't you talk down to me you—"

"You what?" Brandon wanted to know.

"Oh Christ, stop it you two. Richard, you're off the case. Matti will report to both Brandon and me on this. This can't be allowed, and you know it. You know your ethics on this better than anyone, Richard. All I need is the Insurance Commission doing a full investigation on top of every other problem we're facing here. We're talking millions of dollars here, Richard. Millions. Matti, when you've made your travel arrangements let me know."

Everyone looked down at their files, like schoolchildren. Being called to task by Sam in front of the committee was something that rarely happened. Richard's face, reflecting this, was too painful to consider. Luckily, they had more business on the docket.

Everyone had filed out of the conference room, when Sam asked, "Free for lunch?"

"Sure," Matti said, trying to keep her tone business-like. "What time?"

"About 1:30? Why don't I meet you at that little Greek place on India Street, if that's okay. I've got to pick up something en route."

***

At 1:45 he hadn't shown up, and Matti was just thinking she'd order, when he rushed through the door and slid onto the bench seat facing her. She tried not to look too happy to see him.

"Sorry I'm late."

"Don't worry. I'm glad you suggested this. I haven't had a Greek salad in ages."

"A beer?" he asked, "or something else?"

"Why not? I'll have a glass of retsina, go for the ethnic experience."

She looked down at her menu, and when she looked up suddenly, he was watching her. Then he looked down at his menu avoiding her eyes, and she watched him. *Oh boy.*

"So," he said, finally. "That was some performance today from Richard."

"Yes, it was," Matti said.

"I don't feel comfortable with Richard, and never have. I wish I could've convinced you to take the job."

"Well, you know me. I just love to be bossed around by other people." She smiled at him.

"Seriously, Matti. Aren't you getting tired of being on the road? Chasing down information in Third World countries, dealing with claims that are sometimes fraudulent? How would it look if I had to pay you off for a workman's comp claim one day?" Sam smiled making the apostrophes on either side of his mouth deepen and his eyes sparkle. *Damn.*

To distract herself from the smile, Matti looked at her placemat. It said 'Greetings from Mykonos' in several languages. "You didn't invite me to lunch to tempt me to sit at a desk, did you?"

"You know you're my most valuable player as an investigator, Matti." Sam's cheeks were slightly pocked from well-healed acne scars, and she felt an increase in tenderness for him because of it. He also looked worried, in spite of the smile. She had a sudden urge to reach out and stroke him on the cheek, reassure him.

"Are you worried about this banana case?"

"It's a big exposure but we've had worse years, I suppose."

"And the re-insurance?"

"It doesn't cover us across the board. The problem is, we need the big premiums to keep things growing, and we get the biggest ones from buying the biggest risks. Look at Lloyd's. Hard to believe that a company that once insured Betty Grable's legs could have a debt-relief plan of over three billion pounds."

"Two million dollars is still a big pay out—for anyone."

"Yes, and thank God the investment department's having a good year." He sipped his beer, while Matti toyed with the stem of her wine glass.

"The new computer analyst seems to be tightening things up," she said, trying to cheer him up. Sam's fear that Atlas would fail was greater than his fear that it wouldn't grow, which was also substantial. Atlas was an anomaly, a private-held company writing selective high-risk insurance for an international market. A small company with balls of steel, as Willy P had put it on more than one occasion.

Now the reins were fully in Sam's hands. It had to be an awesome responsibility waking up every morning and knowing your whole family's past and future fortunes were riding on the decisions you made.

Matti wondered who else he talked to about his concerns. Ever since The Kiss, she'd laid down some ground rules, though. Sam's personal life was just that. Nothing to do with her. The Kiss had been simply a glitch, a mistake, Benny and the Jets on the juke box, and too much Chianti after lunch. They'd both apologized to each other the next day. She'd been married to Adrian then, and he to Judith. He still to Judith.

It had been a fleeting moment that was now firmly buried in the past. Why did it sometimes play in her head then, like one of those continuous-feed videos?

Sam and Judith, from what she'd observed, seemed to be happily married. Judith, a Radcliffe grad and patent attorney was also the mother of Sam's two sons. They'd been married for sixteen years. In the mentoring department, Sam had a strong, nurturing relationship with his father who'd run the business for thirty years. On top of that, Howard Brandon, Sam's normal lunch partner, was a close friend who'd been on Atlas's staff for more than two decades. Sam played racquetball twice a week with his best friend, Arnold and had many other interests which kept him busy and happy, including coaching hockey for his youngest son's team.

Atlas was in sound financial shape, she knew. So why did Sam suddenly seem so distracted and unhappy? After the food arrived, she thought she'd make a stab at it.

"How's Judith?" she asked him.

"She's fine," he said, not looking up.

"And the kids?"

"Fine too." He finally looked at her. He reached for his drink and continued looking at her. She focused with great interest on her salad.

"This looks good," she said.

"It certainly does." He'd put his drink down, but kept looking at her.

Eventually, he picked up his fork and began eating too. Nothing more of any consequence was said and neither one of them wanted to develop the thread of their conversation. They talked about the Patriots, and the weather. They ordered coffee and drank it and went back to the office.

CHAPTER 3

Matti stopped at the club in Hingham for a swim on her way home. Forty-five minutes later, she washed off the chlorine, conditioned her hair, and pulled on her well-worn jogging suit. The night air was Indian-summer mild, reminding her of school starting all over again.

She headed home, glad that she'd chosen to live in Hull. The sea view from her condo was both spectacular and soothing, and there was a nice little hometown feel leftover from the days when Hull meant Nantasket Beach and bingo games, the roller coaster, and the Jungle Ride. Now the antique carousel had been restored and was historically protected in its own building. Where there had once been hoards of tourists eating salt-water taffy, there were now sedate seaside restaurants, upscale bars, and new condos, such as hers.

She pulled into a drive behind a carved sign that said: White Crest, Residences and parked her 2-year old Pathfinder in the underground parking garage. She got out on five, and opened the door, balancing groceries. As a welcome, Bunny, her white-haired cat jumped out at her from behind the door and attacked her feet.

Matti picked her up, and settled her across her shoulders—the closest she'd ever come to an ermine collar. But as Matti bent down to pick up the cat dish the phone rang, surprising them both. Bunny's claws went out as Matti straightened up, and they both let out a yowl as the animal jumped to the floor and skittered out of the room.

"Hey." It was Brian Donnelly, her upstairs neighbor and close friend. "How goes the life of the working girl?"

"Just great if you like to come home after a hard day to be attacked by your cat."

"Can't you train that animal to *stay?*"

"'Fraid not. But if I do a remake of Pet Semetary up here, I'll let you know. "

"Speaking of Kings, his highness and I wondered if you were free to come up for a drink. I've got enough puff pastry up here to make a body cast."

"Let me feed Claw Girl, and I'll be right up."

Matti put out some food for Bunny, who was still hiding, and freshened up quickly. After her bizarre lunch with Sam, she needed talk. Patrick McDougal, a 60ish rogue with a thick mane of white hair, and merry blue eyes, had an easy laugh and manner that was a perfect counterpoint to Brian's black Irish coloring, sharp wit and relative youth of 47. They'd met in South Boston a dozen years earlier, and survived a dual beating in an Irish pub, several incidents of hate mail, and one instance of car graffiti, before deciding to "head south…away from the proletariat," as Patrick put it.

Hull was the perfect choice. For the price of half a duplex in Southie, here they owned a spectacular vaulted-ceiling penthouse—the only one in the area. Though Hull would never be mistaken as an upper-crust community, Patrick's once-thriving Boston antiques business had rebounded beautifully in snooty Hingham, and Brian had converted their sterile new home into something out of AD. The eight-foot windows were hung with tapestry drapes that crushed themselves on parquet floors layered with antique oriental rugs. The dark mahogany furniture, heavy, rare pieces, were covered with *objets d'art*, silver salvers, candelabras, crystal vases always full of heavy displays of flowers, peonies being a particular favorite. It was like a cross between a downsized five-star European hotel lobby and a cozy museum that served drinks; a great place to hang out and enjoy the stimulating company of these two men who had become like family to her.

She kicked off her shoes as she usually did at their front door. In the sensuous environment of Patrick and Brian's penthouse, where all the finer things in life were displayed and enjoyed, it simply felt more proper to be shoeless and get into the mood of the place immediately.

"Darling Matilda," Patrick greeted her by taking her hands in his, and kissing them. "You look a treat."

In the kitchen, came the sounds of pots and pans banging. "What are you doing out there, Brian?" Patrick asked in a jolly voice. "It's only us commoners out here, not visiting royalty."

"Ha!" Brian said. "Since when did you start drinking gin out of a tea cup?"

Patrick shook his head. "And what will it be for you my dear? A tot of mother's ruin or a bit of the chilled Pinot G?"

Matti had just taken her first swallow of wine when Brian came gliding out of the kitchen with a doilied silver tray covered with assorted puffed treasures. "Tonight we have the béchamel and ham, the chicken liver and gherkin, the smoked trout or the plain Gruyère. Leave the fish 'til last or it will ruin everything else," he said proffering the tray.

"So tell us," Patrick said when the tray had gone around. "How was your day?"

"Mine? Oh...the usual," Matti said, getting in the mood. "An invite from the big drip Richard. Another invite and lunch with a wonderfully *non*-drippy guy, and a new case to be settled on a missing banana baron from Panamá." Matti loved to get her ya-yas out up here. The confidentiality was absolute on both sides, though she'd never named clients' names—a complete no-no. The fact was, her friends had helped her on more than one case with their well-reasoned insights and non-insurance views.

"Banana baron?" Brian repeated, his puff pastry poised in the air.

"The *missing* banana baron," Patrick corrected, swallowing his tidbit in one gulp. "Sounds like soap opera material."

"And what do you think of the invite from Richard? Is he a dark horse, or what?"

"Well," Patrick said with a gleam in his eye. "The old scoundrel's up to something. Will his wife be there?"

Matti smirked. "Presumably she'll be in full view, as it's a dinner party at her home."

"So...what's he after?" Brian asked. "It sounds like he wants something more than a little nookie. There's always the office for that."

"God Brian, you really are *seedy*," Matti told him. "And besides, Richard's not my type, as if you didn't know. Talk about anal retentive. Yuck!"

They looked at each other knowingly, and then back at her.

"And what would Dr. Freud say about the one who *is* your type, I wonder?" Patrick said, burying his smile behind a tidbit of ham and béchamel.

"I'm not telling," Matti said, crossing her arms and looking at them slyly. "I'm not saying another word."

"Stonewalling us again," Patrick said to Brian.

"I noticed. Must have showed us too many cards already."

"I'll tell you he's over six feet tall and has sparkly blue eyes."

"Sounds like *my* type," Brian interjected dryly, and Patrick shot him a look.

"Will he be at the dinner on Saturday?"

"God, no!"

"Then it will just be you and Richard the..."

"And probably a dozen other people! Stop teasing you two," Matti said. "Seriously, I hope this party will loosen him up. He's so...so uncool. And he's blushing more than ever."

"He must be a deeply embarrassed man," Patrick said, draining his drink.

"Maybe," Matti said. Patrick's observations always made the obvious seem more so.

"Enough about that old bore Richard." Patrick said, getting up and filling their glasses. "Tell us about this banana baron. He sounds like quite an exotic species."

"There's not much to tell except that he seems to have disappeared into the ozone, and the family thinks he's dead."

"Well is he or isn't he?" Brian asked.

"That's the problem, we just don't know—yet. There's no body, no witnesses, and no evidence to speak of."

"So in other words, it's just your run-of-the-mill life insurance scam."

"I doubt it. All I do know is that this insured had a big number on his head, an even bigger personal fortune, and a company with almost 2,000 employees."

"My God," said Patrick. "A business that size would make me want to run far, far away."

"That's what's so weird. How can someone so visible just evaporate? The entire town where the company is located is like *his* company for all intents and purposes. So, where could he hide? Where could he run?"

"He had many enemies," Patrick said in his Eliot Ness voice.

"And his enemies hated him," Brian tried to continue, but broke up instead.

"Maybe. Or maybe you're right. It was all too much. He wanted to leave. Just get away from it all...." she shrugged.

"Nancy Drew," Brian admonished her. "Nancy Drew could do better than that. She'd call her father, the all-knowing, always-supportive Carson Drew. Carson would send in a team of experts by helicopter."

"Very funny. But, seriously. We might deny the claim if he doesn't re-appear. We've got a year to decide."

"How can you do that?" Patrick wanted to know, "How can you deny a claim if the terms of the policy dictate pay out?"

"It is not simply a matter of denying the claim, but verifying everything. For example, if different family members' statements vary wildly, and I uncover evidence that there is concealment, or fraud, we can deny the claim and let the courts decide. Remember, the onus is on the claimants to at least show some proof that the policy is redeemable, not on us to prove it for them."

She sipped her wine. "Of course, we try and avoid litigation if we think we might lose. But sometimes a court battle is the only way to force the issue. Sometimes the legal process puts pressure on the claimants in a way that we can't. Sometimes the strain of a legal battle forces hidden information into the open."

"Sounds like legalized torture," Brian said.

"For some people, keeping a secret *is* torture," Patrick said pointedly. "And you ought to know."

"Well, I don't tell everyone *everything*," Brian said in mock defiance. "I didn't tell Matti she was invited to dinner, for instance."

"That's true, you didn't."

"You're going to eat dinner after all this?" Matti said.

"You can watch if you want to. Some people prefer to watch," Patrick the mischief-maker said. "Though it was never *my* thing."

CHAPTER 4

Matti decided if she was going to slaughter Carol Ann's lamb, she'd do it in style. She went to the mall to find some new heels, and bought a gorgeous raw silk plum-colored shawl, instead. Then she went to the club to do laps. Getting into a bathing suit post-summer was a constant reminder she had thighs, and helped check her craving for a chocolate-filled croissant to go with her morning coffee.

As Matti slipped into a channel in the pool, she noticed a new man doing laps. But with his goggles on, she couldn't see him clearly. She glided forward breathing out of the side of her mouth at regular intervals, and began to feel her body give in to the familiar rhythm: chunk, chunk, chunk, breathe, chunk, chunk, chunk, breathe.

She'd been an avid swimmer all her life. Red Cross swimming lessons were mandatory in Scituate where she'd grown up, and every summer morning at 7.30 the whole of her grade-school neighborhood could be found on the beach, ears bright red, huddled together in their soggy towels. She'd gotten her Senior Lifesaving Certificate at 16, and was a certified scuba diver a year later. After a summer as a lifeguard on Minot Beach and many tropical vacations, the swimming habit was hers for life.

After forty-five minutes she pulled herself up onto the pool's edge. The windows looking out to the tennis courts were steamed up, but Matti could see the outline of players lobbing the balls back and forth in the golden sunshine. The gently lapping sounds of the pool echoed in the vaulted ceiling and she perched on the edge of the pool to better catch a glimpse of her swimming companion.

He was still moving, gliding, breathing, and then suddenly at the end of the length he too pulled himself out, pulled off his goggles and smiled at her. Matti smiled back at him. He was a dark-haired man who obviously used Grecian Formula, and was old enough to be her father. Oh well. She went to the changing rooms. It had been more than two years since her divorce from Adrian and she was just getting really interested in men again—Sam being the notable exception to any general statement she made about the opposite sex. Funny, she thought, how being married to a man who cheated on you with his 16-year old students could make you feel skeptical about men in general.

She drove back home, hungry and ready for a nap. With Bunny prancing around her dish like a *prima donna*, Matti drizzled in a little cod liver oil mixed with dry food to keep the peace, and nuked herself some of Brian's leftover appetizers. She took out her black sheath and hung it on the door; she'd never make it as a contestant on *The Bachelor*, but with the plum shawl and the opera-length Mallorcan pearls, it was perfect to get her into Richard's home—and out again before eleven. She expected it to be a boring evening, but what the hell. She could imagine her mother's retort to this line of thinking; Lillian's thought processes seemed permanently frozen in the fifties: "Get out of the house, dear. Remember, every invitation is a potential opportunity to meet a man!" And get married, and have some grandchildren! Matti mentally added.

She couldn't imagine meeting anyone at Richard's house. Didn't dorks have dorky friends? She thought it was a hundred percent likely they did.

At 7:00, dressed, made-up and spritzed with scent, Matti slid into the low-slung '81 pale green Corvette, the only vestige of her marriage to Adrian. He'd gotten the house because she didn't want to live inside those walls ever again, and wanted to divorce him as quickly as legally possible. She got the car, because driving it made her feel so happy it should have been illegal.

The Pathfinder beckoned in the next parking space, a decidedly more conservative and quieter choice. The Vette hadn't been run in a while though, and it was a beautiful September evening for taking it out. Matti pressed her foot on the accelerator, revving the motor. The car growled and she laughed out loud to hear the sound, and at herself for liking it so much.

She drove the back roads to Cohasset, and arrived twenty minutes later at Richard's home. Like the man himself, Richard's house was a study in careful grooming: a slate gray mansard colonial with white trim and scalloped roof tiles set on a leafy one-acre. His familiar classic maroon Jaguar sat gleaming in the drive. Family money, she thought. His or Carol Ann's?

The air was an elixir of fallen leaves heated up, the scent of which reminded her of being fourteen and getting her first kiss on a night just like this on Labor Day weekend, while a light breeze blew in from the Atlantic and touched her skin with brine. Inside the house she could hear small dogs barking.

The bell sounded heavily, as if it was alerting the residents of a grand manor, and Richard opened the door as if he'd been just steps away. The dogs were nowhere in sight. Probably tucked away for the duration of the party.

"Matti! You look lovely!" He gave her a quick, stiff hug.

"Thank you for having me. What a beautiful home."

He led her down a hall which was decorated with careful, expensive landscapes, and into the living room where about eight other people were gathered. As she thought, Richard's friends looked like he did: well-dressed and conservative, like actors in a casting call for a particular type.

Carol Ann was standing on the edge of one cluster and broke away to greet her as Richard went to answer the door again.

"Matti! Thank you for coming," Carol Ann said, giving her an air kiss on one side of her face. "You get more beautiful every time I see you—I don't know how you manage it." Everyone turned expectantly around, and she found herself smiling graciously. Thank God for charm school.

A waiter came by and offered her cocktails on a tray, and she was surprised to see there were only two choices: Manhattans or martinis. She opted for the latter, thinking how this was how her parents used to entertain: with cocktails on trays, not a wine spritzer in sight. In the close distance, she could hear a piano being played. Did they really hire a pianist for such a small dinner party?

She smiled at her hostess and sipped her drink. Carol Ann, as Matti remembered, was a bit too bright and tense, more of a talker than a listener. She gabbled on for several minutes, then left to find about the hors d'oeuvres. Matti, left to her own devices, sidled over toward a table to put down her purse, took another few sips of icy gin, and wondered why she'd been invited. The whole group seemed well known to each other, like old friends, and she felt vaguely out of place, a single woman who was everyone's junior by at least ten years.

She easily wandered away as Richard returned with another couple, and a man called Eddie, who began to tell a joke as soon as he set foot in the room. Where was the piano music coming from?

Curious, she passed through from the living room into the dining room, and saw a pair of French doors leading out to another room from where the music emanated. It looked like a porch that had been converted into a glassed-in conservatory. She could see the edge of the baby grand from where she stood.

She put down her drink on the sideboard and went in. The room was lit only by candelabra, reminding Matti immediately of Liberace, and Lillian's great fondness for him. But this man was no Liberace but a handsome dark-haired Latino who was playing the *Moonlight Sonata* with his eyes closed. Too bad he was the hired help.

He ended the song, opened his eyes, and started to get out a cigarette before noticing her.

"Well, hello!" he said. His accent reminded her of leather—smooth but creaky.

"You play very well," Matti said. "I didn't mean to sneak up on you."

He laughed, then continued in Spanish-accented English, "The *Moonlight Sonata* is for children who want to impress their parents. I'll play for your something more suited to a woman of sophisticated taste." His brown eyes were laughing as he turned back to the keyboard and began playing *Malagueña*. Matti was shocked that he chose one of her favorite songs. It made her think of Andalusia and a far-off summer spent there studying Spanish.

"That was beautiful," she said when he'd finished, meaning it. "One of my favorite songs from a summer I spent in southern Spain years ago."

"Yes," he said, as though no further explanation was necessary. "My name is Ramón," he said coming forward, and she gave him her hand, which he bent his head over in classic style. "I'm a school friend of Richard's, also from years back. And you are?"

"Matti Maitlin, a colleague of Richard's from Atlas."

"Ah, Matti—at last. You've made quite an impression on Richard, I think. And now I see why." His smiling eyes never left her face.

Behind them, people were filing into the dining room.

"Shall we go in to dinner? I think Carol Ann is ready for us." Wine was being circulated now in the tray-worn fashion: two of white, two of red.

Well this was nice. She was going to have an escort after all. Someone nearly her own age, and drop-dead gorgeous to boot, who also happened to play the piano.

Richard, seeing them together, came forward with a big smile. "Well Matti, what do you think of our resident piano player, Ramón?" Oh my God, Matti suddenly thought, this wasn't the *same* Ramón, it couldn't be…

"Very talented," she said, giving Richard a penetrating look. She excused herself to go freshen up.

Locked in the safety of the bathroom, she leaned over the vanity and began talking to herself in the mirror.

"What are you going to do now, smarty pants? Is Richard crazy, deranged? Does he have a freaking career death wish? Jesus!" She vigorously brushed her hair, trying to decide on her next move. Should she bolt for the door? Confront Richard? Sit through the dinner and pretend nothing was wrong?

Five minutes of deep breaths later, she'd made her decision.

She walked back into the dining room just as Carol Ann was seating everyone. Her place was—surprise, surprise!—next to Ramón's, the beneficiary of a life insurance policy worth a potential two million dollars. Ramón Cardozo *hijo*, for God's sake! It could hardly be coincidental that Richard would invite them to the same party. *What a joke!*

She smiled at him as he helped her into her chair, smiled at everyone around her. More wine was served and the meal proceeded. Was this some kind of scam? She kept wondering. After the reprimand Richard had received from Sam, did he feel there was no longer a conflict in introducing an insurance investigator and claimant to cocktails and dinner? If Sam found out, Richard would probably be fired, and Matti wondered if she might be too.

Richard had totally gone over the line this time. This was one of the most flagrantly unethical moves she'd ever seen in all her years in the business.

As the conversation around the table became animated, Eddie dominating with joke after joke, Ramón the Innocent took the opportunity to speak to his tablemate in soft tones.

"I am sorry if you're upset," he said, Old World Charm oozing out of every pore. "This was never my intention."

Matti paused, not sure of how to proceed. "I'm sure Richard out of his fondness for your family thought our meeting was a good idea," she said, trying to keep her voice modulated. "It must be a terrible hardship for your family, Ramón, I understand that. But I'm shocked at Richard for arranging this. He could lose his job over this if his superiors find out."

"I don't think this will happen, Matti," he said, and gave her hand a pat before turning to the woman on his left. Matti felt herself bristle at his patronizing. This Ramón, son of the insured and now acting head of Frutas Tropicales—a big company with big assets—was obviously used to having the last word.

A decent interval after coffee was served in the living room, Matti made her move. "Thank you so much, Carol Ann, for the wonderful meal. You're not only an ace decorator, but an ace hostess. Everything was delicious." Richard rose, and she thanked him too giving him a look that said: We'll talk later.

Ramón also rose while everyone else, save Richard, remained seated.

"It's been nice meeting you all," she said to the room at large. "Good night."

"I'll escort Miss Maitlin to her car," Ramón said, taking Matti's elbow and guiding her purposefully from the room.

They had stepped into the balmy night air, Ramón behind her, his hand still on her elbow, when she turned to him, green eyes flashing.

"What exactly do you want, Ramón? My sympathy? A quick payout? Or were you hoping simple Latin charm would do the trick?" Manipulation in any form made her angrier than any other human failing, except outright betrayal, for which she had Adrian to thank.

"Matti, I'm sorry to see you angry and feel I must apologize. It was my mistake. You must not blame Richard—it was my idea to meet you. As you Americans say, it is a conflict of interest. But I have come to Boston to talk with you about my father—without the company lawyer. Can this be arranged?"

"Of course it can be arranged," Matti said. The anger had ebbed, but it was still there, a mad dog on a leash. "We need to speak about *all* the details of your father's disappearance, Ramón, it's critical to my investigation. But Frutas Tropicales has hired an attorney to represent your family in this case, and if he found out we are speaking directly about his case, he'd be livid."

"Then I'll have to fire him," Ramón said calmly, opening her car door. "There are many aspects of my father's disappearance that don't make sense. Things which even my own family doesn't know, or maybe they do. That's why I wanted to speak to you. I can help you investigate this better than anyone, Matti. You need me," he said, his eyes smiling, "as much as I need you."

Matti was surprised. Not many men would stand up to being skewered like a shish-kabob and come out smiling. And bottom line, he was right. No one's testimony would probably be more important to her case than that of the missing banana baron's oldest son.

"Could we meet late Monday? I'm returning to Panamá on Wednesday." He closed her door, grasped the window's edge. His intensity was starting to set her teeth on edge.

"Okay, Ramón. Call my office on Monday morning. Speak to Ashley. She'll set something up."

"Thank you, Matti," he told her, "and remember: Some things are not what they seem—not even death."

CHAPTER 5

Matti drove home in the dark, feeling the chill September evening wrap around her like a shroud. What did he mean, death wasn't what it seemed? This was obviously a reference to his father's disappearance. Ramón was an unknown, a man who had amused eyes and an easygoing manner. But what else made the man? And why did she have such trouble imagining people having dark motives?

She never saw Adrian's dark side either until it was too late. Maybe—let's be honest, here—she wasn't a very good judge of character at all! Adrian too, had been so magnetically male, that it blinded her to a side of his personality he simply kept concealed.

How long would it have taken her if she hadn't caught him? She drove and thought about it, the memories bursting through as she drove, like flipping through the pictures in a photo album.

Adrian at the charity costume party in Marshfield wearing a Miss Piggy mask, while the rest of him was dressed all in black, leather pants, the works. How he took off the mask and grinned at her, with his perfect square teeth. How they'd walked to the beach later that night, and how he loved the dunes like she did, how the moon shone on their skin, making everything so alive.

She recalled her father's lack of trust in him. Their quickly arranged marriage, everything rush, rush, rush. Why were they in such a big hurry?

A few months after their marriage she'd opened an envelope, anonymously sent, from a "friend" full of black and white stills of her husband, a former porn star, in various compromising positions, taken about ten years earlier, she guessed. He was thinner and his dark sideburns nearly reached his chin.

She remembered the tears, and remonstrations, her father suddenly dying in the middle of it of pancreatic cancer. And then right on the heels of that, the fateful call from someone named Alison, a 16-year-old dropout from Bromsfield High, whom she met in the parking lot of Burger King, who told her all about her meetings with Adrian, her former teacher, and how it was between them, and what he'd promised her, and now she was pregnant. "What am I going to do?" the child/woman wailed. "My parents are going to kill me!"

The therapist helped her see that her relationship to Adrian was no accident: two love addicts drawn to each other like kindling to flame. She'd made an error in judgment, a mistake. She insisted Matti re-examine her life, her motives, and then learn that even the most intelligent, rational people were subject to the laws of humanity. The key was forgiveness, she said. You must learn to forgive yourself.

Remembering, Matti turned up the heater in the car. She thought of Adrian, but couldn't remember the details of his face. The harder she tried, the more she kept seeing Ramón. *Damn.*

Did they really look so much alike? No. Ramón was more European with his dark hair slicked back, brown eyes, expensive scent, hand-made shirts. Monied, mannered, elegant and tall. Adrian was dark but with lake green eyes, a stockier and more rugged build, a man's man, and also—obviously—a woman's man. The perfect porn star. It was absurd, and so comic. And here she was laughing about it! Wow. Time really did heal all wounds, or wound all heels. Three years down the road, and one of the most painful experiences in her life had become like an episode out of *Friends*.

Maybe Ramón was right: nothing was as important as it first seemed, not death, nor marrying someone who turned out to be a narcissistic sex maniac.

She turned into the underground garage at White Crest with a smile on her face, walked into the peace of her condo with a sigh of relief, drank a big glass of water, and crawled into bed. Sometimes being single was so wonderful.

***

That night she dreamed of dolphins and whales swimming together in a synchronized dance as she sat on the dunes and watched. Some man she'd never seen before walked up and put a large pearl in her hand, and then a siren went off and the man ran away.

She woke up to the phone ringing, and glanced at the clock which read 8.38.

"'ello?" she asked. Who the hell would call at such an ungodly hour? Lillian?

"Matti?" the male voice was urgent, and she thought: Richard? And then knew it was him: Richard the Manipulative, the Conniving. Richard the Fixer Upper.

"Do you know what time it is?" Some people were so clueless.

"Oh. Did I wake you? Sorry, the bloody dogs start yapping around here at about six, and Sunday be damned." She didn't answer. Maybe if she waited long enough, he'd just hang up and she could go back to her dream, and the man with the pearl.

"Matti? Oh hell, listen I was going to call on the pretense of making sure you arrived home safely, but the real reason is to explain to you about last night. About Ramón, I mean."

"I'm listening," Matti said, her eyes still closed in the darkened room. She thought Richard sounded frightened.

"Look, I hope we can keep this between us. I mean, you're not going to mention this to Sam are you?"

"I really don't know, Richard," she said sleepily. Forget the dream now, or even going back to sleep. "Why don't you fill me in on your motive and we'll take it from there."

"Well, the thing is, Ramón asked me to invite you," he paused. "You know Ramón is an old friend, an old college friend who's been so good to me. I just couldn't turn him down when he asked me."

"Richard, how did Ramón even know who I was? When you organized the dinner party, did he say, 'Hey, invite one of the company's investigators along. It might be fun'?"

"No, no of course he didn't." Matti could hear the irritation in Richard's voice; he hated to have his authority challenged about anything.

"I told him you were the one assigned to his case, and he wanted to meet you. I didn't think it was a big deal. You'll be meeting him anyway in the course of the investigation."

"That's true. But surely you can see the ethical problem in socializing with the potential beneficiary of a two-million-dollar policy our company may have to pay." Silence. "Richard?"

"Look. They took me in during a time when my parents were divorcing, and became like my new family. I love Ramón like a…a brother, and of course I want to help the family in any way I can."

"Then stay out of it! Your involvement could create more problems for them not less. I'm going to forget that last night ever happened, Richard, and suggest you do the same. I'm passing it off as bad judgment on your part. Just please don't put me in that position again, okay? And listen, thanks again for dinner."

"I'm glad you came," Richard said, and there was recalcitrance in his voice. "Even though it *wasn't* the highest ethical road, as far as the insurance industry is concerned."

Matti thought: He just won't give up.

"Okay, Richard, see you Monday."

"Oh," he said, "that's the other reason I called. Ramón said he'd be calling you for an appointment on Monday, but he had to fly back to Panamá urgently. Some banana crisis."

Matti sighed. "Okay. I'll contact him when I go to Panamá. I imagine you've got his contact details, though I'll need to set up the interviews through the family's attorney."

"That's the other news. He's fired the attorney."

"Oh? And who's the new one?"

"He said that an attorney isn't necessary. You can come to Panamá, do your investigation and deal with the family directly."

"Is that a joke?"

"No. Apparently he wants to get to the bottom of his father's death as much as you do. He thinks a lawyer is going to complicate the situation."

"And what about the demand for early payout?"

"I really don't know. We didn't discuss it."

"Well, I wish I'd put the coffee on before we started this conversation."

"Listen. I'm sorry I called so early…"

"Don't worry about it, Richard, and I'm glad for the update. I'll see you in the office tomorrow then. Ciao." She hung up before he could add anything else.

She threw back the covers to get up, and Bunny, who'd been lying in wait under the edge of the bedspread, nipped her in the ankle, then scampered deep into jungle territory under the bed.

"Damn it, Bunny!" She was really going to have to get that cat some help, either that or a giant Tom cat. Being treated as her cat's only plaything was getting old.

Rio Teribe, Panamá/Costa Rican Border

I have no body. The body I did have, the body that was in my possession, is far, far below. I'm free now truly free.

The night sky is for dreamers and hunters, like me. I own the earth rich smell, the water flowing beneath me. It's mine. All mine. This is my home. This is where I belong.

The sea is not so far for someone who can fly. But why should I return? Why should I leave? The jungle is rich. The feeding is very rich here. Snakes and small rodents are everywhere. They know who I am. They know I am their destiny.

All things were important in their time, but now there is no time. For me now there is only the circle of this jungle, the moments of knowing, feeding, and flight. The Indians understand how it is for me. They understand perfectly. And that is why I am here. That is why I stay.

The hunter is hunted. I know this too. That is why I travel up here in the wind and clouds. Here I am the dominion of all I see. I am the leaf, the river, the sky. I am invisible, except at the moment of death. Then I am seen, but only for an instant.

Only for an instant do they see a blur of whiteness, my black gleaming eye.

CHAPTER 6

Matti spent a lazy, cloud-filled Sunday reading the Globe, having brunch at Brian and Patrick's, and filling them in about Richard, Ramón, and her case in Panamá. The next morning, in brilliant sunshine, she drove to work and pulled into the familiar shadows of the Atlas parking lot. Seeing Chili Wong always put a smile on her face. He always looked so happy the weekend was over so he could put on his uniform again.

Upstairs, Ashley was already at her desk, also looking happy. She had two tiny cups of espresso coffee covered with saucers to keep the contents hot. She passed Matti one. "You're gonna love it," she said. Sam had just installed an Italian-style *quiosco* in their small cafeteria, complete with a red, white and green awning, which had pastries from the North End and an espresso machine. Matti couldn't decide if she should shriek with glee, or register an official complaint. Especially about those sweet, ricotta-filled cannolis. Hadn't Sam ever heard of low carbs, for heaven's sake?

Maybe he just wanted to make sure they were all permanently buzzed on caffeine so they'd work harder. Matti sipped the foamy black liquid from her little espresso cup—no Styrofoam, either. Maybe he was going to ax the Christmas bonus instead.

"So," Ashley asked. "How was your weekend? And how was dinner at Richard's?"

"You just wouldn't believe it," Matti said. True to her promise, she didn't say more. "He and Carol Ann have got a beautiful home, the meal was great. Catered right down to the martinis."

"Wow." Ashley had learned early on as Matti's personal assistant that prying was not in her job description. She was a Katy Gibbs grad, and totally capable; if she had an urge to pry, she didn't show it.

"Anyway, I'm going to Panamá. Make the arrangements for me?"

"When?"

"Wednesday or Thursday. I can't get away before then. I'm hoping I can find out something; there's still no police report, and no body. But I'll need to get back quickly. If I miss my mother's birthday again this year she'll put me up for adoption."

"Is a week enough?"

"More than enough. I'll change it if necessary. Hopefully to earlier, not later."

"Hotel?"

"I don't know. I guess this Platanillo is a pretty small place, and probably very basic. I'll find something when I get there."

"Okay. Anything else you need?"

"According to Richard, the son of the insured has opted out of having legal representation."

"What?"

"That's what I said. I don't know where this might be leading, they're an APC so I need to go and do the PR no matter what."

"That's weird about the attorney," said Ashley.

"I know, but talk about feeling set free! It sure will make my job a helluva lot easier if I can take the family's statements without a high-priced attorney breathing down my neck. Richard said he had the contact details for the family. Once you've made the arrangements, you can notify them I'm coming."

"Notify the son?"

"Yes. Same name as the insured, but with "hijo" on the end, it's like our junior."

"Okay. I'll get right on it." They reviewed Matti's other cases in progress, though Ashley was already well briefed about each of them. They went over Matti's appointments for the period of her planned absence and Ashley swiftly took notes as Matti flicked through her calendar.

"So I guess that covers it for after I leave," she said finally. "I'll ask Brandon to meet with the plaintiff's attorney on the mudslide case, and see if they're ready to settle. Of course our driver was negligent as hell. Who in their right mind would park their 500 SL on the edge of a cliff in L.A. after a torrential rainstorm? Then the car saves him but kills that poor woman who was washing dishes in her own kitchen. Makes you wonder if there is a God."

"Shitith do happenith. By the way, Sam wants to see you. Said it was nothing urgent. Whenever you can. But I got the distinct impression he meant any time *this morning*. That kind of not urgent."

"I'll go up now, then," Matti said, "see if they've got the same perks we've got."

"Ha," said Ashley. "They've probably got tiny doughnuts, if I know Brandon. Little dipping size doughnuts to go with the dollhouse coffee cups."

When Matti arrived upstairs, Sam's secretary Muriel waved her right through. "He's waiting for you," she said, smiling and serene. What was Muriel's secret? Did she drink only green tea?

"Hi, Sam," she said, after a quick knock. She surreptitiously wiped her damp hand on her skirt.

"Hello, Matti." He got up, shook her hand absently and shut the door. "Sit down. Would you like one of our new coffees?" he asked.

"No thanks. I think I've had my caffeine quota for the day. It was a great idea, Sam, especially the cannolis." She rolled her eyes.

He laughed. "Everyone just seems to love the real coffee cups. Funny, isn't it, how a little thing like that improves morale?"

Matti let him run on, feeling his tension as well as her own. Did he know what had happened on Saturday night?

"Judith and I have separated," he said, dropping the bomb. But he looked as if he hadn't digested the news himself. It was not what she expected to hear on the way up to his office on a Monday morning.

"Oh, Sam. I'm sorry to hear that." Was she?

"It's so strange that you asked me about Judith during our lunch the other day. I knew it was coming, just didn't know when. When you've been living for years without…well. Judith is a fine person. It's just that somewhere between the college fun, and the birth of our first son, the flame died…there's no real explanation sometimes, you know?"

"I do know," she said, remembering Adrian. "Did you tell the kids?"

"Last night, assuring them of our love, how we'll spend time together as a family. The usual crap. It was awful."

"Sam, people grow apart. It's horrible when children are involved. I can't even imagine. We all have to do the best we can." She reached across the desk and squeezed the edge of his hand. "I feel for what you're going through. Believe me I do."

"I know you know," he said, looking at her. "I remember when you and Adrian split up, though you never talked about it much, at least to me. God, Matti, you've been such a good friend. I'd made up my mind not to tell you, but then...well, I guess I wanted you to know." He smiled at her in avuncular fashion, and seemed to change gears.

"The reason I *think* I called you up here this morning was to talk to you about the Frutas Tropicales case. I heard from Richard they've fired the attorney. I'd like you to get down there as soon as possible, Matti. They'll hire someone else, of course, as soon as they figure out the risks."

Richard *had* been busy; it wasn't even 11 a.m.

"Have you thought about your travel plans?" He leaned back in his chair, cradling the back of his head in his hands, watching her.

Seeing him in this pose made her stomach do flip flops. She could smell his starched shirt from here, the musky scent of Armani.

"I'm going to Panamá in a few days," she told him. "Ashley's making my arrangements now."

"For how long?"

"A week, maybe less."

"That's good."

"Don't get out the champagne yet. I've spoken to the son of the insured"—that was certainly not a lie—"and he wants to meet with me privately to give me his theory. But, remember, Sam, a team of his own security people has already conducted a *thorough* investigation according to the lawyer's letter, and turned up nothing."

"What?" Sam came forward in his chair. "Do you think the son—what's his name, Ramón—has some inside dope on the kidnapping angle?"

"That's what I need to find out. I'll be down there in a few days, and then I'll know more. But there's still no note, no one claiming responsibility. People are normally kidnapped for a ransom or held as a ransom against some action being taken."

"Unless someone wanted to simply remove him as an obstacle, or perhaps they're still getting ready to demand payout. You know, these executive kidnappings are getting so common, we're selling these K and R policies like six packs of beer."

"I've been reading that some of these kidnappers stay quiet for months. Remember those tourists in Costa Rica who were kidnapped by those Nicaraguan terrorists? They didn't even make their demands for six months."

"Don't remind me! Matti, I want you to stay in touch with this office, understand? Daily. Richard's not sticking his oar in, I hope."

"Oh no," Matti said, trying to give her eyes a transparent, innocent look. The truth of it was, she was a terrible liar.

"You're lying," Sam said at once. "Well he'd better stay clear of me because if I find out he's compromising either you or this company, I'll personally boot his ass out the door. I never liked his damned Hermes ties, anyway."

"Will do," Matti said. She was dying for a glass of water. "Don't worry about Richard. I'll stay in touch."

They shook hands again. "Thanks for being such a good friend, Matti," he said. "I mean it."

"You're welcome." With a pounding heart, she turned and walked through the door. How much more of Sam's one-on-one company would she be able to take?

She made a detour into the bathroom and looked at herself in the mirror. Her lipstick had disappeared, and her hair looked like clumps of spaghetti. *Great.*

She went down to her office and found Richard sitting inside, waiting. *Double great.*

Ashley said in a low voice, "I tried to convince him to wait outside."

Matti walked through the door and went behind her desk. Amazingly, he hadn't decided to sit in her chair, as well.

"What can I do for you, Richard?" she said, trying to keep her voice neutral.

"How did it go with Sam?" He looked worried.

"A promise is a promise, Richard. Let's move on."

Ashley came and put her itinerary on her desk. "Oh, I've go those contact numbers for Ramón." He handed her a piece of yellow-lined paper. On it were Ramón's home, fax and office numbers. There were also the names and numbers of several area hotels.

"You got me a list of hotels?" Now this was a first.

"Yes."

"Did you speak to Ramón already this morning?"

"Oh no. No."

"What? Did you find the hotels on the Internet?"

"No. But I know the area quite well." He looked at his manicure, smoothed his hair.

"You do?" Was there anything he didn't know where Frutas Tropicales was concerned?

"So you still visit the family," Matti said, wanting to close any potential loophole with a statement of fact.

"We *cubanos* stick together." He smiled easily.

"Cubano? You're Cuban?"

"Yes, originally."

"But you haven't got a trace of an accent. *¿Hablas español?*"

"*Absolutamente*, though not as fluently as I used to."

"So, should I start calling you *Ricardo?*" she teased, not knowing what else to say.

"As a matter of fact, that's my given name. My mother was Cuban, you see, my father, too. We Americanized our last name to Parker from Paredes, much easier, you see?"

"Of course," said Matti, though she felt very strange. Was he going to peel off his mustache next, or confess to streaking on weekends? "Well," she said finally, "which of these hotels would you recommend?"

"The Hotel Mariposa is the only option, really. Platanillo is a simple banana town. Pity the circumstances aren't different. The Carodozos have a magnificent ranch up on a hill. You'd be able to stay with them if things were different."

"Pity," Matti said. After he'd left, she took out her own pad of yellow paper and began making notes, lots and lots of notes so she could keep her head screwed on about this case and stop thinking about Sam's starched shirt, how his muscles showed just underneath, and also figure out how one man who'd led a company with 2,000 employees could just disappear in a little, tiny town surrounded by bananas.

CHAPTER 7

She bagged the swim after work, and went straight home. Made herself a cup of ginger tea, and settled with it onto the overstuffed settee. The yellow-and-blue print fabric had come from Provence, a gift from Patrick and Brian two Christmases ago. It made the perfect, cozy counterpoint to the chill over Boston Harbor which was now washed with a pink afterglow from the setting sun. Even Bunny, who was purring at her feet, seemed to like it.

She took a few yoga-style breaths, then picked up the phone.

"Hi, Mom."

"Matti! Well, I thought you'd flown the coop again. I just never know *when* I'm going to hear from you."

"Mom, you know I always call before going on a trip."

"Well, you didn't call me before going to San Francisco that time. And I was worried sick."

"That was three years ago, Mom." She took some more breaths. "Would you like to have dinner tonight?"

"At Jake's?" her mother asked. Lillian could be as sulky as a November rain; luckily it wasn't hard to coax her back into the light.

"Jake's is just what I had in mind," Matti said.

"Oh, honey, I'd love to. Will I meet you there?"

"Yes. It's five now, why don't we meet at seven."

"Perfect," her mother said, and Matti felt relieved, and a

little guilty that, at the bottom of it, Lillian was such an easy mark.

Next she called upstairs. "Hi there," she said to Brian, who always answered the phone.

"Are you home?"

"Yes."

"Can I come down?" he asked in a whispery tone.

"Of course, come now."

In five minutes, Brian was through the door. Matti gave him a hug and could see he was preoccupied. "Tea? Wine?"

"Oh, I guess so. A small glass of wine?"

"What's the matter?" she asked, as he followed her into the kitchen. She passed him a glass and began uncorking a bottle.

"Patrick," he nearly choked. "I think he's having an affair."

"What?" They returned and sat in the living room where the sunset had turned to a dark, brooding magenta.

"He's so distant lately. He's always gone for his morning walk, but now he stays away for two hours or more."

"So, you think he's having an affair *in the morning?*" she laughed lightly, trying to get him to see the humor in this, but he remained grim.

"I know it sounds far fetched, but when I ask him where he's been, he just lashes out at me. It's terrible. He's so angry, and won't tell me why, so naturally I feel it's something *I've* done. Oh God, I know I've got low self-esteem," he moaned, "but knowing it doesn't help."

"No, sometimes not," she said, restraining a smile.

"You know, I followed him one morning."

"You did?"

"Yes, I did," he said defensively. "And you know where he went? To the home of a *woman*, an *attractive* woman for God's sake!" and with that he put his face in his hands.

"Oh Brian, I'm sure it's not what it seems. I know Patrick loves you. You've been together more than fifteen years, haven't you?"

Brian nodded, and blew his nose.

"I want you to come up to dinner tomorrow night. I want you to see for yourself that I'm not making this up."

"Of course I will. I'd love to. I'm going to Panamá on Thursday and wanted to see you both before I left."

"Okay," Brian said. She gave him a hug, and Bunny suddenly jumped out of nowhere and nipped Brian jealously in the ankle before bounding out of the kitchen and out of sight.

"Ow! You damn killer cat."

"You see that? At least you've got someone to be jealous *of*. All I've got is a cat! And hey, remember to get all the facts before you react. Believe me, jumping to conclusions can have disastrous consequences. I'm in the business, remember?"

She arrived at Jake's to find her mother already seated in the booth nearest the door. She waved gaily as Matti walked in and Matti leaned over and gave her mother's pale, cool cheek a kiss. She sat down opposite her mother and and a waitress came over and filled their glasses with chunky iced water. Right behind the waitress Jake appeared with a pencil behind his ear and a big grin on his face.

"Let me guess: two Monday-night twin lobster specials— one boiled, one bake stuffed. Two glasses of the house wine, two more after you get started. One peanut butter pie and two forks to finish." He looked at them and they nodded, and he walked away yelling their order to the kitchen so the whole restaurant could hear.

"That man," her mother said, smiling. "That man has no manners."

"But you like his lobster."

"I do."

"He reminds me of Dad in a way." The waitress brought their wine so quickly, it was as if she had telepathy.

"Oh Matti! He's nothing like your father. Your father was never that much fun. Besides, Jake is Jewish, your father was Irish."

Uh oh, Matti thought, and took a sip of wine.

"But let's not rehash *that* one again," her mother said, surprising her. "At least he left you some money, and *she* didn't get it all."

"I wish I had him back, instead," Matti said.

"Thank God he wasn't completely kookoo," her mother said, ignoring this. "You were a good daughter, and you deserve what you got. And he always loved you so much. Remember when he bought you that pony from the fair? You cried after you'd ridden it, and didn't want to leave, and so he bought it for you right on the spot. Your father was capable of incredible generosity when the mood struck him. I only wish he'd paid more attention to Bob. Poor Bob. Bob was always in the shadows."

"How is Bob?" Matti asked, determined to stay clear of the minefield of her mother's recollections.

"Bob is doing as well as can be expected," her mother said, obviously irritated. "He sees Connie occasionally and is heartbroken they didn't have children even though their divorce is final. It's so sad. I guess in the grandchild department, there's not much hope for me either." She sighed but Matti didn't take the bait.

Their lobsters arrived, and Matti picked up her lobster cracker and attacked a claw. Lillian seemed to take the hint and gracefully changed the subject.

At the end of their meal, Matti paid the check, and they walked out into the chill air. As they approached her mother's car, Lillian unexpectedly grabbed her daughter's hand. "Matti, please don't feel badly about not having children on my account. I know how much your career means to you." Was she trying to bridge the gap, or just having another dig? It was hard to say.

Matti gave her a reassuring smile. In her mother's day a career had a connotation of danger and fast living, and existed in a separate compartment from the world of children and homemaking. It was a place where one wore a suit and women degraded themselves by having to "crawl up the corporate ladder", a favorite expression of Lillian's. Since Matti had been a girl she'd loved solving puzzles and getting to the bottom of things; her job was a natural extension of this. Children had nothing to do with it.

"I don't feel bad, Mom. Trust me." She kissed her mother on the cheek, knowing she thought she was being supportive, even if language and age got in the way.

"I'll call you when I get back from Panamá," Matti said, "and we'll do something special for your birthday."

"Oh good," her mother said. Lillian was as easy to please as a child, sometimes. "I'm so glad you'll be back by then. We'll do something fun." She got in her car and drove away still waving and looking happy. Matti thought how young her mother looked at almost sixty-five. Her life was as simple and compact as a hatbox, safe as a house.

Lillian's father, Malcolm had been a famous portrait painter whose originals hung in the Statehouse and the Museum of Fine Arts. Lillian still lived in the house where she'd grown up on Powder Point. She was an active member of the Historical Society of Duxbury, helped organize all the arts events, and lived off the interest from her father's estate.

Matti couldn't imagine a life like Lillian's. It seemed... well, so boring. Maybe she was a crisis addict, or maybe she just didn't want to pass her days handing out tickets to future art events, or buying all her Christmas presents a year in advance at the Lord and Taylor's after-Christmas sale. She'd already found out what marriage looked like.

She might not have a man in her life right now, but thank God she loved her job.

Rio Teribe, Panamá/Costa Rica Border

I am a force of nature, a man whose soul has flown away to merge again with the elements. I am the smoke that rises from the fire, the mist that rises from the jungle at dawn.

I hunger for life. The hunger is constant and hones me into what I have become: a ravaged beast, a desperate animal. They have captured me, and give me crumbs. What food is this for someone such as I? Who are these poor-spirited ones who would catch and subdue a rare being, and incarcerate him in a bamboo cage?

The sun burns down upon my wings. They give me shelter and water, but I need freedom more than either of these.

I curse these beings who think they are gods but are only greedy men, diminished by their cause. I curse them from the depths of my being. There will be retribution. Oh yes. There will be a mighty punishment. Of that there is no doubt.

The universe decrees: energy does not disappear. They have forgotten. They have tried to strip me of my spirit, but the energy is still here. Transmuted and reduced, perhaps, but still pulsing. Still breathing. Still alive.

CHAPTER 8

Tuesday morning the phone rang through from Ashley's desk to her own, and Matti was surprised to hear Ramón's voice on the other end. "Good morning, Matti. Have you made your travel plans yet?"

"Ramón—what a surprise. I don't have my itinerary in front of me, but I believe Ashley said that my connection from Panamá City to Platanillo leaves Thursday afternoon."

"And the flight here takes approximately one hour. You'll be arriving then on the 5:30 flight in Platanillo on Thursday."

"If you say so."

"There's only one flight daily," Ramón said with a light laugh. "Platanillo is very predictable, you'll see."

"I'll contact you when I arrive," Matti said, trying to sound serious. She'd had a flash of Ramón as he sat playing *Malagueña* in Richard's home, his strong hands moving up and down the keyboard with ease.

"So I am not allowed to pick you up at the airport, Matti? Well. I've made you a reservation at the Hotel Mariposa, and I was hoping you'd have dinner with me when you arrive." She could hear the frustration in his voice. "Otherwise you might have to settle for patacones and greasy chicken."

Matti thought again that Ramón Cardozo, *hijo* was a man used to getting his own way. "Patacones?"

"Plantain that's been flattened and fried."

"That doesn't sound bad, actually," Matti said.

"But not three times a day," he said, laughing. "Nobody can have a *steady* diet of *patacones*, not even a *paisano*. Not even Matti Maitlin." He found this funny, and continued to laugh.

"Ramón, I'm sure I won't starve. And let's not lose sight of why I'm coming down there. I need to have more facts about your father's disappearance."

"My father is dead," Ramón said, after a pause. She imagined the seriousness in his face, the brooding brown eyes switching between laughter and pain.

"Yes, I know that's your belief. But we need more information to proceed with the insurance side, and I hope you understand that. I'm coming on a duty. There'll be lots of diligence I need to do."

"I understand, Matti, of course I do. And I want to assist you in whatever way I can. Which means dinner when you get here, like it or not."

She didn't want to seem churlish or unkind. "Let's talk about dinner later, let's wait and see. Maybe when I'm through with my investigation you'll wish you never saw my face."

"I'd never wish that," Ramón said, and just as easy as that he was charming again.

"Do the other family members know I'm coming?"

"Yes," Ramón said. "But there are only two. Doña Violeta, my mother, and Dolores, my younger sister."

"Fine." She didn't mention she'd probably be having lengthy interviews with everyone connected with the case. "And the local police? I never received a copy of the police report. For some reason, your attorney didn't send it to me."

"I have one here in the office. I'll fax it through to you now."

"That would be helpful." She thought she might need to

make contact with a professional translator when she got there, but this would be something she arranged herself.

"Anything else you need from me?" The unstated intent behind this remark was left hanging like a bat from a tree. These Latin men—did they ever give up?

"Nothing right now, Ramón. You've been *more* than helpful."

"That's the nicest thing you've ever said to me," Ramón said, playing along. " I look forward to seeing you, Matti. *Hasta pronto!*" He laughed, and hung up.

The phone rang again, and Matti wished Ashley was at her desk to answer it. Everyone had taken to hanging around the espresso machine and socializing as if work were really like hanging out at Starbucks. It was stranger still, because Ashley had always tended to keep to herself, especially at work.

"Hello?" she said impatiently, picking up the receiver.

"It's me," Sam said.

"Sam."

"Matti, can we talk?"

"Of course. Should I come up there?"

"I've got a better idea," he said. "There's a new restaurant called La Opera I've been wanting to try. It's over in Braintree. You could go home after lunch, it's on your way home, more or less."

He had obviously given the matter some thought. "You're leaving on Thursday, right?"

Now how did he know that? "Yes, and I planned to take a half day tomorrow anyway to organize things before I go to Panamá." She thought of all she had to do at home. "Sam, how about this? Why don't you come to my place tomorrow? I'll make us lunch there, and then I can stay home and get packing. It's the best view around." She thought: Is this all a setup for The Kiss Number Two?

"I'd love to," he said, and they agreed he'd come at one.

Matti hung up as her mind raced. She'd spent the last three years obsessing over the clandestine kiss, a simple kiss, played over and over in her mind like a mini B-movie. How he'd pulled her into him, how she felt him growing against her. *Jesus!*

She was never going there again with Sam, no way! It had taken her too long to get the brief moment into some kind of perspective. She and Sam could never be a couple, there were just too many obstacles on both sides. He was separating from Judith, but she knew from experience that many couples who split eventually got back together. Age was another thing; he was ten years her senior, the owner of a company where she'd worked for fifteen years. She could see Brandon wagging his finger now: Conflict of interest! He had made his family, had his two sons. She didn't want to have a family, or maybe she did. The list went on and on.

No. She and Sam would be friends; they'd been friends for years. Why blow it? He'd be another male friend to add to her coterie. Why not? She thought of Sam's blue eyes as they'd bored into hers at their lunch the other day. It wouldn't be easy, but she'd had tougher assignments—like getting over her two-year marriage. She changed gears: This was a lunch, so what would she serve? Everyone loved her prosciutto and fig salad. She could make a crab pasta for the main course—without garlic? Should she serve wine? Maybe she should call Brian and get his advice.

"Coffee?" Ashley interrupted her reverie, with a tiny cup and a smile on her face.

"Oh. Yes. Great." Matti said, her mind doing a circuit of the planets.

Ashley sat down in front of Matti's desk, and they looked at each other, their eyes smiling.

"Do you need some more interview forms?"

"What?"

"The forms you use as a guideline to interview people," Ashley asked, omitting the "duh".

"Oh yes, those. Yes I will."

"Did Sam find you?"

At the sound of his name, Matti felt a mild jolt pass through her. "Yes, he just called."

"He was looking for you."

"Oh. Yes, he found me."

"That's good," Ashley said, still smiling. "That's good."

***

That evening she put on her turquoise Chinese lounging suit of baggy pants and shirt, slid on some sandals that she'd be leaving at the door anyway. She got out a jar of almond-stuffed olives, and a box of four Belgian chocolates from a recent first class upgrade, put them in a cute little bag and went to the elevator and up to Patrick and Brian's for dinner.

She rang the bell, slid off her sandals, glad she'd just gotten a pedicure. When Patrick opened the door, though, all thoughts of topcoats flew from her mind. Patrick looked completely worn down, something was wrong, very wrong, but what?

"Hello, Matti," he said tiredly, kissing her cheek absently. "Come in."

They walked into a hall that was twice the width of hers, past the kitchen which was oddly silent, and into the cavernous living room.

"I'm afraid Brian isn't here," he said. "Would you like a drink?"

"Yes, thank you."

"Join me in a martini?"

"We wouldn't want these to go to waste," she said holding up the olives.

"No, certainly not."

He went to the sideboard which was full of antique crystal decanters, and mixed their drinks and brought her hers with a weak smile. They sat in opposite chairs, as they usually did, and raised their glasses to each other. Matti took a sip, and remembered why drinking a silver bullet was something she did on rare occasions. A tiny thread of icy gin traveled to her head like a guided missile.

"Do you have any nibbles?" she asked. "I don't like drinking these on an empty stomach."

"Of course, Brian has a cupboard full. Will Goldfish be alright?"

"Perfect."

He left and came back with a small silver bowl, and placed it at her elbow, and she noticed he didn't have one for himself. This was one of Brian's idiosyncrasies, serving everything individually. "Don't you hate having to get up, and pass things around?" he always asked. Tonight the place seemed totally morgue-like without him.

"So where's Brian?" she asked.

"Oh, he's gone," Patrick said in a resigned way. "Said he couldn't take it anymore."

"Oh?"

"Yes. Seems he has some wild idea I'm having an affair with a woman. The whole idea is revolting, of course, but Brian isn't convinced." He leaned forward, looking sadder than she'd ever seen him. "Matti, I was married 30 years ago, and it was a disaster! Poor Linda, she was so devastated, so ashamed. She came from a very Catholic family, and of course none of them could accept that I was gay when I finally did come out. I think to this day Linda thinks it was all a ploy to somehow end the marriage. The truth of it was, I did love her in my fashion. It made it very difficult, you see, because I really did care about her."

"And Brian, knowing this, thinks you have taken up again with a woman?"

"That's exactly what he thinks. He's terribly insecure about our relationship, and frankly I don't know what more I can do to convince him. I've given him everything I have, including my love. What more is there?"

"Better communication?" Matti said simply. "Why not tell him you have no intention of getting involved with a woman now or ever? He seems to suspect you are."

"Ah, so he's been talking to you, has he?" Patrick was not inclined to raise his voice, but now two angry blotches began blossoming on his cheeks and Matti wondered how many drinks he'd had before her arrival.

"Brian is my friend, as you are," she said gently.

"Well, the little snoop! What has he been doing, following me?" Matti remained silent, waiting, waiting.

"Well, for your information, there *is* a woman in my life right now! But it's no one's business, not his, not yours, not anyone's," he announced. Patrick could be as cold and arrogant as a Tudor king when he put his mind to it.

"Patrick," Matti said calmly, "I certainly don't want to pry into your private life, just remember I'm not the enemy, okay? I care very much about you both. If you don't want to talk about this, it's okay with me."

"It's my daughter," he cried suddenly. "Mine and Linda's daughter! And I never knew she existed. Can you believe it?

A month ago I got a letter asking me to meet her. Can you believe she lives just over in Hingham? In Hingham! She's a beautiful young woman, smart and wonderful. She's recently married. Why should I expose her to my lifestyle? Why should I make her ashamed of me as I made Linda ashamed?" His outburst complete, Patrick bent over and began gasping and clutching his chest.

"My god, Patrick," Matti cried, jumping up and rushing to his side. Quickly she picked up the phone and jabbed 911, gave the address, Patrick's name and his condition.

At that precise moment Matti heard the key turn in the lock. Brian walked in and took in the scene, and sobbed out Patrick's name in shock. Together, they managed to get Patrick out of the chair and onto the floor in a flat position. Together they heard the sirens in the distance and waited for the ambulance to arrive.

Several hours later, Patrick, who'd had a heart attack, was in stable condition in the ICU at South Shore Hospital, and Matti went back to Hull in a cab. At 2 a.m., she finally crawled into bed feeling as if she'd been drugged. At 10:30 the next morning, she remembered Sam was coming for lunch and quickly got some vegetable lasagna out of the freezer, checked that she had salad ingredients, and ran out and got some fresh Portuguese bread, and chocolate mousse at the Flying Gourmand.

She took a long warm bath with aromatic bubble bath, and put cucumber eye gel on her lids to get rid of some of the puffiness. These men streaming into her life with their broken-hearted stories. Was she supposed to be a kind of agony aunt, a sympathetic outsider listening to stories of love and love's demons?

And now Sam was coming into her life. She'd give him lasagna. She'd be the good friend she'd always been to him. She'd listen and not judge. She would not—under any circumstances—kiss him.

She was towel-drying her hair when the phone rang. It was Lillian, asking about her itinerary to Panamá. She told her mother about Patrick, her night at the hospital.

"How terrible! Is there anything I can do?"

"No," Matti said, thinking of her mother trying to mother Patrick. "There's nothing anybody can do but wait. He's stable. I think he'll be okay."

"Thank God for that! I'll call Brian later; you're leaving tomorrow, right? And you'll be back on what date? I want to put it in my diary."

Lillian's diaries had been a constant in her life always. She kept the back copies like a historical record in the attic. Her mother too, had kept a daily diary; maybe it was part of a gene pool that had skipped Matti's generation.

"Next Wednesday, with any luck. What do you think about going into town for your birthday? We could start at Venezia's and then go to a show."

"That would be nice," her mother said. "What show?"

"Why don't you pick one out? Pay for the tickets and I'll reimburse you."

"I'll do just that! Now take *care* of yourself in Panamá, Matilda. Don't do anything foolish."

"I won't," Matti said, rolling her eyes. "Not a chance." Foolishness was a second-place winner behind having to work for a living in Lillian's book.

Next Matti called the hospital and learned Patrick's condition was still stable. She couldn't speak to Brian as there were no phones for patients or visitors in the ICU area. She left a message instead on Brian's voice mail giving him her travel details, and telling him she'd call later.

She packed; her tropical wardrobe consisted of a bunch of interchangeable cotton separates she'd bought at the Banana Republic. She threw in a rain slicker, a travel umbrella, and several pairs of cotton socks. She'd done plenty of time in tropical Latin climates, and knew that, in addition to the socks, sunscreen and insect repellent were a girl's best friends.

She called Kitty Kare next, and arranged for Bunny to be dropped off the following morning. Bunny was currently nowhere in sight, hiding to delay her trip to the kennel as long as possible. As soon as the suitcase came out, Bunny always disappeared.

"Bunny," Matti called half-heartedly. She looked under the bed, knowing that Bunny wouldn't be there. Knowing she wouldn't come out until coaxed out with her catnip mouse and a dab of anchovy paste.

She went through the motions of putting on makeup. This hadn't been her plan yesterday. Her plan yesterday had been to look drop-dead gorgeous but remain aloof and interesting—like fish bait. Ha! Patrick's attack had changed all that. Nothing like almost losing one of your favorite people in the world to see how shallow you really were!

Would Patrick's daughter come to see him? She'd meet Brian, of course, and then Patrick would be out of the closet all over again. She hoped for Patrick's sake, he'd opt for the truth, turn ruddy and full of life again, revert to his old, jolly self.

She remembered her father's own descent, how he'd instantly aged in the hospital: his skin dried out, cheeks sunken, his normally strong, freckled hands looking weak and exposed with their little tufts of silver hair.

She put on her lipstick and thought more about her father. It had been very sad to see him go down so fast; she still missed him terribly. She went into the closet and dug out the softest thing in her wardrobe, a velour jogging suit in pale mauve. So much for making a fashion statement.

It was after one, and she uncorked the wine. Suddenly Sam's lateness, Patrick's heart attack, even Bunny's hiding out seemed calculated to hurt her. Then the buzzer rang. This was going to be interesting, she thought, and found herself suddenly wanting to see Sam's face, have his company.

He came in the door, tie loose, jacket flapping around him, and held out a pale pink begonia. "Starting without me?" he asked, seeing her wine.

"It was quite a night," she said, holding the quivery, delicate flowers. Suddenly she wanted to cry. "A very sad thing happened...." She tried to sniff back the tears.

"Matti," Sam said, taking away the begonia, and pulling her in his arms and holding her while rocking her gently. "What happened?" The smell of his starched shirt, the lingering scent of Lagerfeld made her want to burrow into his chest. He looked into her eyes, and then kissed her long and deep.

"Wow," she said, when the kiss ended. "I swore we weren't going to do that." He smiled at her, and she poured him a glass of wine and excused herself.

"I can't believe it," she said, looking at herself in the bathroom mirror. "Oh my God," she said. The thing she'd feared had not only happened within the first three minutes of his walking in the door, she wanted him to do it again! She took out more eye gel and patted it on her lids before blowing her nose, putting on fresh lipstick, and fluffing her hair. With her swollen eyes, she looked like a sea perch going out on a date.

Sam was in the living room looking out at the view through the September drizzle when she came out. The day was gray, even the gulls seemed without purpose, sailing and dipping their wings on the conflicting wind currents. It all seemed suddenly so poignant though, where moments ago it had only been depressing.

Now Sam too seemed deep in thought, and as she came alongside him he reached behind her, put his arm around her waist and pulled her to his side. "A beautiful if dismal view," he said, kissing her on the cheek. "The view in here is much better."

"Sam..." she started, but he interrupted her.

"Let's not talk about us right now," he said. His blue eyes focused on her with attention and compassion. "Tell me what happened last night." They sat down on the settee.

She told him about going up for dinner, leaving out the part about the daughter and concentrating on the details of Patrick keeling over, what she'd felt seeing one of her best friends unconscious and close to dying.

"But the tears, were they all about Patrick?" Sam asked.

She explained about her father's death still haunting her, and how it had come in the midst of her divorce from Adrian.

"Ah, Adrian," Sam said. "You never really told me what happened between you two."

"Irreconcilable differences!" Matti said, smiling to keep him at bay. She needed time before she'd tell him the whole Adrian saga—if ever.

"What about you and Judith?"

"Changing the subject on me?" They walked into the kitchen and Sam topped up their wine while Matti took out the placemats and began to set the table in the little alcove.

"Judith is a great person. I mean that," Sam said. "But our marriage needs to end."

"Needs?" It seemed a strange way to put it.

"Irreconcilable differences," Sam said, smiling. "Let's leave it at that for now."

The timer went off, the lasagna was done, and she took out the salad bowl and began putting it together while Sam cut the bread.

They went into the dining area and sat down, and Matti realized she hadn't eaten the night before. Suddenly, she was ravenous.

They looked at each other over their glasses. "This is much better than going to a restaurant," Sam said. "Thank you."

"You're welcome."

"Being limited to one committee review a week isn't easy."

Matti looked at him and laughed. She felt exactly the same way. They cleared off the table, and went with coffee back to the settee. Everything was moving so fast; it was like the fantasy she'd always had.

He moved closer to her on the settee. Took the cup from her hand, stroked the hair back behind her ear. "I've never forgotten what happened, you know," he said. "I know it was several years ago, but I never forgot. In fact, the memory of that kiss keeps coming back to haunt me."

"I'm surprised," she managed to say.

"Why is that?"

"I thought I was the only one."

"Matti," he said, and enveloped her neck with his hand and looked her in the eyes. "I've made my share of mistakes, but how could I ever let you get away from me?" He kissed her as he had before, teasing her lips with his and making her flush with sexual heat.

"This is serious," he said after a minute, and they both laughed.

"Yes it is." She kissed him back. She couldn't escape the wonder of his face, his body, his being; desire lodged in her throat. Their passion was like a wave whose destiny is to crash on the beach—nothing was going to stand in its way.

"Ouch!" Sam sat back suddenly and shook his hand.

"Oh my God," Matti said, bolted upright too. "What happened?"

"Something bit me—I swear to God."

"Bunny…?"

"You have a *rabbit* in here?"

"No. Bunny is a cat. A devilish white cat whose behavior is only getting worse." Bunny hardly ever attacked anyone but her.

"They have animal psychologists now," Sam said laughing, as if he'd read her mind, rubbing the back of his hand. "Maybe it's time to check Bunny in."

That night Matti slept fitfully. In her dreams, Adrian chased her through a banana plantation with a Miss Piggy mask on. She tried to get away in her Corvette, but it wouldn't start. Then he took off his mask, but it wasn't Adrian but Sam. He kept trying to kiss her and he kept changing, Adrian one minute, Sam the next. Ramón walked by as if he were the accidental tourist. He was taking pictures with a camera, but it wasn't a camera, but a miniature piano. She finally woke up.

What was in that lasagna, anyway?

Bunny, for once, was purring at the end of the bed, contented and peaceful. What would've happened with Sam if

Bunny hadn't attacked him? The thought made her shiver. Hot milk was the answer. She got up and Bunny began padding around. Matti picked her up, feeling the cool, silky fur and draped her over her shoulder.

She got a heaping tablespoon of Haagen Daz Macadamia Brittle instead of the milk, leaned against the refrigerator and ate the ice cream lick by lick while Bunny purred at her feet.

She still hadn't spoken to Brian and was worried about Patrick. She called the hospital, and talked to someone in ICU who told her Patrick's condition had stabilized. That was a relief. Now she could worry about Sam instead. She got out another spoon of ice cream—three carbs maximum—and started licking again.

Sam had told her he was moving into a condo near the office. Would Matti start paying visits to him, and vice versa, now that he was single again? SBNQD, Single But Not Quite Divorced? The thought gave her a little shiver.

Sam and Judith had been married for fourteen years and had two children, Devon and Rory. There were major adjustments and adaptations to be made, Matti knew—strong feelings, like full moon tides, to be ridden out. She knew what he'd be going through.

As much as she wanted to know Sam—maybe even love him—she didn't want to start making commitments, even though he'd made it clear he had feelings for her. Could they keep it at the kissing stage until he got a divorce?

They hadn't discussed the office situation, and how a romance might impact their professional relationship. It did, obviously, have an impact, a substantial impact. But it was too soon to tell how much it would affect their futures. She mulled over a few more possibilities, got another spoon of ice cream, a total of 73 carbs for the day when you tallied up the bread and lasagna, and finally fell asleep on the sofa under her grandmother's afghan.

At four a.m. the alarm went off, and she woke up feeling rested and ready to go. She showered and dressed quickly, had coffee. Surprisingly, Bunny went into her cage without any resistance. Matti had a 7 a.m. flight to Miami, a quick connection to Panamá City and a late afternoon flight to Platanillo. It would be a long trip, but she'd wrap the case as quickly as possible and get back home. *Get back home to Sam*, she thought, in spite of wanting not to think like that. *Get back for Lillian's birthday.*

She dropped Bunny at Kitty Kare, took the Pathfinder to Logan Airport, and parked. She was dressed in layers that she would peel off as she went further south. She had her briefcase of notes and all her contact details. She was ready to leave her personal life behind and concentrate on her job.

She checked in through airport security with one carry-on and her massive leather shoulder bag that contained a thin briefcase. She had another coffee and ate the contents of a ham and cheese sandwich without the bread. She began reviewing the file and then the flight was called, and she went onboard.

An hour later, as she sat reviewing the police report Ramón had sent her, the telephone in her apartment rang 30,000 feet beneath her, and approximately 1,000 miles north. Voice mail picked it up.

"Ms. Maitlin? This is Dr. Smart's office calling," a woman's voice said. "Could you please contact us as soon as possible? Your Pap smear results are in, and the doctor would like to see you as soon as possible. Thank you.

CHAPTER 9
Platanillo, Panamá

Matti had read many police reports in her day. She'd seen the small town brief, the city formats, reports in French, Portuguese, and Spanish on different colored papers. Long reports and short ones. Reports full of detailed explanations and others which were merely extracts of a crime, or, in the case of a missing person, the description of the individual, familial details, and the place last seen.

In the case of Ramón "Papi" Cardozo, the police report was lengthy, signed and dated by a certain Bolivar Santamaria. Papi Cardozo was not an ordinary citizen; in fact, he was the most visible citizen Platanillo had. He was certainly the most influential. Frutas Tropicales had single-handedly created the local economy, the town, the tax base, and therefore the roads, the schools, the whole municipality.

Frutas Tropicales provided housing, water, electricity, health insurance, and even entertainment for its employees. No one would come to Central America in the early days and become a "*bananero*" for a mere salary. A lifestyle needed to be created and sustained, numerous benefits provided for any man or woman to be lured to the jungle to live.

Now, of course, many indigenous people drove the business in management positions for which Papi Cardozo had picked up the educational tab. Papi was not merely a corporate head, but as his name implied, father to the family of Frutas Tropicales.

This is what Matti could read between the lines of this report and others in her possession. According to the police report, a manhunt had been launched to discover his whereabouts. And it had failed. There was a report from a private security firm that had also come up empty-handed. Ramón said he knew something, but what?

She wondered what had really happened to Papi Cardozo, whose personal empire had to be worth many millions of dollars. She knew that people didn't just disappear. They were killed, ran away, or committed suicide. They had heart attacks in the middle of nowhere. Everyone is either dead or alive, though, those were the only two options. Which one was Papi?

She thought of another case where an insured woman had tried to make herself disappear and had gone to New Zealand. Another "missing and presumed dead" situation; Matti had found the "dead" woman with her hair dyed blond, working as a free-lance photojournalist for a government agency. The insured had lost 20 lbs. and had changed her name in an attempt to escape her rageful, sadistic husband. Disappearing just wasn't as easy as it used to be with all the computer records of flights, passports, IDs, credit cards, and so forth.

Matti had finally located the woman from a travel agent's inquiry list. The claim was denied and the potential beneficiary of the policy, the insured's vindictive husband, was given proof of his wife's continued existence, but not her whereabouts. There'd been a bitter legal fight to get Atlas to reveal the wife's location, but judgment was found in favor of Atlas. Matti's investigation was the private property of the company; they had no obligation to share this information with anyone. Matti was greatly relieved that this had been the outcome, had even written to the woman privately suggesting she move again for her own safety.

Leaning over to study the reports had cramped her side; she felt a rolling pain when she straightened in the seat. She needed a break. She walked up to the stewardess's station to stretch her legs, and got a glass of water and some peanuts. She returned to her seat, and switched on the small TV screen on the seatback in front of her. CNN's star female reporter was covering death and carnage from a place that looked very like the last place she had reported from. And you think you've got a tough job, thought Matti, amazed the reporter could do what she did over and over again. Day after day.

She'd been to Panamá before; there'd been the case of the 500-acre teak plantation that had burned near the canal two years ago, and she'd spent several days in the city. Matti loved Panamá; it offered a combination of western-style comfort, cheap prices, and friendly people. The infrastructure—thanks to the old Canal Zone and the Army Corp of Engineers—was much further along than other Central American countries. The roads were good, the city was safe, Panama City was like a small Miami with waterfront high rises, upscale department stores, big supermarkets, good restaurants, modern hospitals. As the taxi sped down the new highway connecting the international airport at Tocumen with the national airport at Albrook, Matti marveled at the progress made in just two short years. Panama, with its offshore status, U.S.-dollar-based economy and only three hours from the U.S., was growing fast.

They arrived at the Albrook airport, and Matti was not surprised to be able to purchase a same day Miami Herald from a machine at the front door. She checked in at the airport counter, then went through to the little cafeteria. Her flight would leave in twenty minutes. An hour later, she'd be in the province of Bocas del Toro, Platanillo to be specific, with Ramón undoubtedly there to pick her up.

Two big Canadian men came and sat down near her, and she heard them talking about a gold mining operation in Chiriqui. They talked about banks, which one they'd use. There were so many to choose from. They drank beer after beer. Matti stood up and got another bottle of water. If she knew one thing, it was not to get dehydrated while traveling. It messed everything up.

At last they were airborne, flying out to sea and then banking west. She saw a cruise ship transiting the canal. It looked like a fairy tale from up here, the blue canal shining in the golden afternoon light, surrounded by miles of glistening green.

Matti still had her guide book on the country, and did a quick read on the archipelago of Bocas del Toro. Forty-five minutes later they were flying over it: Lumps of green some big some small; gorgeous white beaches to seaward; turquoise water; frilly waves breaking on the outer coasts. There was apparently wonderful diving around the Zapatilla islands where, the guidebook said, the coral sand was pale pink. This is where Survivor was filmed. Maybe if she got lucky she'd get in a day of diving before heading back to New England.

Passing over the island that Matti imagined must be Isla Bocas itself—having the only real town that she could see— she was surprised to find the plane quickly descending over what seemed a short expanse of water between the islands and terra firma.

Suddenly she had a bird's eye view of large, leafy green quadrants stretching as far as the eye could see, and as the pilot made his approach, a few million banana trees came into closer view. As they landed, Matti watched the large torn leaves ruffle violently against the engine's blowback while pale pink plastic bags protected the precious stem of fruit. It was almost dark.

She was in Platanillo, at last.

The flight attendant ushered all passengers into a simple concrete building. Matti's bag quickly came through, and she got it ready to roll. She humped her leather carry-all onto her shoulder, and walked into the main part of the terminal. No Ramón. A well-dressed man in khaki pants and plaid shirt did approach her, though.

"Señorita? You need ride to Hotel Mariposa?"

"How psychic of you," she said, smiling at him, knowing he couldn't be offended by a joke he couldn't understand. This was obviously Ramón's employee, sent to pick her up.

"*Pues, vamos allá,*" she said.

He beamed at her and looked relieved. "*¡Habla español!'*

"*Un poquito, solamente. Vivía en España hace muchos años,*" she explained. I lived in Spain many years ago.

"*Que bien, que bien,*" he said, and picked up her suitcases, hurried through the front door and put them into the back of a new white Land Cruiser.

"*Y como está Don Ramón?*" she asked casually, when she had slipped the seatbelt around herself.

"Ramón?" he repeated, trying to play innocent, and then he began laughing. "He fine. Ramón say to act like taxi. I say yes. Always say yes to Don Ramón." He kept laughing, loving this simple joke, seemingly unconcerned his cover had been blown.

They left the airport's dirt parking lot and proceeded down the main street, a paved but dusty two-way thoroughfare. The driver, Jorge, pointed out the sights as they went. Here was the American supermarket, a favorite restaurant, the bus stop, the bank, but Matti could see that the real retail action was based in a dozen large stores with names like "Almacen Turca" and "Bazar Emilio" that had a motley mix of goods piled outside their doors: plastic tableware, bolts of fabric, children's clothes, buckets, stereos, fans, shoes, and loud stereo speakers blaring Panamanian music into the street.

About a half-mile outside of town, they turned down several streets and into a quiet, greener neighborhood. Matti was surprised to see a golf course, tennis courts, and beautifully groomed gardens surrounding distinctive homes all on the edge of the golf course. Another turn, and they were by the water in a quiet man-made lagoon with several old wooden piers.

The narrow lane where they drove was banked with flowering bushes arching to create a near tunnel effect as the last rays of sunlight broke through the gaps. A short distance later she saw a faded sign with Hotel Mariposa in hand-drawn letters in red. A primitive butterfly had been painted above it with a smiling two-dimensional face. It was an old two-story Caribbean-style wooden house, in faded turquoise, with brick red trim and a mass of fuchsia-colored bougainvillea clinging to its front.

Matti smiled. How perfect, she thought, and watched as Jorge rushed around to open her door, and take out her bag.

An old sand-colored dog lay on the tile floor. It opened one eye when they entered, then shut it. The reception desk had no one behind it. A sign said simply: "Bell" and Jorge banged on it several times. After five minutes, a large woman in a bright print dress appeared from a door in the wall wiping her hands. Her skin was the color of a Hershey bar and unlined except for a herringbone pattern on her brow. She patted her thin white hair and gave them both a big, warm smile. She spoke to Jorge in a rapid dialect that Matti didn't understand.

"I'm Alma," she said smiling, shyly extending both hands to grasp Matti's. "Welcome to Platanillo, Miss Matti. I'm so glad you all could come."

She turned with slow dignity and took a key from a hook that was perfectly within reach for whoever wanted it, and gave it to Matti. It was a piece of wood cut into the shape of a butterfly with the number six painted on it.

"Up the stairs, and go right at the top. That's your room." She paused. "It has a view," she said, and then giggled at herself as though she'd been boastful. "If you want a little supper later, we gonna have some nice fish that Victor caught me. He's my niece's boy. All that child does is fish, fish and catch bait. I'm gonna fry it up nice with a few tomatoes and onions and then make us some coconut rice. You ever had that?" She looked at Matti with the same expectant look she'd given Jorge when they first arrived.

"No, I don't think so. And I'd love to try it. What time?"

"Oh, whenever you come. No rushin, eh?" she jabbed Jorge with an elbow and started giggling again, her eyes twinkling. Matti thought she must be at least seventy-five.

"Miss Alma, I'm going to go and freshen up, and then, do you think I could use the phone? I'm afraid during my stay, I'll need to use the phone quite a bit, so if you want, I can pay you a deposit…."

"What?" Alma said. "Don't be silly! We are all friends here, no deposit required. You just use the phone when you meant to use it, and keep me a little note. That will suffice." She went over to the old black rotary phone, lifted the receiver and listened for the dial tone. "See it's working fine, just fine. Sometimes you need to give it a good bang," she thumped the phone on the desk to demonstrate, "like this. And sometimes it don't work at all. But you'll find your way, honey. No doubt about it."

Matti thanked Alma, tried to give Jorge a tip—which he refused—and went upstairs. She couldn't wait to have a shower and just lie down for an hour. It had been a long day, and she needed to recharge and regroup before calling Ramón.

The room was simple. A single bed with pressed white sheets, neatly folded down, and no blanket. A rectangular white mosquito net suspended from four pieces of fishing line, the side panels folded back over the top. A wood table, a single chair covered with floral plastic, a mirror, and two windows. A bathroom that looked like it had been modern in the '50s. A red floor that was the same color as the trim outside. No screens. A stray piece of bougainvillea had entwined itself into the rotting window frame, but had produced a bright bloom at the very spot, as if in apology. The view over the lagoon was rose-colored in the setting sun, and was perfectly still.

Matti turned on the overhead fan which made a steady whumping sound. She went in and took a cold shower— the only option—toweled herself off, and lay on the bed. It immediately sank down under her weight like a large overused sponge. She closed her eyes.

There was a hard knock at the door. The clock told her she had been asleep over an hour. It was nearly seven, the rosy light had gone, and she had several mosquito bites.

"Phone, miss," said a young male voice outside the door.

"I'll be right down." She splashed water on her face, ran a brush through her hair, threw on a pareo and went downstairs. The phone receiver lay on its side; no one was in the lobby.

"Hello?"

"Welcome to Platanillo, Matti," said Ramón, and she

remembered her first impression of him, his elegant yet masculine demeanor, his Latin charm.

"Hello, Ramón."

"How do you like our Hotel Mariposa," he laughed. "Very cosmopolitan, no?"

"It's charming," Matti assured him, "as is Miss Alma."

"Miss Alma, yes. She's the lead soprano in the Methodist choir, and one of the area's best cooks. You're in good hands. So...how was the flight?"

"Fine, thank you. Luckily uneventful. There's quite a view of the Frutas Tropicales plantation from the air. It's enormous! How many acres are there?

"Two thousand *hectareas*. A hectare is approximately two and a half of your acres. It's easier for you to think of it in miles, perhaps. Frutas Tropicales has more than seven and a half square miles of banana plantation here. In a good year, we ship almost six million boxes of bananas out of here."

"That's staggering! I never thought of bananas in the millions of boxes. I look forward to trying a few."

Ramón laughed. "That's one thing you won't see much of, I'm afraid. The bananas are harvested when they are still green, and shipped out immediately. Unless we ripen a bunch ourselves, they're all exported to Europe. It's ironic, but there are hardly any ripe bananas to eat in Platanillo."

"Is that true?"

"Many of the children like green bananas, they boil them and eat them. But most people here have a diet of root vegetables, plantain and rice."

"For heaven's sake."

"Speaking of food, I guess you'll want to eat with Miss Alma tonight?" Why did she have the distinct impression this had been pre-arranged?

"Yes, I thought I would."

"Good then. I'll pick you up in the morning then, about ten?"

"Earlier would suit me if you could manage it, Ramón. Would you be free for coffee at nine?" She'd had quite enough of having him dictate her schedule. Besides, her number one priority was taking an in-depth statement from Ramón himself, the content of which would largely determine the course of events.

"*Con mucho gusto,*" he said.

The conversation over, the door opened and Alma poked her head through. "Hungry?" she asked.

"Very."

"Come then, my dear," Alma said in her soft voice. "Don't change out of that lovely pareo. There will only be the two of us."

Her kitchen contained a large six-burner stove and oven, an Amana refrigerator like her grandmother used to have, and a big enamel sink. Directly in front of the screen door and incoming breeze was a square table with a vinyl tablecloth, two places laid for dinner, and three rose buds in a vase.

"Victor, he's supposed to eat but I don't know when he's comin'. You know kids, runnin' all day long and don't want to sit down til they're starving." Her laugh caused her cheeks to dimple, then she turned and began stirring something in a pot.

"So, I hear you came to do an investigation about Papi," she said. "We're not accustomed to investigations here, though of course we have our little troubles from time to time, mostly during Carnival."

"Yes," said Matti, drinking from a glass of water in front of her. "I'm the representative for the insurance company here to investigate Mr. Cardozo's disappearance."

Alma got a distant look on her face, and hand on hip, turned and gazed out the open door. Matti thought she might cry. "Oh Papi, Papi," she said. "God willing he has not met some tragic end. *Dios mio.* What a sad state of affairs."

"Did you know him well?"

"Did I *know* Papi? Everyone hereabouts knows Papi like a father. He has a good heart, that man. Heart of gold, like a banana." She started to laugh, then stopped as if laughing about Papi was sacrilegious.

She looked at Matti. "You are gonna find the truth out, aren't you?" The expectant look again.

"I'm going to do my very best."

"Well then, enough chitter chatter." She turned and began putting food on a plate: a whole crispy fish, a cup of rice turned upside down next to it, and some cabbage and carrots that had been sautéed. "No nice vegetables here. People too lazy to grow anything but cabbage," she explained, placing the plate of home-cooked food in front of Matti. "That's why I always got to cook the same: cabbage and carrots, or ñame or ñampe which are some big old roots, or just plain yuca. I tried to grow some nice tomatoes once and onions. The land crabs ate em up, every one. Even the vine." She shook her head in disgust. The scent of freshly cooked fish, garlic, and vegetables wafted up into Matti's face. It was so comforting to be in Miss Alma's kitchen. Like being at home.

They ate, or Matti ate, as Alma refused to sit until she saw that her guest was completely enjoying the meal, and that everything was to her liking. At last she sat, and got into conversation. Alma's husband, George, had gone back to Panamá City in 1975. They'd had seven children, all were grown. Only two stayed close by. Her sister's kids were still hereabouts, three daughters, all married. Victor was Coralia's second boy. Fourteen years old, and barely slept, but when he wanted to sleep he came to Alma's. There was a room in there, Alma pointed off the kitchen, which was his room when he wanted it.

As if on cue, a tall, young boy looking much more like sixteen than fourteen walked in. He was wearing his baseball cap with the peak to the front, but took it off when he entered the house and walked directly over to his grandmother. *"Buenas noches, abuela,"* he said bending to kiss her cheek. He was a handsome young man, Matti saw, with a smile and dimples like his grandmother's.

"Don't be rude!" Alma said, pushing him away in mock dismay. "We have us a guest, an important visitor. May I present my, ah...my grand nephew Victor Robles, Miss Matilda...."

"Maitlin," Matti prompted.

"And none of the *guari-guari* talk. Speak English to the lady as you've been taught."

"Good evenin', Miss Matilda, I am glad to make your acquaintance," he said in practiced English.

"Thank you, Victor. And thank you for the delicious fish."

"Pargo," he said, "it's pargo."

"Delicious."

"Now you want some?" Alma asked him. "You gonna eat today, or wait 'til some other week? Go wash up while I get your plate ready." The old woman rose and walked to the stove slowly on bowed legs. "These children they so skinny, but what can you do? I cook and cook but I think Victor, he got a big worm in there, eatin all the goodness." She put her hand on her hip and inspected him when he returned, smiling in approval.

Victor sat down at the table. He'd washed and his wavy hair was wet and combed. He had a set of perfect white teeth which his face had not fully grown into, and brown eyes that reflected a combination of shyness and curiosity. Knowing how many teenagers were into grunge and how much this image was glorified on TV, in movies, and music, it gave Matti pause to see this young man who was well-mannered and happy sitting before her. Maybe the 20th century had passed Platanillo by, or maybe some kids got the wrong kind of information to begin with.

She and Alma talked while Victor ate, which he did without speaking. When he'd finished, he told her about fishing, and it was obvious this was his passion. Alma stood behind him at the stove watching, and after she'd served him a second helping, finally sat down again. They talked about fish and reefs and bait, about pargo, grouper, octopus, jack, about which fish were easy to catch, and which were not, and the market price: 75 cents a pound.

Matti asked if there were any good swimming beaches nearby, and Victor immediately volunteered to take her in his boat whenever she wanted.

At nine thirty, Matti excused herself. It was easy to get lost in this kitchen with its ease and comfort and forget why she came. The world which she'd left seemed galaxies away.

Tomorrow she needed to be fully rested and alert. This was a big case and a big payout was riding on it. Ramón would tell her what he knew of his father's disappearance, knowledge he claimed no one else had. With any luck, tomorrow she'd also meet with the insured's wife, Violeta, and Ramón's sister, Dolores. With any *real* luck, Papi Cardozo would walk in the door having spent a long vacation in Venezuela with his mistress and plead temporary insanity.

Matti lay in bed, propped up against the wall making preparatory notes. Someone knew more than they were saying. Someone always knew more. It was oftentimes a matter of jogging a subconscious memory; in other cases, she wore people down or intentionally angered them to spark full disclosure.

She thought of Sam. Where was he, what was he doing right now? She tried to imagine and couldn't. Kisses Two, Three and Four had been very real, and now there was no mistaking Sam's feelings for her. But suddenly from being so far away, the old doubts began surfacing like a gang of marauders who smell opportunity in the air. She tried to think of him as he'd been: tender, funny, sexy, and so very lovable. Instead she got a picture of Sam with Judith; an office soirée a year or so ago, she in a black sheath with her bisque skin and dark hair, as elegant and perfect as a porcelain doll. She saw in her mind how she had held Sam's arm as they entered the banquet room. Sam looking at her and smiling. The perfect made-for-each-other couple, a marriage of fourteen years.

Why did it "need to end"?

She went to the window and looked out at the lagoon which was lit up from a full moon. The sheen of light on water made her feel calmer. The palm trees were dark silhouettes, their long, curving fronds in relief against the night sky.

Below she saw Victor sitting on the wall, his feet dangling above the water, watching too, or was he still fishing?

Matti got ready for bed, pulling the net around the bed this time. Thoughts of Sam danced in her head, alternating with visions of Patrick as she'd liked to remember him best: drinking a Silver Bullet, and laughing 'til his face turned red in his big wing-backed chair. She curled into herself smiling, and at last found sleep.

***

Across the lagoon, a short man with a powerful build sat watching as Matti's light went out, and when the moon rose higher, he still stayed hidden in the mangrove along the shore. He'd been following her all day, and now he waited until the moon went behind a cloud before he stepped into his dug out *cayuco*, and paddled silently away. She was all tucked in nice and snug, no need to pull a 24-hour watch.

She was the insurance broad here to investigate the kidnapping, the woman he'd been told to expect. Did she know less than he did? Which is to say about 30 drops short of a teaspoon of knowledge about what the fuck had happened to Papi Cardozo? He would shortly find out.

It wasn't a professional kidnapping, Gerry knew. They were waiting too long for one thing. His partner Larry agreed, and they ought to know being ex-Special Forces who'd worked all the back alleys from Guatemala through Nicaragua, down to the Colombian border through the jungles of Panamá and back again. Latin kidnappings had a certain smell about them, like a moldy, tropical hideaway. The Latinos didn't go for blood, like the Italians. But you never knew. Maybe they had a little psycho in the group who was trigger happy. The Panamanians were great lovers of knives, though, it was their weapon of choice. A nice, sharp machete, or even a kitchen knife.

The sooner they found Cardozo, the better.

In the old days, it was hardly heard of down here. Now, it was like a hot new industry—disturbing as hell if you were the CEO of some big-bucks company. A billion remote mountain camps to stow their prey, and now they had wireless links, and fucking e-mail. They could hole up for months and negotiate their ransoms. Like permanent guests on Wheel of Fortune, they'd only leave when they won, and won big. Let their fingers do the walking in cyberspace, and make everyone else jump through hoops. God, it pissed him off; electronics had never been his strong suit.

They needed to get to Papi before he was exterminated. That was the deal: Find the man and keep him alive. The ransom would be their payoff. The whole thing smelled like a drug operation gone wrong, but who gave a shit?

They'd gotten their expense money up front, no problem there. They'd been contacted late, and he and Larry had headed down immediately. Larry wasn't much of a fun guy, he looked a little like a red-headed Frankenstein, to be honest, but he was a brilliant technician, and was therefore a great partner in situations like this. They'd brought up a whole kit full of goodies from Panamá. They still had friends in the Free Zone in Colón near where they'd had gone to jungle warfare school all those years ago. Friends who thought they were still legit, or chose to look the other way when handed quantities of untraceable cash. Thanks to them, Larry was listening to phone calls both at Frutas Tropicales headquarters and at Cardozo's home, and could pick up the police or anyone else if it suited him. For a big guy, he could make himself practically disappear in his little Daewoo van.

The problem was, the kidnappers still hadn't contacted the family, at least no one was acting like they'd been contacted and Larry hadn't heard anything to the contrary. And that made him worry. Kidnappers did what they did for money. So where the fuck were they? What were they waiting for?

CHAPTER 10

Matti awoke to sparkling sunshine and the smell of coffee. She did the cold water routine, trying not to squeal too loudly, then got dressed. Her uniform was a pair of linen blend khaki shorts, a hemp belt, a sleeveless white cotton blouse, a sturdy pair of putty-colored walking shoes light but durable, white socks and a straw hat. The gold earrings, replicas of pre-Columbian frogs she'd bought a few years back in Costa Rica, gave the outfit an upbeat look.

She got out the leather folder she used as a briefcase when traveling, and brought it downstairs with her. She'd gone over the policy several times, and knew it well. The terms, conditions, restrictions and exclusions. Now she needed to learn the truth so she could make a fact-based recommendation at the next committee review, and move on.

Alma had prepared some sweet pumpkin bread and offered to cook Matti breakfast. Matti declined, had the bread (23 carbs at least), and brought a second black coffee outside where two Adirondack chairs and a table were set up under a lacy tree. She was reviewing her notes when Ramón pulled up driving the same Land Cruiser that Jorge had driven yesterday.

He got out and walked toward her, sunglasses on, smiling His dark hair was slicked back under a baseball cap, he had on a buttoned-down shirt of yellow cotton open at the neck revealing some chest hair, no gold chain, khaki pants, work boots—a beefed-up version of Julio Iglesias. Hey, maybe he could sing, as well as play the piano.

She sipped her coffee so she wouldn't smile outright. He had two craggy ridges on each side of his mouth, a deeply masculine feature that gave him an amused look. She realized he was older than she'd originally thought. Older by at least five years. She wondered if he was married. She wondered how much older *she* looked in tropical sun versus candlelight.

"Hi Ramón," she said, getting up and extending her hand.

"Nice hat," he said. "How was your night?"

"Great. Miss Alma treats me like I'm a member of the family. I also met her grandnephew Victor…"

"Victor, oh yes," he said, cutting her short. "Well, any chance of another cup of coffee? I'm sure we have a lot to cover."

Matti called through the door to Alma, and she brought his coffee out on a tray, no glimmer of her natural warmth in evidence. Ramón still hadn't sat down, was looking now out at the lagoon, as if lost in thought. He seemed edgy as a wild cat.

"Your coffee."

"Thank you."

"You must miss him," she said, playing with her spoon.

"Hmmm?"

"Your father. You must miss him."

"I do," he said, matter-of-factly. "But you know since his… departure, I've been so busy doing *his* job as well as my own, that some nights I'm in bed by 8:30. Not a glamorous life."

"Don Ramón still ran the business?"

"With a larger-than-life presence. You know we have almost two thousand employees here, Matti, and 10,000 dependents. It's like running several towns. We have good managers for each *finca*, or farm, but even so, we're talking about agriculture and there are many risks: floods, wind, pests. Life isn't dull! With so many employees it's necessary to have more than a mayor. One needs many deputies. I was one of my father's deputies and now I'm running the show, as you say in America."

"When did your father start the business, or had it been in the family before him?" Matti took out a small tape recorder and placed it on the table. "I'll need to record our conversation," she said, "and take some notes."

He looked at the small pocketsize machine, nodded at it disinterestedly, and finally sat down. "My father had just turned seventy-two when he disappeared. He started Frutas Tropicales from a two-hundred-*hectarea* farm in 1964 when he was only thirty-six and this place was a jungle, literally and figuratively. Today Frutas Tropicales is the largest independent producer of bananas in Panamá. We've developed our own markets for direct export to Europe. The large multinationals control most of the market, and most banana growers grow for them. We're an exception."

Matti made a note as to time and place of the interview on the standard form, and maintained eye contact with Ramón as she asked: "So you're saying that most bananas are grown for the multinationals. How does that work?"

"Well, a company like Worldwide Produce, for example. They have tens of thousands of *hectareas* under their control in Panamá alone. Though their biggest volume comes from Costa Rica, Brazil and Ecuador. They make contracts with independent growers and give them royalty agreements for every banana grown. It's much more cost-effective for Worldwide to buy from independents than to try and run their own farms in places like this." He picked up his cup of black coffee and drained half of it

"So the banana farmer owns the land, but Worldwide owns the bananas?"

"Exactly. They also own the packing stations, spray the crops with insecticide, provide the boxes and plastic bags, fix the bridges, build the infrastructure and so on. For most producers, it's the only way. Worldwide buys the product onsite, it's packed into refrigerated trucks and then shipped directly overseas. All shipping is handled by the company, and the final delivery to international markets is all arranged. Worldwide is like a *mamita*, a mother who cares for her children. It can be a highly attractive arrangement."

"But your father felt it would be more profitable to stay independent?"

Ramón hesitated. "Yes. I suppose he did."

"And where has he gone now, Ramón? What do you think *really* happened to your father?"

"I think he was kidnapped," Ramón said looking out across the lagoon. "I think he was kidnapped and then killed. Worldwide Produce made my father an attractive offer more than three years ago, an offer that would've yielded them another big farm and now they're trying again. They also like the type of bananas we grow. Valery bananas are bigger and more marketable now. Most importantly though, they wanted our port. This is always a factor: the proximity of the fruit to the nearest port. We've owned the deep-water facility in Platanillo for years. We've leased Worldwide space to dock their ships of course, another profit maker. But, of course, they'd far rather own it themselves."

Matti stared down at her blank interview form where there were headings for name, address, contact tel/fax, relationship to insured.

"Are you saying that you believe Worldwide Produce kidnapped your father and then killed him for not agreeing to sell them his bananas?" she asked him, incredulous. "How could *that* serve them?"

"It would serve them because they thought *I* would be interested in selling, at least I used to be interested. Now I have a different idea, which I'll explain. I think they might have removed my father so that they could do a deal directly with *me*." Ramón looked at her levelly. There was no attempt on his part to convince her or justify himself. There were only his intense brown eyes watching her face for a reaction.

"That's incredible! If Worldwide thought you wanted to sell, and acted as they did because of it..."

"Then what?" Ramón asked, barking out a bitter laugh. She watched his jaw set, his mouth turn down. "I didn't encourage them to do away with my father for God's sake! I'm not *that* much of a bastard." He stood up and crossed his arms across his chest.

"And I want you to know something else. Richard was the one who reminded me we had this K&R rider on the policy. I know it will be difficult to prove, and still think so. But this is why we have the policy in the first place, Matti. Believe me. I know how much more convenient this would be for you if we had a body lying here for you to inspect or a nicely typed ransom note. But we don't, okay? This is not like a Christmas box with a pretty ribbon on it. This is a tragic situation for me and my family, not to mention Frutas Tropicales and its employees who have all lost their leader."

Matti stood up and faced him. "Ramón. Please. I'm sorry if you're upset. It's just a very strange set of circumstances. All I have is your word that these things happened. I need something tangible. I'm an insurance investigator, not a conjurer of evidence."

"There was a time when I thought Worldwide's offer was a dream-come-true," he said, looking off into the distance. "We'd become a member of the club, and I could become rich with little effort. *Mamita* would take care of us through thick and thin. My father always dreamed of returning to Cuba. I thought if we made the agreement, and Castro was out of the picture, he could go one day. We could turn the whole operation over to a management company and we could *all* get a nice income."

"Well, that doesn't sound like such a far-fetched arrangement."

"The thing that's puzzling me, Matti, is this. Worldwide has overplanted and overbuilt in these last few years. All the big ones committed to many new plantations all over Latin America in the last several years in expectation of a huge, open European market."

"So, what's so puzzling about that? You have a great big farm all planted and ready, producing enormous volume. It makes sense to me."

"Yes. But that's was before. Before the quotas, before anyone knew that the European Union would put a cap on certain banana imports."

"Oh?"

"Yes. Worldwide and the others are actually being discriminated against in the European market. They have been limited by GATT, the General Agreement on Tariffs and Trade, as to what they can sell. There is a surplus of 16 million boxes of bananas this year."

"Have I got this straight? Worldwide planted more bananas trees in anticipation of a growing European market, and now their market has been restricted?"

"Exactly. So, why do they still want Frutas Tropicales? We're small potatoes, to them, anyway. There are far bigger farms in Ecuador, for example. So why did they kidnap my father? And why are they still trying to negotiate with me?" He looked at her bewildered, and Matti felt as though she was hearing the truth from his heart. Ramón was acting neither suave nor self-assured. He was genuinely puzzled, and Matti, hearing the facts, was puzzled too.

"And your mother and sister? Do they have the same ideas about this as you?"

"They have many suspicions. But honestly they don't know all the facts. I thought it was better, particularly for my mother, if she doesn't think foul play is involved, especially with Worldwide. You see, they were in favor of his selling. He'd been working hard for too many years. My mother and sister were both worried about him."

"And so why did you change your mind, Ramón? Why did you decide not to sell to Worldwide after all?"

His smile deepened the crags around his mouth. "I'll tell you when we have dinner together tonight." He held up his hand indicating that a refusal would not be accepted. He was once again the old Ramón. A man who was used to having his way.

"Listen. This is not a come-on, Matti. You *are* a very attractive woman. There's no doubt of that. But more than that, I need to try and make sense out of this jumble and you need as many answers as you can get, right?"

"Deal," she said, raising both palms in submission.

A phone rang in the distance and Ramón walked toward his vehicle. She saw him reach in and pick up a slim cell phone and begin speaking. She looked up through the feathery green layers of an acacia tree, and thought about what he'd just told her.

This was the kidnapping scenario that the attorney had originally put forth, and if Ramón was right, and his theory could be proved, the implications were staggering. Terrorists kidnapped corporate heads, but corporations kidnapping the heads of other companies to blackmail them? It was too bizarre to contemplate.

Ramón returned. "Ready to meet the rest of my family?"

"Yes, of course," she said, rising.

She settled onto kid-soft upholstery of the Land Cruiser. The air-conditioning bellowed from two vents in front of her, and she re-directed them away from her chest.

"Do your mother and sister live with you?"

"Oh yes. We're just one big happy family." He laughed. "We each have our separate quarters, our own entrances. There are four wings joined to a great room."

"Children?"

"My children live with my wife, Lesley, in West Palm. It's better for the children to attend school in the States." He paused. "We—she and I—are estranged, as the saying goes. Except of course she depends on me to keep the bank accounts full. In this way, at least, we're not strangers."

"And your sister Dolores? Does she have a husband, children?"

"Dolores is very special. You'll see. She's somewhat—how shall I put it?—different from the norm."

Matti considered this, and looked out the window at the passing scene. Colorful shrubs lined the road as they again drove through the neighborhood of the golf course, the elegant homes. "Who lives in these houses?" she asked.

"Oh, this is where most of the *bananeros* and their families live."

"*Bananeros*, you mean banana growers?"

"Yes."

"You mean there are *other* farms in Platanillo?"

"Nine others. All in the 150 to 200 *hectarea* range."

"And they live here with their families."

"Yes. It's almost like a club. They all signed an agreement with Worldwide at the same time, got this land and developed it with the golf course, club house, swimming pool. There's even a racquetball court. They parceled themselves out lots and built their homes like one big extended family."

"What a lot of collaboration! I would've thought they would be in competition as independents."

He laughed. "That's what works about selling to Worldwide. If these *bananeros* were forced to decide anything as a group, it would never happen. Because they all grow for the same market, and work on the same contracts, they don't have to decide anything. It's done for them."

"Wow," Matti said, taking it all in.

They turned out of the suburb, went quickly down Platanillo's main street, and many people watched as they sped by, and many people waved.

"You're very popular," Matti said.

"Not as popular as my father. Not by a long shot," Ramón said. "The people here love Papi." He turned through two brick pillars laced overhead with wrought-iron filigree. The paved driveway leading to the Cardozo home put the roads of Platanillo to shame.

"And now he's disappeared," Matti continued.

"Yes," Ramón said, rubbing his face with the back of his arm, "I doubt if we'll ever see him alive again."

After more than a mile through an undramatic incline lined on both sides by bananas, they pulled up into a semi-circular driveway. Ramón pulled under a portico in front of a long ranch-style stucco house; the front lawn was bordered by more colors of hibiscus than Matti had ever seen.

The house sat on a hill with trimmed lawns and sweeping views of Banana Bay, an English morph that was used even here. The archipelago of Bocas del Toro lay in the distance, shimmering like an emerald mirage. She could feel the sun burning her skin, even though the breeze was fresher here than below. Rows and rows of banana trees in neat quadrants stretched in all directions as far as the eye could see. Seven square miles of it. In front of the house and down the hill, she saw a large barn in the distance, and an enormous pasture where hundreds of cattle grazed.

"I didn't know you had cows, as well."

"What do you think happens to all the damaged bananas, discarded trees and other silage? The cattle provide milk and beef for all our workers and their families, and because of the ample food supply, they're a bargain to keep. It's part of the cycle."

Ramón led the way into an enormous concrete home with a fieldstone base, upper walls painted in white, molded green trim around the windows which were fitted with ornate wrought iron bars. The red tile roof completed the picture of a modern Spanish-style hacienda. They passed in through heavily carved double wooden doors and into a marble foyer which held an antique grandfather's clock. Many small tables balanced a variety of ferns and orchids. The checkerboard marble floor led into another area which held cascade of white orchids with bleeding heart centers.

The great room was directly ahead, an enormous yet comfortable space with vaulted ceilings and a mixture of antique and modern furniture including a large horseshoe- shaped sofa in burnished leather. A thin, elderly woman stood with her back to them, gazing out one of the plate glass windows that formed the rear octagon of the room. Air conditioning made the room as cold as a meat locker.

The views from the window would be of more plantation, she guessed. More bananas, more greenery, more sea in the distance and clear blue sky. The woman apparently hadn't heard them enter.

"Mother?" Ramón said gently, approaching her. "Mother, I've brought a visitor."

The woman turned surprised, and Matti saw as she approached that the woman's face looked as if it had melted on one side. She smiled warmly at Matti, and extended her hand, and Matti thought: *She's had a stroke.*

"*Buenas días, señora,*" Matti said cordially. "*Mucho gusto.*"

"A *gringa* who speaks Spanish...well!" Ramón's mother, contrary to her visage, seemed alert and lively. Her large, deep-set hazel eyes sparkled, minimizing her disfiguration; Matti thought what a beauty she must have been when young. She still had the coy twinkle of a younger woman, and her handshake was firm, though physically she seemed frail.

She looked at Ramón and her skin seemed to droop as she regarded him. "Offer our guest *un refresco,* Ramón. Please." A command not a request, as if she wanted him to leave the room.

"*Sientase,*" Doña Violeta said graciously when he'd gone, indicating the sofa. As they sat, the woman grabbed Matti's arm and pulled her close. "*Gracias a Dios estás aquí,*" she whispered. "I'm so glad you're here," she repeated, but before more could be said, Ramón re-appeared. A young woman in a maid's uniform followed him with a tray of tall glasses and an icy pitcher of drinks.

"Chicha?" Ramón offered. "It's a fruit drink made in this case from *tamarindo.*"

"Thank you," said Matti, who was skeptical of the brownish liquid. One sip converted her, however. The *chicha* was delicious and refreshing. The air-conditioning continued unabated however, and she wondered if people in the tropics loved the cold so much, why they didn't all move to Boston.

"So," Ramón said, draining his drink. "I suppose you'd like a chance to speak to my mother in private. A good place to begin your investigation, no? I must go to work. Unfortunately Frutas Tropicales does not run itself."

He made a small bow to both of them. "*Llamame cuando la señorita está lista,*" he said to his mother. Now Matti could learn what insights Papi Cardozo's wife might have to contribute. It was a perfect opportunity.

"Doña Violeta. I'm so sorry to intrude on your privacy at a time like this. But I would very much like to know what you know about your husband's disappearance."

Ramón's mother regarded her thoughtfully, and waved her hand. "Oh this is not a private place….and you will hear all the theories. Yes, I am tired. Since Papi left….well, it's been very sad without him. This business would like to swallow us whole. And yet, I still expect him to walk through the door at any moment." She sighed deeply, and took out her handkerchief. Matti, in all her years dealing with bereaved and bereft people, had never seen anyone so wrung dry of tears.

"If you don't feel up to talking to me now, Doña Violeta, I can come back another time."

The woman sat forward on full alert. "Oh no, no! You can't leave before I've told you what I know. I've been waiting for you to come. I've got to show you something. Something important." Matti helped her up, and Doña Violeta did not let go of her hand but led her out of the room, down a long corridor. They turned into a large bedroom with a king-sized bed covered in a pink-dominated floral chintz with matching draperies and a soft green carpet on the floor. A colorized photograph of a handsome dark-haired young man looking very like Ramón was on the bureau. A smaller more recent one showed an exuberant older man holding up a large fish for the camera.

"Is this Papi?" Matti asked.

"Yes, so happy he was to catch that fish. He loves his boat so much! It's a Bertram. He bought it in Florida a few years ago."

She turned and locked the door behind them. Next to a window lay a rowing machine, and the wall was framed by doors at either end of the room. The bedside tables and bureaus, all matched: heavy and ornately designed furniture of a reddish-colored wood.

Ramón's mother went to a bed side table, opened a drawer, and withdrew a manila envelope. "No one knows I have this," she told Matti whispering. "Everyone thinks I am *loca*, a crazy woman. *Pero, sé cosas, sé muchas cosas.* I know many things."

She sat down on the bed, and patted the spread for Matti to sit next to her.

"This is a document," she said. "My husband brought this home the night before he disappeared. I think you'll find it interesting."

Matti took out a stapled document of a dozen pages, the cover page of which stated: CONFIDENTIAL on Worldwide Produce stationery. The second page, also on the company's letterhead, read: "Strategy to Regain European Market Share." Matti read quickly through a summary of the new rules for banana imports into the European Union and learned more about the recent substantive changes. The EU had indeed established "duty-free preferences" for Caribbean and African bananas, and through GATT new quotas for Latin American bananas had been established. The memo described these quotas as "discriminatory", "harsh" and "harmful" to Worldwide Produce's markets abroad.

Following this was a table listing the amounts of bananas produced country by country in the millions of boxes. The figures showed the downturns since the quotas had gone into effect. The impact was immediately apparent, especially in light of increases in capital investment.

Three pages of photocopies of news clippings from periodicals ranging from *The Tico Times* of Costa Rica, to *The Miami Herald*, *The Washington Post*, and *The Herald Tribune* followed. The headlines varied from: "Bob Dole Seeks Punishment of Costa Rica for agreeing to GATT Quotas." To an OpEd article entitled: "Going Bananas: US Companies Fight EU Quotas". Matti skimmed the headlines and turned the last page which discussed the case being brought before the WTO. A positive ruling was expected, it said. And Matti found herself wondering how a case could be decided before it was tried. What was this document not saying, she wondered, that might be tied to Frutas Tropicales and Ramón's theory?

And how had Papi Cardozo gotten this document in his possession, a confidential memo from a multi-national corporation whose buy-out advances he'd refused?

Doña Violeta had been watching Matti intently while she read. She now began turning her hands in her lap. The disfigured side of her face was turned away from Matti's, but she hung her head, making her look even older than her years.

"Is this all?" Matti asked. "Is there any more?"

"No, that's all I could find."

"Doña. Where did your husband find this? How did it come into his hands?"

The woman turned and looked at Matti, her liquid hazel eyes filling with hurt. "Someone faxed it to him on his private line. But...why would someone send him this? Why? It frightens me, because I don't understand. Papi was against joining Worldwide. Always. " She let out a hard, dry sob.

"Doña Violeta, I don't know what to think either. But tell me. Why didn't your husband want to sell to Worldwide? Didn't they make him an offer some time ago?"

She regarded Matti with surprise. "Yes! They did make him an offer. And he was a fool not to take it! The banana business is crazy now! The big ones decided that there is going to be a huge market for bananas when Europe opens up, and they begin planting, planting, planting all over." She continued knotting her hands. "And now the Europeans decide they want to make quotas, and guarantee the smaller countries, their former colonies, a...how do you say...an action?"

"A piece of the action, yes. But why would Don Ramón decide not to sell to Worldwide if the market is so uncertain right now?"

"Because he is so stubborn. So independent," she cried. "All he ever wanted was to go back to the farm in Cuba. That was his dream, you know? That Castro would die, and he could finally go home."

The woman sighed deeply at this admission, took Matti's hand, and patted it. "I will have to rest now," she said. "*Demaciado excitation.* The doctor says it is bad for my heart."

"I understand. But Doña, I need to ask one question before I leave. Do you think that Ramón should sell to Worldwide now?"

"My son Ramón is a man who thinks of himself first," Doña Violeta told her. "He always wanted to sell out to Worldwide so he could go to Florida and live like a playboy. He tried to convince his father many times to sell. Now I don't know what he wants. I don't trust my own son, Miss Matti. I am sorry to say it. *Dios mio*, I don't trust him at all."

CHAPTER 11

Jorge drove Matti back to the hotel. Ramón was too busy to come himself.

"He sorry," said Jorge as they headed back to the hotel. "He say be ready at seven. Wear your pants."

"I beg your pardon?"

"He said wear your pants," Jorge repeated, looking nervous.

"You mean long pants?"

"*Si, si,*" he nodded. "Pants. You go to beach restaurant. *Hay chitras.*"

Alma was in the kitchen and called out to Matti to come in. A spicy home-cooked smell filled the room.

"Alma what are chitras?"

"Mean little fleas you can't see that live in the sand. They come out when there's no breeze."

"Great."

"You going to the beach?" Alma asked sweetly, her dark skin glistening with sweat in spite of the fan swiveling back and forth nearby.

"Not 'til tonight."

"Well, then you'll want a little chicken and rice to tide you over. Nothing fancy. No vegetables around here like I said. Just lots of old roots." She broke into her familiar half-suppressed giggle.

They ate and spoke about various recipes, and when the meal was over Matti asked if she could use the phone. She explained about her calling card. All calls were billed to this toll free number. Alma's number wouldn't be billed. Alma took this in with bewilderment.

"You just use that phone whenever you want," she said, and began clearing away the dishes.

Matti went into the little lobby, picked up the old rotary phone from the phone table, and sat down with it in a green plastic chair. The room was empty, except for the dog that looked like he hadn't moved since her arrival. She went over and patted him to reassure herself he wasn't dead. His tail gave one slow thump. *Whew.*

She dialed her access number and was quickly connected to Atlas's computerized answering machine. With rotary dial, she had to wait for the operator, and at last heard Ashley's voice.

"Matti Maitlin's office."

"Ashley, it's me."

"Matti, hi! We've been trying to reach you."

"We?"

"Sam and Brandon too. Did you make it okay?"

"I'm at the Hotel Mariposa." She gave her PA the number. "Is there a problem?"

"No...I don't think so. It's just that Sam was on my back all morning trying to confirm your arrival, and the number I have just wouldn't go through. I guess we all got a little worried."

Matti assured her everything was fine. "Sam said if you called, to put you through immediately. Shall I put you through now?" she asked. Matti smiled. She was glad he missed her, even though he'd been doing his Siegfried and Roy act in her absence.

"That's fine."

She got patched through to Muriel and found out Sam had gone to lunch.

"I don't really expect him back in the office this afternoon," Muriel said.

"Just tell him I called and that everything is underway here. And Muriel, put me through to Brandon will you?"

"Gosh, Matti, I guess it's just not your lucky day. Brandon went with Sam. So you know they probably went to the Café Budapest for one of their famous lunches. I don't expect Brandon will be back either."

"Not to worry. Tell them both I'll call when I have something concrete to report."

She rang off, and called Patrick and Brian's next; some calls just couldn't wait.

Brian picked up on the second ring. "Matti! Patrick will be *so* glad you called. He keeps talking about how you saved him. Where *are* you?"

"Here in banana land."

"Hey—that could be a new board game. And they even have telephones—wow!"

"How's Patrick?"

"Out of intensive care, thank God. He's actually due to come home tomorrow. I met his daughter Maureen, by the way. She is *so* sweet, not at all like her father, the slime." She could hear the relief in his voice.

"So, that was your mystery woman."

"Yep. It all seems so ridiculous in hindsight. Nothing like a little myocardial infarction to get everything in perspective."

"I'll say," Matti said.

"His arteries were more clogged than the Sumner Tunnel at rush hour; he had four angioplasties. No more eggs sautéed in bacon drippings, that's for sure."

"Eggs and bacon, mmm…"

"I guess you're having a steady diet of bananas down there," Brian said.

"Actually, there's not a banana in sight, just miles of banana trees with pink and blue bags covering up the fruit. It's amazing, Bri; all the fruit is shipped overseas. The people here supposedly *like* green bananas, or maybe that's what they've been taught. I'm getting a crash course in banana politics, that's for sure."

"Now don't go pulling those oars too hard."

"Don't worry. But talk about a banana republic! Papi Cardozo has a seven square mile empire down here; maybe somebody got jealous. There's an abyss between the banana barons and their employees. But so far all I've got is lots of intrigue, suggestions and innuendo, and not a lick of evidence."

"How's the piano player?"

"Still as charming as ever. I'm having dinner with him tonight."

"Don't do anything I wouldn't do!"

"Very funny. Actually, he presented a very complex theory to me today about his father's disappearance. I've met the mother who doesn't trust the son, and has her own theories. I don't have a clue what the sister might say. Fact is, it's hard to find a place to start digging until we find a body."

"Don't you mean that the other way around?"

"Hunh."

"Well…take care of yourself.

"I'd love to. Bri—do me a favor? Check I didn't leave the thermostat up, and give my poor plants a drink, and make sure I didn't leave the thermostat on? I left in kind of a state, I'll tell you more when I see you."

"No problem. Take care sweetie, and by the way, thanks for saving the old fella."

"I didn't save anybody, I'm just glad the ambulance got there so fast. Give him a kiss from me."

"Will do," he said. "I'll fix you a dinner fit for a heart-massaging princess when you get home. Ciao."

***

Matti went upstairs to get back down to business. She made some notes, and also made a decision. She could be weeks down here trying to ferret out the truth. Talking to Brian had helped her crystallize her decision. It was time to fish or cut bait.

She'd move to deny the claim until more evidence was forthcoming. Unless Ramón had something concrete to share with her tonight, she'd finish her preliminary investigation, and get on a plane the day after tomorrow.

Initially it had seemed that having no lawyer to deal with was an advantage. Now that she was here, she could see a certain scenario playing itself out, and she didn't like the look of it. There was too much enmeshment here with the family; and it could only get worse. Ramón had theories, nothing more. The police had uncovered virtually nothing. She'd meet Dolores and get her statement. Meet again with Doña Violeta and take her statement too. She'd visit the places where Papi had last been seen, interview anyone with definite connections to the case, and then she'd leave.

She'd fly back to Boston and wait for further developments, including hearing from their new lawyer. The family would balk at her decision; they'd be upset by what she proposed. But almost fifteen years of experience told her it was better if claimants learned right at the beginning that she was neither a social worker, nor a kind, beneficent therapist-cum-banker. She had a generous spirit but she didn't authorize payout without a clear, provable liability. She cared deeply about treating claimants fairly, but had to have the facts clearly delineated before settling their claims.

If Papi was kidnapped and someone could provide concrete evidence that involved Worldwide Produce, the criminal implications were staggering. The District Attorney (in which state?) would have the complicated task of putting together the homicide case against Worldwide. There would also be a civil suit, no doubt. If it was proved, years down the road, Atlas would have to subrogate against the corporation to recoup their *own* damages on a two million dollar life payout for a dead Papi Cardozo, plus all costs. But lacking the evidence, she could hardly imagine a more ridiculous scenario than Brandon calling the corporate counsel of Worldwide and reporting they had a client who *believed* that their corporation had kidnapped and possibly killed an independent banana producer in Panamá.

The beneficiaries, as it stood at present, had no evidence with which to support either a kidnapping claim or a life payout. Even in the case of missing-believed-dead, some verifying evidence was necessary. Otherwise there'd be at least a year's waiting period. Ramón knew this. It was clearly stated in the policy. Even after a year, some corroborating evidence would still be sought; the waiting period could also be extended if the company felt it could justify such a position legally.

Ramón and his family needed someone who could state unequivocally that they had seen the boat sink, the plane go down, some evidence the insured had left and would never return, that he was dead beyond a reasonable doubt. There'd need to be statements from many people who would swear that they hadn't seen the insured for so many months. In the end, it was a simple fact that Atlas would not pay two million dollars out on a life policy without some verification.

Atlas always paid out in the event of a legitimate claim. *Always*. But if they could legally and ethically buy some time on this one, it was good news. Matti knew Sam would be relieved to hear it; another two million dollar payout, if it could wait a year or more, was definitely going to give Atlas a small but necessary breather. And if Ramón was right, and Worldwide Produce *was* involved, they could save themselves a long and litigious counter-suit with a giant multinational if they had some hard evidence to present before the fact. Matti started to compose a letter to Ramón by hand. Tomorrow, she'd fax it to Brandon for his legal approval, deliver it to Ramón, and shortly be on her way.

She'd come back to Panamá—especially if Papi turned up dead. But for now, she was not obliged to act. There could be weeks of work for her here if she was a private investigator; as a claims adjuster her job was to verify the evidence that was provided, not provide the evidence itself. As she told Ramón, she was not a conjurer.

She thought of Doña Violeta, and her "secret" document which was really nothing more than a position paper that in some ways raised more questions than it answered. She thought of her first meeting with Ramón at Richard's. She thought of Ramón's mildly suggestive behavior, the nuances of his attraction to her. She still wondered how much of it was calculated. She wondered whether a chain of evidence would *ever* be constructed in this case.

There was simply nothing keeping her here, but the trip hadn't been wasted. Frutas Tropicales was an Atlas Preferred Client that rated top treatment in a case like this. The committee knew that a first strike action was an important part in taking control of a claim situation, especially in preventing a claimant from feeling they had no alternative but to instigate a lawsuit. If people were treated fairly from the beginning, Matti found, it made the whole business more economical and the whole situation more salubrious. Insurance, after all, was all numbers at the end, and her part of it was managing the outcome of claims as much as possible, solving things quickly before they got out of hand.

She would have a good basis for a future evaluation and with that in hand she could fly back to Boston and make her recommendation.

She took out a clean sheet of paper, and a pen: "Dear Mr. Cardozo,..." she began.

Rio Teribe
Panamá/Costa Rica Border

I'm near the head of the Río Teribe, I think. The size of the river, the way it runs; this is the Teribe. I'm sure of it. I am not in a Teribeño settlement though, but a small camp where I'm being kept under guard.

I can't remember how long I've been here, no concept of time passing. I seem to be sleeping a great deal, and wake up exhausted, as if I've traveled a long way.

I've seen this jungle path from the air. How this is possible, I can't say. There is the river and dense jungle, the river runs fiercely toward the sea. The Kingdom of the Teribe is near the border with Costa Rica, the Teribeños friendly. I was here a few years ago; we came to deliver some powdered milk for the children. Or is this part of the dream too?

I don't remember my trip here, only a period when I was in a boat at sea. My boat or a cayuco? *I can't remember, though I'm sure I was at sea for part of the time. When I woke up there was a cloud over the moon, and waves lapping and then I slept again.*

I've seen many animals we don't see on the coast: cougar, iguana, even tapir and of course, the monkeys. The howler monkeys wake me every morning with their loud threatening screams. One morning I saw a harpy eagle soaring in the blue sky above me. I wept to see this animal so full of freedom; the greatness of its spirit overwhelmed me.

Now they come again and bring me this drink. I'd like to refuse it, but I can't. They won't let me refuse.

I'm so tired of this place. So weary.

Ah...my sweet dream visits me again, I'm there again. The sweet orange groves of Cuba, their scent fills the air like butterflies. My mother is a butterfly. She brings me tamales on a leaf, and smiles her clever, secret smile. But now she wants to fly away. Wait, Mama, wait. Mama. Mama, don't leave yet! Don't fly away...take me with you, Mama. We'll fly together—you need me to protect you. Just don't go......please...don't leave me here alone. Mama! MAMA!!!!!

CHAPTER 12

Matti got ready at the Hotel Mariposa. She put on the only pair of white cotton slacks she'd packed, sandals, tied a bright red and white summer sweater around the shoulders of a another white blouse, and sprayed herself with Off. She towel-dried her hair and scrunched it in front of the fan 'til it was reasonably dry, then put on her makeup and went downstairs.

Ramón pulled up just after seven, and she walked to his car while Alma waved to her from the kitchen door as if she were going out on a date. She got in and the doors locked automatically.

"Did you bring your insect repellent?" he asked.

"I'm already covered. I heard about the *chitras* from Jorge."

"I don't think they'll bother us tonight. Too much breeze."

"I hadn't noticed."

"Let's roll down the windows so you can feel it, and smell the night air." The smell was floral and ripe, a green sweetness. The word "intoxicating" sprung to mind.

"When do you harvest the bananas? Do they have a season?" Matti asked.

"We harvest the fruit every thirteen weeks."

"That exact?"

"A banana tree grows quickly, Matti. It's an herb, remember, not a tree. So...it grows, opens to fruit, and one of our workers puts a bag over the stem and ties a colored ribbon around the neck. Each ribbon is color coded for different weeks. We know by the color of the ribbon exactly which fruit is ready for picking."

"Of course, I've seen these bags everywhere. What a simple but effective system! I thought the bags were put on at the end."

"No they protect the stem from start to finish. And the workers also brace the plants which is why you see so many lines tied to each tree. A banana isn't a deep-rooted plant and in a strong wind with a heavy stem of bananas hanging off it, it will easily fall over."

"And how many years does a tree live. What is its life expectancy?"

Ramón laughed. "We always say a banana tree lives forever. The banana mother actually produces a daughter, *una hija,* as the stem is ripening, and the *hija* produces a *nieta,* a granddaughter. So, the tree is immortal in a sense. And this is why we also say the bananas walk. Their rhizomes actually travel up to two meters every three years as they have their family."

"Don't they bump into each other?" Matti asked.

"They would if we didn't keep them trained in the right direction. This is another job of our workers, to cut the shoots that will interfere and encourage them to grow in a different direction."

"And on the stem, how many bananas are there?"

"The average stem produces bunches of 8, 9 or 10 hands. There are normally 18 to 20 fingers on a hand."

"You call a banana a finger?"

"We do."

"For heaven's sake. You just never think about these things when you're peeling one to eat."

"No, coming from where you do, I suppose not. And your family, are they American for many generations?"

"No second generation in both cases. My mother is of Lithuanian descent, my father was Irish."

"So, a true green-eyed blond. With a temper?"

She smiled. "I think you've already had evidence of my temper first hand."

"Hmm. Yes, I guess I have. Does it get much worse than that?" he asked her, smiling

"Not much," she said, looking away, out the window.

They pulled into a dirt parking lot next to a building that had no walls but only a large thatched roof whose dried leaves were piled thickly on top of a rustic frame and hung over the edges. Ramón described the building as a *rancho*. There were several couples sitting at some bare wood tables, a few others at the bar. Everyone looked at them as they walked in, and Ramón nodded and smiled at everyone.

The sea breeze was refreshing after the heat of the day, and the sea was illumined by a nearly full moon on the channel. There were a few white caps, little chips of froth on the dark sea.

They sat down, and everyone turned their attention back to a color TV mounted behind the bar.

"We have three choices of drinks. A Cuba Libre, popularly known as a rum and coke, a cold beer or a soft drink. What would you like?"

"Do they have light beer?" Matti said. The barman came over, and Matti settled for a rum and diet Coke.

"You look very lovely tonight," Ramón said.

"So do you," she answered, grinning.

"A woman with a sense of humor." He looked at her frankly, a gesture that was so Sam-like, it gave her a jolt. "They've got all kinds of seafood here, Matti. What would you like to eat?"

"Do they have lobster?"

"Not like your Maine lobster, but I think you'll like it."

They drank their drinks and made small talk. Huge plates arrived a half hour later: Grilled lobster tails swimming in garlic butter, rice, fried plantain and a mixed salad. Everthing was fresh and delicious. As they ate, the breeze picked up, giving the water a frothy appearance. The air, though still balmy, grew a few degrees cooler and she put on her sweater.

"This channel," she asked him. "Does it lead out to sea?"

"Yes. This is this is where the ships come in from Europe. Our port is around the corner from here," he pointed in one direction, "inside Platanillo harbor. To the south are the islands of Bocas del Toro in the middle of Banana Bay."

"It seems strange that a place in Panamá would have an English name."

"That's because the founders of the banana business were from Boston, did you know that? They came down here, experimented with bananas, found out they grew well, and the rest is history. People by the thousands came here from the Antilles to work, many from Jamaica. The company set up schools where only English was spoken. Most all of our older residents speak English, or a perversion of it, called *guari guari*."

The waiter came over, and they ordered coffee, declining dessert.

"Tell me, Ramón," Matti said, "where did you go to school? Richard said you were classmates."

"That's a long story; we were roommates in Florida when his parents were both killed in a plane crash. He became my father's adopted son after that." Ramón shook his head, sad at the memory. "He came to Panamá for awhile after we graduated. Eventually, he headed back north and opened up an insurance agency."

Matti remembered seeing Richard's CV several years back, when Sam had decided to split the claims department into two divisions: national and international. Matti, though Atlas's Latin investigator, still took on big cases in the States. It was one of the many anomalies of her job.

"I'm puzzled about something, Ramón. You said you'd had a change of heart about staying involved in the business. What happened to change your mind?"

"Did you ever think of taking up investigative reporting?" he asked her, smiling. He had a very sexy way about him when he teased her and suddenly it seemed warmer than it had been a moment before. Was the temperature going up or down? She couldn't decide if she should take her sweater off or leave it on.

"My change of heart didn't happen so long ago," he said, "and now, with Papi gone, it's become a fait accompli." He looked hurt as he talked about his father. Matti knew the look, and the feeling.

"For years my father tried to instill in me a love of the business. I was his heir, his son; he wanted me to take over when he retired. After Miami, he sent me to study the banana business in Ecuador. Unfortunately, I was always more interested in the extra-curriculars than education. I met Lesley one year during spring break, another spoiled kid with too much time on her hands. She got pregnant, and we got married. Stayed in Florida and tried to make it work for the next ten years. We have two kids." He paused, and swirled the ice cubes in his glass with great concentration. "It was during this time I decided life was very boring. I took up gambling—a very short term cure." He met her eyes, looked humble for about a millisecond, then shrugged. "I came back to Platanillo to get my life back in order."

"How long have you been back?" Matti asked, a journalist trying to stick to the facts.

"Just over a year. I was totally burned out. Too many parties, too much fun, fun, fun. My mother was concerned about my father's being under so much stress, and I was nearly insolvent. Since then, it's been one crisis after another. It's like jumping into a current. You just get swept along, and can't get out again. And that is the true reason I have stayed, and one reason I am against selling. Where would I go? What would I do? My old lifestyle just about killed me. Now when my father disappears, Worldwide contacts me. Isn't that the ultimate irony? All the years I wanted to sell, and my father didn't. Now that I *can* sell, I don't want to."

"Have they made any concrete offers?"

"They haven't begun real negotiations. Yet. But they will. All these calls inquiring about when my father will be back. It's a scam, a joke. They want Frutas Tropicales, I'm sure of it."

"I wonder why."

"Who knows why a multinational corporation does the things it does. I may not have an MBA, but I won't sit down at the table with the people who murdered my father. I think they were hoping without Papi the business would fail. They didn't count on me. That's one thing my father made sure of: that I got the training to run the company."

Matti considered this. "But surely your father didn't plan to stay in the business forever. He's 72, right? "Did he have any health problems?"

"One heart attack, a double bypass."

"I don't remember seeing *that* in the file."

"It happened two years ago. After the policy was written, as I recall."

Matti let it slide. "And you say he was in good health before he disappeared?"

"Excellent. My father was one of those people who took his heart attack as a serious warning. He changed his diet and exercised daily."

"And what of Dolores, your sister? Is she involved in the business?"

Ramón laughed. "Miss Bananita? Oh my God, she's daddy's right arm. A CPA specializing in international tax law. Her job is the books. Or I should say the screen. I think sometimes her brain has been absorbed by that computer of hers. She's the CFO of Frutas Tropicales, but if you're asking if could she run the business the answer is no. She may be brainy but she has no managerial flair, not much flair of any kind. She's always been a loner, never married, has always lived at home."

"I'll need to meet her," Matti said, as a gust of wind swooped down on them from the north, rattling the dried palm fronds on the roof like paper. The noise increased as the wind whipped up. The rain sounded like it was coming down in pellets instead of drops.

Ramón raised his voice to be heard over the din. "I can't say Dolores would like to meet you too. Dolores doesn't like anyone or anything except the company and her daddy."

The rain was now a steady thin wall of water between palm frond and ground, and occasionally gusts of wind flung it into the restaurant, though Ramón seemed not to notice. The other patrons had merely huddled closer to the bar, and were all still staring at the color TV, oblivious to the wind and lashing rain, mesmerized by a couple who were pushing each other back and forth on the screen. A Latin soap opera, Matti guessed.

"I'll need to get Dolores's statement," Matti said, wrapping the sweater tighter around her shoulders. "In fact, tomorrow would suit me. I'll also need to see the local police chief, if that's possible. I need to squeeze in as much as possible before I go."

Ramón looked startled. "You're leaving?"

"I'm afraid so," Matti said, bracing herself. "I have no choice, Ramón. There's just not enough evidence to make even a preliminary finding on this case. The policy stipulates a minimum six-month waiting period in the case of disappearances like your father's. Just be glad that this is not a run-of-the mill life insurance policy. Otherwise, you'd be waiting for a legal declaration of death according to Massachusetts's law. In which case you'd be waiting five years."

They heard a gunshot, and Ramón turned and looked back at the TV. The glossy, black-haired actress still held the small elegant pistol pointed at the blonde-haired actor who was bleeding in the chest. Her eyes remained wide and unblinking, framed by inch- long eyelashes, and not a suggestion of a tear.

"Jesus. What about the kidnapping?" Ramón said, his voice raised against the wind.

"There's no evidence that your father has been kidnapped, Ramón, I'm sorry." Sometimes the best way to deal with policy beneficiaries was to deal it up plain and simple.

Ramón rubbed his face in anxiety. "So now I've got to not only run the old man's business, but prove his death myself. Great. Thank you. Thank you very much."

"Let me do my investigation," Matti said, in a calm tone, "and see what I can turn up. Let me talk to some of the people who were close to your father. The people who saw him last. In one of my files, a man named Quintero is mentioned. Who is he?"

"Quintero? He's an old man, the overseer on Finca 8. My father and he are old friends. If they weren't, he would've been gone long ago. Besides, you can't speak to him now. He went to the States on vacation; Papi had been insisting he take time off. After my father disappeared, I made sure he went. He was completely beside himself over my father's disappearance."

"What is *his* theory?" Matti asked, her interest piqued.

"Oh, the usual paranoid ramblings."

"Such as?"

"That there is a faction inside Worldwide that wants to gain control of our port, not for bananas, but to run drugs to Europe inside the banana boxes. He believes my father knew of this ring—have you ever heard such nonsense? Quintero's got infiltration theories, and kidnapping scenarios that make mine seem tame. He's completely out of his mind."

"That does sound far-fetched," Matti thought. How many more theories were there?

"And now that *you're* leaving, how should I deal with Worldwide?" he continued sarcastically. "Do I string them along, or try and flush out an admission? Maybe I should try and shake down some of these poor Colombian banana pickers, and try and squeeze the truth out of them."

The rain had misted her hair, and her back was wet. "Let's take things one at a time, okay, Ramón?" "I may not be Carmen Miranda," she told him nodding at the screen, "but I can do a hell of an imitation of a woman seeking justice."

"You're soaked," he said, suddenly, as if seeing her for the first time. "Let's get you home."

On the drive back, Matti could feel herself shudder, even though the temperature was in the mid 70s. She felt chilled, and a little achy.

"I'll make you a hot rum and lemon juice at Alma's. *Mañana,* Matti. *Mañana* you will feel better. I guarantee it."

They pulled up to the front of Hotel Mariposa and Matti was relieved to see that someone had taken the time to close her shutters against the rain. At least her bed wouldn't be soaked through.

Alma's place was as quiet as a church when they went in. Ramón went into the kitchen as if he lived there and she followed. He turned on the overhead light, found the rum under the kitchen sink. He took two lemons from the fruit basket near the door, cut and squeezed them into a mug and put on the kettle to boil. In minutes she had a steaming hot toddy placed on the table in front of her, while overhead the neon ring buzzed bluely making the room and everything in it seem unreal.

"*Gracias,*" Matti said, wiping away wet strands of hair from her face.

"*De nada,*" Ramón said with a wink. "Drink that down, and then get into bed. You're probably a little run down from all the traveling."

She smiled at him. "You sound like my mother."

"I don't *look* like your mother, I hope."

"No," Matti said. "There isn't the slightest resemblance." Why was she feeling so randy all of a sudden?

He leaned over and kissed her on the cheek. "You look very sweet when you're wet."

"Now I'm getting flustered." She could actually feel herself blush.

"Don't be." The deep smile lines on either side of his mouth were starting to work their magic.

"So, will I be able to see Dolores tomorrow, then?" Nothing like changing the subject to stop thinking about kissing. Kissing Sam. Kissing Ramón. Soon Brandon would need to whip out Atlas's Canon of Ethics for a little tutorial.

"I'll ask her."

"Could you also draw me up a list of other people who knew your father best?"

"Of course," Ramón said. He kept smiling. He hadn't mentioned again about her leaving the day after tomorrow. What a mature man! What a thoroughly attractive, adult male he was turning out to be. She stood up.

"Goodnight, Matti," he said, and this time there was no mistaking it, the buzz of his attraction, coming so close she could smell his skin. Suddenly the spongy sofa in the lobby seemed like a great idea.

"Goodnight," her mouth managed to say while her brain gave instructions. Leave the kitchen and walk up the stairs. Go to bed. Go to bed now!

"*Hasta mañana*," she said, backing away. Was she growing up, or what?

Probably "or what". She headed up the stairs for bed.

CHAPTER 13

She woke up in the dark, feeling headachy. It was six am. At least she'd had seven hours. She got up and threw open the shutters to a streaky orange-tinged sky. The palm trees ringing the lagoon looked like ghosts in the mist.

And Ramón was right. The fever had broken, her sinuses had almost cleared. With a little luck and a few Advil she'd be feeling fine in no time.

She walked out to the landing, and called down to Alma, who luckily was within earshot, to ask for a glass of juice. She washed her hair with a minimum of water; how could water be so icy in the tropics? She had a bathrobe on by the time the knock came at the door.

"Come in," she said, combing out her hair at the little vanity table.

Victor poked his head in the door shyly. "Juice?"

"Thanks Victor, just put it here on the table. I'm trying to keep the doctor away."

He put the juice down, and then backed up to the door, smiling. "You want to go in the *cayuco*?" he asked. "I'll take you today."

"Let's see how I feel. Maybe this afternoon we can go for a swim. Will you be around?"

He shrugged. "Already went fishing."

"You've been and come back?"

"Yes'm."

"Well. You're certainly more diligent in your job than I am," she said. "Did you catch anything?"

"Plenty pargo," he told her grinning. "I see some funny boats go by."

"Oh?"

"Yeah, big *cayucos*—big boats. Not from here, though. And big motors too."

"Really?" she asked. "How many were there?"

"Two, going out."

"Out to sea?"

"Yes, to sea," he said. His curiosity about the boats had piqued her own.

"Maybe they were going fishing," she said.

"Maybe."

"If you're around later, maybe I'll take you up on that ride, alright?"

"Al*right*," he said.

Matti dressed and went downstairs. She wanted to call Sam and have a nice leisurely chat. Until she realized it was Saturday. The office was closed, and she didn't have his new home number. *Damn.* She didn't want to leave some short message on his voice mail. She wanted to talk. No point calling her mother, who'd immediately assume something was wrong. She'd already talked to Brian.

She sighed, picked up the phone and called Ramón's home.

A young woman answered. *"Allo?"*

"Me pondría con Ramón, por favor." Matti asked.

"Como?" the woman asked. *"No hablo ingles."* It was a source of constant amazement that Matti could speak Spanish to certain people who, upon hearing her accent, thought she was actually speaking English.

"Está Ramón?" Matti asked, louder than usual.

The woman sighed. *"Si, si. Espera."*

Ramón sounded happy to hear from her. " Matti. Feeling better?"

"Much better, thank you," Matti said, glad beyond belief that she hadn't attacked him in the lobby after all. Funny the little things that made you feel happy to face another day. "Did you speak to Dolores?"

"Yes. She'll meet with you at eleven, is that okay?"

"Perfect. I'd be delighted to meet her."

Ramón paused. "Dolores doesn't get delighted, Matti. But she's agreed. Will you join us for lunch?"

"Thanks Ramón, but I think I'll pass."

"I'll send Jorge to pick you up. I drew up the list you wanted. It's not a very long list. And these people have already been interviewed by both the police and our private investigators. You're welcome to have another try." Pessimistic to say the least.

"I'll see you later," she told him. "And Ramón. Thanks for dinner last night. Except for the gale-force winds, I really enjoyed it."

Matti went into Alma's kitchen, and found a cup and saucer laid out on the table with a note: "Help yourself. Gone to church for choir practice. Eggs and bread in fridge. Alma." She scrambled some eggs, made coffee and went outside.

The morning smelled like ripe fruit and fresh cut grass. The sun was already warm. After she ate, she took out her briefcase and made some notes, and finished the letter to Ramón. If she didn't have a break in the case in the next two days she'd dictate the letter to Ashley, who would send it by fax and then certified mail to the family, declining coverage until more evidence was forthcoming.

Ten-thirty. She had half an hour, and decided to stroll around the lagoon under the palms and around the corner. Maybe she could see the Frutas Tropicales port from the head of the lagoon. The water was clear and green, even though a half dozen waste pipes were apparently emptying their gray water directly into the sea.

About fifty yards away, she noticed a stocky man sitting in a *cayuco* with his back to her. A gringo. He looked out of place, reading a paperback under the hot sun without a hat on. As if reading her mind, he suddenly got up, stepped out of the boat and disappeared behind a clump of mangrove. What a funny place for a tourist.

She couldn't reach the head of the inlet, so headed back to Alma's. Jorge came for her at just after eleven. Already the heat of the day had risen, little drops of sweat clung to her upper lip and she kept wiping them away. This time she was glad for the air conditioning in Ramón's car, at least it helped her feel like she wasn't growing a mustache. The cold air blasted away, and she felt he chest tighten. She wondered if all the changes between hot and cold would give her bronchitis. Perfect! Then she'd have her mother bringing over her Garbage Soup, a truly toxic combination of mystery meat and root vegetables that Lillian had always insisted was a cure-all for viruses of every description, including yeast infections!

Matti buttoned the top buttons on her blouse, smiled at Jorge, and switched down the a/c fan. She needed to get the facts and get out of here. The lack of evidence in this case was starting to get on her nerves.

Maybe Sam was right. Maybe she needed to travel less. Maybe Sam—in mentioning an office job—wanted her closer. But would she ever be ready to trade international travel and adventure for a nine to five life? A career of sameness? The thought made her shiver, and concentrate. If she didn't start to get some facts in this case soon, maybe the whole career question would be a moot point!

Jorge turned into the Cardozo compound, and up the hill they went. This was good. The primary interviews could probably be wrapped up in two days; she could fly back to Boston on Tuesday and do the rest of the diligence from there.

Jorge ran around to her side of the car but Matti was already out the door, pen in hand. She strode to the big wood door, and banged the brass knocker, and the door fell open, revealing a wan-looking Doña Violeta standing in the middle of her lobby full of orchids. She greeted Matti with a frail hand.

"Bienvenida, señorita," she said, as if they'd never met. A glassy-eyed serenity had replaced the desperation that had marked their first meeting. Matti wondered if Ramón's mother was on medication, and if so, who had given it to her.

I'll have what she's having, Matti thought, suddenly overwhelmed. How was she going to nail down any facts in just two days if this was what she had to work with?

She shook Doña Violeta's hand, and pressed forward into the house. She wasn't going to be put politely out to pasture any more. With Dona Violeta trailing behind, Matti walked forward into the living room just in time to see Ramón finish speaking angrily out of the side of his mouth to a woman who could only be Dolores.

Seeing Matti, their discord evaporated, as Ramón took Dolores's arm, and they came forward to greet her.

"Matti Maitlin, my sister, Dolores Maria."

"Hello," the woman said without emotion. Matti put Ramón's sister in her mid-thirties, but like many plain women, Dolores Maria could have been any age. Her long, dark brown hair was shiny, her best feature. Her skin was lackluster and pale, devoid of makeup. Wire rimmed glasses were held in place by a patrician nose, and though she shared Ramón's large brown eyes, she lacked the long, dark eyelashes that framed his. Unfair, really, that her brother had been blessed with all the beauty in the family. Also, it seemed, the charm, as after the introduction she just stared at Matti blankly.

"Pleased to meet you, Dolores," Matti said, releasing the damp, boneless hand. "Thank you for taking the time to see me today." Everything about this woman screamed dull and shut down. Her navy skirt was a convent-style A-line worn with a plain white blouse.

These were usually the easy ones, she'd found. Introverted people were invariably easier to open up than gregarious ones. Bubbly people knew how to duck and defend themselves. She'd get right to the point with Dolores, Matti thought. Then move on.

"Is there somewhere we can speak privately? " Matti asked brightly. She didn't want Ramón lurking in the background, or Dona Violeta fussing over them during the interview.

"Of course," Ramón said, trying to accommodate himself to this sudden rush to action. "You can use this room for your meeting. I'll take my mother back to her room. Mother?"

Ramón extended his arm, and his mother took it unquestioningly. She nodded at Matti and smiled weakly. "*Hasta luego*," she said, waving at her with her blue-veined hand.

Dolores and Matti went to the sofa and seated themselves. Matti took her folder into her lap, opened it, took out a pen, and smiled at Dolores. I guess I can skip the opening warm-up, Matti thought. Dolores was sitting primly, ankles tightly crossed. Was Dolores a product of convent school? Or just a stiff, humorless woman with no sex life?

When Dolores reached over to a wooden box on the coffee table, took out a cigarette and lit it, Matti couldn't have been more surprised than if she'd started to peel off her clothes.

"I hope you don't mind if I smoke," Dolores said in a surprisingly strong, husky voice, remarkably like her brother's. Her English was perfect, nearly without an accent.

"Not at all," Matti said. The covers of all books were not so revealing. Maybe Dolores had a secret other life, or maybe she was just addicted to nicotine.

"Dolores," she began, "I'm hoping you can shed some light on your father's disappearance for me." Co-opting was always best in the interview situation. If she reverted to badgering, she'd lose control.

Dolores nodded, her face stoic and impassive as she looked at Matti. She put the cigarette in her mouth and inhaled deeply, looking away. Maybe this wasn't going to be so easy after all.

"I know you've been already given a statement to the police and have probably gone over and over the events leading up to your father's disappearance a hundred times, but today I need you to tell me the story again. I'm going to record everything on this tape. It will be your story of the day your father disappeared. So just tell me what you know in your own words, and to the best of your knowledge, alright? Just relax. If you forget something we'll just add it in later. So take your time." She paused to give the woman a chance to digest this. "Any questions?" she asked, and Dolores shook her head.

Matti removed her tape recorder, pushed the On button, tested the machine, then began talking into it giving the date, time and place of the interview, also the case number.

"Could you give me your full name please?" Matti asked, starting to relax. This was familiar territory, getting a statement from someone involved in a case.

"Dolores Maria Mercedes Cardozo."

Matti remembered that in Spain, the children took their mother's maiden name followed by their father's. "Are you married Dolores?"

"No."

"Children?"

A slight hesitation. "No."

"What is your date of birth?"

"December 29, 1970."

"Dolores, you're the daughter of Sr. Ramón Cardozo. Is that correct?"

"Yes, I am." A sudden tearful look.

"Anytime you need a break, Dolores, just tell me, and we'll stop. Alright?" Dolores nodded.

"You are also the Chief Financial Officer for Frutas Tropicales. Is that right?"

Dolores nodded, and reach for another cigarette. "You need to answer out loud, Dolores."

"Yes, I am the CFO for my father's company."

"Fine. Now. Can you tell me please what you remember about the twenty-second of August? Start in the morning when you got up, and tell me everything you can remember in your own words."

Dolores dragged deeply on her cigarette and leaned back on the sofa. She looked at the tape recorder and began speaking in her strangely masculine voice. "I'm an earlier riser. I am the first one up in the house, except for Luz who gets up to make breakfast for the family. She gets up normally at five thirty. I take my shower by six, and that day was no different. It was a Monday." Tears brimmed up along the bottom of her lower lids again but she blinked them back. Her face otherwise remained as impassive as stone. "It was a sunny morning, but threatened rain. From up here we can see far out to the horizon, and see the weather coming. 'Before the weatherman,' my father always said."

She looked around the room like a little girl who's lost her way. "Anyway, the rain did come later, lots of rain. And we were glad because the bananas were dry. It had been a drier winter than usual and they needed the water."

"Does your father get up early too?" Matti asked, steering her back onto a chronological recollection of events.

"Oh yes, we had breakfast together that morning." A dreamy look, not unlike Dona Violeta's. "We had papaya. We always had papaya and other fruit for breakfast. And then some *tostadas* and coffee. We would plan the day."

"And your mother, and Ramón? Did they join you?"

"No, Mother and Ramón would breakfast after we left, generally at 7:30 or so. Ramón hates to get up in the morning, and mother, since her accident also sleeps later."

"Your mother had an accident?"

"Yes, her face—you must have noticed. She was in the kitchen. She slipped and grabbed the handle of a small pot of soup she was heating up. She got second degree burns on her face."

Matti winced. She remembered the melted quality of Doña Violeta's face which she'd assumed was a stroke. She'd obviously been a great beauty in her day. Now scars on one side mutilated her face.

"Of course, she's had plastic surgery," Dolores said. "But I don't think it helped much. She used to be a minor movie actress, you know. She was devastated. Has never been the same since, really." The distant look again, with just a dash of spite.

Jealous of her mother's former beauty?

"So, back to the events of that morning," Matti said, bringing her back on track. "You and your father had breakfast together. What did you talk about?"

Dolores stabbed out her cigarette, and began twirling her hair again. "Well, we had an interview scheduled that morning with a potential new accountant. Someone to help out in the bookkeeping department since Inez got pregnant. We spoke about that, about the person's qualifications. It is not easy to find someone locally who has knowledge of the computer accountancy programs we use. This individual did, and we thought we would definitely hire him. Other than that we talked about the rain, you know. The usual."

"And then you left for work?"

"Yes."

"Did you and your father often travel to work together?"

"Every day." Her hair play had developed a definite rhythm. Twist, tug, flip, twist, tug, flip. All that repressed emotion, Matti thought. Did it ever find release?

"And then what happened?"

"We drove to work, and….that's right. We were heading down the hill—it's a narrow driveway—and we saw Julian coming up. Julian seemed to be in a hurry and my father swerved out of the way. Then he backed up, and rolled down his window."

"Who is Julian?" *Play dumb.*

"Julian Quintero. He is one of the overseers. He's in charge of Finca 8."

"The fincas? Oh yes," Matti said, "Ramón explained that. The entire farm is divided up into sub-farms, and each is run as an autonomous unit."

"Yes," Dolores said, with a grimace that might've been a smile. Luz, young, slight and energetic, appeared with coffee and sandwiches on a tray.

"Do you remember what they talked about?" Matti asked.

"Something about the Colombians," Dolores said. "Problems with the Colombians."

"And what did your father say?"

"He was used to problems with this faction of the work force. They're always wanting to strike."

"I see," Matti said. "So your father had no comment."

"He said: 'We'll talk later', something like that."

They entered a twilight zone of silence then, instigated intentionally by Matti to see what insights she might gain by just shutting up. She poured herself coffee then stirred it with a spoon, just waiting.

After a five-minute vacuum, Matti smiled at Dolores as though she were the most fascinating person she'd ever met, and started in again. "Were Quintero and your father close?"

"Yes, they've known each other for many years. My father had been feeling that Julian needed to retire, though, and he didn't want to hurt his feelings. Julian is a worrier, and always has been. The Colombians have worked for us for years, and are reliable. Believe me, if there were problems on Finca 8, my father would know about them." There was a change in Dolores's body language as she said this, a slight tightening of the jaw, the hands clenching, even more defensive, if that was possible.

"Do you trust Quintero?" Matti asked, taking a stab in the dark.

"Not really," Dolores said, looking away, as if bored.

"And why is that?"

"He was too close to my father, too *friendly*," she said, as if this explained it. The class system in Platanillo was apparently alive and well.

"And Ramón? Does he feel the same way?"

"Ramón's only been back a little over a year. He doesn't know what's *really* going on." Dolores laughed dismissively. "Ramón is only in charge because my father is *not here*."

"So, you and your father went to work together," Matti said, switching gears. "Any other conversation in the car on the way?"

"Nothing I can think of," Dolores said dryly.

"What mood was your father in that day, Dolores?" Matti asked, thinking: there's got to be some little morsel on this bone somewhere!

"Mood?" Dolores asked. "I don't know what you mean. My father was not a moody person."

"I mean was he in good spirits? Was he happy? Sad? Pensive?"

"Well, I guess he was somewhat quieter that day than usual. But I couldn't describe him in your terms. He was strong-willed, fast-moving, my father. Driven. I guess that would describe him best. He was always restless, wanting movement, as if he was running a race against time. A perfectionist." Dolores looked off into the room again, twirling her hair compulsively.

"Dolores?" Matti asked. "What do *you* think happened to your father?"

"I think he was kidnapped," she said, her voice turning low and venomous. "Kidnapped and killed by Worldwide Produce. They wanted him out of the way so they could buy Frutas Tropicales and all it holdings."

She looked at Matti, with eyes full of rage. Moving on, it seemed, would not to be a part of Dolores's agenda for years. She'd been daddy's little girl, and was now a wounded woman who'd been abandoned by the most important man in her life.

"But Worldwide made a mistake," she told Matti. "If they wanted the company, they should have killed *me*, not him. Because they'll only get the company over my dead body now that they've murdered my father. It's as simple as that."

At least there was some collaboration in theories. Dolores and Ramón, though seemingly full bore into a deep sibling rivalry, shared the same thoughts on their father's disappearance. They both believed Papi Cardozo had been kidnapped by Worldwide Produce, and then killed.

"And how are the shares currently distributed?" Matti asked neutrally, for this was one of the big questions she wanted answered.

"Twenty-four percent each to Ramón and me. My father held a controlling interest of the remainder, or fifty-two percent."

"And if it's proven he's dead?"

"Ramón will have a controlling interest of fifty-one percent, and I'll have the remainder." She looked grim at the prospect. "My mother will receive a generous stipend until her death, and of course this home is hers." Dolores had retreated behind a big wall of rage and passivity. Getting her out again would take more than a jackhammer.

"Does Worldwide Produce still want to buy you out?"

"Oh yes," Dolores said. "They even had the nerve to call here, an attorney by the name of Corcoran in their Boston office. He pretended he didn't know Papi was missing."

Matti made a note. Corcoran/WWP, she wrote. Check it out with Brandon.

"And what about that? Can either of you sell your shares to Worldwide?"

"Ramón can't sell without my approval, and I can't sell without his. Plus, we have to give each other a right of first refusal before selling to a third party," Dolores said. She reached over, and took out another cigarette and lit it, while the sandwich bread stiffened on the plate in front of her.

"Is there anything else you want to tell me about the morning before your father disappeared? What happened when he got to the office? Did he receive any phone calls, faxes or special e-mails that you know of? Did he meet with anyone?"

"No." Dolores shook her head. "It was a perfectly normal morning. He went out late in the morning to go to Finca 8. There was a problem with heavy winds and he needed to talk to Quintero about windbreaks."

"And then he returned to the office?"

"Yes."

"Was he by himself?"

"Yes." She paused.

"Then what happened?"

"He went into his office, and came out to go to lunch at about a quarter to one."

"He went by himself?"

"Yes."

"And he went in his own car?"

"Yes. I was going out at the same time, and saw him leave." Dolores seemed to find the memory painful. Her lower lids brimmed with tears that never fell.

"We're almost finished, Dolores," Matti said. "Where did they find your father's car?"

"Near the rancho."

"You mean the restaurant? Was he meeting Ramón there for lunch?"

"No. Ramón and he always ate in town at the company restaurant."

"The rancho—is it outside of town near a beach?"

"Yes."

Matti remembered a winding dirt road through wooded terrain and the rain that had soaked her skin as it blew in across Banana Bay. The rancho, Matti thought. How many places were there to abduct someone along that road? And why had Papi been going there in the first place?

"But he didn't go to the rancho—did he eat there before he disappeared?"

"No, his car was pulled over on the side of the road, about a half mile before the rancho."

"Well, Dolores. I think that covers it. I'll only need to have your verbal verification on one last important point: Have you or any member of your family received any notice, threat or demand from anyone claiming to have killed or kidnapped your father?"

"No."

"No note, no call, no hint of foul play from anyone. No threat from Worldwide Produce or any of their representatives."

"No.

"And yet you're sure Worldwide is involved."

"Oh, yes. You don't know how vicious they are. They kidnapped that executive in Honduras, remember? He convinced some of the company's farmers to produce for another big consortium in Europe."

"No. I didn't hear about that."

"Or the Indians who were told to vacate lands that they bought from the company in Belize? Or the governments they have manipulated in the Far East? The markets they have flooded and choked over the years. Believe me, Miss Maitlin. There's a lot more than meets the eye with Worldwide than a pretty pink sticker on a banana. Much more. And now they want Frutas Tropicales. Wait and see what they do next. Just wait."

"I hope you're mistaken, Dolores, for all our sakes."

Dolores smiled grimly. "You think it's the money, don't you? Well, it's not. The insurance payment means nothing to me. I want justice done, Miss Maitlin, and I'll use any means to get it. If the authorities launch a high-profile investigation against Worldwide, it's fine with me. If your company has to sue Worldwide for damages, that's fine too."

"I can see you've really thought this through, Dolores," Matti said. She reached over and shut off the tape recorder. "Unfortunately, pursuing the kind of scenario you describe would take years, and I imagine some very hefty legal fees. Atlas would only go against Worldwide if all the evidence was irrefutable, and then only after a final legal verdict was made."

Dolores looked away, and for a minute Matti saw the rage that ran beneath the surface of Dolores's demeanor like an icy stream.

"Thanks for your time, Dolores," Matti said. "I'm sure we'll be speaking again." She tried a warm smile, like trying to win over a polar bear inside a meat locker. "I guess I'll need to see your mother another day. She didn't seem very well."

"As you like," Dolores said. A Latin lady with a subzero personality, Matti couldn't remember ever meeting the type. "I'll send Ramón out." She shook Matti's hand hard this time, before turning and leaving the room.

Alone in the great room of the Cardozo home, Matti went to the large plate glass window and looked out at the bananas rolling down the hill and into the distance in an undulating green wave set against a vivid blue sky.

What did it all add up to?

If Papi's death, or even his kidnapping, could be proved, payout was assured. A hundred percent on that one. If one of the *beneficiaries* of the policy had done the deed, that was a different story. She'd once had a case where this had happened. The courts had implicated one of the sons of the insured in his murder. Still, the other beneficiaries—not implicated—had received their full benefits from the policy. Actually, each had received *more* than their original percentage because they didn't have to share the proceeds with the perpetrator.

If the allegations could be proven against Worldwide, Atlas could in theory recoup the damages. The whole scenario was messy and far-fetched beyond belief. Matti hated cases like this: Suits and countersuits that remained open for years and didn't solve anything. Meanwhile, where was Papi Cardozo? Was he dead? Kidnapped? Or kidnapped then murdered? This was the heart of the case; why she was here.

Unfortunately, a large part of the information for her investigation came from the family itself. The beneficiaries were also Atlas clients in a manner of speaking. They'd receive payout based on the facts. She had the letter to the family declining coverage already in her briefcase. But timing was everything. If she didn't handle it right, lawyers would be brought back *en force*, a litigious nightmare begun.

Meanwhile, what other choice did she have for this family who had as many theories as blue gel caps in a super-size Advil bottle, and nothing but circumstantial evidence to back them up? Could she appease them and convince them to wait for further investigation? Should she keep the letter, or not?

Early settlement on a policy worked like a psychological massage. If claimants didn't have anything to hold onto, a nice fat check always made them feel on some level that life was fair. She could handle it this way, too. Unfortunately, she'd found that too often the feeling wore off and the beneficiaries wanted more than they'd originally agreed to.

She also needed to keep the Cardozos from suing Atlas. And for that she needed Brandon Howard. He was brilliant at coming up with successful strategies in cases like this where clients needed to be put on hold. She needed his input, and needed it now. She'd call him first thing on Monday morning. She'd keep interviewing people throughout the weekend, and keep the ball rolling.

Matti walked over get her notepad, and it was at that precise moment that Ramón walked into the room. His face was as white as the limp piece of paper he held in his hand.

CHAPTER 14

Instinctively she moved toward him. "Ramón, are you alright?"

"They've made contact. Can you believe it? I went to settle Mother into her room, and thought I'd have a look in my father's study. I just hadn't thought to go in there the past few days. He has a private fax line, and I found this…I can't believe it! It's two days old!" He passed it to Matti, and began pacing the room, as she read in chunky hand-writing:

LISEN GOOD. YOUR FATHER ALIVE. GET READY TWO MILLION DOLLARS IN HUNREDS. UNMARKED OR HE DIES. NO POLICE OR HE DIES. WAIT INSTRUCTIONS IN TWO DAYS. YOU PAY, PAPI LIVES.

"My God, Ramón, that's today. Right?"

"Jesus! How could I be so stupid not to check his fax machine? I expected a phone call….maybe an e-mail. Why didn't I think?" Ramon's normal golden skin had turned an angry red. "I'll fucking kill the bastards! I'll kill them, I swear it." He began rubbing his hands through his hair, pacing up and down.

"Has Dolores seen this?"

"Yes, she came to find me. When she read the fax, she just ran out of the bedroom saying she'd find the bank manager." As they spoke, Matti heard the sound of a car being gunned near the house and burning rubber as it departed.

She took a deep breath. "God, I wish it wasn't Saturday." She'd never needed to get authorization on a two million dollar ransom payment on a weekend before. "We need to think clearly, make a plan," Matti said, trying to take her own advice. "Ramón, there is no guarantee, none at all, that the kidnappers will make good on their promise to keep your father alive. They are thugs. Remember that. You can't just throw money at people like this, because too often you're buying nothing but an empty promise. Do you hear me?"

"Ha! But now we have *coverage*, don't we, Matti?" he said. "We didn't a moment ago, but now we do. The kidnapping clause in the policy. Remember?"

Matti remembered very well. It could take up to 24 hours to get the money wired down, maybe sooner if it was a weekday. Should she contact Signa Security? They were contracted by Atlas as consultants for cases such as this. Unfortunately, time was against them. They were 48 hours late in even seeing the kidnappers' message. They'd be making contact again today, any moment, perhaps. Signa was based in Cincinnati. How long would it be before they could get down here?

"Yes, I *do* remember, Ramón," she said, trying to sound more in control than she felt. "And it looks like the decision will be up to me."

She walked over to the window and stared out, folding her arms across her chest. Think, Matilda, think. Thinking was always easier if she focused on some benign object or view. Her mind-to-mouth connection could work like a well-oiled machine if she didn't have to maintain eye contact as well. Many people were disconcerted by this well-ingrained habit, her way of focusing, and would look where she looked to see what was so fascinating. Ramón did this now, peering out the window behind her to see the source of her absorption.

"For the time being we'll act on this ransom demand as if it were bonafide," Matti said to the window. "This is what the policy dictates. We must act to save your father, but in the most thoughtful way possible. We'll need to contact the police, of course...we'll worry about verification later."

She finally looked back at Ramón, who snapped from his reverie at the same time her words sunk in.

"Verification? Are you out of your mind? Do you think this demand isn't *valid,* for God's sake? Are you saying it's a fake?" Ramón asked, incredulous

"I'm saying," she told him, "that we will follow up on this aspect later."

"You're a bitch, you know that?" he told her coldly. "Just another blond bitch who thinks she can sweep all the balls in the room into the corner." The deep lines around the corners of his mouth, which usually emphasized his smile, were now apostrophes to his rage.

"I don't believe you just said that," Matti said, pulling her arms closer around her.

"And no police," he said, pointing a finger at her.

"Calm down, Ramón," she said, mad now too. "I'm not your ex-wife—not even close." *Whatever that meant!* Her father's temper hovered above her head like a storm cloud ready to throw off a few bolts of lightening. She took a deep breath. "We need to concentrate as a team, not behave like adversaries." Luckily, the cloud was passing with only a little thunder, and no direct hits.

"This fax...I can't believe it was just sitting there for the last two days," he said, sadness taking over.

She took it from him, and read it again.

"I thought my father was dead, and now he might be alive. Keeping him might be in my power! These are big emotions,

Matti. Bigger than I've ever experienced. You're the professional here. Help me."

She remembered a short course they'd been given by Signa Security on clients who are victims of violent crime. First came denial, then sadness, then more denial, then deep grieving.

"And I'm here, Ramón, here to help in whatever way I can." She was trying to calm herself too, knowing that adrenaline once released into the blood takes almost three minutes to dissipate.

They walked into Doña Violeta's bedroom, and found her lying on the bed in darkness very much asleep. "I sedated her," Ramón whispered. "The doctor gave me the prescription. She doesn't need to know what's going on right now, it would probably kill her." They walked softly past the bed in the big room, past the rowing machine near the window. Ramón opened a set of double doors that looked like they led to a closet, and Matti saw it was really the entrance to Papi's study.

They went in. A typical home office, Matti saw, with a large wood desk, a computer turned off, a neat blotter with no notes, no diary, only a calendar that was torn to the last day anyone had seen Papi Cardozo alive. A yellow legal pad lay vacantly to one side, a cup filled with pencils at the ready. These were the marks of an organized man, Matti thought, and wondered whether Papi's small study had ever been searched, things removed, in the course of the police investigation.

"The police were here, the private investigators too," he told her, anticipating her question. "There was a list on the pad, but it was very ordinary. A list of things to do, nothing else." He sighed deeply. "Quite honestly I hadn't given this place another thought until today."

"Well, better late than never at all, I guess we can say in this instance. Imagine if the kidnappers left all these messages and no one ever saw them until after the fact." They both looked at each other.

"So, I guess we have to wait," Ramón said. He seemed more resigned than angry now. "Dolores has gone to find the bank manager. She'll want to get her hands on the ransom money. I know her, Matti. She won't wait for you, or me, or any insurance company to decide what to do. Trust me."

"Maybe Luz can make us some coffee," Matti said.

"Of course," Ramón said. He pressed an intercom button and put in the order.

They looked at each other in silent acknowledgement. Truce, their eyes said. I accept your apology if you accept mine. Let's move on.

They both turned and stared at the fax machine as if at any moment it would come alive.

"This is your father's study and you said his fax number is private. How many people would have access to him here?"

Ramón shook his head. "My father was a very open man, Matti. He encouraged all his deputies and overseers to contact him at home whenever they felt there was a need. It was a good system. People felt they could come to him with anything and he'd give them a decision or a response personally. In that way, the company was run very much like a family."

"Which is why he has the name he has," Matti added.

"Exactly."

"And has anyone used the fax machine since his departure, do you know?"

"I don't think so. Not unless my mother's been using it. But I doubt she even knows how it works."

"So, we could get a journal print-out for the last 20 calls sent and received. Did anyone do that yet?"

"What a great idea! No I'm sure they didn't. Fax machines are not used much in Platanillo, believe it or not—they're considered old-fashioned now. Most people seem to have gone from hand-written correspondence to e-mail. If I thought about it, I could probably tell you everyone who owns one in the area."

"I'm not sure that would help. You said you thought the threat is from Worldwide. If your theory is right, they could send a fax from anywhere in the world. Of course, the kidnappers themselves, if they were hirelings of the company, will presumably have the smarts to eliminate their caller ID. Then again...I saw a couple of obvious spelling mistakes in their message."

"Let's do it," Ramón said, as Luz came in with a tray of coffee and cups. Ramón poured while Matti studied the machine, pressed the journal key, and got a print out of eight out-going faxes, and twelve incoming. All were dated prior to August 22nd, but one. Three of the eight outgoings and two of the incoming faxes were of the same number. Prefixes of 617 and 781. Both in the greater Boston area. Where Worldwide Produce had their headquarters. Well, well, Matti thought.

Ramón ripped the sheet off and scanned it. "These are the area codes for Massachusetts, aren't they? I knew it."

"We can check out the numbers on Monday through my office, but off the top of your head, do you know if your father had any contact with anyone in Boston other than Worldwide?"

"Not a soul. His whole life is here. Most of his old school friends live in Florida, a couple in New York. That's it. Worldwide is his only connection in Boston as far as I know."

"This looks very implicating," Matti said, "but something just doesn't smell right here." Ramón nodded, and let her evolve the thought for both of them. "You said Worldwide killed your father to remove him. The theory was, *your* theory—Dolores's too—is that they wanted him out of the way so they could buy you out. Get rid of the non-assenting party, and buy your shares. Fine. That makes sense. But if it's true, why didn't they kill him? And why are they now seeking a ransom of two million dollars nearly three weeks after they took him? A multinational corporation would hardly go to all this trouble for two million dollars. And I can't honestly imagine them using this hostage scenario to throw you off their scent. It's just plain weird."

"Maybe they decided killing him was too cold blooded. Maybe they decided to hold him for a while and scare us into a decision. It wouldn't be the first time."

"Yes, but it's an awful lot of trouble, and they're getting into complications that they could have avoided by actually killing him...though I don't mean that *heartlessly*," she emphasized.

"No, I see your point."

"The other thing that bothers me is this: Dolores told me you're not the only shareholder. That in fact you have a majority on your father's death, but she still maintains a near-equal share position."

"And she told you that I needed her permission to buy out her shares, right?" Ramón said, shaking his head. "She's deluded, Matti. I have a copy of the will that I can show you. In it my father specifies that she must sell to me if I make a formal request at a fair price which he also spelled out. She can't refuse. Papi wanted to avoid any in-fighting after his death, and this was how he handled it. If Dolores becomes a problem, I will buy her out. Simple as that. Maybe my father fed her that line about the right of first refusal. He often manipulated my sister like that and never wanted to have a scene with her about any of this. He is a true Latino macho, Matti. And poor Dolores.

She really suffers from the most severe Electra complex, one reason she poured that soup on my mother's face."

"She *burned* her?"

"And she told you how my mother slipped, and pulled some hot soup off the stove onto herself?"

"Exactly."

"Well, unfortunately, dear Luz heard my mother fall and then scream, and arrived to find Dolores standing over my mother with the pot in her hand. Just standing there watching her scream and doing nothing. Mother of course, who was half-conscious at the time, defended Dolores afterwards. But we all knew the truth."

"And your father? What did he think?"

"Let's say he saw a side of Dolores he hadn't seen before. After the quote unquote *accident*, he began to cool off his relationship with her. Of course, it was about the time I came back from Florida.... so Dolores blames me for the change in their relationship. "

"And of course, she's still CFO of the company..."

The fax machine rang softly, interrupting them. After three rings it stopped, while Matti and Ramón held their breath and waited. There was no caller ID on the screen, just a line that said: Caller Unknown. The message began to spool itself out.

RAMON. GO TO PAPI'S DOCK AT 7 TONIGHT. BRING TWO MILLION CASH IN HUNREDS. TURN ON RADIO CHANAL NINE. WAIT FOR NEWS. NO POLICE OR PAPI DIES. NO MONEY PAPI DIES.

"My God," Ramón said, his eyes glazed over in a combination of horror and disbelief. "Are they holding him out at sea?"

CHAPTER 15

We have to call the police," Matti said. "Who do you trust to help us handle this?" That was another Signa caveat: Don't by mystified, and controlled, by what the kidnappers are telling you. Don't go it alone.

"Bolivar Santamaria is the Chief of the Policia Nacional here in Platanillo, *el jefe.* I trust him completely. He's a bit long-winded, but he's a good man. An old family friend. If I didn't tell him about Papi, I'd hate to stick around for the consequences."

"Good. We need him. We'll be needing some manpower standing by. God knows where they might have your father." *If they have him at all.* "You know Ramón," Matti said, "these messages from the kidnappers are no guarantee your father's alive."

"I know." He looked grim.

"Let me say this: The policy will indemnify Frutas Tropicales in the case of the kidnapping of one of its executive officers, we will pay the ransom and try to negotiate on your father's behalf to keep him alive. As we don't have two million dollars on hand, though, you'll have to use your own funds and we'll reimburse you. " Ramón nodded mutely. His expression said: Don't you ever give up?

Matti ignored him, took a large barrette out of her bag, twisted her hair up, and clipped it firmly in place. "Will Dolores be able to get the money?" she asked.

"I really don't know. If the bank has that kind of money in its safe, we'll get it. I just don't know if on the weekend, after payroll, they'd have that kind of cash lying around in the vaults."

"Let's see," Matti said, breaking into another of her fugue-like states involving a plaque mounted on a wall. "It's almost two now. We need to get hustling, whether we've got the money or not. We need to get some provisions on the boat and be prepared to move. We need to call Boli Santamaria as well. Let's do that now."

"We?" Ramón said. "What's this about *we*? Are you planning on coming to the big event? I thought you were going back to Boston." He smirked at her.

"Who me?" she said, arching an eyebrow. "No, I can't leave now. Believe it or not, this is what Atlas pays me to do. We didn't have any evidence of a K&R before, now we do. That changes everything."

"That doesn't mean you should be involved physically, Matti. I just can't allow you..."

"Don't give me that Latin routine, Ramón, I have to go, in any case..."

"In any case—what?"

"The ransom *might* be recoverable, Ramón" she said. "You never know." Brandon would never agree that this was part of her job description. Sam would be furious if he heard these words pass her lips. But they were there, and she was here. Besides, she'd never forgive herself if she let two million dollars of Atlas's money get away, and not tried to *do* something about it.

Ramón gave her a look like she was a few peels short of a banana. They heard a car screech to a halt outside and quickly left the study. Passed by the still sleeping Dona Violeta, and were greeted by the sight of Dolores staggering toward them across the massive lounge a bulky Mickey Mouse bag swinging in front of her.

"The manager gave me a million," she told them both breathlessly, "in his daughter's gym bag." The black bag holding part of the ransom had Mickey Mouse dancing with Minnie in a pink polka-dot dress. "He can get the rest on Monday." She looked from one to the other desperately, and Matti was shocked to see her transformation. Dolores the Passive. Dolores the Cold and Wary. Her marble skin had flushed pink, her brown eyes, without the glasses, glistened with Bambi-like fear. When she began running her fingers through her hair in a near duplication of a favorite Ramón gesture, Matti wondered if they might not be twins.

"We got a second message," Matti told her, trying to stay calm. She was going on that boat. That Mickey Mouse bag wasn't leaving her sight.

"And?"

"And they've given us more instructions." Matti passed her the limp piece of paper. Dolores devoured the information.

"Chanal. That's misspelled, isn't it?"

"Yes." Whoever was doing the writing was no English major.

"We have five hours to get ready," Dolores said. Apparently, she was going too.

"You're not going," Ramón told his sister. At least his machismo still carried some weight with someone.

"Que?" she spat at him. She bored into him with more Spanish epithets than Matti had heard in a barroom once, in a back street barrio in Barcelona.

Matti tried next: "Dolores, the fewer people the better. Trust me. Your emotions are running very high, it's better if you stay out of it."

"*Puta!*" Dolores said. "I knew it. I knew you wouldn't let me go." She seethed not at Matti, but at Ramón. "Always the big brother. Always Ramón gets to be daddy's big star!"

"You're not going, and that's that," Ramón said. He seemed to enjoy taking charge again, putting his sister in "her place."

Matti tried a different tack. "Look, Dolores. We need you *here* to monitor the situation and keep everyone else informed. What if another fax comes in? You have to stay here, and stay in charge," she said in an even voice. "We can't leave your mother waiting for the next kidnapper's message, now can we?"

This seemed to strike the right chord of conciliation. Dolores nodded. Her jaw was still set, but she seemed to soften. "We need to work as a team," Matti said. She was on a roll now, and didn't want to lose her momentum. "So let's get started."

She led the way to the sofa and they all sat down. "Here's what I think may happen," she told them, and began to lay out a scenario in which she and Ramón would be liaising with the kidnappers somewhere at sea. The sky outside was an opaque blue without a cloud in sight. As far as boating went, it was perfect weather for going to sea.

They laid out some rough plans, and Ramón left to call Bolivar Santamaria.

Dolores went to find the VHF Papi used to stay in touch with the family when he went fishing. Dolores explained they always monitored channel 64. Matti hoped the kidnappers would be monitoring only 9 and 16, though obviously when the time came for more explicit instructions they'd switch to another, less public, band.

Dona Violeta continued to sleep. Luz, blissfully unaware of developments, came and offered Matti some pineapple *chicha*.

When she'd left, Matti reiterated the need for absolute secrecy. Only she, Dolores, Ramón and Boli Santamaria would know exactly what was going on; Papi's life might be at stake if the kidnappers felt their conditions hadn't been met.

Matti called the bank manager. Unfortunately, he already knew from Dolores about the reason for the large cash withdrawal. Matti reminded him of the need for absolute confidentiality. If word got out, Matti told him, they'd come and question him first. *"Entiende?"* she asked.

"Si, si," he assured her, hurrying to get off the phone— Matti thought—to intercept his wife before she called everyone in town.

"We can't be sure of how far the news has already traveled, but it will be much less confusing the fewer people know. If the kidnappers are locals, they'll have their ear to the ground for gossip; we don't want to scare them away."

***

The front door knocker reverberated through the room, and Ramón got up and let Bolivar Santamaria into the house. The *Jefe de la Policia Nacional* strode forward in his perfectly-pressed green khaki uniform. He was a short, compact man with a handsome moon-shaped face that showed evidence of his black, Indian and Chinese ancestors, and a round belly that spoke of his fondness for rice and beans. He looked both friendly and commanding, an officer with a big heart. His boots were spit polished to a hard gleam, and he was hatless, his clean pate gleaming with sweat. Matti could feel the short blast of heat which had followed him through the door.

She stood up, so did Dolores, to greet him. He took both their hands in turn, then they all sat down, Bolivar in a big planter's chair across from them.

"Well, then," he said, in accented English, "Tell me what happened."

Ramón told him the story of the faxes, showed him both copies. The police chief studied them quietly for a moment, then started talking. And talking. "Reminds me of the time the Nicaraguans stole Jimbo Johnson's *cayuco*. Didn't know he was in it 'til the next morning and they'd sailed it half way to Límon. Jimbo wakes up, says 'Where am I?' They hit him over the head with a big paddle and knocked the poor man out. His mother Renalda, she was German you know, brought all her antiques here in 1912 and had a big mansion built and put them all in it? Well, she married Mr. Johnson from the American consulate, and they had Jimbo—but THAT CHILD WAS NEVER ANY GOOD. Was peeing in the bushes in the front of the Governor's house when he was nine. I CAUGHT HIM! And then he drank, and well….they kidnapped him just like Papi."

So this is what Ramón meant by long-winded! Matti noticed Bolivar Santamaria finally draw a breath and rushed to interrupt him before they all were buried by an avalanche of more words.

"Captain Santamaria," she began firmly.

"Oh, I know. I know what you're thinking! THAT I'M A LOCAL. Don't know nuthin, right? Well, ha! I know a few things, don't you worry about *that*! I was sent to school in the U.S., ya know. Came back after Torrijos fell, just in time for the Noriega years. I was in the same party as him, and I'm not ashamed to admit it. I didn't know he was into the drug thing then. OF COURSE I DIDN'T. I have three children, would string them up like Christmas lights they ever touch any drug. He was wrong to do what he did. But he won't be coming back now, will he? Not if the French have anything to say about it. And now they get a mayor in Platanillo with a sixth-grade education. Ha! DO THEY THINK THAT'S AN IMPROVEMENT? I…."

"Captain Santamaria, please!" Matti fairly screamed. "This is all fascinating but we don't have the time right now to discuss it." Bolivar's mouth snapped shut like a wounded clam, and he eyed Matti with fleeting indignation, before giving her a nod. He was a consummate politician, Matti saw, not easily thwarted, but adaptable, thank God.

Matti drew in her own breath, and was suddenly at a loss for words, and the police chief rushed in to fill the gap. "Forgive me...I do tend to get sidetracked, Miss Maitlin. Please call my Boli. My brain you see..." he touched his temple, and laughed lightly, "it just races away, totally out of control. I never forget anything, that's the problem. And so it has nowhere to go, just around and around until it has to finally spill out." He opened his hands in a conciliatory gesture, and Matti found herself liking him in spite of the fact she knew she was being played like the major chords on a piano.

Boli Santamaria was as flamboyant as an actor, yet he was also obviously a survivor. An educated man, he was probably lonely living in this small banana town and loved having a new audience. There was intelligence in his eyes, but she wondered if it could be harnessed to help them in their quest. She wondered too what had brought him back here after his U.S. education. Like most small towns, Platanillo was full of characters and dramas woven and rewoven into an intricate tapestry.

Matti was no anthropologist but for the first time she considered just what an outsider she was. She was entering a potentially dangerous, maybe life-threatening situation with people and a culture she hardly knew.

If Sam knew what she was about to undertake, he'd be beyond furious with her. In spite of The Kisses, he might fire her for this level of involvement.

Still, he was there, and she was here. She'd been thrust into a situation where action had to be taken. Because of the timing, she was involved whether she wanted to be or not. If Papi Cardozo was alive, she might help him. Could she help it if she also loved the idea of saving the company two million dollars? This was a far greater buzz than finding Donna Karan outfits at the end-of-summer sale at Filene's Basement.

Matti Maitlin, insurance investigator, was about to go to the Panamá Kidnappers' Sale instead. She had half the demanded ransom in a pink Mickey Mouse bag, no gun, and an abiding sense that the good guys usually won. She looked at Ramón and wondered what he knew about boating. Considering they'd be headed out to sea at night, she hoped he was more than a novice yachtsman.

CHAPTER 16

I can't swim," Ramón told her as they arrived at Papi's dock at six-thirty with all their gear. "I thought you should know."

Papi's fishing boat was a beautiful classic white Bertram with a flybridge and twin screw diesel engines. Ramón ran his hand affectionately over the rail as he described it to her. It was 31 feet with an 11-foot beam, a boat in which to go fishing in safety and comfort, cruising at 25 knots. The big fish—the tuna, marlin, and giant snapper—he explained, shunned Banana Bay, preferring the beginnings of the deep blue Gulf Stream to the calmer lagoon.

They'd come alone to the boat, fearing the kidnappers would be watching their every move. Boli had stayed behind but was monitoring them too. "Indian methods," he explained to Ramón, mysteriously. "Don't forget my mother was half Guaymi."

Across the boat's transom, Matti read: *La Boca Grande.* The Big Mouth. A perfect name for a fishing boat, or a fisherman with big stories to tell. Two fighting chairs were bolted to the wide afterdeck, and two big ice chests stood sentry on both port and starboard sides, for fish storage and beer, Ramón explained.

A few steps below, the joinery was teak, oiled and gleaming. A U-shaped settee doubled as dining room with its big square table, and a tiny galley to starboard. Forward of that she found was the head and a V-berth cabin converted into a triangular queen-sized bed. Surprisingly there was no boat smell. Every power boat she'd ever stepped on had earned its moniker of "stinkpot" with its lingering smells of residual fuel and tainted bilge which could be sickening in a toppling sea.

They stowed their few belongings in the cabin, some supplies in the galley, and Ramón opened windows and hatches, and immediately switched on the radio, passing the receiver to Matti. She checked "home" with Dolores on channel three, their agreed means of communication, to be used as little as possible and only in code unless some emergency dictated otherwise. Matti had designed a quick list of code words before departing just in case the kidnappers were monitoring all stations. They'd be listening for Ramón's voice in Spanish, most likely, not hers in English.

She switched the radio back to channel nine and they sat down and waited.

They'd left Dolores to perform a radio check for Boli whose under-funded department possessed only an old hand-held VHF transceiver. Matti insisted that only she and Ramón be seen as coming to Papi's private dock and boarding the boat. Matti would later appear to disembark. Who knew who was watching their movements as the sun had begun to throw its last fire into the sky?

After the kidnappers gave the next instructions, which would almost certainly involve their going to sea, Boli would organize the police launch to follow at a distance with four of his men. They'd depart in darkness, and follow Papi's boat and hope they'd remain undercover. If they were well-funded, the kidnappers would have long-range radar, trackers, GPS, and God-knows what other technology to make their job easier and less predictable to their adversaries. Matti could only hope they had none of these things and were only some locals trying out their luck.

Luckily, the sea, like the weather, was September calm. This was the month to go to sea, Ramón told her. It was invariably the same every year: sky so blue it made your eyes ache, and a sea as flat as glass day and night. The banana leaves didn't rustle, even here, right down to within twenty feet of Papi's dock where the trees had been planted and bore fruit.

This inlet was an extension from the main port, Ramón explained. She'd see when they got underway. If they got underway. So far, the radio lay silent. They sat in the two fish-fighting chairs, and looked at it. It was ten past seven now. Ramón ran his fingers through his hair several times, unconscious of the gesture. He was a man used to holding all the cards. Now his power had been reduced to waiting for a call on the radio.

Matti felt ready. The adrenaline had started its strumming entry into her bloodstream, calling every sense into focus like those old tap-dance recitals when she was a kid. She'd already started to build toward the challenge that this night would demand. If she was alert enough to execute the right movements at the right time, she might be successful. If not, they might both end up too involved, too emotional. Not only drained, but dead.

Like a fish charmed to the surface by a twisting silver spoon, she could feel herself rising too. This wasn't the first time she'd delved into the action of one of her cases; she was sure it wouldn't be the last, either. On some level, she craved the excitement, but was she addicted to the buzz, the danger or simply being part of the solution? Sam had warned her about this before. Brandon too.

What are they going to do, fire me?

Besides, she was hooked and could already feel the energy pumping through her veins. In this state she was able to make highly intuitive, focused decisions. In most instances there had been a positive outcome when she'd become—ah—involved in her cases. The down side was that she'd feel so exhausted and drained afterwards, she'd have to sleep for a full twenty-four hours to recover: Home if she could get there, a five-star hotel otherwise. Standard procedure.

"What are you thinking?" Ramón asked. "You seem very far away."

She smiled at him. "Human reactions to stress."

"The kidnappers'?"

"No, my own." They paused and looked at each other, their eyes glinting in the darkness. She thought Ramón was attracted to her and that the feeling was starting to become mutual. "We certainly have been thrown in at the deep end together, forgive the pun," she said, trying to lighten the mood. Stress also made her feel very sexy.

"Yes," he said, his voice husky. "We have. Would you like some coffee?" He got up to go below deck, and as he did the radio crackled to life, giving them both a jolt.

"Boca, Boca, Boca, do you copy?"

A man with an American-accented voice that held strong traces of his Latin roots. Ramón nodded at Matti, and she switched on her tape recorder as he lifted the receiver.

"This is *Boca Grande*. Go ahead,"

"Hey big mouth," the speaker said, laughing—that laugh! "Switch to the channel number on the note to the right of the receiver, and don't say it aloud." They could hear fumbling in the background, as though papers were being shuffled. The caller was making the classic mistake of talking too loudly into the microphone and not letting go of the transmit button.

Lack of experience? Suddenly there was silence, then a loud: "Are you listening?"

"I'm all ears." Ramón switched to channel four, as Matti leaned in closer to capture it all on tape.

"You're going to Escudo," the voice continued broadcasting. "At the second channel marker, follow a course of 64 degrees southeast. Get there tonight. You'll be met." A pause, and then as if someone else reminded him to do it, he pressed the button again. "Over," he said.

"I have the ransom money." Ramón told him, his voice calm and assured. "But I need proof my father is alive. Otherwise I'm not coming. Over."

The voice came back, gruff and unflinching. "If you do not come your father will die. If you do not come alone, your father will die. If you do not bring two million dollars, your father will die. Do I make myself clear?" Matti wondered if this one of the kidnappers or just a hired guy with a tough voice. He sounded like a Mexican extra on a bad cowboy movie.

"Oh you're clear," Ramón said. "You're so fucking clear I can't believe I'm not talking to air! So listen up, airhead! I'm not leaving this harbor until I hear my father's voice. If he *is* still alive, I suggest you let me speak to him *now*. Three weeks is kind of a long time to be tied up, you know? I'm not forking over *any* money until I hear my father's voice."

The radio went dead. In the police boathouse Boli might not have heard everything, but Matti could call Dolores and relay the information to her on channel three. How frustrated Boli would be not to hear this transmission himself. He and Papi were old friends. Two *politicos* with different agendas, but the same constituency. Matti thought of him, his garrulousness now silenced as he waited and hoped to hear proof of Papi's survival.

As much as Boli had argued, Ramón had insisted that no police would come onboard. It was simply too great a risk to take, and wasn't having Matti along bad enough?

In a few minutes, she'd pretend to leave the boat. It would appear to any observer that Ramón was alone on *La Boca Grande*. One of Boli's detectives with a blond wig was lying on the floor of the front seat of the Land Cruiser waiting to do an imitation of Matti driving away when the moment was right. If they were being watched, the kidnappers would think Ramón was coming by himself, that he was agreeing to their terms. She pointed out that she'd taken a course in self-defense, and had her pepper spray. Ramón found this funny. He'd brought his .38, insisting that this was the only tool they needed.

"The only reason you're here," he told her again, "is that technically we're using your company's money for the ransom."

"That's right," she said. "Exactly." *Whatever.*

She continued to sit in silence. Waiting. Thinking about the gang mentality, and cowards who found safety in numbers.

Three weeks was a long time to hold someone hostage. Why had there been such a long gap between Papi's disappearance and the kidnappers' demand? It had been the biggest factor in her original assumption that no kidnapping had taken place. Now, here they were.

She sat and watched the moon begin to rise getting angrier by the minute at the delay. How dare they prolong the torture like this. Poor Ramón! He looked like he was going to chew off the inside of his cheek.

She might not be doing the most professional thing in being here but she was doing the right thing personally. Humanly the right thing. No doubt about it. Professionally, well…probably not. She thought of Sam, how critical he could be of unprofessional behavior. "Sorry, Sam," she said softly.

"What?" Ramón asked.

"Sorry. Thinking out loud."

"Jesus, how long do they have to wait? Are they pulling him out of a shallow grave, or what?"

"I don't know," Matti said, placing a hand on his arm.

"This is the worst torture I've ever known."

"I can't imagine," she said, squeezing his arm harder.

It was now nearly a quarter to eight.

Suddenly, the radio crackled with static. "Stand by," the speaker said in a rough tone.

"*Hijo?*" They heard the sound of Papi's voice sounding small and confused, calling for his son. "Ramón?" A sound of snuffling. "*Mi hijo…mi vida!!!!*"

"Papa?! PAPA?!" Ramón screamed down the receiver in response to his father's call.

"*Si, soy yo, soy yo. Mi corazón, eschuchame……*" "It's me, a weak voice said, "listen to me…" struggling to make itself heard. A drugged voice, fighting up from the depths.

"*Ya*," the caller's voice again, cutting him off. Then, almost politely: "Over."

"You fucking bastards. If you have hurt my father, I'll kill you. I'll kill you all! Put him back on now, I want to know if he's hurt."

"Do what we tell you, follow the course, and you can have your precious Papi." A pause. "Over and out."

Matti had already found the chart and was heading down the hatchway with it to locate Escudo. It was an island about forty miles offshore that looked utterly inaccessible as it was surrounded by reefs.

"We've got a GPS, so let's just plug it in to that," Ramón said, slamming the receiver into its cradle. He rushed down below and opened a cabinet crammed with electronic devices. He pulled out something that looked like a large hand-held calculator with a big display screen. Ramón laid it flat, and pressed some buttons.

"I know he's got the *rumbo* for Escudo in here somewhere."

"Rumbo?"

"That's Spanish for rhumb line, or course."

"Aren't you going to follow the course they gave you?"

"As soon as I can see if they're not trying to run us over some rocks, I will."

"Let me look," Matti said. "I can still plot a course on a chart. Back when I spent summers on my father's sailboat, he made me practice. Over and over. I'm sure I can remember how...."

"Here. It's here. I found it," Ramon said. They looked at the screen, and then at each other. "It's 63 degrees, 52 minutes—close enough."

"Ready to leave? It's going to be a solid two hours to get there."

She followed him topside, dropped over the starboard side onto the dock and turned and waved at him. She went to the truck, opened the door, slid into the seat, then wiggled over to the passenger side and slipped out the door with a dark blanket enfolding her. The blond-wigged detective crawled out from the back seat got in the driver's seat and sped off. Matti stayed hidden among the banana plants until Ramón was ready to throw off the lines and temporarily turn off the running lights. Then she crept to the dock's edge and slipped back into the boat under cover of complete darkness. Matti pulled herself into the cockpit and crawled down the hatchway as *La Boca Grande* got underway.

Ahead of them in the inlet, a man, invisible under the overhanging mangroves which cloaked both him and his low-slung dugout, watched with night vision Heatseeker binoculars as Papi Cardozo's yacht left the dock. "They're leaving now," he said into a closed circuit walkie-talkie. "Hell no, I don't know where they're going! On a midnight booze cruise. Maybe on a fuckathon. How the hell do I know?"

He listened to the answer. "No. They did this cute maneuver like she was leaving the boat. You know? Totally amateur. Then she climbs back over the side. Jesus." The observer was Gerry Velásquez, a former SEAL from Hawaii, his mother's home state. Short and powerfully built, Gerry looked like a native and spoke fluent Spanish. His father was Mexican, after all.

"You think they're going after Papi? Shit—he's alive? Do you have confirmation?" He listened as an explanation was made. "You picked up the radio signal? *Excelente, hombre!* Escudo? Yeah, I was there about twenty years ago." He chuckled. "They took us out there for some underwater training. The place is fossil heaven. These lime cliffs, crusted with the shit. Reef's a bitch, though. Yeah. Wear your best shark-repelling suit. It'll be like a wedding, without the honeymoon. Okay. 22.00. See you there. Out."

"Fuckin A," the agent said, looking up at the stars with an ironic smile. "Kidnappers on Escudo. Well, well, well."

CHAPTER 17

The moon had risen, and in its light the Bertram's wake came alive. Otherwise, the sea was as dark and still as a glass of merlot with only the contrast of their white wake and an occasional long, low sea swell to break the pattern.

No sign of anyone following. No evidence even of Boli and his men.

Ramón gave Matti an all-clear signal and she came up on deck. The breeze created by their forward motion was gentle and warm with the faintest smell of land they were leaving behind. A truly blissful night to be at sea…..except somewhere ahead lay Papi, his abductors, and more danger than Matti wanted to think about.

She went below to get the coffee, and passed him up a mug. In spite of everything, she was mesmerized by the beauty of being at sea at night.

Wouldn't it be wonderful if Sam could be at the helm, instead of Ramón? (her brain continued to natter). Why couldn't this be Cape Cod Bay? A trip to Nantucket for the weekend, instead of to some island off the coast of Panamá to rescue an Atlas insured?

As she looked back at the boat's wake she allowed herself to swing free of the moment, and indulge in a reverie of Sam, his face, his sternness at meetings, his surprisingly muscular body, his tenderness when he kissed her. As much as she missed him, she loved missing him. Loved that she knew someone whose absence could make her feel some passion at last. After Adrian, it had taken a long time to even want to be with a man again.

She and Sam had made out like teenagers on her couch and now her whole body had come alive again. Now here she was on a boat in the tropics with a single, gorgeous Latin man, who'd let her know he was available. She looked at Ramón's craggy profile etched against the moonlight. He was so different from Sam. So much more…what was it? Carefree. More romantic in an overt way. More smiley. More Latin. She didn't doubt that they'd be good bed mates. They had a charged relationship, and like a mild electrical current their mutual attraction was getting hard to ignore.

Get a grip!

Adrian had taught her about relationships based on lust, had she forgotten the lesson so quickly? There was something soul-destroying about loving someone who wanted to get physical with everyone else, too. She and Ramón had a long boat trip ahead to Escudo, a mission to save a kidnapped man. How could her damn libido come roaring forth at a time like this?

A splash over the side brought her back to reality, and Ramón pointed. "Look, Matti, dolphins. On the bow. Two or three. Do you see them?"

Matti went to the port side. She'd dreamed of dolphins not long ago and here they were, like the fulfillment of an omen. What a thrill to see their dark shiny bodies, their compact shapes scalloping through the water so effortlessly. She wished she could dive over the side and join them. Maybe that would cool her off.

"They're gone," she told him.

"They'll be back," he said. "They love to come and go. It's like a game."

He gave her a long look before turning away.

"How long before we reach Escudo?" she asked, feeling his heat, like a pounding heart, next to her.

He looked at the GPS. "According to this, we'll be there in about two hours, maybe a little less. I'm going at nearly top speed. We need to use the time to talk about strategy. Like how the kidnappers will react when they find out we've only brought half the money." She leaned over to look at the GPS too, and he clasped her around the waist. He pulled her close to him, rubbing her arm.

"Cold?" he asked. She lifted her face to say no, she wasn't cold in the least, and he kissed her. A deep, passionate kiss that made her burn like a falling star.

"Ramón, we can't do this now," she said, wanting him to do it again.

"Tell me you weren't thinking about it too." His black T-shirt smelled of an Armani-like musk.

"I can't tell you that," she admitted.

"Good," he said, kissing her on the forehead. He squeezed her on the shoulder and held her away and smiled. "Why don't you get us some more coffee—intermission."

She went down and filled the mugs, knees shaking. She managed to pass him one without spilling a drop; Matti Maitlin Woman of Steel.

She said: "I guess stress does that to you."

"What? Makes you want to make love?" He dismissed her explanation with a laugh. "I wanted to do that before now, Matti. I wanted to do it since I first saw you that night at Richard's."

"I'm definitely blushing now."

"Luckily it's dark, and I can't see it." He laughed his easy laugh for the first time in hours. He looked back over the transom. "Boli is a couple miles behind us."

"He is? How do you know?"

"He uses a red flashlight. He's used it for years patrolling the turtle beach for poachers; nesting turtles hate bright light. I guess he's just used to it."

We're not turtles, Matti wanted to say, but didn't. She realized she'd been hoping the police would apprehend the kidnappers, rescue Papi, and save their asses at the last minute. Reality hit. Boli with his good intentions, well-preserved vocal chords, and old VHF—Boli who was following them in an under-powered boat, with a red flashlight—might not be their savior, after all.

Ramón, luckily, interrupted this train of thought. "The first minutes of our contact with the kidnappers are the key. Everything hinges on it."

She nodded. "I don't think we're dealing with expert kidnappers here, Ramón." Was this the truth, or wishful thinking? "They seem disorganized, somehow. And look how long it took for them to even make contact with their ransom demand. It's like *The Gang Who Couldn't Shoot Straight*." She was still trying to quell her pounding heart.

"I have the same feeling. I'm also hoping that if the kidnappers contacted us from Escudo, they're holding Papi there too. He had to be close enough to get him on the radio. I know Escudo pretty well. If he's there, I'll find him."

Matti said, "If we're dealing with professionals, they'd never do a money exchange at the same place where they're holding the victim." Yet another tidbit from her crash course at Signa Security. "There's no security if something goes wrong. These guys are under pressure now. You could hear it in the man's voice on the radio."

"Yes." Ramón said. "He sounded angry, but also scared."

"Exactly," Matti said. "As the deadline gets closer, they'll be as adrenalized as we are. *Except they probably won't want to have sex, as a result,* she wanted to add. "They've had three weeks to mull this over, day and night. I think that's an advantage for us."

"I'll be the one to physically give them the ransom," Ramón said. "I don't want you anywhere in sight."

She didn't think arguing would do any good, plus, one can of pepper spray probably wouldn't be enough to pull it off.

"And the gun?"

"I'll have the gun."

"What if they find it on you?"

"That's a risk I'll have to take. You just stay below, Matti. Promise me," Ramón said. "Promise me you won't come up here when we make contact."

As much as she hated to think of an unsecured million-dollar ransom going over the side and into the night, she knew he was right. Now if she only had her stun gun...

Ramón continued, "And don't try anything stupid, like rushing into save me, okay?"

Matti looked at him silently for a moment. "There's no guarantee they won't gun you down, Ramón," she said. "No guarantee they won't..." She left the rest of the sentence unfinished.

"If they kill my father, they'd better have a hiding place on another planet, because if I enlist my employees I'll have an army of two thousand people looking for the men who did it." His jaw hardened, adding to his dark masculinity, if that was possible.

She looked out to sea so she wouldn't have to keep studying his profile. She suddenly remembered Victor telling her about the large *cayucos* he'd seen. Going out, he'd said. Toward Escudo? She told Ramón, and he agreed. It was unusual to see large *cayucos* that weren't full of traveling families, or laden with fruit, livestock, or piled with nets. No one could afford the fuel to drive a big *cayuco* if there wasn't a sound economical reason for it.

"So, how will they react when they find out we brought only half the money?" Ramón asked. "What do you think they'll do?"

"Don't admit it," Matti said. "That would be my tack. Counting a million dollars takes time. If they ask, you'll tell them it was the best you could do. Which is the truth. We need to put them on the defensive, if possible. Admit you never saw the fax until this morning. The banks are only open on Saturday til noon. They can have the rest of the money Monday. Tell them it can be handled, but not on Sunday. Tell them you want proof that Papi is alive—again. Keep them engaged. Maybe they'll decide it's not worth the wait, and bolt. Hopefully, the million will look good enough; maybe they're sick of waiting, and will want to cut their losses and run."

"Hopefully if they *do* count it they won't be so pissed off that they decide to kill my father and keep the money anyway."

"That's true. But remember, Ramón, your father will always be worth more to them alive than dead, keeping them waiting for half the ransom buys a lot of time. But you must keep insisting on proof. Proof that he's alive."

Ramón grew pensive. "Who the hell *are* these guys? That's the real question. The caller definitely spoke American English but with a Latin accent that I can't place."

"I thought the same thing. An accent that was a meld of different accents, as if the speaker had lived in different Latin countries."

"I have a nagging feeling about that voice, Matti. As if

the speaker is someone I know, or knew. Every time I try and concentrate on it, I lose the thread."

She took out her recording machine, rewound the tape. "Want to try again?" She re-played the conversation three times. But the more Ramon listened to it, the more frustrated he became.

Matti moved back to the present. "Well. The speaker isn't acting alone, that's pretty clear. Now they've waited all this time, and decided the time was right now. Why? Maybe Papi got sick. Maybe they were afraid he might...you know...before they even got paid. It wouldn't be the first time: Too many drugs, not enough liquids. Simple oversights."

"Well, he *is* alive. I heard his voice, and would know it anywhere. The bastards! He did sound weak, though. He did have that by-pass"

"Right—the by-pass." She'd forgotten about that.

"But the doctors said he's in great shape," Ramón said, trying to keep the spark of his hope alive. "He's very fit for his age." He paused, smiling into the distance. "I hope you get a chance to meet him. He's quite a macho character. Not at all like the weak voice you heard on the radio."

"I'm sure." If Ramón was a chip off the old block, she could only imagine what his father was like. She brought up the thermos again.

"Do you do this often?" Ramón asked.

"What, pour coffee?" She smiled at him

"I mean pursuing kidnappers, overseeing ransom payouts? That kind of thing?"

"Not usually. But I wouldn't say I've *never* gotten involved."

"Part of your job description then?" Ramón asked.

"Not exactly," Matti said, thinking of the ramifications if Sam found out where she was. "But you're an Atlas Preferred Client, Ramón, what we call an APC. So you do rate better treatment than most." She tried not to smile.

"Very funny," he said. "Listen, I was thinking that they may try to intercept us before we reach the island."

"That's true, they might. The element of surprise." She'd been thinking the same thing. Why else would the kidnappers give them an exact course to follow?

"Exactly. So when we get closer, I want you to go below, into the forward cabin, and lock the door."

"So I can put on my bathing suit," she said.

"Your *bathing* suit?"

Matti said, "From what I could see from the chart, there's pretty much all reef protecting Escudo's bay. The Bertram will never make it inside."

"What's your point?"

"That if we need to, one of us might have to swim to shore, Ramón. As you can't swim, it kind of narrows the choices, don't you think?"

"No, it doesn't. As it's not an option. *La Boca Grande* has gone inside the reef many times. I can do it." He could see from her expression she wasn't convinced. "What are you thinking about now?"

"That the kidnappers don't know I'm onboard. What if they decide to search the boat?"

"Forget it."

"I was also thinking, that if we get in close enough, it wouldn't be that far to swim. Then I could see what's going on."

"You mean try and spy on the kidnappers? That's ludicrous!"

"Not it's not." She was getting that stiff Irish lace feeling.

"You're not going, and that's that." Why were men always trying to boss her around?

"Hunh," she answered. "Let's see who does what when we get there, Ramón. Let's see what happens when the time comes."

Above them, in the darkness, a microlight engine droned.

CHAPTER 18
Hull, Massachusetts

B rian had fed Patrick his chicken soup with parsley dumplings, had plumped his pillows, and found an old movie on cable which they sat and watched half-heartedly. He'd never seen Patrick more docile, or happier. It was as if the heart attack had given them both a whole new take on reality, reminding them of how much they loved each other.

Brian, bored by the movie, began flicking through a magazine, when suddenly he remembered something and stood up.

"What?" Patrick asked. "What's wrong?"

"Oh hell. Matti asked me to check her place, and I completely forgot 'til I saw this advert with a cat. Reminded me of Kung Fu kitty herself. I better go down and check it out."

"Surely she didn't leave her cat….."

"No. But I think Matti was a little nerved up leaving. Other things on her mind. She asked me to check the place out." He walked from the room. "Back in a flash."

Brian grabbed a set of keys Matti had given him several years ago, went down in the elevator and let himself in. The place smelled of Matti and made him realize he missed her. There was a soft citrus smell under a lingering scent of *First* that permeated the air. He flipped on the kitchen light. Everything immaculate. Stove off, good. Coffee maker too. He went in to the livingroom. Thermostat down to sixty, well he could feel that, without checking.

He noticed the blinking red light on her answering machine, and thought: What the hell. He played back the messages, and heard the one from Doctor Smart's office.

"Shit," he said, playing it over.

He left and locked the door and went back upstairs. Patrick looked at him expectantly from the bed. "Sounds like Matti's gynie wants to see her sooner than later."

"Shit," Patrick said.

"My sentiments exactly."

"Well, for God's sake, don't call Lillian."

"I wouldn't dream of it."

"Who then?"

"What's her PA's name? "A" something."

"Anne? Amber?"

"Ashley! I just remembered. Tall, black woman, big, sculpted hair. A looker."

"I remember now. Matti's Christmas cocktail. A couple of years ago."

"I'll have to wait 'til Monday," Brian said. "Unless she calls me in the meantime." He paused. "I wonder who the new man is."

"Why? So you can call him up and scare the shit out of him?" Patrick was definitely feeling like his old self again.

"No, just hoping she won't hook up with an Adrian look-alike again."

"Matti's too smart for that," Patrick said. "Isn't she?"

"Hopefully she'll never forget that divorce," Brian said. "It was like watching someone go cold turkey from a heroin addiction ."

Patrick didn't seem to be listening. "There's only one reason a gynie calls back after an appointment."

"I know."

"Because something isn't right. A positive PAP smear, for example."

"I know," Brian repeated.

"I don't want to even think about it," Patrick said.

"Maybe she left her umbrella behind in the doctor's office," Brian said, and they were both silent.

"We need to call Ashley first thing Monday."

"*I* will call Ashley. Now try and get some sleep," Brian said. He stroked his partner's forehead and turned off the light. He closed the bedroom door softly, went into the library and got down the medical encyclopedia. He looked under "Female Organs" and studied the diagrams and learned about everything that could go wrong down there. Jesus. He'd never thought about it before, why would he? Compared to a man, a woman's machinery looked like a the plumbing diagram for a seven-story condominium. Which frightened him even more. He put the book back on the shelf and sat in the darkness, watching Boston Light blink in the distance wondering when Matti would be back.

CHAPTER 19
Escudo, Panamá

W e're almost there," Ramón told her.

Ahead of them lay a dark island with lots of palm tree silhouettes. Escudo had no residents, and no electricity. In the moonlight, Matti could only see a thin strip of bluish reflection from the white sand beach.

"Depth sounder," he said. "The last two miles there's a shelf that becomes a reef. Depth shallows off from 17 to 5 meters. We're over the reef now." Ramón cut their speed. "I thought they would've contacted us before."

"Yes," Matti said. She'd gone below a half hour earlier, locked herself in the cabin and put on her bathing suit. Fifteen minutes later, she'd come up again because she couldn't stand the suspense.

Ramón didn't seem to notice that she wasn't stashed below, as per his earlier insistence. Instead he wanted to talk. "Do you really think they're holding my father on Escudo?"

"I think so. They could've worked it so your father was prompted to speak on the radio from a different location, but I doubt it."

"Even if he was on Escudo they could've moved him again," Ramón said.

"Using the same *cayucos* that Victor saw?"

"Perhaps. At night an unlit cayuco is virtually impossible to see, they're very low in the water. Everyone is always running into them in the bay, they even run into each other."

"What's the range of the VHF radio?" Matti asked.

"That varies a lot. Mostly VHFs rely on line of sight of the antenna, and we have a good tall one onboard," he said, pointing up at it.

"And the kidnappers…."

A booming voice sent them reeling backwards. It wasn't coming from the radio though, but from somewhere over the water, through a megaphone.

"SLOW YOUR SPEED," the voice said. "SLOW YOUR SPEED NOW."

Matti immediately ducked below. They'd caught her off-guard and now it was likely they'd seen that Ramón hadn't come alone. *Damn.*

Ramón pulled the throttle down and gradually slowed *La Boca Grande.*

"PUT HER IN NEUTRAL," the voice commanded, sounding strangely like the voice of the Wizard of Oz.

True to type, Matti began shaking like the Cowardly Lion. Boli Santamaria wouldn't be able to help them now, not in this remote place. Why hadn't she thought it through more carefully? The kidnappers had decided to skip the radio and simply show up; it was clever, and unexpected. But through the porthole in the dark cabin she couldn't see any other craft, not even a dark shape.

Ramón had the boat idling; Matti could smell the blowback from the exhaust on this windless night. She heard:

"WE WILL COME ONBOARD. PREPARE TO HAND OVER THE MONEY."

"I'M NOT HANDING OVER *ANYTHING* UNTIL I HAVE PROOF MY FATHER IS ALIVE!" Ramón yelled back in an impassioned voice.

There was a pause, and Matti could hear nothing but the idling engine of *La Boca Grande*.

Then suddenly the radio burst into life. *"Hijo! Hijo!"* Papi's voice, weak, sounding desperate. Then: *"Pagales!"* Pay them, Matti translated.

Ramón answered him. *"Papa. Ciudate, CUIDATE."* Be careful. *"PAPA? PAPA!"* he said into the void. No response.

Again the voice from the other craft. "WE WILL LEAVE HIM ON THE BEACH ALIVE ONE HOUR FROM NOW. A pause. *AFTER* WE HAVE THE MONEY." The voice on the megaphone was like the radio voice, Matti realized, only more amplified.

Ramón whispered down the passageway. "Now what do I do? When they see only half the money is there, maybe they'll kill him!"

"Give them the ransom," Matti whispered back. Words carried over water extremely well, she'd just re-discovered. "When they've left we'll get in closer and I'll try and swim to shore."

"This is fucking insane," Ramón whispered back, angrily. Then: "I think I'll try and shine a little light on the situation."

"I HAVE THE MONEY." He yelled across the water, and at the same moment, he pulled up the high-power spot light and shone it in the direction of the voice. Two figures in black atop two dark-colored jet skis sat approximately fifty yards away. They both wore helmets with full-face visors.

"TURN OUT THE LIGHT, ASSHOLE," said the Latin-accented voice, hoisting the megaphone. "THERE'S NOTHING TO SEE OVER HERE. AND BESIDES WE'RE ARMED AND DANGEROUS." A snickering laugh carried across the water sounding like it came from five feet away.

"PUT THE MONEY ON THE STERN WHERE WE CAN SEE IT. TRY ANYTHING FUNNY AND YOUR FATHER DIES." They heard the whining engines of the jet skis starting up.

Matti handed Ramón the pink Mickey Mouse bag from down below. Too bad they didn't have an electronic bug in it. But the kidnappers would change bags, all the smart ones did. There was nothing else to do but give them the money and hope for the best.

She wrapped her pepper spray in two plastic bags and tucked the bag down the front of her suit. These were the first jet skis she'd seen in Banana Bay. The kidnappers—with their fancy helmets and fluent English—weren't as uneducated as she'd thought they'd be. Then again, they were damn close to the Costa Rican border up here. Maybe the kidnappers planned to make their getaway through another country. There were miles and miles of deserted coastline between Puerto Viejo and Limón. She'd driven down that coast once herself. Her mind reeled with dozens of scenarios. Anything was possible, now. Even Papi's murder.

Ramón placed the bag as directed on top of the boat's broad transom and stepped back from it.

"LEAVE THE BAG AND GO BELOW," the voice instructed.

Ramón backed away from the bag toward the hatch so he could watch the maneuver. He had his gun out, Matti saw. The jet skis came speeding up, one man stood on the swim platform while the other opened a bag, and the money was transferred. The empty Mickey Mouse bag was flung to the deck.

"WAIT ONE HOUR. WE NEED TO COUNT THE MONEY," the voice said, and they sped away, as quickly as they had come.

Ramón put the gun down. "I've never felt so powerless..." he said. He sat on the yacht's wide rail, and put his head in his hands.

Matti called Dolores on channel three to tell her that the ransom had been handed over. "Tell Boli we're just outside of Escudo," Matti said. "Just outside the entrance to the harbor. Tell him to please be very, very careful of being seen." Dolores wanted all the details, and Matti hushed her. "We can't talk now." She switched back to channel four.

"They're not going to be happy," Ramón said. "You don't short guys like that."

"Let's wait and see what their reaction is, it's impossible to predict. They might have everything all arranged to leave now. Sticking around could totally disrupt their plans."

"Meanwhile, we'll wait."

"I'm going to swim to shore," Matti said. She was pumped up too, and ready for action—any action. "Is this shark country?"

"You must be kidding," Ramón said.

"Look, I swim about ten miles a week. I'm totally prepared to do this. I'll go in, see what I can see, then swim back out. It'll take less than an hour."

"Of course there are sharks—this is the Caribbean, for God's sake! God only knows what might be swimming on that reef at this hour."

"Oh Ramón, don't you ever watch those nature shows? Sharks hardly ever attack humans, especially out here where there's an ample food supply. I just thought I'd ask—maybe put on some shark repellent." She tried a smile.

It took him a minute to realize she was kidding. "I can see you've made up your mind." He put the boat into gear, and seemed resigned. "But let me get in closer. I can get in a lot closer than this."

"Great."

"I've got an inflatable liferaft. Why don't I blow that up?"

"Fins would be better, and quicker, also a mask and snorkel so I don't have to keep my head up."

"I can't believe I'm going to let you to do this. Are you insured?" Now it was his turn to smile.

"Workman's comp," she told him, as she grabbed the gear, and slid over the side.

He leaned over her. "Matti, don't go exploring, please! Just go to the beach, see if Papi is there then swim back out here pronto."

"Will do." She had the mask on now, and the flippers.

"Just be careful. Christ, be careful."

"I will," she said. "They'll probably have a lookout on the beach. I'll see what I can."

"I've got this waterproof flashlight," he said passing her a thin cylinder in bright yellow. "Take this with you."

"Two clicks, and I'm heading back to the boat. One click, I have to lay low." She tucked the light in with her pepper spray, put the snorkel in her mouth, and swam away.

CHAPTER 20

They sat in a circle. Three figures dressed in black, counting the money around a small battery-powered lantern whose light was concealed to any outsider by the bodies huddled around it.

"It's short," one said. "I think they shorted us."

"Keep counting," another one said.

A few feet away Papi Cardozo lay, bound, gagged and inert. They'd given him more of the *psilocybin mushrooms,* and he would start hallucinating again soon. He was very pliable in this state. Non-resistant.

"They fucking shorted us a million bucks!" the first one said, throwing down the last packet. They looked at each other, the reality of this sinking in.

"Fucking Ramón! He knows he's going to get it back from the insurance company, the cheap prick! It's not even his money, and he decides he'll play cute. Well, fuck him! Eh, Don Ramón? What do you think of that? Your son has screwed you old man. He screwed you good. Only paid half the ransom."

They all looked at Papi. He looked dead already. Then he twitched, *"Bueno,"* he said out of the sides of his mouth around the gag. The group all spoke Spanish, but they spoke English fluently too—learned in their line of business.

"Now what?" one of them asked.

"We try again," said the one in charge, the voice on the radio.

"I told you we should have left him at the Rio! And now we have to get him out of here," the other one said. "And hide him *again*."

"Call him on the radio. I don't like this hanging-around shit. Too many things can go wrong, especially when we have *el jefe* in tow."

They extinguished the lantern and began organizing their few belongings by the light of the moon.

***

In the shadows, ex-Special Forces agent Gerry Velásquez prepared to drop a gas canister in their midst and break up their little party. The person who'd hired them had been firm on this point: keep Papi alive at all costs.

Gerry had made his landing in Escudo a scant ten minutes earlier, and Larry was outside on the reef waiting for him in a sleek, silent water-jet powered inflatable that had landed with them on the microlight they'd flown to a tiny atoll two miles away.

Now he was lying here and couldn't believe what he was hearing. The kidnappers had been stupid enough to bring Papi along. What a bunch of fucking amateurs! From what he'd overheard, they'd gotten one million from the son and were confident about getting the rest. Too bad for them. They'd wake up on Escudo in an hour or so, and have no Papi, and no money either. He'd hoped for the whole two million, but he and Larry would settle for a million, not a bad piece of change for a few days' work. They'd extract the victim as agreed, collect their fee, then go to the Maldives for awhile and hang out. The insurance broad would leave empty-handed too, she'd been dumb enough to come with the son on this wasted mission. It was getting to be like *American Idol* out here, all these amateurs thinking they could make a big play and be Famous Kidnapper of the Month.

Didn't these people get it? Why didn't they hire a pro to do a pro's job instead of sending in some half-baked blonde who probably sat at a desk three hundred days a year?

Gerry waited for them to make a move so he could get closer, undetected. As they were getting ready to move Papi, the timing was perfect. He had the canister out and was crawling forward on his belly when he heard a noise behind him. He froze. The lookout from the beach had come back to camp shortly after the ransom pick-up. So who the hell was out here creeping around?

He heard the noise again. It was a very soft sound, barely discernible. The kidnappers didn't hear it but he was trained to detect small noises, things that didn't fit into the surroundings.

They were headed down toward the beach now, having strapped Papi onto a litter. Gerry remained frozen in place waiting to hear what was coming up behind him. He couldn't imagine...there were no animals on Escudo. And this wasn't a lizard noise, or a bug or a bird or a snake. He knew that. He slowly turned his head to measure the distance and realized the individual behind him was now within ambushing distance. He came to a quick squat, reached out and grabbed the crouched shape that was moving toward him. Twirling the body around, his knife was instantly at the throat, and all sound was silenced by his manipulation of the windpipe. He then pinched a nerve bundle and the body slumped forward.

It was the insurance babe!

And here he sat while the kidnappers with Papi in tow were making their getaway. "Fucking hell," he said under his breath. In the distance he could hear the kidnappers starting the big Yamaha and revving the jet skis that would get them out of here in the blink of an eye. And here he was with this limp blonde slumped in front of him. He looked for his radio to signal Larry, and realized it had fallen from his belt. He rolled her over, and found it underneath her. The case had popped open, the tiny battery had rolled out, and it was as dead as a dodo bird. Now even Larry couldn't give chase. Goddamn it to hell.

He pulled the woman forward, and her head lolled on her shoulders. He pinched her nostrils and covered her mouth to force off her oxygen. That sometimes worked better than smelling salts.

It didn't work, so he humped her over his shoulders and down to the beach. He undid a plastic satchel she had strapped around her middle, then rolled her into the water face down for a few seconds. She lifted her head from the shallow water and vomited.

He dragged her back up to the sand, and rolled her on her side so she wouldn't choke. He was pissed off beyond belief. He found the soaked plastic bag sticking out of the top of her bathing suit.

"And what might this be?" He yanked it out, unrolled it and found the pepper spray. "Oh, now isn't that cute," he said. "Wet pepper spray—and a light! A waterproof flashlight. Well now. Too bad it's not in pink." The kidnappers were gone, their engines a fading whine.

He could see the starboard light of the yacht twinkling about a quarter mile away. *What the hell*. He flicked the light a few times, then flicked it in Larry's direction, too. Matti just groaned and retched again, and he looked at her in disgust. Reminded him of a date he had when he was fifteen on Waikiki Beach. Too many Mai Tais, then after some decent hokey-pokey, he took her for a swim in a rip current and she almost drowned. After that he'd developed a distinct prejudice against blondes.

***

Ramón saw the light, and so did Larry. Ramón had inflated the liferaft; the small outboard was already attached to it, ready to move at her signal. He wasn't going to let her swim back to the boat—no way.

Larry was in his inflatable, too.

They converged at the reef entrance in perfect sync, like extras in a Ester Williams' water ballet.

Ramón looked at Larry and wondered if he was coming face to face with a kidnapper or one of Boli's reinforcements. Then he changed his mind. The guy was definitely not Panamanian, he was white as chalk, and looked like that guy who played the butler on the *The Addam's Family*. "Who the hell are you?" Ramón asked.

"The Easter Bunny, you dickhead," Larry said, not a hint of a smile on his face, as he gunned his jet-propelled craft toward the beach.

Ramón followed, yelling Matti's name. This was getting more bizarre by the minute. He'd seen the big *cayuco* and the jet skis leave Escudo—the kidnappers, for sure—and head in a northerly direction. To Costa Rica? They didn't say anything as they sped past; there was no radio contact. Was Papi with them? He had no way of knowing and he couldn't leave Matti and chase them. If he followed without subterfuge, they'd try and kill him. Maybe kill Papi, too, if he was with them. He could only hope they'd decided a million was enough and left his father on the beach.

He tried to alert Boli on the hand-held radio but couldn't raise him.

He had no choice but to follow the Munster, and so he did, landing on the beach to find Matti laid out like a rag doll next to a short guy in a wetsuit who had a chest out of *Pumping Iron* magazine.

Ramón looked at the man—Polynesian or Latin?—who seemed preternaturally calm. Were these guys the kidnappers, a few leftover thugs that got left behind?

"Matti, Matti?" Ramón bent down over her prone shape.

"She fucking snuck up on me, okay? I had the whole thing laid out like The Last Supper and she decides at that precise moment she's going to join the fun. What great timing!" He wiped his nose with the back of his hand and sighed deeply.

"What the hell is going on here?" Ramón demanded. "Where's my father?" These two were the last thing he'd expected. Neither one had a Latin accent. They were obviously professionals, though. Professionals who did hand-to-hand combat before Pop Tarts every morning.

"Sit down," said the man who reminded Ramón of a samurai. He looked resigned. "You're Papi's kid, right?"

"Yes," Ramón looked over at Matti who groaned and sat up, holding her head. He went and put an arm around her. "Who the hell are you?"

"We'll get to that. So, you shorted them, huh? They weren't too pleased about only getting a million. Gonna drop back ten and try again. Hey, listen. Sorry about your old man. I'm Gerry, this here's Larry. We want to find your father too."

"You do?"

"Yeah." Gerry had worked up a story that would be acceptable to these two, and now he tried it on for size. "We're on special assignment here, government business, you know?"

"No I don't," said Ramón. "What government?"

"Well, that gets a little tricky, Ramón. We're operating strictly undercover here trying to protect your father and others like him. His life may be at risk from certain subversive groups and he's not alone. You know kidnappings of corporate executives are getting to be a chronic problem in Latin America.

"We were asked by our government who was asked by other governments to act on a free-lance basis to intercede in these cases. The idea is we kind of insinuate ourselves into each incident, though usually know one ever knows we're involved, even after it's over. We go where governments can't go, *capisce?* We try to extract the victims using our own unique methods. It's kind of a cross between search-and-rescue and covert ops."

He looked at Ramón and shrugged. Now that sounded good. Even he was convinced. He and Larry were just a couple of guys that came to do a job. Nothing to be suspicious about.

"So. Let me see if I've got this right. You're working for the U.S. government which has a deal with Panamá for kidnapping intervention and prevention?" Ramón asked, incredulous.

"Not just with Panamá which hasn't very many incidents, thank God. It's with a lot of the Latin countries, plus some others." Gerry paused, to let them digest this. The woman was up now, and listening to every word.

"This is Larry, by the way. I'm Gerry." He extended his hand to Ramón, trying again to keep the mood friendly and non-threatening. Ramón warily introduced himself and Matti, keeping his focus on Gerry. "Do you have some ID?" he asked.

"Not on me," Gerry said, laughing. "They teach us at Jungle Warfare School to leave that stuff at home. But hey. I guess you don't have much choice," Gerry said in his reasonable voice. "If we're gonna work together on this, you're gonna have to trust us."

"Matti, what do you think?" Ramón asked.

"I think he's right. We don't have much choice." She rubbed her head and was shivering. "Let's get back to the boat. We need to talk to Boli and be next to the radio in case the kidnappers try and make contact again."

"Sorry about the ambush," Gerry said, helping Matti to her feet. "I think if we can team up we might help each other instead of getting in each other's way." He looked at her with his almond-shaped brown eyes, he could make them go all satiny and soft at will. It was a trick he'd learned years ago in Hawaii to get the tourist girls onto their backs on a chaise on the beach.

"Don't worry about it," Matti said, smiling. "You're just lucky I didn't have my pepper spray handy." She picked up the canister where it lay at her feet, and blasted it into the air about three feet from his face. He grabbed her by the wrist.

"Don't worry, Gerry. That was only a test. I hardly ever use my pepper spray. I mean, you don't want to go spraying people in the face with something like this—unless you really need to." She blinked at him ingenuously—she knew the same trick as Gerry—and they piled into the two inflatables and headed back to the yacht.

CHAPTER 21

They all clambered aboard the Bertram and Matti went below to shower, change into dry clothes and take some Advil. On deck, Ramón offered the two men coffee, and they spoke about recent events. The kidnappers still hadn't made contact. Nor had Ramón heard anything from Boli Santamaria. The best news was that Gerry had seen Papi near the campfire, and he was still alive.

"I heard them talking," offered Gerry. "They were pissed off by the shortfall. Said the deal was two million. Then they strapped the old man onto a litter and dragged him down the beach."

"Their *demand* was two million," Ramón corrected him. "I never even saw the fax they sent 'til this afternoon. They should have done a little more checking instead of just assuming I got their message on Thursday."

"Yeah. That wasn't too bright," Larry put in. They turned and looked at him. Larry looked as thick as two short planks, but Gerry knew that where Larry was concerned, looks were deceiving. His partner wasn't only smart, organized and daring, but had a low adrenaline threshold. He'd try anything if he thought it had even a remote chance of succeeding.

Which was why he was so in demand as a commando-for-hire and his P.O. Box was regularly filled with requests from his advert in *Soldier of Fortune* magazine.

"So. Did you hear them say anything else?" Matti asked, coming topside as she toweled her hair dry.

"Yeah," Gerry said. "As a matter of fact I did. They mentioned a place. They said the word "rio". I heard that distinctly, and then "terry", something like that. Couldn't hear more, not close enough." He tried not to look at Matti as he said this. The memory of her arrival still pissed him off.

Matti looked at Ramón. "Do you have any ideas?"

"There are dozens of rivers along this coast. Literally thousands of places they could bolt to and not be seen by anyone. The dugout and the jet skis…I did notice when they sped past that hey were all headed northwest."

"Toward Costa Rica?" Matti asked.

"Closer, I think," Ramón said, "Let's get out the chart and have a look."

They went below, unrolled a chart and peered at it. "Río San Pedro, Chiriquí, Veragua," Ramón read off. "Río Calovébora." Matti's eyes moved across the chart: Peninsula Valiente, she read, then noted the various entrances into the lagoon from the Caribbean Sea to the northern landfall on the other side of Banana Bay. "Swamp" was printed in large simple letters, and above it: Río Changuinola, and above that, Río Teribe.

"Could this be it, the Río Teribe?" But even as she asked, her heart pumped in anticipation.

"Yes!" said Ramón, excitedly. "That makes sense. It's remote, but still navigable." He looked expectantly at Gerry.

"Sounds right to me," Gerry said, folding his arms across his chest and nodding. "Terry. Teribe. These people love remote places where only they know how to get in and out."

They all kept looking at the chart, listening to Gerry, mesmerized by the black squiggle that indicated the river. And

Matti's eyes kept wandering to the word "Swamp" beside it. Oh well, what was a little swamp after shark-infested waters?

Now maybe they really could rescue Papi and capture the kidnappers. With Gerry and Larry in tow it was doable. These two were experts in jungle operations—government agents who were trained for this kind of work. It had to be better than a long-ago Signa Security seminar. Boli was still nowhere to be seen or heard and Matti knew he was out of his depth, too.

"Let's hope we're right," Matti said aloud, the double meaning clear to all of them. She still didn't trust these guys. "Ramón, can you get us up the river?"

"No," Ramón told her, flatly. "We need a local guide and a cayuco. Most of Boli's men are from Platanillo or down near Robalo." He grew thoughtful. "What about Victor?"

"Victor Robles?" Matti said. "Alma's grandnephew Victor? He's just a boy."

"He's fourteen and that counts as manhood around here," Ramón said. "Victor knows that river probably better than anyone I know."

"Sounds like our man," Larry said which sounded like kidding, but when Matti looked at him his implacable features hadn't moved a millimeter.

"Problem is, how do we get him here?" Gerry asked.

"We need to talk to the police chief," Ramón explained. "He and his men were supposed to be following us but we lost radio contact."

Ramón went over to the handset and tried again. Nothing. *"¡Hijo de puta!* And why haven't the kidnappers been in touch?"

"Oh they will be. I'd bet a million dollars on it," Gerry said, chuckling.

"Right," Matti said, finding the humor grating. Gerry had knocked her senseless then almost drowned her, and that was part of it. The rest had to do with his demeanor. He looked like a man who enjoyed his power a little too much, and who found women an annoying and expendable commodity. He was the type of man, Matti thought, who would prefer never to find a woman in a decision-making capacity. Earlier, he had given her this Svengali look as though he was trying out a little romantic mind-control. Now he was finding the ransom comical. Well forget it. She thought she'd fill him in now about her own jungle code of ethics.

"The way I see it," Matti began, "is you need *us* to help *you*. We have the vessel to make this trip and all you can do now is either terrorize us or make your way out of here on that inflatable with your gear. You'll have to find transport to get you up the Teribe, and you'll need a local guide. We have no proof who you are, *Gerry,* but when the police arrive you'll need to give him some details so he can verify you are who you say you are. You appear to share our goal of recovering Mr. Cardozo alive. And you haven't killed us yet, not quite. That's the good news. The bad news is your glib manner could endanger Mr. Cardozo and this whole undertaking. Unfortunately, it's Saturday night and I….."

Gerry raised his hand. "Excuse me. *Excuse* me. But don't you think you are jumping to a helluva lot of conclusions there, Miss…(Bossy Bitch, he wanted to say) Maitlin?" He had to keep his total cool at all costs. She was like a wound-up ticker waiting to go off. A blonde bombshell who would look better exploded into a million teeny pieces. Why the fuck couldn't women stay at home or at least behind a desk?

He gave her a sheepish look (that usually worked). "Look, Miss Maitlin. I'm sorry if I gave you a headache. And I know you think I'm a bastard—excuse my French—for doing that. But believe me, you didn't give me any choice." His Royal Humility Act usually did the trick. They needed this boat with these resources. Too much time could be lost otherwise. If they didn't cooperate, he and Larry would have to eliminate them both—which would be way too messy.

"Oh, you mean when you did that little Leonard Nemoy trick so I'd pass out?" she said, evenly. Did this guy really think she was going to buy his phony apology? Did he really think she could be fooled by his polite little *act?* What a macho asshole!

"Well, I apologize," he said, grandly, proud of himself for not reacting. "Please accept my apology for hurting you again."

"Hey you two," Ramón said. "Do you mind if we get started on a strategy here?" He went over to the radio and tried to raise Boli again, and everyone was surprised when he was successful and Boli's loud, exuberant voice began spilling down the airwaves.

"Ramón! *Hijo! Gracias a Dios!.* Thank God this thing is workin' again. Poor Dolores. She's worried SICK. We are still about five miles from Escudo. The engine broke down. I told that stupid *encargado* not to buy a re-built Mariner. *El estupido!* And now where are you? What happened? Did you see the kidnappers? Did you get Papi?" Finally he took a breath.

"Boli, *eschuchame.* Listen. The kidnappers left with the ransom. They found out it was short, and they've taken my father. But we think we know where they might be. We've also run into....a...ah...situation. Come to the boat so we can fill you in. We're still in Escudo harbor. Over."

"Okay. You okay? Nuthin' wrong with you or that pretty one? You both safe? *Cambio.*"

"Yes, we're fine. We'll come to you. I can see your running lights. Over and out."

Gerry and Larry went over the side to pull in their craft. Ramón told them they could lash it onto the bow deck. There was something that looked liked a bumper too, but Gerry undid a clasp and it came open like a miniature suitcase. It was filled with tightly rolled clothes and some electronic devices that didn't look familiar. Gerry made no attempt to conceal the contents. In fact, he stood and announced that he and Larry would need to change. Could they please go below? Ramón offered the shower, told them where the towels were, and they went below giving Ramón and Matti a chance to speak alone.

"Do you think they are who they say they are?" he asked her.

"I really don't know. But why else would they be hanging around Escudo? Unless it's a scheme to kidnap your father from the kidnappers. It wouldn't be the first time."

"Well, if they were going to do that, they would have done it before now. Their story sounds reasonable. Also, they look like who they say they are, and they've got all this high tech equipment."

"Yes," Matti agreed. "And let's face it, I don't think you and I have the skills to go and recover your father from a bunch of terrorists. The kidnappers are under more duress now. Plus they think we tried to cheat them; they can't be happy about that."

"I can't believe they haven't re-contacted us. Why not, I wonder?"

"I really don't know. They like to keep us guessing, that's for sure."

"Should we go back to port and get some reinforcements?" Ramón asked. "Some people we know and trust?"

"We need a guide, and I agree that Victor may be our best bet. We'll have to pick him up and get some supplies. Can Dolores arrange for the rest of the ransom? We'd better have it available."

"Not until Monday at the earliest. We cleaned the local bank right out. We'll need Victor's *cayuco* too," Ramón said.

"We will?"

"Hell, yes. The river is only navigable by dugout. Anyway, the Bertram is one of the most conspicuous boats around. We'll have to go in the *cayuco*." He looked at her. "It's going to be a rough trip. Are you sure you want to go?"

"Hell, yes," Matti said. She didn't remind him that a million dollars of potential Atlas money was lying somewhere in a duffel bag in the jungle. Rough or not, this was an excellent reason to be going along for the ride.

"You want to get the money back, don't you?" he asked.

"That's part of it," she admitted. She looked at Ramón's handsome face in the dark. Had they really passionately kissed just a few hours ago?

"When this is all over," Ramón said, not taking offense, "I'd like to make you a job offer, Matti. I've never seen a more dedicated employee."

"I love what I do," she said, trying to explain.

"I can see that!" Ramón stroked her cheek. "You're all flushed and excited. And I thought it was me."

She smiled at him. "I'm exhausted," she said, feeling like she could simply drop to the deck where she stood and fall deeply asleep.

"It's the shock," Ramón said. "You'll be in bed as soon as we've talked to Boli."

"Can you talk to the chief, get him to stay in the background? I think we need to use these guys, much as they creep me out. They're obviously trained to do this work. Boli can still look like a hero at the end of it if we're successful."

"I think you're right. We can ask him to do a background check. What did they say their full names were?"

"Gerry Velásquez and Larry Knight," she said, and as if being cued, the two agents walked up onto the deck looking like ordinary people, except for Larry's height, which would make him stand out everywhere, except maybe the NBA.

Gerry turned first, hearing the sound of the police boat's approach. Out of the darkness they could see a red light blinking, and then Boli's moon face appeared. He was surrounded by half a dozen men in drab green uniforms who were all carrying guns.

CHAPTER 22

One of the men had a semi-automatic that looked like a Woolworth's machine gun for part of a Halloween costume. They all looked to Matti as if they wanted to start shooting just to alleviate the boredom. Thank God they'd arrived after the fact, and not before.

On deck, Boli grasped Ramón, hugging him tightly. Then Gerry stepped forward with military precision and presented himself. "Gerry Velásquez. Special Forces, sir." He snapped off a salute. Matti noted a subtle shift in Boli's body language, a slight lifting of the chin. She realized that Gerry was stroking Boli's pride, deferring to him as the officer in charge. Oh, brother.

"At ease, soldier," Boli said, looking to the military-manner born. "And you?" He looked up at Larry as though up at a two-story building.

"Special Agent Larry Knight, at your service. Sir!" Larry also saluted, and Matti thought: What a bunch of crap! Was Boli really that naïve?

"What is your mission here, soldier?" Boli asked Gerry in the manner of an Army colonel. All we need now is Noriega showing up, Matti thought, to complete this ridiculous tableau.

"We're here on a special mission from our government to assist Panamá in intercession of terrorist activities, information gathering, and extractions, sir." Gerry was the epitome of a military professional. Even Matti found herself grudgingly impressed.

"I've had no orders...er...information about this. Why wasn't I advised?" Maybe Boli was shrewder than she'd first thought.

"These operations are high level, sir. Strictly on a need-to-know basis."

"And now I am being told?"

"Yes, sir. We'd like your permission to continue in our mission to rescue Sr. Cardozo and capture the kidnappers alive, if possible. Sir."

Boli looked into his boat at his "men". Only of them was over twenty-one. They'd been trained, in a manner of speaking, but kidnapping and "extraction" was way out of their depth.

"I'll need to see some ID. I take it we're going back to Platanillo," Boli said.

"Yes," Ramón said. He took Boli to one side, away from the earshot of his men, and filled him in on their plan to go up the Teribe.

"We'll keep you fully informed, sir," Gerry told the chief of police. "The kidnappers will be yours to deal with as the law sees fit. We need to remain undercover. I hope you understand." Gerry Velásquez, Matti thought, could win the prize for Mr. Congeniality.

"What do you think?" Boli turned and asked Ramón. "He's your father. Do you feel comfortable with this plan?' For once Boli wasn't screaming, or shouting instructions. Matti thought he looked about ten years older than he had yesterday.

"I think they're right. If we have the assistance of these men, we should use them. I'm afraid my father is in a weakened state, tio. He sounded drugged. We have no time to waste."

He asked Boli about using Victor. "Victor is young, but he's smarter than a lot of grown men I know," Boli told him. "And what about the woman? What about Miss Maitlin?"

"She insists on coming," Ramón told him.

"This is no place for a woman," Boli said, but without his usual enthusiasm.

"No. But it's her company's money. I don't think we have right to stop her. Besides, she and Victor can keep an eye on each other in the boat. I don't expect we'll just sail up to the kidnappers' camp and disembark. We'll have to leave the boat at some point, and go in on foot."

"Well, these men are professionals, and this is their job. I am afraid, *hijo*, that I can only get in the way."

Ramón looked at the older man, his father's old friend whom he called "uncle". He clasped him on the shoulder. "We still haven't heard from them, *tio*. Maybe they're going to change tactics. Maybe they'll take him over the Costa Rica border. We have to try and find them before they set up the next meeting, it's our only chance."

"Ramón, did you speak to Dolores?"

"No, we haven't spoken. Does she have some news?"

"YES," Boli said, "yes! The kidnappers sent another fax."

Ramón raced to the radio, picked up the transceiver and switched to channel three. "Frutas Base, Frutas Base, Frutas Base. Do you read? Over."

Nothing.

"Dolores, Dolores, Dolores," he tried. "Do you copy? Over."

A squelch, then Dolores's voice finally came through. It was distant but clear, and full of choking emotion. "Ramón? This is Dolores. I can hear you loud and clear. Where is father? Over."

"Dolores. The kidnappers still have father. I'll fill you in when I see you."

"A fax arrived," they could hear paper rustling.

"Not on the radio, Dolores…"

"It says…." more crying, now building into a sob. "It says: The ransom's short you fucking asshole. Get the rest, or Papi dies. Stay onboard. You'll be contacted."

Ramón heaved a big sigh and everyone watched him as if in a trance. Boli broke the spell. "Tell her I'll be there soon," Boli said. "Tell her no more talking on the radio. I'll be there soon."

Ramón gave his sister instructions, and signed off, looking shell-shocked. Matti wasn't the only one who needed sleep. First though, they had to go back to Platanillo, round up Victor and his boat, and provisions—and another million dollars.

The mouth of the Río Teribe could be reached from Platanillo in two hours. They could negotiate its length in a half a day, or night. They'd probably start out tomorrow, early. Which meant she'd be out of touch, again, when the office opened on Monday.

Ashley would call Alma at the Hotel Mariposa, who'd probably put her in touch with Dolores. Dolores would tell Ashley where Matti had gone, why she hadn't called, and Ashley would tell Sam. *Uh-oh.*

Thinking about this chain of events made her lethally tired. Her head was still pounding. She told Ramón she needed to go below for a few minutes. She sprawled face down across the forward berth, just for a minute, she told herself. After Boli had gone, they got underway. Ramón came down and covered Matti with a blanket. Asleep and curled up, she looked like a little girl who'd been playing too hard, and finally fallen in her tracks.

Two hours later they were back inside Banana Bay and Matti awoke from the lack of movement, the stillness. She pulled herself up and looked out the porthole. The boat was tied up at the dock. Dawn was breaking. She'd slept through the entire trip back. She splashed water on her face, drank a big cold glass of it from the fridge and saw a note from Ramón that they'd gone to find the bank manager, get provisions, round up Victor, and get Alma's permission for him to go up the Teribe in his dugout. They'd be back, hopefully, before the kidnappers made radio contact again.

No word on Gerry or Larry, who Ramon had hopefully dropped at the police station so their credentials could be verified. She poured the dregs of the coffee from the thermos into a mug, brought it up on deck and sat in one of the fighting chairs. She looked at the transom, the scene of so much action last night. Had it really been just a few hours ago that she'd kissed Ramón, swum to the beach, been ambushed by an undercover U.S. operative, and watched a million dollars get snatched away by two men on jet skis?

It wasn't even 7 a.m., and the enormity of what she'd done began to make tiny inroads into her brain—not to mention how much more she'd have on her plate before this day was over. On top of that, she didn't even have a clean pair of panties never mind insect repellent, face cream, or a fresh T-shirt. And there was no transport around here. No taxis cruising by, no boats either for that matter. This was a private inlet with only one installation: Papi's private dock. If she could get to Alma's, she could at least get organized, instead of sitting here obsessing and trying to make sense of it all.

If the kidnappers raised the call before they made it to the mouth of the Rio Teribe, the timing would be against them. They might name a rendezvous point far away. Of course, Ramón would always have the handheld radio with them, act as though they were still on the Bertram, act as if they were just hanging around waiting to pay the ransom instead of (hopefully) sneaking up and capturing them on the Rio Teribe.

She still had the feeling that Papi's captors weren't professional kidnappers but some group looking for a quick, easy score. Atlas was so careful with these K & R policies not to advertise that they even sold them. The policyholders themselves were a closely-guarded secret. It would be too easy for potential kidnappers to select insured individuals over non-insured targets. Those with insurance coverage had ransoms that were practically guaranteed!

And so it didn't make sense, again, about Worldwide Produce being behind the kidnapping scam. If they wanted to bring pressure on Papi, there were far more effective ways. Removing him on the chance of doing business with his son was a long shot, at best. And Ramón claimed he didn't want to sell. Yet the family seemed convinced that some people in Worldwide were behind it. Perhaps the family knew more than she did. Perhaps there were hidden motives she couldn't see.

Gerry and Larry were the kind of guys Gloria Steinem would've liked to have on her dartboard. Gerry defined the word "misogynist". His attempts to be polite were just an act; the way he *handled* everyone showed what a control freak he was, and he had all these fake steroid muscles—icky in the extreme.

Meanwhile, they were a couple of high-tech bruisers who had the know-how to help save Papi. She'd be present in a logistical support role. She and Victor would study the charts, look for the most likely hiding places. Gerry and Larry might not be future dating material but they were both armed, dangerous and here. They might even save Atlas two million dollars—and wasn't that also part of the bottom line? If they made a meaningful contribution, she'd make sure they got a generous reward from Atlas for their time, trouble and risk-taking.

The minutes ticked by and her thoughts whipped themselves into a rat's nest of conflicting possibilities: *If* the kidnappers were up the Rio Teribe and could be found. *If* they weren't seen (and kidnapped and killed) before the bad guys could be apprehended. *If* the kidnappers hadn't killed Papi already and left the area hours ago. *If* Victor didn't get lost in the "swamp". *If* they didn't run out of food, water, or get heat stroke. *If* they didn't get dengue fever from a mosquito bite, and if the boat didn't sink. *If* the kidnappers thought a million dollars was really enough and the last fax was just a ploy. She thought she'd get out some paper and make a list when she heard a car motor coming toward the dock, and then suddenly Ramón's Land Cruiser came into view.

He and Victor emerged from the car. Ramón looked strung out, exhausted. Victor smiled shyly at Matti. The two agents got out of the back seat and they all walked around to the back of the vehicle and began unloading supplies. Matti helped take the stuff on board.

She asked Ramon, "This is too much to fit into Victor's dugout, right?"

He nodded. "We'll use *La Boca* as a mother ship. We'll bring the boat around and leave it near Changuinola. Victor will follow in his boat with the agents who will stay out of sight. Then we'll go up the river in the *cayuco*—all of us lying flat so the kidnappers don't get suspicious."

"How big is the dugout?" she asked, avoiding comment on what a long shot this whole expedition seemed.

"Thirty feet, right big guy?" Gerry answered, knuckling Victor in the upper arm. Matti noted a little mutual admiration society in the making.

She reminded Victor, "This isn't a game, right? You're

not going to play some Ninja turtle warrior. You're just our guide—right Gerry?"

Gerry rolled his eyes and got busy with something else.

Victor was so eager to please. "*Si, si*. Ramón already told my mother and *abuela*. We will stay on the boat."

"That's right," Matti said. "You're coming with us so we don't get *lost*."

"I know the Teribe," Victor said. "I know it real good."

"Great, Victor. That's really great. I'm so glad you're with us." *And I'm glad you're such a good liar.*

Ramón passed her a sandwich. "Your breakfast," he said. "I also picked up your bag from Alma's."

"Oh, God! Thank you so much, Ramon."

She asked him, "Did you get the rest of the money?"

"It's all here." He picked up a black back-pack style satchel.

"And no more radio contact on this end—did Dolores get anything new."

"Nothing."

"I hope we're doing the right thing," she said, following him below. "What if it isn't the Teribe? What if they're somewhere else?"

"We can't sit here and wait, Matti," Ramón said. "Gerry's ninety percent sure he heard them say the word "Teribe". Besides, if I just sit here I think I'll implode."

"You need to sleep, Ramón. Let me put this stuff away. Go and lie down, at least for an hour."

Surprisingly, he agreed. "We'll leave after lunch."

Matti ate her sandwich. *What carbs?* Then she began stowing all the food and other supplies. She'd have to wait a few days before she could call the office. Hopefully Ashley wouldn't press the panic button between now and then and alert Sam.

Gerry came down below, followed by Victor. "Hey, how about rustling us up a sandwich?" She thought about this.

"Here's the bread—and how about tuna?" She asked Victor. "The mayo's in the fridge, the bowls are over there. Help yourselves."

Gerry looked at her with barely managed contempt. "You're a real babe, you know that?"

Matti looked at him and smiled. "That's what they all say."

Rio Teribe, Panamá

The day is clear, the sky is blue. The sun dapples the ground beneath the tree. I'm lying here, chained like a dog. The river water is cloudy from sliding over the fine sand, a murky gray green. All around us the vegetation crowds in: stalks of caña blanca over 20 feet tall, nance, guanabana, laurel and breadfruit trees. Wild banana, plantain, and avocado. The Teribe Indians have lived near these banks for the past 2,000 years and live here still in villages: Sieyik, Solon, Bonyik. I'm not at a village though, but a nameless camp, one of Noriega's old training camps, I think.

The Teribe have a kingdom, the only one left in this part of the world. Their king is called Santana. I met his father years ago. The Teribe are kind and peace loving. They fish, they farm, they make wood carvings to sell. Why have the Colombians brought me here and not to the Darien where they said they would?

Quintero told me: There are problems here that don't have to do with bananas. He said he'd bring me the proof. If only he had stayed out of it! And now, because of him, I'm held captive by the same Colombians who are on my payroll.

I know what they're capable of, these men. I've watched them work. They are farmers first, and know the bush completely: that the root of the marijuana plant works well against asthma, that sage is also good for this purpose; that clove is good for intestinal parasites; that coriander is good against colic. They know which herbs are valuable against headache, hunger, and heart palpitations. Which plants can be eaten; which plants can be used as balms, hallucinogens, poisons. Especially they know about these.

They say they want more money, that my life will be held against payment of what they are owed. I can't argue with them, they know I'm worth two-million, not one. Ramón will get the money, I know he will. The Colombians will disappear, and I will be free to pursue my goal, once more. They won't kill me—I'm sure they won't. We've know each other for too many years. It would be like murdering their own father.

These men are not simple campesinos, oh no. One of them just came back to camp swinging a bushmaster at least ten feet long and laughing. This is one of the deadliest of snakes. He tells the others about disturbing her habitat, how she leapt out at him like a demon from the bush. Her tiny offspring followed, fresh out of their eggs, they lash out at anything that comes near. Congenital aggression. Like these men who hold me now.

The Teribeños are peace-loving people. If only they would find me, maybe they'd remember. Maybe they'd help to set me free

They come now with the milky drink they put into a coconut shell. I cannot refuse it; they won't let me refuse. It's dark at first, very dark, but then I fly. I fly as high as any eagle in these mountain currents.

I have the strength to return to Cuba, at last.

CHAPTER 23

"Everybody ready?" Ramón asked, sipping a Coke. He'd slept for two hours. Everyone had eaten. Gerry and Larry had made Victor's dugout into a mini-wooden-warship. All the rest of the supplies had been stowed on *La Boca Grande*

No one at Atlas knew where the hell she was, or what she was up to—thank God. As soon as she had resolution she'd call the office and fill them all in. Hopefully the outcome would be worth the pain and suffering she would have to endure from Sam and Brandon when they found out about her over-involvement in this case.

Ramón had bought a new hand-held VHF and brought it along with a spare battery pack. So much depended on the radio, Matti thought, it couldn't fail them. The kidnappers still hadn't made contact; other than the one angry fax they'd sent nothing. Their silence nibbled at the edges of everyone's nerves.

Matti must've been looking more worried than usual because Ramón came and gave her a squeeze on the shoulder, ruffled the back of her hair.

"Don't look so worried," he said.

They went up on deck, Ramón started the engines. They finally saw Victor streaming past, the two agents concealed from view. To the casual observer, Victor was simply going off on another of his frequent fishing trips.

They threw off the lines, and *La Boca Grande* headed out of the inlet and into the bay behind Victor. Victor didn't even look back and Matti found herself admiring his pluck. At fourteen, he was already showing signs of adulthood.

The sky was all jewel-colored, the sea as calm as a lake; Matti had never seen a sea so calm. What a difference from the north Atlantic.

They'd made a series of plans around the galley table, Gerry listing the contingencies calmly and thoroughly. Still, she didn't trust him. He knew a lot about Papi, for example, though Matti knew neither she nor Ramón had filled him in. It was spooky to think that governments could have this kind of information about private citizens, and that their agents— albeit in the name of altruism—would seem so opportunistic.

Matti couldn't shake the feeling that somehow Papi Cardozo was a much more important person than she knew. How, why or by whom he was considered so valuable, she'd maybe never know. Had Papi really been kidnapped—in broad daylight—by someone not from the area? She doubted it.

Meanwhile, it wasn't her job to know every detail. Her job was to pay out on the K&R policy, and go back to Boston. The ransom for Papi's life and recovering Papi himself had become so inextricably linked that she could hardly separate them in her own mind. Wouldn't Sam be happy if they saved the insured and also the ransom money? It might make him so happy he'd forget how angry he was.

Once the kidnappers made contact, again, Ramón planned to tell them he had the other million dollars and it was agreed Gerry would make the exchange. If they didn't find Papi up the Rio Teribe and apprehend his captors, first—and this was obviously what they were all hoping. But there were so many hiding places, secluded bays, coves, inlets throughout Banana Bay. Perhaps the kidnappers had already come and gone from the Teribe and were hunkered down in a new hiding place just setting themselves up for the next drop off.

In less than an hour they reached the hidden inlet that Ramón had decided would be the base for *La Boca Grande*. It was only an hour from the river in case they needed to go back and meet the kidnappers elsewhere. Victor went ahead of them, and was already obscured by the bushy, tall mangrove outcrops. They entered the inlet carefully and Ramón swung the bow toward the entrance, dropping the anchor into black mud.

Victor had the dugout under some overhanging mangrove in the shade; Matti could just make out Gerry and Larry—they were nearly invisible in their camouflage gear. They had additional T-shirts of the same material for Matti, Ramón and Victor. Matti passed them two square boxes of food over the side. Gerry had done the provisioning inspired by Basic-Training Cuisine: dozens of tins of sardine and packages of soda crackers competed with tinned cookies, and bottles of Gatorade. A five-gallon jug of drinking water was already in the dugout, as were 15 gallons of gas, a large tarp, towels, insect repellant, sunblock, hats, rubber boots, flashlights, a cooler with icepacks, a first aid kit, a tent, and Gerry's "bag of tricks". It was planned as a twenty-four hour trip that could turn into two days. They'd know soon if Papi was in a camp on the river or not. A search into the bush was not practical for obvious reasons. They either found him and got out, or, if he wasn't there, they'd have to come back out and wait to hear the kidnappers' next rendezvous point.

Victor pulled alongside the swim platform and Matti stepped into the dugout—Banana Bay's answer to all-purpose transport—carved out of a single tree and powered by a 75 hp Yamaha. Matti had seen other *cayucos* since her arrival that were so low to the water, they nearly disappeared into the surface.

From Alma's place, she'd seen many different varieties: a gaff-rigged sail made out of old flour sacks sewn together; others with paddles, outboards of various sizes. Victor had managed to find himself one of the bigger ones with a high freeboard. The Yamaha looked like an older model, but seemed reliable.

They stowed the food, to which she'd added two thermoses of coffee. Essential, in her opinion, and no one disagreed. She saw that Victor had brought his fishing gear which consisted of a big roll of Styrofoam wrapped with fishing line, and a bucket of minnows for bait. Even on this mission, Victor wasn't going to miss out on his fishing time.

Someone had also brought several bunches of small, wild bananas—*primitivos*, Victor called them—and she ate one as they got on their way. It was the best banana she'd ever tasted, firm and sweet with a mild clove flavor; what a difference from those big yellow ones with a Worldwide Produce sticker.

She offered bananas to everyone. They all were in a sitting position; Gerry reckoned that the danger of being seen in the bay was now behind them. There were no other craft visible in the area. If they spotted someone, they could all hunker down.

The radio was in Ramón's lap, the extra battery pack in a waterproof bag at his feet.

"I'll try Dolores," he said to no one in particular, and turned the radio to their agreed channel.

"Frutas base, Frutas base, do you read? Over."

"Loud and clear, big brother," Dolores's voice came back crystal clear and more friendly than Matti had ever heard her.

"We're in position," said Ramón simply. "Over and out."

***

They mouth of the Rio Teribe, when they reached it, was roiling with white water, but it calmed as the mouth expanded—

though the currents remained strong. Egrets lined the shore like one-legged soldiers. Green foliage hung over the banks.

The kidnappers still had made no contact. What were they waiting for? It seemed a menacing silence, Matti thought, which became more so with each passing minute. She had used this technique in interviews with claimants: by shutting up, the other party often felt compelled to speak, blurt things out, make mistakes, give away truths that were meant to be dissembled. It was unnerving technique that worked wonders.

The Teribeños were gentle, peace-loving people, Ramón had explained. But there were corrupt people in every culture, and maybe the kidnappers were among their ranks. Gerry was emphatic on this point, that no one see them all sitting in the boat. It would raise too many questions altogether, and their presence could well get back to the men holding Papi hostage.

Ramón agreed: In this part of world, word traveled as fast as the river flowed. Matti estimated that this would translate to about a 30-knot-per-hour rumor mill. God help them, either, if anyone went overboard. It would take only minutes to slide out to sea—if anyone survived the trip over the rocks.

Gerry and Larry sat like the soldiers they were, in the bow, their backs to her. She sat behind them, Ramón behind her. She turned back to see Victor, last of all, as he readied the boat to take them into the churning white water and up the river. He looked calm and in complete control. Ramón passed her a life jacket. They all held on to the sides as the dugout surged forward, sprightly as a pony.

The placidness of the delta was behind them now, the water cascading past them on its way to the sea. And this was the dry season!, Matti thought. Around the boat, swirling eddies and surges from the intersecting currents became progressively more intense. She wondered what would happen if they suddenly lost power, and were forced backwards through these roiling waters, and decided it was better not to think.

She held on, too frightened to even turn and look at Victor. They'd put so much trust in this young man and his abilities. Her swimming skills would be useless if they capsized; the best she could hope for would be to get thrown up on a rocky shoal. There were small crocodiles in the pools at the river's edge, and many large fish too, according to Victor; but Matti was mesmerized by the murky green water, the color of a black cat's eyes.

She turned and saw Ramón frowning as he studied the bank looking for any sign. Victor, behind him, was smiling, his perfect white teeth lighting up his brown face. Someone else was paying for the fuel and he was having the time of his life. Her hands were frozen claws, gripping the gunwale as their big cradle of a boat rocked upriver.

Ahead of her, Gerry and Larry looked like sensory machines, taking in every detail of the banks hanging with clinging vines, the tall stands of cane, the trees and thick jungle undergrowth. If the kidnappers camped, they'd have to find a clearing. It was unlikely that they'd be camped right at the water's edge in plain view. Were the Teribeños involved? Who knew?

Gerry turned and made a signal to Victor to navigate toward the left-hand bank. The white water was absent here by the bank, and on the other bank, Matti saw, there were little stagnant pools, emerald with slime. The trees were hanging low over the water on the bank. Matti saw that Gerry wanted to get into position to see more clearly upriver so they could continue to navigate as surreptitiously as possible.

This wasn't going to be as easy as it sounded, Matti observed. They had passed only one person going downstream, a young man poling on a log raft. There were rock outcroppings, pools of spinning current, many high banks. There were not all that many places to pull into and hide. The most they could hope for, she realized, was to be lucky enough to see the kidnappers' camp before they were right on top of it.

Gerry and Larry had also specified: no talking. Voices carried remarkably well over water as did engine noise. Paddling was not practical: the river was too long, there was too much current, the boat was too heavy. If they were nearing a known Indian encampment or village, Victor would advise them in advance and the two agents would go in on foot.

While upright, everyone was instructed to look for any signs of encampment; at Gerry's signal they'd immediately lie down in the bottom of the boat. Gerry made them practice this now, and Ramón nearly knocked over the radio. They moved the provisions, and made space so that everyone could lie prone. If they encountered another craft, Victor would look like a lone fisherman on a fishing trip, nothing more.

Matti was beginning to sweat profusely in the rising heat of the day. The breeze from traveling up the river was considerably reduced when they stopped. She felt her face chapping from over-exposure to the wind and sun.

They were all covered with sunblock, but nevertheless she felt the sun burning her skin. The camouflage shirt she wore was soaked through, she her arms were already bursting with freckles where the sunblock had been sweated off. She ate another banana to take her mind off this extreme un-makeover.

Gerry gave the all clear signal, and Victor turned the craft back into the navigable part of the river, and they continued upstream.

Sam appeared unbidden in her mind's eye. What would he be doing right now? Playing racquetball in Milton? Going for Sunday lunch to his parents' house? Maybe he was re-decorating his new condo. Maybe he'd chucked the whole thing in, and was back with Judith?

The first few months after a separation were the hardest, Matti knew. Depression fought with euphoria, anger bubbled up to displace the fear. She had tended to stay at home isolating for long periods, then would burst forth for a frenzied round of partying, dancing and drinking. It took her nearly two years to normalize her routine; at first she acted as if she were no longer hurting, and eventually it became true. She developed real friendships with the people around her, Patrick and Brian being her particular favorites. Her women friends were spread out all over the world, and she kept in touch with all of them and visited them whenever she could. This was her world family, and she was loved by her friends, loving them deeply in turn. If only they could see her now!

Gerry snapped her from her reverie by pointing in an exaggerated way at a plastic bottle floating by. It was mustard yellow with a red cap, the words "*aceite*" printed on its side. Gerry made the signal to get down, and they all obeyed. A cooking oil bottle, Matti thought. Is this the way they dispose of their garbage? Is that what's on the bottom of this river, not crocs, or tarpon, but the 20th century refuse of the Indian nation?

They slowly made way, Victor having reduced speed so Gerry could anticipate what might lie ahead. Victor's calm demeanor indicated to Matti there was no settlement near here; they could no evidence of habitation on the banks. Outboards would have been nearly impossible to hear over the din of the river, but people here were more likely to use paddles than outboards, she guessed. Was someone camped up just ahead? Or had the bottle had floated miles downstream?

Suddenly the radio crackled to life in Ramón's hand and she was so startled by this burst of life and what it might portend that she started shaking from pure adrenaline. Her heart, picking up the signal from her brain, also and began hammering. The voice from the radio was firm and loud and sounded like it was coming from someone standing ten feet away:

"*Boca Grande, Boca Grande, Boca Grande,*" the voice demanded. "Do you read? Over."

They all sat up in the bottom of the hull and Gerry motioned to Victor to cut the engine as he scrambled back from the bow so he could cue Ramón. They'd practiced Ramón's response repeatedly on the way out but now that the moment was upon them, he looked like an actor who's forgotten all his lines.

"This is *Boca Grande*, go ahead," he managed, sounding much calmer than he looked. Gerry nodded.

"Hope you have the other million, *hijo*," the voice said, emphasizing the last word with venomous sarcasm. "Over."

Gerry nodded. Go ahead. "Yes, we have the money. You can have it when I see my father alive. Where is he?"

A chuckle responded to this. "Easy does it, *nino*."

Gerry grabbed Ramón's arm. "Don't react," he told him in a low voice, "just do as we agreed."

"I repeat," Ramón said, pressing the transmit button. "You can have the money when I see my father is alive."

The kidnapper—who they had nicknamed Radio Man— answered with a cold: "*Espera.*"

"Wait!? Wait?!" Ramón yelled before Gerry could intercede. "I want to know if my father is still alive. Put him on so I can hear his voice now!" He released the transmit button, and the radio reverted to a deep, dark megalithic silence which went on minute after excruciating minute while they all waited.

Gerry took the radio out of Ramón's hand, put it inside the waterproof bag, and pulled out a paddle to turn them around.

"They've gone to get him. They'll be in touch again." He nodded at Victor to keep going.

Everyone hunched down once more as they were propelled upstream toward the Kingdom of the Teribe. Matti lay back and wondered if Papi was looking at the same cloudless, blue sky, or had he died waiting? The old man had a heart condition and was probably not getting the best of care.

If he were dead, the kidnappers had nothing to lose by an ambush.

It depended on who saw who first.

A long hour passed uneventfully. Larry strung up the tarp which gave some shade, but increased the temperature and blocked the view completely. The prickly heat caused Matti's chest and arms to burst into a rash, and she was grateful beyond belief when Gerry indicated they should pull over to the bank and take a break. Under the cover of a leafy tree, she waded into the shallows and tried to cool down. Gerry dispensed cans of sardines and crackers and Matti felt as if she could drink the entire five-gallon jug of water single-handed.

"Easy," Gerry said, indicating that she should take small sips, or risk cramping up. She would have skipped the sardines entirely and settled for more bananas, but again Gerry insisted: she needed the salt to guard against dehydration. On this kind of mission, he told her, you ate what you could when it was put in front of you. Three squares a day were not an option.

Larry, who'd not spoken a word in at least ten hours, now let out a deep belch and a sigh. What a charmer! Is this what being in boot camp was like? If so, thank God she'd never signed up.

Gerry and Larry walked onto the bank and began conferring in low tones. What were they planning that couldn't be shared with the rest of the group? They motioned for Ramón up to join them, and they all began nodding their heads.

Now wait one minute...

Gerry put on his polite act again. "We think it's better if you stay here," he told her. She had the early symptoms of heat stroke, he said. They could make her comfortable here. Clear the underbrush with machete and leave her sufficient provisions. She looked at him in horror. "No way," she told him. She immediately jumped back into the boat, and clung onto her seat, smiling as if it were a joke. "I'm not staying behind."

As many dangers as might lay ahead, she refused to be left here in this wild place with whatever animals, snakes or other reptiles decided to show up. To her going—not staying—seemed much less of a risk.

Ramón went forward to the cooler, took out an icepack wrapped it in a towel and passed it to her. "You're being foolish," he said. "And stubborn."

She pressed the ice pack to her hot, flushed face and felt it melting on contact.

"I'm fine," she said. She'd slathered on more sunscreen, and put on a thin cotton long-sleeved shirt on to protect her arms and neck.

There was no more argument, and they started up the river again. They'd only passed two other dugouts going downstream. Victor waved to them, and tugged at his fishing line like an actor. He merely had to play his innocent self, and troll an unbaited line.

"Later," Gerry had said earlier, removing the minnow from Victor's hook and putting it back in the bucket. "Later you can catch us a big snapper, or we might have to eat these for dinner."

Victor, as always, took this good naturedly, and smiled his beautiful toothpaste-ad smile.

CHAPTER 24

The first Teribe village was just up ahead.

They pulled over to the bank where Gerry and Larry took unrolled camouflage netting and covered the boat with it, leaving Matti, Ramón and Victor, mercifully in the shade on the bank. In minutes they had disappeared into the bush and Matti lay on the bank, pressing the melting icepack to her face. The leafy overhang and moss covered bank was the perfect picnic spot; too bad she wasn't a tourist and this wasn't a secluded spot on the grounds of a 5-star hotel.

The river was shining with golden light when the two agents returned at almost five o'clock. The Indian settlement contained neither kidnappers, nor any sign of Papi, Gerry reported.

"We'll camp further upstream—less activity," Gerry said, which seemed like a sensible plan. He and Larry dismantled the tarp, pulling it over Matti, Ramón, themselves and all the gear in the bottom of the boat before Victor headed upstream once more.

Matti could hear children and women along the banks, and smelled burning charcoal as they made their way up river past the village. Someone shouted to Victor from the shore, a dialect that sounded completely foreign to Matti's ear. Did these people really live completely isolated from the rest of civilization? Was it such a bad idea not to have cable TV, or fast food, or cars?

Matti could feel herself tensing up listening to their exchange, and forced herself to take deep breaths. Thank God the sun was beginning to set. She could soon take a swim and cool off.

Victor kept his tone light and friendly. The person on shore laughed and said something that Matti couldn't hear. They progressed further upstream and the smell of smoke faded and the sounds too. Victor peeled back the tarp as an all-clear signal, and they all gratefully crawled out from underneath it.. To Matti the river was a lot less frothy now. The water was deep and eddying, swirling around them. The banks were further apart, and hung heavily with greenery, the trees huge and stately. There were no signs that they'd just passed an Indian settlement at all; it was pure wilderness once more.

They traveled a bit further until Gerry found a suitable site. Victor steered the boat to the bank. Larry jumped out and began expertly cutting the underbrush with a machete. Soon they had cleared a spot to rest and re-group.

Gerry spoke to Victor. "Okay, buddy. Time to do a little fishing if we don't want sardines again." Victor broke into a grin and went forward to get the bait. In minutes he had a handful of minnows, jabbed the hook through half a dozen, and flung the line into a passing current. Matti waded into the water with all her clothes on. For someone who'd spent much of the day lying down she felt exhausted and was still overheated.

Gerry reached into the boat and pulled out their box of provisions on top of which some wilted greenery lay. "Salad anyone?" he asked, and after offering it around, stuffed what smelled like coriander into his mouth. Larry did the same while Ramón and Matti watched.

"It's an acquired taste," Gerry said, sucking the green bits from his teeth.

Ignoring the epicurean comment, Ramón asked, "How much further will we go?" Like Matti, Ramón was growing ever more skeptical about the chances of running into the kidnappers up here—not to mention that they had never radioed back.

"We need to go upriver until it's no longer navigable. Tomorrow morning should do it. Remember, going downriver will be much faster than coming up. The only thing that could screw up our plans is if they want us to be in Escudo or some other place that's a long distance away tomorrow morning. Then we'd be fucked. Excuse my French," he said, smiling patronizingly at Matti.

"Why French?" Matti wanted to know, feeling annoyed as she usually did when Gerry opened his mouth. "I mean, why not 'Excuse my Spanish, Italian or Portuguese?' Better still, why not 'excuse my English?'"

"I think you're right," Ramón said, ignoring her. "You overheard them saying Teribe. It makes perfect sense to me that they'd be up here. It's close to the lagoon and yet well hidden. I think we're in the right place because we've traveled up here all day and not passed them. Perhaps they'll move down river tonight to be closer to the bay and a pickup point. I don't think they'll meet us in Escudo again, though. It's too predictable."

"Yes," Larry said, somberly. They all looked at him in amazement.

Gerry picked up the slack. "If they are up here and need to head down to be in the area tomorrow, they'll most likely come down tonight. Then we ambush them. We'll hear their motors and they'll never know what hit 'em. Right, dude?" Gerry said to Larry, who grinned in long-toothed affirmation.

Victor jumped up. "I got one," he said, and began pulling in his line with delicate overhand motions. Two black rubber tubes covered his forefingers and prevented the line from sawing into his flesh, and in minutes he flung a big silver fish onto the bank. It surely weighed at least five pounds. "It's a robalo," he said. His smile nearly reached to his ears.

"A snook," Ramón translated. "My favorite."

"My God, Victor, well done!" Matti said. "But what can we do with it? We can't build a fire," she said. "Anyone for sashimi?"

"We're going to make a very small, hot fire in a pit, and bury it," Gerry told her with satisfaction. "An old Maori trick and their version of the American barbecue. In Hawaii they do it too, bury the whole banquet: meat, fish, vegetables, the works."

"It sounds like a New England lobster bake," Matti said.

"Exactly," said Gerry, "so let's get digging."

Later, they sat around feeling the after-effects of the meal, the sun, the emotional strain of being on guard the entire time. Sitting around the smoldering pit, Matti remembered her long-ago Girl Scout camp-outs. There'd be no giggling and ghost stories tonight. Larry pitched the tent and she crawled into it. Let them all figure it out; they'd call her for her watch around midnight.

She fell fast asleep. In her dreams, she was swimming in the river, but it was much wider, and each time she thought she was nearing the bank it would recede. She began to struggle, and then suddenly Ramón was beside her, pulling her to safety, and kissing her. Then her cell phone rang, and it was Sam demanding to know where she was. "Matti..."

"Yes?" she was immediately awake and alert.

Gerry had crawled into the tent with her. Oh my God— Gerry in her tent! What was he doing in here?

He put his fingers to his lips, pulled her up to a sitting position and motioned her out through the opening. The moon had set, her watch said 4:10 a.m. Still she couldn't imagine what Gerry was after. His every action was sure and calculated. She stuck her head out and watched as he roused Ramón, then Victor, who was curled up under the tarp.

Larry was nowhere to be seen. Gerry made a hand signal to get in the boat, and put his finger to his lips once more. Quietly. No sound.

They left the tent and other gear, except for the tarp, and crept forward.

Matti saw Gerry watching the river with the concentration of an animal about to do battle. It was frightening. Later she realized he was gauging the current, and his ability to maneuver in it. Seconds later, she heard the sound that Gerry had known was coming. It was a sound that she had been anticipating and dreading since the trip began.

There was a boat approaching. It sounded like a powerful engine going at low speed. As she listened more closely, and came fully awake, she thought she was hearing not one engine, but two. Were these the kidnappers? Coming downstream before daylight to get ready for the ransom pickup somewhere in Banana Bay?

Gerry hustled them into the dugout. Matti burrowed into the bow and pulled a corner of tarp over her. She was suddenly deeply frightened; what had ever made her think she should come on such fool's mission. Victor's head was in resting on her feet and she stroked his head; instinctively wanting to protect him. He was trembling more than she was.

Ramón crouched forward peering over the bow. No one could see their boat tucked here under cover of darkness, but the kidnappers had that advantage, too. Visibility was no more than twenty yards, the total width of the river was only about thirty yards across. The as-yet-unseen boats wouldn't be visible until they were practically in touching distance.

Everything came down to split-second timing. They risked Papi's life and their own if they alarmed the kidnappers prematurely. She prayed Gerry knew what he was doing and that no one would die in the next few minutes.

Gerry waded into the water, whispered to them to stay down, and stay hidden. "Don't move," he told them in a fierce, low voice. "And don't get out of the boat under any circumstances." He had emphasized this point before and Matti was not about to go against his orders now.

She peeked over the side, though, and watched him disappear into the water. Still no sign of Larry, and the boats—indeed there were two, she could see their dark outlines—were getting closer.

Now she could hear mumbles that more distinctly became voices as the *cayucos* came closer. They were men's voices, talking just loud enough to be heard over the engines. No problem about having to keep it down, Matti thought. So what if they talked loudly? It was almost four-thirty in the morning, in the middle of the jungle, on a remote river in northern Panamá. Who could possibly be listening?

The voices became more animated now. Somebody was telling a joke, and laughing as he told it. That laugh again! It was Radio Man's without a doubt! But before she could react it was as if she was frozen in time and space. The motor on one of the boats spluttered and died.

The *cayucos* came to a stop mid-river. Pulling the cord repeatedly yielded no result and they started to drift. Someone threw out an anchor and Matti held her breath. They obviously didn't want to careen downstream without power. Matti peeked out and watched as the men tried to figure out what to do. One of them moved to the stern to tilt the engine out of the water and see what the problem was. There were consultations in low voices, several men crouched together now in the one craft. It seemed as though the prop was fouled with fishing line, or something similar. The man near the engine asked for a knife to cut away the obstruction.

At that moment Gerry and Larry struck.

A net came sailing over the heads of all the men who were congregated in the stern, who were bunched altogether, with no room to maneuver.

Larry burst over the side looking like a huge slick white monster; even from here Matti could see his pale skin flashing in the low light like the underbelly of a giant fish. In seconds, Gerry had boarded the other craft, and started the engine again while the three netted kidnappers swore at him in crazed Spanish from the other, fouled *cayuco*.

"Papi's alive," she heard Gerry say. "The ransom's here too."

Larry, meanwhile, had made a neat package of the four men and the fishing net in the other broken down dugout. If any of them moved, the boat immediately became unbalanced. Matti couldn't believe the speed of the whole undertaking; in less than ten minutes the two agents had ambushed the kidnappers, found Papi, and segregated him. They had even recovered the ransom—what perfect timing! They'd be getting a big reward from Atlas, that was for sure.

Larry left the four kidnappers and boarded the other boat which held Papi and where Gerry waited with the engine idling. They had brought Papi to a sitting position, in spite of the fact that he looked inert. He was probably filled to the gills with tranquilizers.

Ramón watched too, his face slack with relief, and joy. "Papa, Papa," he cried. If it hadn't been for the treacherous currents, he would have swum to the boat immediately.

Gerry and Larry said not another word. They merely turned up the engine to full throttle and took off without a backward glance.

"What?" Matti said, watching slack-jawed as they sped downstream in the fast moving currents. "Jesus, Ramón. Holy shit!" Matti cried. "They're taking off!"

Ramón quickly went to the stern of their own craft and tried pulling the Yamaha to life while Victor looked on, his mouth hanging open. The engine didn't even splutter.

"The bastards! The animals! I knew we shouldn't have trusted them!" She thought of Ramón's .38, safely back aboard *La Boca Grande*, at her insistence.

"They took the black bag!" Ramon cried. "Jesus. They got the other million."

She began running along the bank after them. "Gerry!! God *damn* it, get back here this instant! Do you hear me? Gerry! Larry! That's enough—this isn't a joke." It was as if they were in a different dimension; they didn't appear to even hear her, though she knew they could, quite clearly.

"Ramón, do something!" she screamed.

"*Chuleta!*" Ramón yelled, as he pulled the starter cord again and again. She and Victor collided as they tried to help, looking more by the minute like extras in a slapstick comedy. Meanwhile, Gerry, Larry, Papi and a two-million dollar ransom were all heading quickly downstream.

They collapsed onto the hard bench seats. Matti looked at Ramón, tears of frustration stinging her eyes. "I knew we shouldn't have trusted them, the bastards! I just *knew* it!'"

"We were all fooled," Ramón said. "Let try and call Boli and see if he can head them off." But of course, when they looked for it, the radio was gone along with the battery pack.

Mid-river, the kidnappers stood muttering, but still. What were they going to do about them?

"What's the plan?" Matti asked Ramón, as the sun began to rise, lighting up their semi-secluded spot under the branches.

"For a start, I brought the gun you told me not to bring... although I didn't couldn't get it out fast enough to stop Gerry and Larry."

"Oh!"

"Matti, I need you to use it now to keep these men under control."

"I can't use a gun, Ramón, I never learned how."

"Well, don't worry about it," Ramón told her in a low voice so the men standing in the other *cayuco* couldn't hear. "Gerry took all my bullets."

"Did they leave us anything besides sardines?" Matti wanted to shriek in frustration. How had they been so completely duped?

"Okay, Matti, this is the plan. We need to tie them up and get them lying in the bottom of the boat while one of us holds the gun to their heads. Which one do you want to try?"

"I'd better hold the gun."

"My thought exactly. You don't have to shoot anyone, just pretend you might. You can finally put that Irish temper to some good use."

"Very funny."

"I want Victor to stay onshore." He turned and told Victor. "We'll drag your *cayuco* upstream along the banks and then paddle down to them. Once they're secure, I can try and restart their engine. Victor will help me unfoul the propeller, and you'll kick anyone in the *cojones* who tries anything funny."

Matti replied, "Speaking of *cojones*, I could just *castrate* those two. I thought Boli checked them out."

"I thought he did, too."

They pushed the boat into the river, wading upstream with it. When they were fifty yards from the kidnappers, they climbed aboard and Ramón guided the boat downstream. In seconds, they were alongside the other craft, causing the kidnappers' blabber to stop immediately. One of the men, seeing Ramón, began an outpouring in Spanish that sounded to Matti's ears like a very self-pitying apology. The other two began aggressively wiggling inside the net, and the dugout began to wobble precariously.

Ramón grabbed hold of the gunwale and steadied it. "*Los colombianos,*" Ramón said, calm as ice. "Why am I not surprised?"

"I will tell you everything, Don Ramón, it's not how it seems…we only wanted to take Papi on a little vacation, get him away from the *finca* for awhile."

"Save it," Ramón told him savagely. Matti picked up the gun, and pointed it directly at the man's crotch. He tried to cross his legs in protection.

"Don't say anything to piss us off," Matti said. "I might enjoy this."

Ramón said, "All of you move forward. Go slowly, or you might drown, and I might sit here and watch." Gerry and Larry had bound them so tightly inside the net, that no one could sit down or move without affecting the others. Matti had never seen such an ingenious yet simple method for keeping people contained. It was like a tiny prison where everything had to be decided by a committee of four.

They began to inch forward, all looking down at their feet as they slowly made space between themselves and the motor.

"Victor," Ramón said, "Get in the water and see if you can free the prop. It looks like fishing line." In minutes, Victor was hanging on to the stern, a knife between his teeth expertly clearing away the fishing line that had been wrapped around the prop and frozen it.

The big Yamaha fired up on the first try, and Victor turned to Matti and smiled. She felt her entire body sigh in relief at the sound. The went to the bank where Victor's dugout slammed against the shoal with its dead engine.

"Okay, Matti, help Victor get his *cayuco* secure so we can tow it behind this one." The kidnappers stood watching quietly to see what would happen next.

On shore, Ramón cut some of Victor's anchor line, and re-tied the kidnappers hands behind their backs before partially removing the net so they could all sit down. Matti trained the gun back and forth between them, aiming low. She was starting to enjoy this. At least they'd captured Papi's original kidnappers. Maybe now they could start getting some answers.

Gerry and Larry, she knew, would be gone from Panamá in a matter of hours.

Papi would only slow them down. He was just temporary security to enable them to get away with two million dollars. But who were they really, if not government operatives?

And would Papi survive another harrowing ordeal?

"So, those guys weren't with you?" Radio Man asked, curiosity overcoming his good sense.

"None of your fucking business, *amigo*," Ramón told him. "Now lie in the boat face down while I tie up your feet." Everyone obeyed, watching Matti out of the corners of their eyes.

Victor stood in the stern looking from Matti to Ramón and back again. This obviously hadn't been part of the kid's wildest fantasies when he'd left Platanillo to make this trip. Now, in addition to losing Papi again, and the ransom, they had these four Colombians lying prone in the bottom of the boat.

They started downriver. "Apparently, you know these men," Matti said.

"They're FT employees, from Finca 8—unless this is a bad hallucination."

"Nothing surprises me in my line of work," she said. "These must be the men your father's *capitaz* Quintero spoke about."

"Yes," Ramón admitted. "And I didn't believe him. But it still doesn't make any sense, Matti."

"Two million dollars doesn't make sense?" Matti asked, arching an eyebrow. "If you ask me, it's a hell of a big motivation. Look at all the trouble Gerry and Larry went to get the whole ransom."

***

Meanwhile, the questions in Matti's mind seemed to be growing exponentially. Were the kidnappers hired by someone like Worldwide to kill Papi? Did they then become greedy and decided to play for a ransom, too? Why the delay in making their demands? And what about Gerry and Larry who had "re-kidnapped" Papi and gotten two million dollars into the bargain. Were they hired guns too, or just a couple of thugs who had gotten wind of the whole scheme and inserted themselves into the outcome?

The Bad Ass Boys (as she'd began thinking of them) were certainly not government agents, but seemed to have military training. Something nagged on her consciousness, but she couldn't fathom what. There was so much to take in, so many factors to consider all at once. Thank God the sun was coming up. At least they didn't have to land at the Teribeño village in darkness, and startle everyone.

Victor had more difficulty steering having to tow the other *cayuco* behind him and the kidnappers were grumbling. It was nerve-wracking and Victor kept losing his concentration. Going downriver was much faster than going up, like slippery spaghetti being tipped out of a pot of boiling water. And now as they came to a swirling patch where the water was churning madly, the kidnappers heard it, and began moving and jostling. Ramón yelled to Victor to be careful, and just then the line towing Victor's boat snapped and the dugout went ahead of its own accord. Its canoe-shaped stern whipped around beam-to just as Victor careened into it, giving their own craft and all its passengers a good walloping bang. Matti clung on to the gunwale. She'd almost gone over the side. Being on the river in these currents was like being in a skid on ice without the freezing temperatures.

Suddenly they were through it.

Victor put the boat back into gear, and Ramón put out the big flat paddle, steering them to the bank. They needed to regroup. Ahead of them, Victor's *cayuco* had lodged between some rocks, looking innocuous and calm, when a moment before it had almost killed them. She felt herself surge with gratitude that they hadn't capsized.

Ramón and Victor began discussing methods of getting down to the village as safely as possible, and at that moment Matti looked up and saw a group of three small, low *cayucos* paddling their way. Indians, a pair in each boat riding so low in the water she could barely see their sides.

"We've got company," she told Ramón, pointing.

"Thank God," Ramón said. "But somehow they don't look like they have a radio."

"They're fishing," said Victor, smiling at the thought.

They watched as the Indians paddled closer; going upstream without a motor wasn't easy. Matti wondered if the king was an understanding sort. Would he believe their wild tale of kidnapping and counter-kidnapping? Would they believe that the four Colombians bound and gagged in the bottom of their boat had tried to ransom Papi Cardozo?

Or that the victim, two more thugs, and two million dollars in cash had just passed his village and escaped?

She remembered Ramón explaining that up here the king acted independently in matters of crime and punishment. Maybe he'd put them all in jail while he tried to figure out the truth.

Ramón looked at her and shrugged acceptance of their new fate. "Welcome," he told Matti, "to the Kingdom of the Teribeños."

"Did you find her?" Sam asked, leaning over Ashley's desk. It was now 11 o'clock on Monday morning.

"No sir, the woman at the hotel said she checked out."

"Checked out *where*, Ashley?" Sam asked. He looked menacing as a prizefighter, and Ashley had a strong urge to back away from him. She managed to hide her fear by setting her jaw, something she'd picked up from Matti.

"The woman didn't know, Sam," she said. "Someone came and got all her clothes, and said they were going on a boat trip."

"Come in here now," Sam said, leading the way into Matti's private office, closing the door behind them both. "Look here, Ashley. Does this sound likely to you? That Matti would allow someone *else* to check her out of the hotel? What kind of hotel allows other people to check their guests out?"

"Her name is Alma," Ashley said. "She owns the place. She said Matti went up to the farm the previous day for an appointment, and then went on this boat trip."

"Why hasn't she been in touch with this office since she left? It is not only out of character but completely against company policy. I asked her to check in daily on my voice mail. Why didn't she?" Ashley thought he might start pawing the ground in a minute. She was sure Matti was fine, had just gotten sidetracked. She wasn't about to share this feeling though with the owner of the company.

"I've tried to call the insured's home but there's no answer. The number rings through to an answering machine so I know the number's right. Maybe everyone has gone on this boat trip together. Maybe they found out where the insured was, and went to get him." Ashley tried a weak smile, which didn't sell.

"I want you to call every contact we have down there. And get Richard on it too. Where is he, by the way?"

"Don't you remember? His wife had a medical emergency and he took vacation time to stay home and help out. He won't be in all week, he said."

"Call Frutas Tropicales then. Call the agent in Florida. Get every number you can lay your hands on and call until you find out where she is. Call me immediately when you know something." He strode out of the office.

Ashley began going through the file and making calls. She tried the Frutas Tropicales office. No one there knew anything. She tried another call to the insured's home for the sixth time. A nervous-sounding woman finally picked up but she spoke only Spanish. Ashley resurrected her few basic Spanish phrases, and the woman, obviously not understanding, simply hung up. She sent an e-mail to the agent in Florida who was out when she called. She was going to call Richard at home when the phone rang. It was a man named Brian. Did she remember? He was a neighbor of Matti's in Hull. They'd met at Matti's Christmas party a few years ago.

"Yes, I do remember you. Patrick too. How is he by the way?"

"He's fine, thanks for asking." Brian told her about going to Matti's apartment over the weekend and checking her messages. He told her about the message from Dr. Smart.

"Oh no," Ashley said. "Wait 'til he hears this."

"Wait 'til who hears?" Brian wanted to know. Who cared so much about Matti's well-being that he'd be upset to hear this news? Matti had been so close-mouthed about the identity of the guy with the sparkly blue eyes. It had to be somebody in the office.

Ashley replied, "Sam. Sam Adamson."

"The president of Atlas?"

"The one and only."

Bingo. "I suppose his interest is only...professional?"

Ashley hesitated. "As a matter of fact, I believe it's more than that." *Matti's going to kill me.*

"Well," Brian said, trying to keep the thrill out of his voice, "*someone* needs to call Dr. Smart and get the lowdown. Gynecologists who leave urgent messages aren't really my forté. Matti needs to know what's going on."

"Don't worry. I'll call the doctor. The trouble is, we can't locate Matti at the moment. We've had no contact with her since last Wednesday and it's not playing well around here, let me tell you."

"I can only imagine."

"Brian, please give me your number and I'll call when I've get any updates," Ashley said. "I'll call the doctor now, and then I'll have to go tell you-know-who. Hope he doesn't shoot the messenger. Know what I mean?"

"Do I ever," Brian said. Ashley thought he was great friendship material. No wonder Matti liked him so much.

She hung up and thought about what to do. Her brother-in-law was a gynecologist, one of those people who had an unending fascination with his career and thought everyone shared his interest. He had spent hours over holiday dinners regaling the family with the minutiae of his subject. Therefore

Ashley knew that fifteen percent of positive PAP smears were false positive. Most of the women she knew had had a false positive test at some time in their lives; she hoped Matti was in that lucky group.

She tried the doctor's office but the line was busy.

"Damn it," she said, slamming down the receiver and a few people looked her way. All these calls and she just couldn't connect. It was like a curse.

She picked up the phone again and punched re-dial with a vengeance.

CHAPTER 26

Matti, Ramón and company were treated well by their Indian escorts. But cordial didn't translate to warm and fuzzy in this culture.

King Santana, Ramón told Matti, was the one who would decide if they were accepted, or not.

Meanwhile, Gerry, Larry, Papi and two million dollars in cash were reaching the mouth of the Teribe River and there was nothing anyone could do about it.

Matti fantasized about how she would get even with them. Atlas also had its resources, and government contacts.

Sam and Brandon probably wouldn't be jumping up and down to help her on this one, though.

***

The big dugout hit the white water where the sea met the river, and they all held on. Papi, jolted, tried sitting more upright, his eyes glazed. He had the look of someone who'd become intimate with Timothy Leary's proclivities.

Gerry looked over Papi's head and yelled to Larry. "Mushrooms," he said. "And probably something else too."

Larry nodded and lay Papi against the inner hull so he wouldn't fall over the side. Gerry picked up speed, and soon they were through the mouth and heading for Banana Bay. Papi was conscious but barely so. He studied Larry with deep furrows between his eyes.

"*Quiénes son?*" he managed before lapsing into unconsciousness again.

***

Matti concentrated on looking like a diplomat as the Indians gathered round. She smiled heartily.

Ramón had told Matti that the Teribe had previously forbidden foreign visitors in their territory. *Uh-oh.*

Inside the dugout their four captives continued to grumble and shake against the ropes that bound them. One of Indians pointed into the boat and spoke in a low, rapid-fire voice to the others, looking back and forth between the captives and Ramón.

"*Momento,*" Ramón said, raising his hands. They glanced his way for the briefest of moments before resuming their intense chatter.

Two of the Indians now reached in and began jabbing the men. This inspired a near hysterical outburst of jabbering and laughing from the other Indians; the captives were like pigs bound for the market.

Matti looked at Ramón, who shrugged, and Victor, easily swayed, joined in their laughter. And suddenly they were like an audience at a comedy club, sharing a crazy joke.

In protest, one of the kidnappers began an angry diatribe in Spanish. This provoked more laughter, and a comment by one of the Indians—it sounded like a warning to Matti's ears—shut the man up. Without more explanation, one pair of Indians paddled forward , picked up the bow line of the dugout and began towing it with the kidnappers, Matti, Ramón and Victor all inside. The others paddled over to rescue Victor's craft.

They were in the Teribe Kingdom. On the stony shore, many Indians were in the water: women washing, filling pots with water, and bathing their children. The men stood back watching the approaching *cayucos* without expression. This was a characteristic Matti had noticed even in Platanillo: the Indian tendency to stand still and speechless as the world sped by. Behind them stood the village: a gathering of thatched-roof houses on stilts. In the center, on a hill, was a large rancho, its thatch roof a clean, neat pyramid shape.

"The palace," Ramón told Matti.

"You've been here before?" Matti asked.

"I'm hoping they remember. I came with my father to bring powdered milk for the children. The current king's father was also called Santana."

They got out of the boat, and walked toward the palace. Behind them, Victor and the Indians got the kidnappers into a standing position and cut the rope around their ankles so they could walk.

The villagers, seeing the men bound and pieces of netting hanging off them, began to point and giggle at the captives. It was like being in a Monty Python skit; any minute now John Cleese, playing the king, would appear in a grass skirt.

"What are you smiling at?' Ramón asked.

"The absurdity of our situation; I can't quite get the reality of where we are or how we got here."

"I just hope to God the king has a radio. If I can get to Boli, we have a chance of stopping Gerry and Larry."

Behind them, the men had arranged the captives into a line, and were marching them forward. The well-worn path led under a grove of cocoa trees, and up the hill to where a short, rotund man stood and waited.

"Is that the king?" Matti asked. Somehow when she said the word conjured up visions of ermine collars and jewel-studded crowns. This was an ordinary man wearing a freshly pressed shirt that looked slightly newer and of better quality than everyone else's. Otherwise, he was undistinguished.

Ramón greeted him in some dialect that Matti didn't understand.

The King nodded and answered back.

Matti heard Ramón repeat his father's name several times, and pointed at the kidnappers. The King nodded sagely and looked at Matti.

"Come in," he said, in stilted English.

Inside the palace, the only ornamentation was a picture of the Virgin Mary holding Baby Jesus. In front of it was a little altar with some blue plastic flowers and a candle.

A wood-frame sofa suite looked like it had been new in the sixties.

A round-faced woman in a cotton dress came and offered them *chicha.*

Ramón explained the situation again and the king smiled at Matti.

"What do you need?" he asked her. *Did kings prefer blonds?*

"Oh. Thank you, ah....Excellency? Thank you. We need a radio, most of all. You see, we thought we were with government agents, but they stole two million dollars and took Mr. Cardozo, as well..."

He nodded as she spoke as though absorbing every word. When she finished he shrugged. *"Como?"* he asked, looking at Ramón.

Ramón interceded smoothly in Spanish. Nothing was going to happen quickly here. Gerry and Larry were long gone, and had taken Ramón's father with them. Would they try and ransom him again? Kill him? Drop him somewhere in Banana Bay?

The King indicated they should go outside and see the kidnappers. Seeing their leader, a group of Teribeño men forced the captors to lie on the ground. Then they stood on their backs for good measure. Surprisingly, the Colombians didn't resist this treatment, or even express their outrage. More Latin pride? Or were they simply beginning to accept that they were outnumbered?

Ramón added more detail and the King raised his hand, pointed at a nearby building, and the men were led away.

"Where are they going?" Matti wanted to know.

"To prison," Ramón said, satisfied.

"That was quick."

"They'll hold them until Boli can come and get them back to Platanillo. Meanwhile, they're not going anywhere."

Suddenly something occurred to her. Something that had been forming in the right part of her brain over the past several days, was finally taking shape.

"Ramón?" she said. "I've got a theory…"

"Not now, Matti," Ramón told her firmly. "Santana has invited us to breakfast. He doesn't get much company here. So I suggest we accept." His eyes told her that this was a delicate diplomatic moment not to be tampered with. Later, he told her. There'll be time for theories when we get the hell out of here."

Matti smiled graciously as they were led to an open-sided rancho filled with long tables and benches. Over a roaring wood fire, a large pot boiled and tossed to the surface large chunks of what looked like pigs' feet.

"Sit," said the King, indicating a rustic table and some stools. "Drink," he said, as Indian women passed them each a plastic glass which contained a brownish liquid that Matti hoped was tamarind *chicha*.

A woman put a plate with two large pigs' feet in front of Matti, smiling as if this was a great honor. There were no forks or knives, noticed, and no napkins either. Matti gave the King a smile of delight and picked up a pig's foot and bit into a rind of pure fat, or was that softened hoof? She tried to recall childhood tricks of disposing of food. Unfortunately she had on a T-shirt with no cuffs, and the pockets of her jeans just would not suffice for anything so large and meaty. Plus the whole community had gathered 'round to watch them partake of this astounding feast.

Victor, who joined them, luckily loved pigs' feet and Matti was able to smuggle him one of hers under the table. Matti rolled the other one about on her plate and after a few minutes and patted her stomach indicating she was full.

The King laughed heartily as he took out his bowie knife, stabbed her meat and put it on his own plate. Ramón laughed too as though women who didn't eat big greasy chunks of meat for breakfast were just hilarious. Matti smiled coyly. When would they be able to use the radio, and try and stop those two bastards? Discovering a new culture was always fascinating, but right now she wasn't in the mood.

God, if she ever saw that Gerry again! He had lied so smoothly—only had come with them up river so they could abscond with the million the kidnappers already had, and take the other million from Ramón. They'd probably pushed Papi over the side at the earliest opportunity and were now on a microlight flying to Costa Rica.

The breakfast dishes were cleared away, and the King wanted to give them a tour. He was particularly proud to show off the new school and health center. Ramón, Matti and Victor followed him, trying to look engrossed.

Finally, she pulled Ramón aside. "The radio," she said. "Jesus, Ramón! This is a matter of life and death, remember?"

"If you rush it," Ramón told her, smiling for the King's benefit. "We could be here even longer."

Eventually, they turned and followed the bandy-legged King down a path into the bush. As Matti wiped the sweat moustache off her upper lip for perhaps the twentieth time that morning, they headed toward a concrete building with a large antenna.

Maybe it was one of those modern municipal buildings with indoor plumbing too.

Life was always full of surprises.

CHAPTER 27

Later that afternoon a small plane took off from Platanillo airport.

Gerry and Larry were dressed like paramedics. Their patient—unconscious on a stretcher—had a gauze-wrapped face. The few people at the small airport were told he was a burn victim from Platanillo hospital.

They arrival in Albrook Airport an hour later without incident. This was a regional flight on a private plane, and therefore not subject to the same scrutiny as a commercial flight. The pilot explained to the immigration official that there had been an accident in one of the gold mines near Chiriqui Grande. The unfortunate Canadian executive on the gurney had had a bad fall, and they were transporting him to the Johns Hopkins Hospital in Punta Pacifica for special treatment. Gerry and Larry lifted the gurney to the tarmac while the explanation proceeded. As the pilot kept the patter going, the two operatives hustled Papi Cardozo into a waiting "ambulance" and sped away.

"Easy peasy," said Gerry, as they entered the stream of city traffic.

The clinic they'd chosen an unmarked building surrounded by high fences thick with greenery. It looked like a large private home and was in one of Panamá City's better residential neighborhoods. It was actually a drying-out center for the rich and famous and had such a high level of anonymity that the real entrance into the facility was through a tunnel from a garage fifty yards up the street. Here the clinic's clientele could enter and exit the facility, and their cars wouldn't be seen. Many men and women who had had recent plastic surgery also came here while their bruises healed. The building was divided into individual suites so that—God forbid—the convalescents would never come face to face with each other.

It was into this sanctum that Papi Cardozo, tranquilized and re-hydrated, was now admitted as an alcoholic. His name was given as Carlos Mendez, his age 72—the only true fact—and his nationality Costa Rican. His suite was equipped with a telephone/fax machine and a socket for wireless internet, necessary tools to liase with the individual who had hired them. There *was* honor among thieves, as far as Gerry was concerned.

Therefore they would fulfill their contract: deliver Papi alive, and keep the ransom as payment for their trouble. The thing was, they needed to get out of the country as soon as possible. Gerry had learned long ago never to underestimate the power of local authorities. Sometimes they had quick response teams that could turn your life into a nightmare. He'd been doing free-lance work for six years now and never had a problem. He had a few million in CDs in a Swiss bank, and was almost ready to retire. Why mess with fate?

The wall-to-wall carpet in the suite created a mood of quiet luxury. Papi lay on top of the quilted bedspread and snored steadily. The admitting nurse hadn't asked too many questions; she'd been prepped by the patient's attending "physician" from a nearby hospital. They just couldn't risk a plain hotel suite. When the moment came to leave, Papi would need the medical attention this place could provide. He was not to die or there would be hell to pay.

There were fancy lamps by the bed, a sofa and two chairs in striped silk, a refrigerator and wet bar complete with wine glasses. Larry held one up and shook his head.

"I thought this place was for drunks."

"Maybe they like to keep their customers that way so they keep the place full," Gerry chuckled. He walked over and drew the drapes which further darkened the room, and sealed the lushly planted patio off from view. Papi Cardozo began rolling back and forth in the bed moaning.

"*Aguila*," he cried, as though he'd lost his best friend. "*Aguila*."

"There he goes again," said Gerry.

"Who's aguila?" Larry asked.

"Not who, what. An aguila is an eagle. If he's having a hallucination, it's probably of the harpy eagle, a native of Panamá. It's an incredible predator, the harpy. A symbol of strength."

"Fantasy Central?"

"Either that or the man had a favorite pet harpy who just died."

"The mushrooms," Larry said.

"Shit's never been my thing. I prefer a good snort, myself. Ah, well," Gerry said, "Might as well get some kip, dude. Then we'll make the call. You take the sofa. I'll cuddle up with Papi, here."

Larry nodded and rose. "Wonder if they've got any cold brews in here." He hunted through the cans in the refrigerator.

There was a knock at the door, and a male nurse entered the room with a rolling IV and a blood pressure kit. So much for kip time.

"Hey, hombre," Gerry said. "Seems like my uncle here is suffering from delirium tremens."

"*Sí, señor,*" the nurse agreed. "We will need to do blood tests and an EKG," the nurse said, switching to English. The other big, pale man looked about as Latin as Gomez's butler.

"'preciate it," said Gerry. "Don't want old *tio* to kick the bucket." He laughed.

Papi Cardozo rolled around in his bed. The palms of his hands were sweating and he seemed to be having a bad dream. Somehow he looked familiar to the nurse, but then, many who came here did. Keeping his job meant having a short memory.

"His blood pressure is high but not dangerous," the nurse said, rolling up the equipment. "The doctor's ordered electrolytes to re-hydrate him. She'll be in to see him shortly."

The nurse left and Gerry decided it was time. He dialed the number he'd been given by the man who'd hired them. No time like the present, so why wait? Their mission was accomplished and they needed to go away—far away—and lay low for awhile.

***

Matti sat inside the Teribeños' municipal building wondering if it was possible to sweat to death. She knew that strictly speaking it was true: perspiration was nature's way of cooling the body down; when there were not enough liquids coming in to be sweat out, one could indeed die. But more than the heat, her stomach was the main focus at the moment. It seemed to be having a serious rebellion over the one small piece of pork fat she'd forced down her throat. Her abdomen felt strange and bloated.

Combined with the incredible humidity, Matti felt herself growing more sluggish by the minute. Now it hit her full force: the pounding head, the incredible nausea. She had food poisoning, or a close cousin to it. She ran out the door and was sick. If she could just lie down in the shade for awhile...

Ramón finally had contacted Boli by radio, and filled him in on all that had happened. After that, the urgency was gone. The kidnappers were locked up. Gerry and Larry had gone down the river hours ago. To think about pursuing them now was pure folly.

They had Papi, and they had two million dollars.

She knelt down in the dirt outside the building feeling like she would faint.

Ramón came running to her side. "Matti, what is it?" She was almost too sick to answer; was it too much to ask that she could find somewhere soft to lie down and then die peacefully? Ramón and Victor helped her to stand, and walked her back to the King's palace. Somehow she managed the stairs.

"I'm so sorry," she told everyone before collapsing on the sofa and curling into a sweaty ball.

The King left them and came back a short time later with a tiny wizened man who had half a coconut shell filled with a whitish liquid. It was simply lime juice and salt, Ramón explained. It would help her body deal with the partially-digested fat. Some people were particularly sensitive to pork fat, he said, especially if they weren't accustomed to it. Matti drank the liquid hoping they'd all go away and leave her alone. She was amazed that she didn't throw it up immediately. Ramón wiped her forehead with a white handkerchief but she curled away from him. All she wanted now was to be alone and try not to move.

Ramón and Victor went back to the *cayuco* to prepare for the trip back down the river. As soon as Matti was feeling up to it, they were heading back to Banana Bay.

***

Ashley gave her report to an unhappy Sam early that afternoon, leaving out the news from Dr. Smart. She'd called Dr. Smart's office to let them know Matti's travel plans, and that she'd be in touch as soon as she got back, hopefully later this week. Dr. Smart himself had come on the line and given Ashley his beeper number.

"Have her call me," he said sharply. "As soon as she gets back."

A positive PAP smear, Ashley thought. It was the only thing it could be.

She told Sam about her numerous calls to the Cardozo's home, how the same Spanish-speaking woman continued to answer, but every time she heard Ashley's voice, she hung up.

"And where the hell's Richard? I thought he said Ramón Cardozo was an old school friend. Find out what contacts he has."

"I did call, sir. He's not answering."

"I thought he took this leave to take care of his sick wife. Did he sneak off to Mexico instead?"

"I don't know, sir," said Ashley.

"Well, stay on it," he told her fiercely. "I want some answers as soon as possible."

***

In Papi Cardozo's home, his only daughter waited by the fax machine in her father's private office, where the radio was set up and a cot had been added for sleeping. For more than twenty-four hours Dolores had not left this room except to use the bathroom. Boli Santamaria had visited several times; her brother had been here very early yesterday morning, but it seemed like it had been years since she'd seen him. She had listened in on the kidnappers' conversation with her brother yesterday on the radio, but since then had had no news at all, nor had Boli. Luz the maid brought her food and drinks on a tray, though eating was the last thing on Dolores's mind.

Luz, knowing a little bit about the drama being played out, wanted to do her part. She imagined herself to be like one of the servants in her favorite soap opera: caring, selfless and always available. She had made Doña Dolores's favorite orange cake, and been tending to Doña Violeta, and making sure she got her medication on time.

Dolores was not a soap opera fan. Her mother had been a character in one called *La Tormenta* which had been syndicated through LATV for almost ten years. The last thing she needed now was her mother's histrionics. She told Luz to make sure Violeta got her medications regularly, and Luz was following instructions. It was becoming obvious to both of them now who the real lady of the house was.

"Ha llamado alguien en la otra linea?" Dolores asked, who thought she'd heard the phone ring earlier.*"Nadie,"* Luz told her smiling as she brought in yet another tray with a clean cup and a dainty napkin. Someone had called, of course, a woman not speaking Spanish. A wrong number obviously, and an unnecessary disturbance to Dolores who was so concentrated on her father's return.

She chased any residual thought of the call from her mind and poured the cream into Dolores's coffee.

CHAPTER 28

Richard Parker, former insurance agent, and current claims' manager for Atlas International, sat in the music room of his home and picked up the mandolin. Its case was warped from water damage, but it was strung and polished. He plucked its dead strings absently. It was strictly an *objet d'art*, something Carol Ann had picked up in her interior decorating quest, to go with the piano and the battered antique trumpet.

Too bad neither of them played.

Like so much of their life, Richard and Carol Ann's existence was divided as neatly as the two halves of a cherrystone clam: appearances on one side with reality clamping down hard on the other side. Of Cuban descent, they had adopted the surname "Parker" the day they got married, and had fooled everyone ever since.

Even their old Yankee neighbor, Mr. Grimes, thought they were *puro americano*. It was a joke he and Carol Ann (formerly Consuela) shared about Yankees in general who thought that only Americans who were born in America and descended from the Mayflower could qualify for the title.

Perhaps it was Carol Ann's blonde hair and fair complexion; perhaps it was because they'd spent twice as many years in the U.S. as they had in La Habana. Perhaps it was simply that they'd chosen to live outside the Cuban enclave of Little Havana and went to school with *gringos*, so their English would be perfect. No one had ever questioned the Parkers' story: they'd lived in Florida, had met while attending the University of Florida (which was partially true). Richard had become an insurance agent who'd then taken his current job in Boston. They'd lived in Cohasset for two years now.

They had been among the lucky ones who'd been sent by their parents to be educated in the U.S. in January 1961.

Two years after Castro's revolution and four months before the Bay of Pigs, they'd met on the plane to Miami, and become inseparable. Richard's father had been a shirt manufacturer during the Batista years. He'd stayed behind hoping he could still make a living under Castro. It would take him several years before he realized how badly he had miscalculated the new "freedom" of the *comunistas*. Carol Ann's father had been an executive with Bacardi—like doing salsa in a minefield (as he'd described it). Both families had stayed in Cuba and sent their eldest children to the U.S.

After the failed Bay of Pigs invasion, things worsened quickly and dramatically. Carol Ann's father was among the Cuban participants who'd helped the CIA organize their anti-revolutionary invasion by mostly American-based Cuban exiles. Her father was not among the 1,200 participants later ransomed to the U.S. for $53 million in cash and food; his sin of operating within Cuba exempted him from this deal.

Richard's father and mother were also presumed dead; too many lines had been crossed, too many political indiscretions had come to light. But Richard would always remember his father, a robust man with thinning hair, a barrel-shaped chest, a man who loved to run his big hands over the fine cotton he manufactured.

In their last semester of college, an *amigo* and fellow student named Ramón Cardozo came into their lives. Ramón knew their struggles and arranged contact for them with a

Cuban community group that worked to integrate their people into American culture. They also were active in resettlement programs throughout the U.S., a frightening prospect for most Cubans who had deep attachments in Little Havana. Unfortunately, the group was badly underfunded; they could hardly afford office space and phones, let alone college tuitions. Ricardo and Consuela used the little money they had left to get married. Richard and Carol Ann Parker were granted full American citizenships a year later.

The next day Richard started letting his hair grow longer. Carol Ann dyed hers blond. They wore jeans and granny glasses, bought albums by Crosby, Stills and Nash. They uncleaved from their memories of Cuba as much as possible, and didn't talk about the "old days". They prided themselves on their improved English, ate pizza, practiced their new names, and pretended they were fine. Gradually, they gave up even calling Cuba—it was too painful to talk to aunts and uncles who could not confirm anything.

They were out of funds, and needed to leave school when a miracle happened. Ramón appeared again, marveling at the changes in them. He'd taken a semester off, he said, to party with some friends in the Bahamas.

When he found out about their plans to drop out, he grew serious. He'd speak to his father, he said. His father had left Cuba in the early days of Castro and had gotten his money out too. He'd gone to Panamá at an ideal time and was now a successful *bananero*. Large blocks of land were available very cheaply, and for his father Papi—who was trained in agriculture, anyway—the timing was ideal. His father had started growing *abacá* or hemp and cocoa, but the big, growing market was in bananas. He was aggressively buying up all the land around

Platanillo he could with an eye to buying the deep-water port eventually.

Ramón was sure his father would help two college kids from Cuba who were so close to getting their degrees. If he could raise the money, would they stay at college and finish their senior year? They merely looked at him stunned, and nodded.

"I have to do one good deed while I'm here," Ramón continued with his convincing smile. "Otherwise even *I* will feel my education has been a waste."

Within two days it was all arranged. Papi Cardozo, a Cuban exile living in Panamá, wired the funds to Ramón, and Richard and Carol Ann graduated. To Richard he was like a God, the father he'd never had.

Richard plucked the strings of the mandolin, and picked up an odor of deeply imbedded mold. In spite of the lacquer, the mandolin was obviously in a slow state of rot. A pity really. Carol Ann would be broken hearted to see one of her little treasures in such a state of disrepair. That had been the problem with Carol Ann in the end. Always thinking so small, wanting the surfaces of everything to gleam, wanting to play the "fine game" forever, not to mention her little "problem" with Ramón.

They graduated in 1970 and Papi invited them to come to Panamá as a graduation present. It was love at first sight for Richard, and it seemed for Papi too, who offered Richard a job.

As Ramón Jr. played away his days and nights in Florida, Richard stood by Papi for more than five years and learned the banana business inside out. He helped build dams against rising rivers, sprayed against the dread black sigatoka, the deadly soil-borne fungus that could destroy whole plantations. He tied up banana trees in the middle of the night against high winds, helped install miles of motorized cable which snaked through Papi's growing plantation, bringing the bananas so much more efficiently to the railway station than mules. He worked at the business as diligently as a son, and became Papi's true right arm. No one had been more loyal. And when Carol Ann became pregnant and lost their baby son in her sixth month due to lack of proper medical attention, and when he almost lost her because of severe edema from the heat and humidity, still he stayed.

In Ramón's absence, Papi seemed happy that Richard was there to fill the gap. He and Ramón were the same age after all. They were both of Cuban descent, had somewhat similar looks and a similar build. Papi included Richard in all areas of his life, shared his vision of a Cuba without Castro, the means needed to accomplish it. They fished together, ate their meals together, and Papi treated Carol Ann like a daughter. Dolores was still young then. Her mother, a minor actress, was often away filming, and so she seemed to develop a fixation for her father, instead, following him wherever he went.

Papi often spoke about Ramón, and his eyes lit up with hope that one day he'd finally settle down. Meanwhile, in Ramón's absence and lacking his own family, Richard worked hard to develop a father/son bond with Papi. Richard trusted Papi completely; he would never let him and Carol Ann down.

There would always be a place for Richard in the Frutas Tropicales empire, even when Ramón returned.

Richard was obsessed with financial security. Carol Ann couldn't get pregnant again and Richard wanted to make it up to her. He built her a beautiful home that he could barely afford, and bought them a new pickup truck. Life had been good in those days, if stressful. It seemed there was never enough money to pay all the bills.

Richard remembering all this was hit with what he thought of as simply "the pain". The pain was wedged between his heart and his belly and felt like a red balloon of heavy rubber that was being squeezed by giant fists. This was not pain that could be cured by an over-the-counter remedy, and he'd been to countless doctors who were unable to determine its source. At times it would simply make itself manifest, during periods of high stress, for example, and nearly always at Christmas.

Richard loved Papi, truly loved him like a father though Papi had never truly loved him—not like Ramón. Papi had only two loves: his son and Cuba. Papi had always spoken of Ramón's return, but couldn't he see how inconsiderate Ramón was? How Ramón *used* him? Ramón gambled, drank, got himself into terrible debt, and Papi always bailed him out. The only request he made of his son was that he come to Panamá. Over and over he asked. It was like begging! And Ramón just ignored his father and continued to live his life as selfishly as he always had.

It wasn't until Christmas of 1975 that Ramón finally came home. As father and son hugged and joked, Richard felt his gut squeeze in jealousy and grief. No matter how hard he'd worked, he'd never replace Ramón in Papi's eyes. He was an outsider yet again, had lost another father, and it was simply unbearable. He felt truly sickened seeing them together, turned to Doña Violeta, but she too was caught up in the joy of their reunion, the first real Christmas "the whole family" had shared in Panamá.

Even Carol Ann had responded to Ramón as though to some lost love. She flirted with him, sang old Cuban songs as he banged out chords on an old upright piano, everyone dancing and gay. And Richard, his smile so tight his face hurt, clapping mechanically while he thought of ways to get even with his adopted brother, Ramón.

He stayed in Panamá another year before selling his home and returning to the States to find work. He was gut sick of Panamá, and the banana business, and could see there was going to be no future for him at Frutas Tropicales as long as Ramón was still alive. Papi had sadly acquiesced to Richard's departure, and given him $50,000 to start his new life.

Meanwhile, Ramón continued to play his way through a fortune in Florida, buying and selling a succession of clubs and restaurants. Doubly frustrating for Papi was Castro's continued hold over Cuba. Finally, a little over a year ago, Ramón decided to come to his father's side. Twenty-five years of not caring a whit about the business, except knowing that it supported his egregious lifestyle, and then he'd suddenly changed his mind!

Carol Ann, oh Carol Ann, he thought, as he sat in the music room and watched the dust motes make their chaotic paths in the sunlight. Why did you do it, you bitch? He felt the blood and bile rise, the red balloon squeezing his gut.

How could you have loved Ramón more than me?

He heard the phone ringing insistently in the other room, and let voice mail pick it up. It was too late now, too late for him, and probably too late for Papi too.

He walked over to the piano bench, sat down, began playing one hand of a simple two-handed tune that Papi had taught him called Dominoes. And wasn't that typical? Richard thought. I learned to use two fingers, while Ramón learned to play the classics.

The pain started again so he went to the bar and poured himself a shot of neat scotch, quickly tossing it down. It burned like hell, but eased the clenched fist slightly. He went back to the piano and attacked the keyboard with his two fingers like a maniacal five year old.

The next morning, he decided he would really learn to play the piano. He still had John Gardner's *Piano Pieces You Like to Play,* a piano primer. His favorite selection was "A Country Garden," in the key of C but with some nice little chords which he was managing now after a weekend of practicing. Still he couldn't quite keep pace with the metronome which clicked persistently back and forth as though mocking him. He threw it against the wall, and when it ticked weakly back and forth a few more times he kicked it into submission. Having won this battle, he laughed out loud. Winning was so easy. You just had to know who was in charge.

***

Henry Grimes saw nothing particularly alarming at the Parker residence, and he was a detail man. Had once gotten the number plate of a getaway car that had hit the 7-Eleven down at the corner and the cops had caught the bastards. Across the street at Richard and Carol Ann's both cars were in the driveway but he hadn't seen either of them in a number of days. That was a bit unusual. She was an avid gardener, had said just the other day she planned on getting the mums in by the weekend. But that hadn't happened. Maybe she was sick. Maybe they'd gone on a trip, and used the limo service to get to the airport.

But this morning when he went down to get his mail, he'd noticed a curl of smoke emanating from the chimney over at there. Odd, he told himself. But Mrs. Grimes had passed on more than four years ago and so Henry didn't waste much time on it. Unusual occurrences were only good fodder when you had someone to share them with.

He stood in the driveway, instead, sorting through the junk mail: a free visitor's pass to the new Hot Tub Gym, and a special on six pairs of non-run pantyhose for only $19.95 with a lifetime guarantee! He walked to the rubbish bin, chucked in the whole lot, and looked again at the smoke. A wood fire in the morning? Maybe Carol Ann was burning her flyers in the fireplace. The thought made him chuckle, but still he wondered about it. They never had fires in the morning, only at night, when they got cozy with their cocktails or entertained those Latino types. Oh yes. He'd seen them. Arriving in their fancy cars. They weren't from around here; nobody could kid him on that score. He was a Yankee, after all. Born and bred. He knew damn well what another Yankee was supposed to look like. Now Carol Ann with her pretty figure and fluffy blond hair; she was a real Florida girl. Richard was handsome in an Ivy League way, a very fastidious dresser, obviously with a rich daddy.

Henry Grimes turned, snapped his suspenders, and headed back up the driveway. Maybe they were having a little romance. Rolling around on the rug with a little fire to keep off the chill? Carol Ann would be the type to enjoy a good bedding, though he didn't know what she saw in that husband of hers. He was handsome, okay. Monied, probably. But there was something about Richard that was too prissy, too perfect. It was like he had a monkey on his back and couldn't shake it off.

Henry walked through the kitchen door letting the screen door slam. Which reminded him to take it down and put up the storm windows—he could almost hear Mrs. Grimes reminding him. Weather service said there'd be a chance of a nor'easter before Wednesday so he'd better get the storms up instead of standing around thinking dirty thoughts about his neighbors. He snapped his suspenders and went to get his screwdriver.

CHAPTER 29

Ashley stayed at work late to book up for Friday's insurance exam and to look through the Frutas Tropicales file one more time to see if she'd missed anything.

Richard hadn't answered his home or cell phone in two days.

She'd checked the sign out sheet, and in it he had clearly stated that he was taking the week off because he wife was due for surgery. Surely, she couldn't still be in the hospital? Richard was due back in the office on Thursday and he didn't even have his answering machine turned on.

Richard wasn't her most favorite person, it was true. His rigidity was a turn off, and everyone groaned behind his back wishing he'd loosen up. But his self-consciousness seemed to override any awareness of what other people considered normal. He was fussy and ill-at-ease, well-groomed as a Ken doll—and just about as flexible.

Ashley sighed and started going through the policy section of Frutas Tropicales files. These consisted of the underwriter's notes, main coverages and their limits, named the insured party, and these files never, ever left the office. She found what she was looking for easily in Matti's pile. Matti had her own particular system for files, a far cry from Richard's style, which had everything alphabetized and in file drawers. One of her habits was never to file an active case, but to put it in a stack on top of a long table behind her desk and up against the wall. The stacks themselves had an order, though not alphabetical. Matti stacked things according to how new or old the case was. She had a separate pile of cases which were being litigated, and the oldest of these were in boxes underneath the table. New cases were on top in this instance and therefore Ashley had had no trouble locating Frutas Tropicales's file.

Going through it took time and she worked late. She'd already called the Miami agent, Jorge, who spoke in machine-gun English with a heavy Hispanic accent. He had the same contact numbers as hers and could add nothing more.

Ashley dug deeper.

Parts of the file were indecipherable and in code. The underwriter's notes, for example, included these codes: CA-025P and CA-026VP & F. What the hell did that mean? The policy itself was also in code, and was called a "COR. K/BE/PE/CK/E." Someone had scrawled in a margin "70% of incidents result in fatality for SWAT/hostage/ or hostage taker." Now that was clear and to the point. She hoped to Matti was staying out of it. She always tended to bite off more than she could chew. The fact that she couldn't be reached wasn't a good sign. It meant she wasn't sitting on a chaise by a pool.

Would Matti ever learn that being an insurance investigator had its limits? As her PA, Ashley felt herself frustrated and a little frightened. What if Matti was in trouble and needed help? What if she simply disappeared and never called? The thought gave her chills.

She continued to work through the file page by page and at almost 8 p.m. she came to a page of scribbles with a name and Panamanian number different than the others. It was too late to call the Chief of Police in Platanillo tonight but she'd try first thing in the morning. Maybe he knew what was going on, or could find out. Hopefully, he spoke some English. Although after this, Ashley vowed, she'd start taking a night course in Spanish.

She pulled on her coat and passed through reception saying goodnight to the security guy—who was a looker, by the way—and went down in the elevator. When she reached the lobby, she was startled by Chili Wong, who jumped into the elevator as soon as the door opened.

Her immediate reaction was to scream. "Chili, you scared me to death!"

He just grinned at her. "Going to the Jewish deli tomorrow?" he asked her sweetly. "You bring bagel, I buy." She patted his shoulder and said she would.

Meanwhile, she thought she'd pop into Bertucci's for a slice of pizza before getting on the "T" and heading back to Quincy. She was still shaken by Chili's sudden appearance, and knew the if Matti hadn't called, her position had probably been compromised. Thoughts of the security guard danced around the periphery of her consciousness, and she decided she needed something more than pizza. She turned and let her beautiful black legs carry her across the cobblestones to the Long Wharf Marriott.

She wanted to stop thinking about work for awhile. It was time for a nice big daiquiri—hold the bananas.

***

The sun had set before Matti finally was able sit up without nausea. She'd apparently slept for hours. The medicine man or *sukia* had given her something that tasted of clove but was dominated by a foul bitterness. Amazingly, she'd hadn't thrown it up, but merely gone to sleep.

And now it was almost eight o'clock at night. The whole day had been lost.

Ramón sat nearby in a chair, watching her.

"Oh my God, what time is it? Did you get in touch with Boli? What happened?" She sat up so quickly her head spun.

"Easy does it," said Ramón. He passed her a glass of water. "You want to try some of this."

"Yes, about a gallon of it. I'm hungry, too. Are there any crackers?"

"I'll find you something." He went into the King's kitchen, and came out with a round disk of bread. "A johnny cake, ok?"

"Thank you." She nibbled at the moist white bread. "Tell me what happened?"

"I finally made contact with Boli, but it was through an intermediary, a sport fisherman named Captain Tom based in the lagoon, who has a big aerial. He relayed the message to Boli, who's on his way in the morning. I told him Gerry and Larry have Papi and the money and left the Teribe, no everyone in the province will know. But maybe that's not such a bad idea. More people will be on the lookout for them."

"That's good." Matti still couldn't believe that Gerry and Larry had managed to abscond with Papi, the ransom, and one of the kidnapper's *cayucos* in a few short minutes.

"As soon as you're feeling up to it, we'll go down the river. The King has agreed to keep the Colombians here until Boli takes them back to Platanillo. The Teribe Indians are peace-loving people, and the King doesn't want to upset the applecart. He said we could stay the night."

"What did you just say?" Matti asked him, suddenly alert. There was the thread she'd been groping for, but now it was more like a rope, dangling in front of her. She just had to pull it to recall...something Ramón had just said.

"About the Teribe being peaceful?"

"No," Matti said, trying to shake off the fugue of many hours of pork-induced food poisoning. "The applecart," she said. 'Don't upset the applecart with Frutas Tropicales.' Richard said that on the morning we spoke about the case. Ramón, Richard was very involved with your family. Was there any way *he* could be involved here?"

Ramón squinted into the distance. "I've been over and over it. Richard worked in Panamá with my father for years and is like a son to him. But obviously this whole kidnapping had a mastermind. Two masterminds. Because Jerry and Larry had nothing to do with the Colombians."

Matti's heart started to pound. "I'm wondering how Frutas Tropicales came to own a kidnapping and ransom policy with Atlas in the first place. It seems an extraordinary coincidence that Richard worked for Atlas in this high-level position and that he was also so close to your family."

Ramon said, "I think the policy was written before Richard went to work for Atlas. In fact, it might have been written while he still had his insurance agency in Florida."

"Of course," Matti said, knowledge filling her eyes.

Ramón said, "It's just not possible," he said. "He loves Papi as much as I do."

"But two million dollars is a lot of money," she said. She realized that Richard was one of the only people who could have knowledge that such a policy even existed on Papi Cardozo. That is why the files were coded, to protect the identity of the insured in case the files were ever burglarized.

"And envy is one of the seven deadly sins," Ramón said. They sat in silence, pondering this.

"So, Richard was jealous of you?" Matti asked.

"Yes, he was," Ramón looked past her. "But I thought it was a boyhood thing. That he'd outgrown it."

Matti thought of all Richard's attempts to fit in, his expensive wardrobe, his home in Cohasset. If someone suffered from low self-esteem it could be a life-long affliction.

Ramón continued, "But if he did do it, what was his motive? He and Carol Ann have plenty of money."

"I'll be damned if I know," Matti said. "Let's walk down to the river, watching the water always helps me think. Also, if I don't have a bath soon, the King will lock me up for 'sloth'."

***

Papi Cardozo no longer believed he was a harpy eagle, Gerry realized. This fact had apparently depressed him, for he was non-communicative, and alternately stared at the wall, cried, or slept. Clinically depressed, the doctor had observed, but stable. He was on a IV drip that probably contained a mild sedative and anti-depressant.

Gerry thought he would live, and it was time to call the client and let him know. Even mercenaries had their professional ethics.

The doctor turned out to be a petite brunette with hair cut bluntly and turned under, so that every hair seemed to hug her jaw. She had a peaches and cream complexion that reminded Gerry of a Devonshire milkmaid, but her accent was pure north England, even her Spanish was accented with it. She called herself Doctora Louise, and she had hazel eyes irises like cut glass that seemed to pierce right through him.

"Not enough drunks for you in the U.K., doctor?" Gerry began, chuckling.

"Oh there are plenty of those," she said, serenely. "But drunks are drunks the world over, Mr. Velásquez. And the treatment we employ is the same no matter what the culture." A working class family, he guessed, determined to educate herself so she could leave the poverty behind. People's weaknesses and how to exploit them was a big part of Gerry's business. Dra. Louise had this aura of perfection that wrapped around her like spun silk; if he could piss her off, it would just tickle him pink.

She paused. "Now your *uncle* here, doesn't fit the profile. For one thing, he doesn't show the classic symptoms of alcohol withdrawal." She didn't elucidate. "Nor does your uncle strike me as someone who would seek an entheogenic experience."

Gerry shrugged, thought about the word "entheogenic" briefly, and said with a smug smile. "Are you saying he doesn't like *getting high?*" He loved to tackle broads like Louise Sands who thought they could use big words and intimidate everyone.

But this one was completely non-reactive. Most babes took the bait hook, line and sinker. But not Louise Sands. Maybe she meditated in her spare time. His ex had been into that, and after two years, had become completely beyond his reach.

"It appears he may have ingested something. Do you have any idea what?" she asked in a neutral tone. "His B.A.C., or blood alcohol content is zero."

"Excuse me..." Gerry said, his defensiveness easy to act out at this point.

Dra. Louise continued, "He seems to be suffering some form of psychosis—but it's not delirium tremens." She had the blood tests back, and her patient's liver was fine. Strange to say the least for someone who had apparently come into the facility to dry out.

"Well, I'm sorry *doctora*. I'm not the man's keeper. Just someone who was given the job of straightening him out. My aunt isn't very good at these things." Gerry's nostrils flared, a classic sign. He was lying, but about how many of the details, she couldn't tell. Too bad her patient wasn't well enough to tell her himself.

Dra. Louise went calmly to Papi's side and gently stroked his forehead. Even in the air-conditioning, his face had a sheen of sweat. "You will soon be well, my friend," she told him in Spanish. "Soon you will feel better. I promise."

Gerry watched as she checked his vital signs, shook the IV bag which was almost empty, and pushed the big red button which called the nurse. He watched the pretty doctor bend over and minister to her patient, and noting her white jacket, her shapely legs, the flush of her cheeks. He felt himself becoming aroused.

"The nurse will come and give him a sponge bath. We need to keep him cool, and try and bring his blood pressure down." His breathing was labored and his blood pressure was in a dangerous range.

"I'll be back in a few hours," she told Gerry. On the sofa, the big, pale man sat with a can of beer in his hands, and didn't say anything.

She walked calmly from the room, more calmly then she felt. Something strange was going on, something very strange. She'd call the referring physician to try and get more information. Maybe the other doctor had more background information than what had been forthcoming from the man who called himself Gerry.

CHAPTER 30

Matti was eating a banana by the river when Boli pulled up with his men. It was now Tuesday morning. Glad as she was to see him, she felt reticent. Being in Boli's presence was like having a breaking wave sweep over you with no life jacket on.

There were now three boats in which to travel back to Banana Bay, Victor's, the police's, and the kidnappers'.

"I'll go back with Victor," she told Ramón, "if you don't mind. I'm not ready for Boli yet, or a ride with the prisoners either." Ramón nodded his agreement, and they both stood to greet the man Matti knew would've have paddled here with his bare hands, if only to tell them another story.

Boli, true to form, jumped out of the boat, light on his feet as a dancer. "Thank God you're safe," he said, grabbing them both in turn. "Now don't tell me! You're both exhausted. I can see that. I'm not blind. Bet you're hungry too." Boli smiled at the King, knowing he didn't understand English. "Only got that wild pork up here. Yes? Don't I know it! I had to come up here for a banquet once, nearly killed me. How are you my dear?" he asked Matti.

"I..."

"Lookin' a little green, don't mind if I say so. Now—"

Ramón grabbed Boli by the arm. "*Tio*, we need to wrap this up. Gerry and Larry could be in Costa Rica by now. They..."

"He, he, he," Boli said. He began slapping his thighs.

"*Tio*, what is it? What's so funny?"

"They think I'm a *campesino*, no? How do you say in English, *a country bumpkin*, right?" More laughs at this joke. "Well, I did a little checkin'." More stabs in the air with his forefinger. "No such thing as an anti-terrorism unit in Panamá. Maybe in Colombia, they got some Yanquis runnin' around in disguise, but not here, especially after the invasion. I got my friends—they didn't count on that did they? Thought those fake IDs would fool me, didn't they? Mr. Gerry and Mr. Larry. Ho, ho, ho."

"You found them?" Matti asked in disbelief.

"Not yet, but we're narrowin' it down. One thing's pretty sure, they're still in the country."

"Really?"

"Yes, really, *mi vida*. We gotta find our Papi, that's the main thing, and we're gonna do it. They flew outta Platanillo on a private plane. One of my men thought it was funny, man on the stretcher, his fact all wrapped up. Then when I put the word out, he put two and two together. That tall one, Larry, he's pretty hard to disguise. They got Papi in that plane, bet my life on it. Just gotta track it down. Hey, did I tell you 'bout the time that duster couldn't land? Out of fuel. Couldn't make it to the runway, so hooked his landing gear on one of the banana cableways? Thing got pulled back like a giant slingshot—think I'm kiddin'?. There was a zapatero tree—*muy grande*—about this close. Just missed it. Luis, Mari's Uncle saw the whole thing first hand…."

"Goodbye," Matti said, squeezing Boli's forearm, and starting to walk away.

"Tio, let me get Matti in the boat," Ramón said, walking with her.

"If I don't call the office soon, they'll be calling the American Embassy. I've got to go. Come on Victor," she motioned. "Let's go."

Matti and Victor left the banks of the Teribe where a crowd of children gathered to see them off, giggling and waving. The turned to wave, but the rapids carried them slickly out of sight and Matti felt as if she were riding a thirty-foot noodle. It took them approximately a tenth of the time it had taken them to go up the Teribe to reach the mouth again. As they hit the incoming waves of the Caribbean, Matti turned and saw Victor grinning widely. It was a beautiful morning, and she knew Victor would have his line out soon looking for snapper.

They passed the inlet where *La Boca Grande* still remained hidden from sight and Matti went to retrieve her clothes and papers. So much had happened since Saturday it was becoming difficult to assimilate. Her report, if she made it, would look like a novella. She couldn't believe so much could be squeezed into 96 hours. Had she really visited the last bona fide kingdom in the hemisphere, only to end up barfing her guts out in front of its King? Boli claimed he was on the trail of Gerry and Larry. Was he really? Or was this another of his great tapestries, woven with embellishment and wishful thinking?

Worst of all was the revelation about Richard. Did the Prince of Conformity really have a dark side that stretched to Central American kidnapping plots? As they skimmed across Banana Bay, Matti admitted she knew little about Richard as a person. But this only amplified her suspicions. The dinner he'd arranged. The push to travel to Panamá. Did he just want her out of the office, so he could pull the strings from Boston? Some of the most twisted people could be concealed behind innocent faces, nice clothes, and colonial homes in suburbia.

She didn't have to look further than Adrian to know how true that was.

Atlas's K & R policies were highly confidential, and with good reason. If terrorists knew what ransoms were already bought and paid for through insurance companies, the insureds would become the most likely targets. He'd probably sold the policy himself!

But motive. What motive did he have? He and Carol Ann seemed well off. Matti had assumed there was family money. They lived in a lovely home in one of the South Shore's most exclusive towns. No expense had been spared to furnish and decorate it, right down to the baby grand piano.

As they sat at dinner, did Richard already know where Papi was? If so, why hadn't the extortion happened earlier? Perhaps he'd arranged for the kidnapping with the locals, then planned to use his vacation time to fly down when the ransom was paid out. Meanwhile, he'd shown up for work as usual, was present even for the committee review on the case! She remembered his defense of the family, saying they didn't want the money, just wanted justice served. Sam had removed him from the case due to conflict of interest. The more she thought about it, the more she kept returning to the same conclusion: Richard had known the family. Richard had known that Papi personally was insured. And yet something else nagged. Something else that seemed obvious but refused to come to the surface.

She let it go. The wind streamed past, cleansing her face, washing away the residues of sickness she'd felt on the Teribe. She thought how wonderful a cool shower would feel. It was still early. A cup of Alma's coffee first? Then a shower. Then maybe some pumpkin bread. She was starving.

She'd make some notes, then call the office. She'd test the waters with Ashley first, then talk to Sam. He was sure to be very angry about her lack of communication with the office, her enmeshment in the case. The company's policy was clear on the handling of such situations and she knew she'd overstepped her bounds. The manual was : In kidnap/hostage emergencies these were the following priorities. 1. The safe return of the victim(s), ideally without giving into hostage-takers' extortion demands; 2.Apprehension or containment of the kidnapper(s) without violence, if possible; 3. Maintaining continuity of operations (meaning Frutas Tropicales) during the absence of someone (in this case Papi Cardozo) whose skills are essential to the organization.

The policy manual also specified that an emergency *team* deal with the above. In Atlas's case, that meant Signa Security, people who had the right training, not a lone insurance investigator taking things into her own hands.

Her theories about Richard would quickly put all that on the back burner. If not, maybe she'd be taking a very early retirement. Maybe Sam would punish her by making her sit at Richard's desk after all, especially if Richard was going to jail.

Sam would rant and rave but she could live with that. Her father's Irish temper had inured her to other people's tantrums, and anyway, she could defend herself gustily if needed. She could only imagine Brandon Howard's reaction when he found out; it was Brandon's job to check out everyone's credentials before they were hired. Hopefully, Brandon would be able to move swiftly to get Richard arrested. She could imagine him vacuuming up the facts like a machine. Brandon was could be very single-minded and had lots of resources. He'd construct a case that would throw its own net around Richard's transgressions and compile enough evidence to create an airtight criminal case against him. If Richard were guilty, justice would not only be served but expedited.

Actually, the whole scenario made her wish that Richard *did* have a personal stake in the Cardozo kidnapping. It would be worse, much worse, if he'd merely been selling information at random to interested parties. With his nearly unlimited access to confidential files, it could be disastrous. Hopefully this was an isolated incident. Richard's very personal, sick scam. She'd be sure to mention this to Brandon so he could evaluate the company's vulnerabilities. In any case, new security procedures would need to be implemented to prevent this kind of thing from happening again. Brandon was great at damage control, and Matti knew that Sam would need Brandon's level-headed approach when it came time to deal to with Richard's deceit.

The boat finally left Banana Bay and turned into the channel of the port of Platanillo, its calm waters a soothing balm after the long ride. They turned into the lagoon and Matti suddenly remembered that it was here she'd first seen Gerry, he'd been pretending to read a book, then disappeared. He'd been spying on her from her arrival; had Richard hired him and Larry?

The sight of the Hotel Mariposa on its lopsided foundation with the tangled fuchsia bougainvillea, the Adirondack chairs under the palms, and her own little opened window upstairs made Matti want to leap out onto the grass and cry: "Yes!"

But before she could disembark, a worried-looking Alma came running across the lawn as fast as her bowed legs could carry her.

"Phone!" she cried. "Phone call! Miss Matti they been callin' here for you til I thought you were dead myself." She gave Victor an assessing look. "And you, young man. I thought maybe you all drowned together in one big package. Come in now and clean up," she said in the gentlest tone Matti had ever heard Alma use with her grand-nephew.

Matti went into the little lobby, and picked up the heavy black receiver.

"Hello?"

"Thank you, God," she heard Ashley breathe a big sigh of relief. "I thought you were a goner this time, and I'm not the only one."

"Ashley! It's so good to hear your voice. I just arrived this minute. What timing."

"Nothing to do with timing," Ashley told her. "I've called so many times, I was sure to get lucky sooner or later. Like playing Bingo."

"God, Ash, I'm sorry," and gave her an abbreviated version of the past five days.

"So basically you're saying the man got re-kidnapped? Jesus, that's a pretty major complication. Hopefully we won't have to pay out twice! But hey all of that's gotta wait. You need to get back here rapido."

Matti laughed lightly, thinking of Sam. "Why? Is *el presidente* on the war path, or what?"

Ashley was quiet.

"I don't know how to tell you this girl," she said finally. "Nobody died, or anything, but your doctor called. Dr. Smart? He wants to see you asap, and I mean now. You gotta get home girl, and that means on the next flight."

"Oh, for heaven's sake...did he say why?"

"Doctors don't *talk* about these things over the phone, honey."

She said, "Well, I'll call him myself, then. I can't leave now, Ash. There are some things that have to be wrapped up here before I can come back."

"Oh my God."

"Ashley, I know you're concerned," Matti told her, as she opened a barrette with her teeth and clipped it into her hair. "But you're just going to have to trust that I'm making the right decision."

"Yeah," said Ashley. "I just hope you don't die making all these right decisions, know what I mean?" She gave her boss Dr. Smart's number. "I'll put you through to Sam."

Seconds after Muriel took the call, Sam was on the line. "Matti?" To Matti's ears he sounded anxious, but something else lurked there too. All in that one word, spoken in a certain tone.

"Sam," she said, "I'm so sorry for not phoning in. There was absolutely nothing I could do about it."

After a heartbeat he answered. "Matti. I know you've got your reasons. But you cannot, I repeat—cannot—do this any more. To say I've been worried about you doesn't begin to cover it."

"Thank you. I've missed you too. I'm fine. A little tired, and definitely dirty, but otherwise fine. Let me fill you in." She told him about the family Cardozo, the banana plantations, *La Boca Grande*. Gaining courage, she told him about going to Escudo, then up the Río Teribe with Ramón. She told him about Gerry and Larry, the kidnappers and re-kidnapping. She told him about the lost two million dollars. She told Sam that Boli Santamaria, the local police chief, thought the second set of kidnappers was still in the country. She didn't mention having breakfast with the king or about the food poisoning. She didn't mention anything about Richard. She was thinking, seriously, she needed to save that one for Brandon.

"No wonder you didn't phone." He didn't sound as aggrieved as she thought he'd be. On the other hand, he didn't sound exactly happy, either. Like a parent seeing a report card with lots of A's but two D's. "We're going to make some policy changes when you get back." Now that sounded ominous. "Some *firm* new policy decisions. This can't go on, Matti. It's as simple as that."

Now it was her turn to pause. "Sam. There's something else. I prefer to speak to both you and Brandon about it. Can you get him in your office, and turn on the intercom? And turn on the tape, Sam. This is going to take awhile."

Sam summoned Brandon and within minutes Sam indicated they were both present and sitting down. They were both listening. Matti started from the beginning, painful as it was. She told them about having dinner at Richard's house, meeting Ramón, sitting at the table next to him. Discovering later the other guests were all Cuban, and her not knowing yet if that was salient, or not. She recounted everything she could remember. She apologized twice, yet something still nagged, an inconsistency she couldn't quite grasp.

It was Brandon, with his well-ordered mind, that placed the morsel before her.

"What was *Ramón* doing at Richard's dinner in Boston if his father was kidnapped, maybe dead, in Panamá?" Matti felt her stomach flip. This was exactly what she'd unconsciously been ruminating on. So focused on Richard—so unsuspicious of Ramón—she'd simply overlooked it. Why, indeed, was Ramón in Boston when he was supposed to be running Frutas Tropicales? Why had Richard invited them both to dinner, and paired her up with his charming adopted brother? Were they in it together?

Ramón had kept insisting that Worldwide Produce was the one behind the kidnapping. He was the one who had found the fax from the kidnappers in his father's study—conveniently when she was in the other room. Had this all been a set-up by Ramón, not Richard? After all, he had potentially a lot to gain: a ransom payout, 51% of FT shares, and a life insurance benefit in the case of Papi's death. Matti's mind whirled like a Ferris wheel. Was Ramón broke? Still gambling and not able to meet his debts? Was she such a rotten judge of character that she'd actually been duped by Ramón's charm and good looks? She had kissed him for God's sake! Had she been blind, or was there some other explanation? She knew there was one way to find out.

"Brandon, until we get to the bottom of this, you need to seal everything in Richard's office. Is he *in* the office, by any remote chance?"

"Hah!" came Sam's disgusted reply. "His wife went in for *surgery* he said. He signed out for nearly a week's leave that is supposed to end tomorrow. If he is still in the country, it would be a small miracle."

"He may well be. Can anyone find out if he is home? This isn't just your run-of-the-mill insurance scam, take the money and run, and I suspect there may be a lot more motives we haven't uncovered yet. You know, Ramón told me that not only did Richard know his family, they actually took him in. Paid for his college education. God, what a mess." She listened to herself and thought she must sound just like Boli.

"Matilda." Sam's voice now came through the muddle of her thought. She knew that voice well, and knew it broached no argument. "Matilda. Come home. *Now.*"

"Of course, we don't know where Gerry and Larry fit in yet, and Boli Santamaria. He's the local police chief. They took Papi out of here on a private plane. Boli thinks the thugs and Papi will be found soon. Hopefully the ransom can be recovered as well. I can't come home today, Sam. But I will very, very soon. In fact, I promise I'll be home no later than the weekend, no matter what."

There was no response from Sam to this, but Brandon picked up the slack. "Remember your contract, Matilda. You're an investigator. So stop acting like a dilettante. Is that clear? If you want, I can set you up an interview with Signa Security; maybe that's more your kind of work." Part of Brandon's posturing, Matti knew, was for Sam's benefit. Brandon secretly loved that she got so involved in her cases, because she often uncovered evidence that helped him win Atlas's biggest cases. "Call us as soon as you know anything. We've obviously got plenty to keep us busy on this end."

***

Alma came in carrying a tray with a large glass of fresh-squeezed orange juice and a cup of coffee. Matti thanked her, picked up the juice, and drained it in several gulps.

"Thirsty?" Alma asked in her sweet tone.

"You haven't got any pumpkin bread, have you?"

"Hungry too. I wonder why. I'll be right back."

Matti had two pieces of pumpkin bread and two cups of coffee before heading up the stairs. "I'll need to burn these clothes," she told Alma, grinning. "Have you got an extra towel? I really need to wash my hair."

"Of course, my dear, " Alma said, and patted her hand. "Go right up to your room. I'll bring some towels and fresh soap right up." Matti felt again the force of Alma's warm nurturing enfold her. Thank God for the women in my life, Matti thought, who truly understand and don't try to control me with their supercilious attitudes.

Matti picked her butterfly key ring off the board and headed up the stairs.

After her shower, she wrapped her hair in a towel and sat at the little rickety table that faced the window with the embedded bougainvillea, and the view of the lagoon, and began writing.

One banana, two banana, three banana, four. With any luck she'd start to unravel all the hanging—and seemingly unrelated—details in this case and start to connect the dots. If she didn't get some answers and get the hell out of here, she might well be going to an interview in Cincinnati. The thought made her squeamish. Along with all the counter-terrorism tactics, search and rescue, psychology and PR, you had to do an intense course on first-aid.

And Matti just hated the sight of blood.

CHAPTER 31

Dra. Louise Sands—a woman whose petite size belied her strength—was growing more and more concerned. Her patient's name, listed as Carlos Mendez from Costa Rica, was undoubtedly an alias.

She was used to lies in this place, and had once made quite a liar herself. Twelve years clean and sober had done wonders for her powers of observation, not to mention her bullshit detector. The two thugs who had brought "Carlos" in smelled like mercenaries to her. Maybe they were security guys, maybe the whole thing was political. But drugs and politics to often went hand in hand in Central America. She's seen it in Panamá, and Nicaragua, too.

Now she had a patient who was either hallucinating or having flashbacks, whose blood pressure was too high and who had been drugged. Maybe it was some kind of bush poison, or maybe slow poisoning from over-ingestion of hallucinogens. She didn't really know. Bush drugs were not her specialty; today everything was refined and chemical—and identifiable. Normally, hallucinogens could not be ingested over long periods, the body rejected them. But whatever combination of junk this poor man had been fed, he was spiraling inexorably downward, out of her grasp.

As a doctor, she knew there was little you could do for a patient who'd given up the will to live, and this man had lost it. She knew it, could see it in his eyes, though he wasn't talking. Except for one whispered word: *"aguila"*. She had heard him say this with such heart-breaking sadness, it pierced her to the core. They knew from the intravascular ultra-sound that he had had a heart attack. There was the stent to prove it. She thought his age was correctly listed as 72 years old. She sensed that he was ready to die.

The one who called himself Gerry was pathetic with his black muscle T-shirt over all that pumped flesh. Knowing about the range of human vulnerability, she felt sorry for him. Given the circumstances, she would never let him know it, however. Gerry was the type of man who would use whatever it took to empower himself, and women would be his easiest and most vulnerable target. There were plenty of women, Louise Sands knew, who would be swept away by a man like Gerry Velasquez.

The patient's breathing was shallow, his heartbeat slowing. She turned to Gerry, ever present in the lounge chair near the bed, legs extended straight out, thumbs twiddling over his crotch, looking at her intently.

"What's his real name?" Dra. Sands, asked. "I'd like to know."

Gerry smiled. "His name's on the chart, doc. Didn't ya see?"

She said, "I saw what you told admissions to put on the form."

"Well," Gerry said, enjoying himself. "If you want to get a date with him later, after he's cured, I can arrange it myself."

She almost reacted to that, but caught herself. "You have a very sick man here. I hope you realize that." She'd tried to contact the referring physician, but there had been no reply on the cell phone number she'd been given. It rang and rang, she'd tried half a dozen times, and nothing. She couldn't even leave a message.

The man known as Carlos began wheezing, hyperventilating, and in minutes was having what appeared to be a massive coronary. Dra. Sands rushed to the bed, and leaned on the red button calling "stat" though the intercom. In the space of less than a minute, the room was full of equipment and people all focused on saving the man called Carlos Mendez.

The patient was lost.

This was no surprise whatever to the doctor who had inexplicably left the room soon after her patient flat-lined. In the confusion, even Gerry didn't notice her absence.

What she didn't want to happen now was to lose the one link to her patient's real family. Maybe he was a kidnap victim. Maybe he was a politician from some other country. All she knew was that "Gerry" had some questions to answer, and she'd make damn sure he did. She had her own friends in Panamá, had even dated one of the President's cousins who just happened to be best friends with the police chief of Panamá City. They had one padded room at the clinic, fortunately little used, for restraining out-of-control clients. Happily the clinic also had a top-notch security team to protect the anonymity of its wealthy and famous clients. These men, mostly ex-Army, were only too glad to see some action in the peaceful days of post-Noriega Panamá.

They came with guns drawn, handcuffed Gerry and Larry, and put them into the padded cell until the police could arrive. These men had brought a dying man to her clinic, and she wanted some answers. If they were truly innocent, they had nothing to fear. She watched Gerry pacing back and forth like a panther in a cage. If he was ever released, he'd probably come gunning for her. She was sure of it.

However, Louise Sands was a woman who'd committed many courageous acts in her life, not the least of which was recovering from her own heroin addiction. The Gerry Velásquezes of this world didn't worry her much. She went back to her former patient's room to see what she could find. They'd already wheeled Sr. Mendez out under a sheet, though the air was still charged with the banging molecules of trying to save him. There was surprisingly little in the room, a smooth, hard case by the bed that turned out to contain sunglasses. A cylindrical case in the closet which was locked. A duffel bag stuffed into the corner which had some white uniforms on top which she dragged out, because she'd gotten the scent of it before she even saw it.

Strange that. Average people came regularly into contact with one of the biggest germ carriers of all, and didn't even think about it. They touched it, sweated on it, held it out with love, and clutched it in fear. And that is why, Dra. Sands thought, money had such a distinctive smell. The unexpected thrill of finding so much of it, filled her with a feeling of vindication. Her instincts had been right.

Sr. Mendez had died, and she had a strong feeling this money was his estate—maybe only a part of it—and was definitely not the property of the two goons locked in the padded cell. She'd find the owner of this money (hopefully a worthy widow and not the some drug cartel) and make sure it was returned. Maybe there'd be a reward and she could start that clinic for indigent drug addicts after all. In the meantime, she couldn't just leave it here moldering, and so she dragged the bag out of the closet, and across the room, and dragged it down the hall to the administrator's office, where they counted out two million dollars and stacked them in the safe.

Then she called the President's cousin.

CHAPTER 32

Outside the picture window Henry Grimes could see the leaves swirling in the wind. The oak leaves in his front yard always tended to turn brown rather than colorful, and this disappointed him. His little birch tree was looking pretty flashy, but with the increasingly high winds its small leaves were starting to float through the air like confetti.

He turned the TV on to the local news, and there was that silly weatherman again with that dumb-ass smile on his face. Did he think the storm was entertaining, or what? Natalie now, she was something else. He loved watching her read the news, which is how he got stuck with Dicky Doo.

Anyway, he was saying that tomorrow there'd be a front heading down the coast from Maine. High winds. Read that: Full blown nor'easter. There, he finally managed to say it. He finally got it out. A classic nor'easter with gusts up to sixty miles per hour. That was a good blow. Not as bad as some, but a good one. Better check the supplies, now he was doing Margaret's job as well as his own.

The storm windows were up, at least. And they could all kiss the fall foliage good-bye. He poured himself his third cup of black coffee, Chock Full O'Nuts. He'd drunk the same brand for his whole married life, and was still drinking it, though he'd switched to de-caf now. Doctor's orders.

He stared out the back window over the sink, watching birds scurrying into the bird feeders, and thought he'd better dig out the plywood sheets to cover the picture window. The thing would cost a fortune to replace if a branch whacked it. The rest of the windows he'd criss-cross with silver tape.

Some people didn't give a darn about their property and were clueless about New England weather. Those Parkers, for example. During one of the blizzards, Carol Ann came over to borrow in succession: butter, sugar, flour, and what really got Henry, a bottle of booze! Of course, they made up a big basket full of stuff afterwards and Carol Ann lugged it over. The husband was obviously too proud to come begging and too much of a coward to come and say thank you in person. Still, he couldn't fathom how some people could be so unprepared with a storm building around them.

The cars in their driveway still hadn't budged. What was it, four days now, or five? Unless they had slipped out for ten minutes and he hadn't noticed. He'd seen the red flag up on the mailbox earlier, so somebody was sending out mail. Henry suddenly remembered something else strange at the Parker residence and it caused him to ponder. The little yipping dogs, Pansy and Daisy? Little white fluffy dogs, not really like dogs at all. He hadn't seen them running, barking, peeing or digging up anything over there in days. Well, he'd just go over there later to check and see if they needed something from the Stop and Shop. Maybe they needed a hand buttoning up for the storm. Didn't do to be un-neighborly these days. You never knew when you might need a neighbor yourself.

***

Matti lay on the bed wrapped in a pareo, letting her mind float free. Ramón, she thought, God help you if you're lying. You are on top of the Maitlin hit parade. Get ready.

Just after noon Alma called upstairs to her, but when she opened the door Ramón himself was standing there. He smiled at her, and stepped into her room, closing the door after him.

"You smell good," he said. He gave her a quick kiss on the cheek. "Did you call your office?'

"I did."

"Well, you don't seem very happy," he said. She pulled the pareo tighter around her and looked at him.

"Sit down," she said. "We need to talk." He sat on the little metal chair near the desk.

"What's going on?" he asked. "What's the matter?"

"Plenty, between you and me. I need some answers, Ramón, and I'll tell you now I'm in no mood for any bullshit."

"What?"

"Lies, Ramón. Fucking lies."

"Please....spare me the pretty language," he said, holding up his hands. She actually reached over and swatted at them. The thought of his betrayal, after all they'd been through, made her feel like she was married to Adrian all over again.

She crossed her arms firmly across her chest and began. "There's been something nagging at me since we started on this little adventure, and finally I figured out what it is." She took a deep breath and plunged in. "What were you doing in Boston, Ramón? Meeting me at Richard's house, socializing with a man who you claim is a jealous adopted brother? What in fact were you doing in Boston when your father had just been kidnapped and might be dead or dying?"

Ramón said calmly, "Well, I suppose I shouldn't be surprised. You're very low on trust, Matti. But my reason for being in Boston is none of your business."

"None of my business! You are the largest beneficiary of your father's estate, Ramón. You have more to gain than anybody, both if the ransom is paid and if he dies. You stand to gain four million dollars, in fact. Which is a damn good motive for kidnapping and murder."

Ramón raised his eyebrows, and then began laughing. He took out a cigarette and lit it—the first time she'd seen him smoke. "You think I'd kill my own father for money?"

"It wouldn't be the first time someone did such a thing."

"And then what? Richard and I would divvy up the proceeds?" He took a drag on his cigarette. "And about this dinner party. You feel it implicates me, but don't forget Matilda, you were there too. Does that make you guilty as well?"

"I don't have an intimate relationship with Richard. I'm not Richard's brother or adopted brother, whatever you call yourselves. I was merely *invited* to a party which I was led to believe by Richard was a social gathering. Then he seated me next to you and the whole thing feels like a set-up."

"Yes, I can see how you'd think that," Ramón said. He looked distracted now. "I think now I finally understand why Richard called me just after Papi was first missing. He expressed shock and concern, and wanted to know all the details. I thought to myself—how did he find out so fast?"

"He did?"

"Yes. Didn't I mention that? It seemed innocent at the time and was very welcome. A brotherly act."

"So why did you go to Boston, brotherly love?" She still had to be convinced.

"Not exactly." Ramón threw the last of his cigarette out the window pausing for moment before deciding to continue. He took a deep breath. "I went to see Carol Ann. She called me too, just after Richard had. She told me how unhappy she was with Richard. He'd been acting more and more strangely, she said. Complaining about a pain in his stomach that no CAT scan, or X-ray or MRI could find. The doctors all said it was psychosomatic. She was worried more about the 'psycho' part."

"Did Richard know you'd spoken to her?"

"No, I don't think so. I told him I needed to come to Boston anyway and meet with Atlas's attorney about the policy. See what help they could give us with the investigation. Richard thought it was a great idea. He said he'd set it up himself."

"And so you flew all those miles. Left the business, and your missing father to check on Carol Ann's welfare?" Matti asked.

"Remember I only went to Boston for the weekend. I flew back on Monday. An exhausting trip, I admit. But Carol Ann was like a sister to me, Matti. I'd do anything for her. We've know each other for many years."

"A sister?" Matti asked, for she suspected something else. At the dinner in Cohasset, Carol Ann could hardly take her eyes off Ramón's face.

Ramón hesitated. "We did have an involvement, many years ago. One Christmas. I flew down to Panamá for the holiday. Carol Ann was so depressed; she'd just had a miscarriage. Richard was in a hateful mood. She just seemed desperate for some attention…and well, I gave her the affection she was craving."

"Did you notice any change in Richard when you saw him in Boston?" No point in belaboring the relationship with Carol Ann. It was an obvious source of embarrassment to him.

"No, honestly he seemed the same. Just smiling away with this big wall up that no one could penetrate. Or least I couldn't. Richard always seemed…ill at ease, I guess is the best way to describe it. If we had five minutes alone, he'd leave the room, walk the dogs, make an urgent phone call. Maybe he was finalizing all the arrangements of the kidnapping. I still can't believe he'd do such a thing. Richard was like my father's son, though he was never officially adopted."

"But was money his only motive?" Matti persisted. "It seems like he wanted to get back at you, and back at Papi. A grudge kidnapping."

"I've been thinking about this ever since we left the Teribe, and this is my theory. Richard's first thought *was* maybe to kill Papi. I'd get a big life insurance payout, and he'd think I would wanted to return to Florida. He could then take over as head of Frutas Tropicales. It was his greatest ambition to return to Panamá."

Ramón looked out the window and Matti watched him piecing it together in his mind. "His fantasy, I guess, was to find vindication at the helm of the business, a place reserved for me. He knows the business too. Hell, he's worked in it longer than I have!" He told her the history of Richard and Frutas Tropicales.

Matti said, "He told me he knew the area, not that he worked in your family's business. And you thought Worldwide Produce was involved."

"Well, I'm not sure how they fit in, but I still feel they do, somehow. Maybe we'll never know."

Matti continued, "Let's get back to Richard. If we follow your theory, Richard kidnapped Papi so you could get the life insurance to lure you away from running the company. When you came to Boston, he saw your determination to stay at the helm. Maybe then he figured he'd at least get a ransom payment out of it?"

"Maybe. But it sounds pretty complicated," Ramón told her.

"I'm sure Richard wanted to facilitate the handling of the claim from the beginning. He really pressed me to settle quickly and probably hoped that by introducing us, the process could be sped up."

They both gazed at the bright bloom of bougainvillea at the window, and Matti noted for the first time its long, sharp thorns.

"He also knows," Matti continued, "all the reasons that claims like this are denied. He knew that for you to collect the life insurance quickly the body had to be discovered."

"Maybe he lost heart," Ramón said, a dim sort of hope in his eyes. "Maybe he simply didn't have the nerve to go through with it and decided to kidnap him and leave him alive, rather than murder him."

"Maybe," Matti said, gently. "But we still need to find out who hired who. Maybe Worldwide hired Richard to implement the whole kidnapping/ransom/murder scenario. Maybe they found him more tractable than you. With the family Cardozo out of the way they could deal with Richard directly."

Ramón looked weary. "I wonder if we'll ever find all the answers. Until Richard is investigated and the kidnappers shaken down, my main concern is my father. I'm afraid all this may have been too much for him." He stood up. "And now you suspect me."

Matti said, "I can't honestly say I find much credibility in you as a suspect, Ramón. Besides, why would you have gone up the Teribe to find your father if you had hidden him there? You would have sent us all on a false trail."

"Does that mean I'm free to go home and have a shower?"

"You're not under house arrest."

He smiled at her. "Let's get together later. See what more ideas we can come up with." He started to walk out the door, when she called to him.

"Ramón," she said.

"Yes, Matilda?" A quasi-stern tone.

"It's my fault for not asking about the dinner at Richard's before. I'm sorry I pounced."

"Don't mention it," he said, and winked at her.

Matti watched him through the window as he walked across Alma's front lawn to his car. She wanted to see if he could pick up the fact that she was watching him, a simple entertainment to test her telepathic abilities.

Instead, she saw Boli drive up in his police vehicle, park and nearly fall out the door. Immediately her heart picked up a beat. There was news, but from the look of his expression, it wasn't good.

"*Hijo, hijo,*" Boli cried, his voice projecting easily to Matti's window. "*Sientate, sientate. Dios mio!*"

Matti rushed out the door and into the garden in time to hear Boli say, more quietly than she'd thought him capable: "*Esta muerto, mi vida.* They found him in a clinic in Panamá. The doctor said it was a heart attack. Nuthin' they could do to save him."

Ramón leaned his head into the older man's shoulder. Matti put her arm around Ramón's waist and held him too. He broke down as he got the reality of it. They had tried so hard—but it hadn't been enough.

Alma came out and joined their circle, all of them holding each other. After a few moments, Ramón pulled himself up. "Where is he? I want to go to him now."

"Then we must go to Panamá, *hijo,*" Boli said. Matti had never seen the jovial man so serious.

"We'll go in the Frutas Tropicales plane," Ramón said. "It is a four-seater. There's room for you, Matti, if you want to come."

"Of course," she looked at him sadly. They both knew that her job wasn't over. That she still needed to finish her job as an insurance investigator and that meant a death certificate.

"They found those two. *Los hijos de putas*," Boli added with such venom, she almost missed the point. She could see Boli as the military man he'd once been: precise and deadly, not kidding with the prisoners.

"Gerry and Larry?" she asked, astounded. "They *captured* them?"

"*Exactamente.*" Boli affirmed, all flamboyance gone. "Some woman doctor got 'em locked up in a padded cell. They're Americans, so they gotta stay there 'til the officials at the American Embassy decide what to do. Better for their own protection." A look of rage cast a dark shadow over his normally sunny features.

"A padded cell," Matti mused, and when she looked up, she saw Ramón a tiny crack of a smile on his face. "Perfect."

"Let's get down there," Ramón said. "I need to get home and tell my mother and Dolores what's happened."

Matti nodded, glad she didn't have to go with him. She went up to her room to change clothes, grab her suitcase, and check out of the Hotel Mariposa once more.

CHAPTER 33

Let's go," he said, strapping himself in. "Dolores was better than I thought she'd be. I think she was expecting the worst. She'll broadcast a message to all FT employees on the radio in a little while. There'll be five minutes of silence in the banana fields." He rubbed his nose with the back of his hand, and they were quickly aloft.

Mellow golden rays of late afternoon filled the small cabin, and Matti looked out the window at the miles and miles of bananas below. What a visionary Papi Cardozo had been. A Cuban immigrant who'd come to Panamá as a young man and built an empire in the middle of a tropical jungle.

She normally loved the tropics, but was looking forward to getting home to some crisp fall weather. The trees would be coming into their color and this case would be behind her—except, she imagined, for testifying at Richard's trial. She reassured herself she'd get a clean bill of health from Dr. Smart. Maybe she and Sam would take a couple of days off and drive up to Ogunquit to have dinner somewhere in Perkins Cove. Cuddle up in one of the inns that was open off-season along the hauntingly beautiful coast of Maine. She wondered if this was pure fantasy. Since their lunch, she hadn't talked to Sam at all about his personal life. Had he really left his wife and moved into his city condo? There was so much she wanted to know.

"What are you thinking about?" Ramón asked her.

"Oh, nothing in particular," she lied.

"You look happy," he said. "You must be thinking of going home."

As the came closer to Panamá City, the Panamá Canal came into view, yet another feat of engineering and vision. In the distance, Punta Paitilla and its gleaming high rises made her feel like she was landing in Miami.

Boli talked by radio to the people who be involved in organizing Papi's funeral. Thousands of people would attend, he said. It would be like the burial of a head of state. An event to be remembered and recounted for years to come.

***

Henry Grimes sat in the living room all prepared for the pending storm. He had his tunafish on wheat in front of the TV and the lamp on. It was only just coming up to one o'clock, but the plywood covering over the picture window and the darkening sky made it seem more like early evening.

He thought: I'll skip the nap. Storm building fast now. Get over to the Parker's, see if I can lend a hand.

He put his dish and glass in the sink and buttoned up his cardigan. He'd have to make a quick dash to the store for milk, coffee and bread. Maybe a pint of that Cherry Garcia ice cream they made up in Vermont. The freezer had plenty of chicken and vegetables. No more beef since the time a piece got lodged in his throat at Laredo's and they had to do a Heimlich maneuver on him in front of everybody. The salad, he reckoned, could wait til next summer. He was strictly a frozen peas and green beans man from mid-September until the local farmstands opened again and he could buy fresh tomatoes, sweet corn so tender and juicy it plucked at your heartstrings. Too bad summer was over.

He looked carefully both ways for oncoming traffic. This was one of the backroads all the commuters used to get to the Hingham exit and into Boston. Thank God he was retired. Thirty-two years at the Fore River Shipyard as a foreman had been enough for him.

He looked up at the Parker's driveway which went slightly uphill. It was pretty house since they fixed it up, they weren't in the best Cohasset neighborhood to be honest. The town had this fancy pants reputation, which is why, he thought, the Parkers bought this house in the first place. They'd had the driveway sealed twice, so it had that glossy look. Smoke still curled out of the fireplace, so somebody had to be in there, adding logs.

Hmmm.

He reached the crest of the drive where it curved around and walked to the front door. At the side was a covered parking space for two cars, and there they both sat looking dusty, leaves blown all around them.

Henry Grimes took in the cars, the leaves piled into the entry against the fancy mullioned door, and had a strong urge to turn and rush back home. The wind was building now, violently tossing the treetops. By five o'clock it would be a full-blown nor'easter, then the branches would start to crack and fly, trees would fall, icy needles of rain and fallen leaves would combine to make the roads lethally slippery. Why not just go back down the hill, get in his Dodge and drive up to the supermarket? What was he thinking coming up here? These kids should be checkin' up on *him*, seeing if *he* needed anything instead of the other way around.

Standing there in front of the door he had just decided *not* to ring the bell when he heard the music. Carol Ann, he knew, loved the opera, those big bulky tenors. He had listened when the windows were open in the summer.

But this wasn't a record.

Someone was playing the piano, though it sounded more like banging than playing. With the wind it was hard to hear. He moved around to the side of the house, where the big bushes grew in close to the walls. He'd hinted to Carol Ann awhile back that she should prune them. They'd rot the siding if she wasn't careful.

He slid between the bushes and the house. Was he a prying old fart, or what? Margaret would turn over in her grave if she could see him peeking in the neighbors' windows. But he couldn't help himself, like he was meant to do this, though he couldn't explain why.

He edged up to where the music was coming from and peeked inside. It was a quick peek, but he saw that it *was* piano playing. The husband, Richard, sitting there banging away. Sounded like some kid's music. He snuck another look. No worry about Richard seeing him, he was completely engrossed. Henry noticed a glass of some gold liquid on the piano ledge— whiskey? The man didn't look plastered, but had a red flushed face and faraway gaze that Henry didn't like one little bit.

The old man's heart picked up a few paces as he stood there, only half-concealed now trying to make sense of what he was seeing. Suddenly the wind hurled some of the bushes' branches at the window right next to where he was standing. This got Richard's attention, he stopped playing and looked at the window and straight at Henry, and Henry's eyes grew wide with the sight of him. Henry Grimes had seen his share of gore and craziness in World War II, and there was absolutely no doubt in his mind now. He was looking into the eyes of a madman, and the sight turned his blood to ice.

He never looked back, just pushed his way through the thicket of sculpted bushes and jogged as fast as his could down the grassy slope—the shortest distance between the Parkers' yard and his own front door. His peripheral vision took in the lack of traffic as he darted across the street, and when he was on his own front stoop and fumbling with his keys, only then did he turn back.

Richard was standing at his door, hands on his hips, looking at him.

Henry didn't need to see more. He went inside, bolted the door, and went directly to the back of his closet and got out his old hunting rifle. When he finally had it loaded, he double bolted all the doors and with shaking hands, sat down and called the police. Then he went down to the cellar, where he knew he could see the Parkers' house from one of the windows. He brought down his binoculars and rifle, and waited like he was in a bunker.

***

At the American Embassy, the ambassador received a transmission on the secure line that meant it was coming directly from the State Department.

Two Americans had been detained by the Panamanian authorities earlier in the day and remained under house arrest at a private clinic at the behest of the ambassador who needed to buy some time and find out who these men were. Maybe they were mercenaries. God forbid, they had some undercover assignment about which he knew nothing.

Southern Command had no record, however, of either Gerry Velásquez or Larry Knight, and it was making the ambassador nervous as hell. If these guys were CIA, he'd make sure the President himself knew the timing couldn't be worse.

The negotiations for the Latin drug center to be based in Panamá and staffed with American military personnel was a hard enough sell. If *La Prensa* ever got hold of this!

Years of effort had gone into making the reversion of the canal to Panamá a success. The American invasion of Panamá was less than two decades old. Development was well underway on the reverted canal areas. There were marinas now, boutiques, high-rise condo projects, shopping malls, and parks. Foreign investors were arriving in droves to buy chunks of Panamá's premier real estate and take advantage of the Panamá's offshore status, U.S.-dollar economy, and low taxes. The country had proven it was modern, sensitive to business, and most importantly, was politically stable. And now two bozos who claimed to be "consultants"—read that thugs for hire—were being held pending advice from Washington.

He'd sent their passports for verification, coded urgent, and the response had been given a Top Security designation. It read:

REF: GV & LK, REF Nº P0081
EX-SPECIAL SERVICES, NOW WORKING IN PRIVATE SECTOR. SEE HOW THEY LIKE THE SUITE AT LJP.

The ambassador sighed deeply. His liaison at the department loved to squeeze in a little humor now and then. They wouldn't say what these two were doing here, only that they were not sanctioned agents of the U.S. government. They were therefore subject to the laws and justice of Panamá. The LJP reference referred to La Joya Penitentiary, a theme park of Danté-esque hells which contained some of Panamá's toughest offenders.

The ambassador was approaching sixty and did not feel hale and hearty, though he groomed himself to look the part.

He saved the message, sitting back in his big chair in the plush office.

He sat like that for a few moments, stroking his nearly bald head, then took several deep breaths. Like a fighter getting ready to step into the ring, the ambassador readied himself by smiling. Someone had once told him people could *hear* if you were smiling or not. He lifted up the receiver with a flourish. In less than two minutes the head of the *Ministerio de Relaciones Exteriores* came on the line and the ambassador began chatting to her with an ease that was as ingrained as the swirl patterns on the wall-to-wall carpet.

A kidnapping and murder charge was serious enough, but there'd also been the small matter of two million dollars in a duffel bag. It sounded like a drug deal to him. These two men, Gerry Velásquez and Larry Knight, had really screwed up his public relations effort but good. Now it was up to him to make it right with his Panamanian counterparts.

He kept smiling and talking.

CHAPTER 34

Papi's mortality had brought her own into sharp relief. What if she wasn't okay? What if the PAP smear was positive? The trip to the clinic was the first free moment she'd had to think about it.

"Matti, where are you?" Ramón asked. "We're going to need to identify Gerry and Larry, you know. Both of us."

"Of course," she said.

"Matti, are you listening?" Ramón demanded. Even Boli turned around in the front seat and regarded her sternly.

"I'm fine," she told him. Fine, fine, fine, her brain repeated. She sat up straighter and tried to focus. "Are we almost there?"

"I will deal with Mr. Gerry and Mr. Larry," Boli told them. "Don't worry about a thing." The jovial Boli was nowhere in evidence, and Matti found that, in a strange way, she missed all his babble.

They showed their credentials and we allowed to enter a sealed driveway in front of a large, white stucco home with a red Spanish tile roof. The property was surrounded by an attractive wrought iron fence at least ten feet high that doubled as a security fence. Red palms grew in lavish displays on the sod lawn; ornamental shrubs framed an understated sign that said *Casa Esperanza* in gold script. Two uniformed guards stood at the door.

Boli jumped out of the car before it came to a complete stop, and flashed his badge at the security guys who led the way inside.

A petite woman with shining dark hair came forward to greet them, and introductions were made.

"I am Louise Sands," the woman told Matti, putting her doll-like hand into Matti's large one. Matti nodded taking in the English accent, but not wondering much about it. She kept having this vision of herself lying in South Shore Hospital, the doctors shaking their heads. *There's nothing more we can do, the chemo didn't take. Sorry...*

They followed the doctor down a hallway passing a little chapel, and several numbered rooms, before she stopped in front of one of them.

"Your father's in here, Ramón" she said. "Are you ready?"

Papi looked like the photograph on his dresser, but fast forwarded by a time machine. They'd moved his cheek muscles, Matti noticed, so that he had a small contented smile on his face. Ramón went immediately and knelt by the bed, grasped his father's hand and began kneading it. Boli shoved both forefingers into his eyes, his back quaking with emotion.

"Is there somewhere I can lie down for a few minutes?" Matti asked. Seeing Papi, whom they'd tried so hard to save, now dead under a sheet, made her feel like she'd keel over any minute. Dra. Louise led her from the room, down a corridor, and into a beautifully-furnished suite. She pointed at the bed, and took Matti's pulse. She took a thermos by the bed, and filled a glass with water.

"You're dehydrated," she said, leaning over Matti's eyes with a flashlight. "Were you sick lately?" she asked. Matti told her about the King's wild pork fest.

"You do look drawn, I must admit," Dra. Sand told her in her strong English accent.

"Does this mean I can't assault Gerry?" Matti asked.

"You *know* Gerry?" the doctor said, and cracked a smile.

"Unfortunately, yes," Matti said, smiling back. Thinking about Gerry and Larry in a padded room definitely cheered her up.

"He's quite a sample of manhood gone wrong," said the doctor.

Matti said, "You don't know the half of it."

"So it *was* a kidnapping," Dra. Sand said, exhaling at the end of Matti's abridged version of events.

"Yes."

"I'm glad we found the family before any link was lost." She paused, and grew thoughtful. "I was harboring a small hope...I want to start a clinic for homeless drug users here in the city."

Matti smiled. "And you were hoping there was a reward?"

"Why are you so happy all of a sudden?" the doctor asked.

"Because, Louise. Because," Matti told the petite dark-haired doctor. "Atlas *does* offer a reward policy. It's not a Bin laden bounty. But it's something. I'll have to check with the office, but if I'm not mistaken, that reward is yours."

"That is such *excellent* news." She stood back and regarded Matti, tiny hands clasping tiny hips. All that brain and savvy, Matti marveled, packed into a size four.

"Now, about you," the doctor said. "I want you to lie here and rest for awhile," she smiled. "I want you to try and drink two of these," she told Matti, swishing the jug of water. "I'll get Ramón to fill out all the forms to release Papi, and there'll be more to-do about the return of all that money. It should be a couple of hours at least. So just rest. I'm going to send in a big bowl of fruit and ice cream. You've been such a good girl, you deserve your sweets." Louise winked at her. "You need the sugar, so eat it—right?" *Roit?* "Is there anything else I can get you?"

"Actually, yes." Matti said. "There is something. I don't know if you can arrange it, or tell me where I might go." In spite of her desire to be straight forward, she suddenly felt reticent.

"All those nights in the jungle—like being dragged backward through a hedge," Louise said. "Don't I know it! We have a hair dresser on staff, Matti, or a maybe you'd like to try Magic Bob our in-house masseuse?"

"Magic Bob sounds wonderful. But actually what I need is a…ah…gynecologist." Matti told her the Dr. Smart story, and swore she could see Louise Sands' broken-glass irises shift and re-group into a different pattern as she considered the problem.

"Well, we don't have anyone on staff, let me see what I can do."

She insisted on Matti's spending the night at the clinic, which was as good as any good hotel and free of charge. A short while later she was back. A friend who was retired, Dr. Julio Contreras, would come by in the morning. They'd have the results by mid-day.

Matti slept out of pure relief, and awoke to find Ramón standing over her.

"Hello," he said. His eyes were red, but still he managed a smile.

"Hello," she said, beckoning him closer. She sat up and hugged him around the waist, looked him in the eyes.

"A full service insurance company?" he said, trying on a grin.

He sat down on the edge of the bed and she held his hand.

"We've been through a lot together," Matti said. She really wanted to kiss him now—he was an excellent kisser—but if they got started in this beautiful private suite, would either of them be able to stop?

He explained that his evening would be full. There were so many people to see, so many relatives right here in Panamá who needed to hear about Papi's death in person. Boli would come with him, like the uncle he claimed to be.

Matti told him she'd be staying the night here. She felt cozy and safe. She'd probably fly back to Boston the day after tomorrow.

Ramón was absorbed now by his father's death. For once they didn't talk about kidnappers, ransoms, or motives. They didn't talk about Richard, or their theories. Ramón's grief would ebb and flow, Matti knew. Action would give way to interstices of numbness. There would be denial, anger, and eventually peace and remembrances of love.

The ransom money would be on its way back to the bank in the morning, Ramón said. Boli had smoothed the way on that score. He was still well-connected with law enforcement personnel in the country's capital.

"And Gerry and Larry?" Matti asked. "Did you see them? Do I need to see them? They must have Gerry in a strait-jacket by now."

"There's no need of that," Ramón said. "Boli did that particular deed, identified them, I mean. I never saw him with such a big smile on his face when he told me they'd be spending the night locked up at La Joya prison."

***

A blue and white squad car pulled into the driveway of the Parkers' house, and two officers stepped out. Henry Grimes tensed to see what would happen next. He couldn't see if Richard came to the door or not, but the cops finally went in through the screen door. Moments later the younger one came running out again. His face was pale as fresh snow as he leaned over the hood of the car and vomited.

In less than ten minutes two more squad cars had pulled up. He hated like hell to go over there, but he knew he must.

The cops were conferring, the radios loud and alive as Henry came up the driveway.

"You Grimes?"

"Yep."

"The one who called in?"

"One and the same," Henry told them.

"Woman dead in there, Mr. Grimes. Looks like the husband killed her 'bout a week ago." As he said it, the back door came open and Henry Grimes smelled an odor that brought back memories from the Pacific front—and odor he'd hoped and prayed to God he'd never have to smell again.

"Jesus God. Young Carol Ann?" he said. "A little blonde?"

"Was that the wife here? Carol Ann." He looked down at his clipboard. "Parker? Is that right?"

"She was such a pretty little thing. Sweet as she could be. She never got her mums in...." Henry said, feeling dizzy all of a sudden. Dizzy and just plain gut sick.

"Close the GD door, will ya'!" the officer screamed to one of the others. "Smell's gonna kill us out here. Where's Billy? Tell him to get his ass outta there and wait for the crime scene people. Jesus H. Christ, these kids." Henry reckoned the officer in charge was no more than thirty-five himself, though he was big. Bigger than six two, with a hefty gut.

"Where's the husband? " Henry asked. "He was playing the piano...he..."

"Shot himself," the officer said, and gulped. In a small town like this, the worse the kid had ever probably seen was some roadkill. He was trying to beat it though, and hiked his gun belt up trying to look the part. Henry knew if he had seen the whole story in there, really had a good look, he'd probably have nightmares for at least a year. Maybe more.

Henry Grimes didn't want to hang around and see the waste of two young lives. He was too damn old, and brought back too many sad memories. Besides, the wind was whipping their asses out here and he needed to go back home and sit down. Maybe have a medicinal. That's what Margaret called a shot of brandy she claimed warmed the body after shock. And Henry needed a medicinal, oh yes. If only a medicinal could make you turn the clock back. He felt like he'd aged about a hundred years in the last few hours. Worse was, there was hardly anybody to call. Joe lived up in Keene now. His sister Ruthie was closest, but she was down on the North River.

Maybe Ruthie would invite him down there for a few days. Suddenly the idea of spending the night alone in this howling wind didn't have the same cozy feeling it had earlier. He knew they'd be hounding him. The cops, the reporters, all the looky-sees. They'd be pounding up the walk to see him: the eyewitness. That's what they'd call him, he could see it now.

Are you the one who called the cops, Mr. Grimes? What made you suspicious? Oh, I was just thinking about buying some ice cream, when I strolled over there and happened to see this maniac playing the piano through the window.

He saw a vision of Richard's face again, red-flushed; ashamed he looked, and crazy as a loon. But still the question loomed: Why? Why had Richard done it? He had a pretty house, a pretty wife, a good job, a nice car. So, what had driven him so far? Maybe, Henry Grimes told himself, if you hadn't been such an old Yankee codger you could have done something. Something to help. Times could be bad, God only knew, horrible things could happen to a man, but there was so much, always so much, to live for.

CHAPTER 35

B randon Howard went down one floor to Richard's office with Atlas's head of security in tow. Richard had locked his office and his secretary, Audrey, said he'd forgotten to leave his keys. She was a young, freckled- faced girl with a genius IQ and a degree in stastics from U. Mass. Brandon didn't want to raise any flags, so he simply smiled at her. Told her that he needed some files urgently. The security guy had the master keys, so that was alright.

Audrey had tons of data to put into the system, and she wanted to get it finished. When Richard came back tomorrow, she wanted to have everything ready for him.

Brandon told her he was looking for some files related to a case in Panamá. Audrey found this a little strange; it wasn't like Richard to hang onto files that other people needed. But she knew that there were many oddities at Atlas and didn't question either Brandon's authority or his motive. Richard hadn't come back from vacation yet. That was all she knew. And she missed him.

Audrey still lived at home with her mother, and had a rich fantasy life that revolved around Richard taking off his glasses and sweeping her into his arms. He often told her she was "indispensable". It was just a matter of time before he left his wife and they could run away to Bermuda, one of those hotels right on the beach.

Brandon could see that Audrey was engrossed in her work. He closed Richard's blinds, and the door, and got down to work. There was very little to investigate. Richard was meticulous in all the details of his life, Brandon saw. His desk looked barely used. The blotter was immaculate, the trays empty. The bookcase behind his desk revealed nothing but insurance manuals. There were no details of the man himself, his family or any personal detail. Brandon looked through the file drawers, and found roughly two dozen current files. These he took out and placed on top of the desk.

He tried the top desk drawer next. Locked. But in the top file drawer there'd been this small key, which he tried and it fit. Too easy, Brandon thought. He opened the shallow drawer, usually reserved for the ephemera of office life: pens, pencils, erasers, and the like. But in Richard's drawer, there were none of these things, only a plain white business envelope neatly addressed in Richard's hand to, Brandon Howard, Esq. The lawyer was about to pick it up, and then his lawyerly instinct kicked in and he decided to get Sam down here as a witness. He re-locked the desk drawer, picked up the files, and relocked the outer door.

"I'll keep these for the time being," he told Audrey lightly, tossing the keys in his hand.

"Sure Mr. Howard," the PA told him. Richard would be mad as hell to find out Mr. Howard had been snooping around in his office, but what the heck. He was a powerful guy, Atlas's corporate counsel. What was she supposed to do? Tell him no?

The lawyer turned around and came back to her desk, perching on the edge of it. Normally, Mr. Brandon wasn't so friendly. He had on the most beautiful socks, she noticed, silky gray ones that perfectly matched his suit. "Looks like there's a helluva storm building out there, Audrey," he said. The wind could be heard howling down State Street even behind these thick layers of insulated glass.

"Yes sir. I guess the northeaster's arrived."

"You live with your mother, don't you?" Brandon asked with charm. Too bad the woman hadn't seen clear to giving her daughter some orthodontic work, he thought. The kid was all teeth and gums.

"Yes. Yes I do."

"Well...why don't you call it a day and go on home? We'll probably lose power later anyway." He smiled, and she thought that Mr. Howard was really quite handsome in a swarthy kind of way, especially when he smiled.

"Well, we have the emergency generator, no problem," she told him. If she left now she'd have to listen to her mother babbling for a full six hours, instead of the usual three. Worse, she'd never have all these reports finished for Richard when he arrived tomorrow.

"Really sir, I'm fine," she said. Her grin reminded him of horses who snickered with their upper lips drawn back. Did Atlas's corporate dental cover orthodontia? He couldn't remember.

"No, I insist," Brandon told her. He wasn't going anywhere. "And don't worry about Richard, okay? Just shut down that computer now, and get your things. Trust me. This storm is going to get much worse before it gets better." He smiled again but Audrey got the impression there was more going on with him than his worry about her and the storm.

"Yes sir," she said. It quickly became apparent that he meant to wait and watch her shut down and pack up before he left. Was he going to escort her to the door too?

She suddenly became nervous. This was her first job. Had she screwed up? Maybe he was firing her, and she didn't know the protocol.

CHAPTER 36

On Wednesday Dr. Julio examined Matti and by noon, as promised, she had the results: a clean bill of health. "Whoopee!" said Matti. She gave Dr. Julio a kiss on the cheek. She was free to go, free to leave. Her body wasn't going to give her a death sentence after all.

She met with Louise, and got Papi's death certificate. They exchanged phone numbers and e-mails. Matti said she'd be in touch about the reward as soon as she could confirm it with Brandon back in Boston.

At Louise's suggestions, Matti booked into the Hotel Miramar for her last night in Panamá. She'd need to meet with Ramón again before she left; maybe they'd have a real dinner, this time.

It was a hot, sunny day with a pure blue sky and she was back in the world.

As soon as she was checked in, she'd call the office, tell Ashley the good news and hopefully, finally, talk to Sam. Maybe call Patrick and Brian as well. Then tomorrow, she'd fly back to Boston. It might be cold there now, and gray, and rainy there, but it was all hers. The tropics, perfect as a postcard, were starting to wear thin.

***

Brandon and Sam went down to Richard's office. Many staff had left early due to the increasing intensity of the storm. Together, they entered Richard's office. Sam watched as Brandon went to the desk and opened the top drawer.

He removed the thick business envelope, and showed the face to Sam. "A will?" Brandon said, hefting it.

"Or the Greatest Story-Ever-Told-That-No-One-Wanted-to-Hear," Sam said.

Brandon said, "We'll soon find out." He slit open the envelope with a letter opener he'd brought for the occasion.

They both gazed down as Brandon unfolded the thrice-folded sheets, the top of which read: Last Will and Testament.

"Bingo," said Brandon.

"Does this mean he's dead or just pretending to be? Maybe he decided to do a disappearing act."

Brandon scanned the document quickly. "Doesn't leave anything to the wife. Everything, listen to this: 'All my worldly possessions I hereby bequeath to *La Familia Cubana*.' The Cuban family? What the hell does that mean?"

"Nothing at all for his wife?" Sam asked. Finding this will in Richard's drawer made him feel like a spider was crawling up his back underneath his shirt.

"No," Brandon said and sat down with a thump in Richard's chair. *Tarump, tarump, tarump*, his fingers drummed on the desk. "Meaning this was all planned out. The leave of absence, the kidnapping. This envelope was only meant to be found in the event that things didn't go according to plan."

"Maybe he meant for it to go wrong so we could pay out to his favorite charity."

"God, the guy was as polished as a Gucci loafer. Could it be he was hard up and we didn't know it? We ran a credit check on him, and he came out squeaky clean. Who the hell is *La Familia Cubana*, anyway?"

"I think they're one of these organizations that help re-settle Cuban exiles," Sam said.

"Matti was right. This wasn't just about the money. This Cuban thing. There's gotta be some connection. Wasn't the owner of Frutas Tropicales Cuban-born too?"

Sam said, "Didn't Matti tell us the insured's son was of Cuban descent? Or was that Richard? Jesus. I can't believe we all sat there and listened to Richard tell us he knew the insured during the committee review. He really *was* trying to manipulate the claim."

Brandon continued to scan the documents as Sam recalled the details and possible scenarios that had led them to now be sitting in Richard's office reading his will.

"Uh-oh," Brandon said.

"More good news?"

Brandon peeled off more papers from the back of the sheaf, and they both stared down at it. "Life insurance," the lawyer said, but though the policy was standard issue for all Atlas employees. "I had a funny feeling that just got a helluva lot funnier."

"This a standard life insurance policy, right? So...."

"We gave him a policy without a suicide exclusion," Brandon said. "I remember now, he brought up the point specifically when we were reviewing his benefits package."

"You think Richard killed himself?" Sam asked. That espresso he'd drunk an hour ago was now tossing around in his stomach.

"So the Cuban whatevers, the *Familia* just got about a half mil richer." Brandon was never a big one on sentimentality and he'd never liked Richard. He looked at Sam.

"Don't even think about," said Sam. "There'll be copies, so forget it. We're not going there."

"Just a thought," Brandon said. "Just thinking."

"Well forget it." Sam repeated. "Richard was an Atlas insured, right? That's the way the cookie crumbles, as my father always said."

"I was only thinking," Brandon said not letting go, "of how criminal intent in a case like this could be used to nullify our contractual agreements with our former claims manager. And I mean nullify *all* our contractual responsibilities. This policy is a benefit we give to Atlas employees, a kind of bonus, not a *de facto* benefit. Management personnel don't pay even one cent for it."

"Okay...keep thinking by all means. But I'm going back up to the office to call the police. I think there's a good reason why Mrs. Parker is not included in Richard's will and why no one has answered the phone at their home for the past five days."

***

Matti shook out her white dress from the wreckage of her bag, called the maid to iron it, and went into the bathroom and began to get ready.

The dress was a simple sheathe with mandarin collar and cap sleeves that de-emphasized her square swimmer's shoulders and upper arms. A "man's shoulders" Lillian had always told her. And a square jaw that had gotten her into trouble on more than one occasion because without even trying she looked determined and willful.

She smiled at herself in the mirror. Lipsticked and mascaraed, she looked fully different than she had throughout the duration of this eventful trip. Even her hair was right tonight, falling in unhumidified dignity two inches from her shoulders. She affixed her silver earrings from Thailand. "Lucky" they spelled in Chinese, and maybe she would be, tonight.

The Miramar was perfect with its seaviews out across the bay and over the marina. In spite of his many commitments, Ramón had called to invite her for drinks and dinner. He sounded harried and out of sorts when they spoke, but she was looking forward to seeing him. After all they'd been through together, Ramón had become more than a client to her. How much more, she still wasn't sure.

Her calls to Atlas had been answered only by the automated system. On the fourth try, the switchboard operator finally picked up.

"Helene? Matti Maitlin, here."

"Matti, hi! How are you? I bet you want Ashley, right? Sorry, love, but she's gone, so has half the office. We're having a big storm here. Brandon's been sending everyone packing."

Matti looked out her window at the calm Panamanian sky, which now had fingers of orange and red and gold streaking through it. "Is Sam still there?" Just saying his name made her heart pick up a few paces.

"Somewhere, I think, but there's no answer in his office Muriel's gone too. Can I take a message?"

"Tell Sam I'll be back in Boston tomorrow; I've got an early morning flight. Tell him everything's fine."

"I will," said Helene, "take care." And rung off.

Matti took out her silky, tasseled wrap as a buffer against the air-conditioning, and went down to the fifth floor to the cocktail lounge called Sparkles, feeling equal to the name. It was just after six, outside in the atrium a grand piano was being played by a handsome Latino piano player, reminding Matti of meeting Ramón for the first time.

At last they'd have some time to get to know each other in a civilized atmosphere.

She walked into the lounge smiling in anticipation. Directly ahead of her sat Ramón, and with him, a stunning platinum blonde with ice blue eyes.

"Matti," Ramón said in a too-hearty voice. He jumped up to greet her, and whispered "sorry" in her ear when he kissed her cheek.

Then, with his typical Latin charm, "Matti Maitlin, may I present Lesley Bancroft. Lesley, Matti."

"Nice to meet you," Matti said, still stunned by this bombshell of a woman with her glistening hair and glacial eyes. Her lips formed into a perfect, glossy-pink pout.

"I'm still a Cardozo, the papers aren't signed *yet*, darling," the nearly/former Mrs. Cardozo told her husband. She smiled at Matti. "We're sharing a bit of this white wine. Will you join us?"

"Actually," Matti said, smiling back, "I think I'll have a martini, Bombay if they've got it." She could imagine Patrick standing up from his wing chair and applauding: *Bravo!*

Ramón hailed the waiter and ordered her drink. "Lesley heard the news and decided to fly down immediately."

"That was sweet of you," Matti said.

"I came on the first plane," Lesley said. "I was so fond of Papi. He and I were like *this*." She crossed her fingers and Matti caught a glimpse of a flawless three-carat diamond.

"And how are the arrangements coming, Ramón?" Matti asked. She sipped her drink and shifted down a gear, as if she'd hit a curve on the back roads in her old Corvette. *Don't hook in*, she told herself. *Don't even go there.*

"Fine," he said. "Fine."

"Ramón said you and he planned to have dinner tonight. To discuss Papi's insurance? I guess I'll be joining you…" Her laugh was girlish. "If I'm not *intruding*."

Ramón and Matti both turned and looked at her. "No," they said, together. Matti added, "Of course not." She realized at that moment she hadn't brought any of the paperwork down with her. She twirled the olives in her drink and thought about this.

"It's really become a much more straight-forward matter now than before." Could she excuse herself and go up seven floors and back down in the time it took for to "freshen up" in the ladies' room? She and Ramón exchanged glances, and Lesley caught them.

"It must be so *interesting*, your line of work, Matti," Lesley said, making it sound like people who worked for a living might be one small step above people who begged in the street. "All that travel, meeting so many interesting people…"

Matti let her eyes twinkle. "You have no idea."

Now it was Ramón's turn to laugh. "If you want to call the Rio Teribe interesting. Eating wild pork for breakfast. I thought the King would…"

"May I have some more wine, Ramón?" Lesley asked. "And maybe you should arrange for our table. It's been an awfully long day."

That just got a hell of a lot longer, Matti wanted to add.

"I'll handle payment of Papi's life insurance as soon as I get back," Matti said to Ramón. She plucked the olive out of her drink and ate it. "And if you don't mind, I think I'll pass on dinner. As Lesley said, it's been a long day, and I've got an early flight."

"Matti, please let me treat you to dinner…" Ramón's insistence seemed to further inflame some mechanism in Lesley's brain. The lids of her ice blue eyes blinked rapidly.

"It's been nice meeting you," Matti repeated to the other woman, shaking her hand and getting up. "Ramón, what can

I say? It's been nice meeting you too." They both laughed. He rose, took her extended hand and pulled her toward him. Gave her a meaningful kiss on the cheek.

"I'll be in touch."

"Take care," Matti said, and left Sparkles cocktail lounge. She walked to the elevator hungry but smiling. What curve could life possibly throw her next?

CHAPTER 37

Matti had an hour to kill at Miami Airport, so she called Lillian. Her birthday was two days away now. Better to call and reassure her then suffer the consequences later. Lillian loved her birthday. It was her one big moment a year to be the absolute center of attention, and God forbid if either of her children forgot it.

"Hi, Mom."

"Matti! Where *are* you?"

"Back in the U.S. Florida, actually."

"Florida! I thought you said you were going to Panamá?"

Don't say it, Matti told herself. *Don't hook in.*

"Mom," she said. "I said I was *back*. I'm on my way home. I have a *layover*." A woman at the next pay phone, about Matti's age seemed to be having a similar conversation. When she heard Matti's tone, she turned and pointed at her own receiver and nodded sympathetically.

"So you made it." Lillian said with relief but a little skepticism still in her voice.

Matti thought of her ordeal in the jungles of Panamá, the PAP threat come and gone, the near death experiences and a romance in ashes, then realized that her mother wasn't referring to her job but rather to the fact that she had made it back in time.

"Yes, Mom. I didn't miss your birthday. I'm still alive to take you to dinner."

"Oh honey, I didn't mean it like that. Now you sound angry."

"I'm tired. I thought I'd call." She took a breath. "Did you get some tickets to a show?"

Now it was Lillian's turn to pause. This was followed by giggling. "That's what I wanted to tell you."

"What's that?" Matti asked. *Now what?*

"Well the funniest thing happened. The other day I was just in the garden pulling up all the bulbs and dividing them, you know how I do? And this handsome man walked right up the walk!"

"No kidding." Lillian finding a man handsome? Now that was one for the books. "What did he want?"

"'Are you Mrs. Lillian Maitlin?' he asked, very serious. And I said I was. 'Well, Mrs. Maitlin,' he said, 'this is your lucky day. You have won a free year's subscription to *Arts and Leisure*. My favorite magazine. Do you believe it?"

"Wow," Matti said. She hadn't heard Lillian sound so happy or, what was the word?...*effervescent*—in years.

"And then we started to talk. We went to the same grammar school, but had different teachers. What a small world! The next thing I know he was sitting in the kitchen and I gave him some of my Virginia cookies, you know those crunchy ones you like? And we had coffee, and just talked and talked the whole morning away."

"Fantastic," Matti said, wondering if this guy was the real thing, or an ax murderer.

"And then we went out to dinner," she said. "Ralph drives a Cadillac. He used to be a salesman for a pharmaceutical company, and now he's retired. He just does these promotions for a PR firm to get him out of the house."

Matti thought: *Ralph?* "That's great. I'm so glad you have a new friend."

"Plus," he mother said undeterred. "*Plus* he's invited me out for my birthday. Do you mind if we don't do the show this weekend?"

"Don't worry about me," Matti said. "I'll be fine."

"Well, of course you will!" her mother said, missing the irony completely. "You're the most capable woman I know."

Now that was a new twist, thought Matti. "Try and squeeze me in for dinner some time next week, then."

"Of course I will!" Lillian sounded sixteen. "You're going to hit it off, you two. I just know it."

"Love you, Mom. And tell Ralph I said hi."

"Love you too, honey. Bye bye."

"Ralph." Matti repeated when she hung up the phone. The woman in the next phone booth, hung up too, and raised an eyebrow.

"I could've sworn you were talking to your mother," she said.

"I was. You?"

"Me too. Who's Ralph?"

"The new boyfriend." They both groaned.

"I thought Ralph Nader was the last Ralph on the face of the planet."

They giggled, then shrugged, two professional women living in a parallel universe colliding like electrons in Miami Airport, who now turned and went to their separate gates.

***

Logan Airport was still buffeted by winds. The storm had passed, but barely. She got in her car, and headed south. Signs were blown over, leaves stuck greasily to the pavement, and an eerie after-storm brightness filled the sky. She wouldn't go to the office now. It was Friday afternoon. She'd go home, call Sam when she got there, and organize her notes. Now that Lillian's birthday was taken care of, her weekend was free.

Would Sam come over? She wanted to see him, but was uneasy too. The Kisses seemed like they'd happened in some other lifetime. Would he be glad to see her or still upset that she'd openly defied him about coming back to Boston two days ago? He said "major policy changes". Maybe he'd be chaining her to a desk after all.

And Richard. Where was he now? Sitting behind bars, or in the office defending himself to Brandon? On a plane to Santiago with Carol Ann? Or heading down to Panamá for Papi's funeral?

The traffic wasn't bad, pre-rush hour semi-bliss through the Ted Williams Tunnel. Within an hour she was parked in the garage in Hull and turning the house key in the lock. A huge bunch of orange and yellow tiger lilies had been placed on the coffee table in the livingroom. "From Patrick and Brian," the note said, "With our un-dying gratitude. Come to dinner soon."

She drew back the drapes, and found the mail that Brian always insisted on bringing in whenever she was away.

She put on the kettle as she sorted through it. A Filene's Basement bill, the normal flyers, a birthday card without a stamp for Lillian (Patrick and Brian again), and a long white business envelope. She put a tea bag in her favorite china mug, poured in water, and opened it. There was no return address, but the handwriting was familiar. Disturbingly familiar.

Richard's.

Matilda,

It's over now. All over. By the time you get this, there will be nothing left: of me, of Carol Ann, Papi, or this case. There will only be the payouts, Atlas checks cut and sent. This is the only legacy I leave, sad but true.

Dolores called to tell me that Papi is dead. What a bitter end to a brilliant idea! We were in it together, you see. Not Papi and Ramón, but Papi and Richard. Papi and me! He always loved me more than Ramón. I know that now.

Years ago, Papi had a vision. He wanted to assassinate Castro. For years, he'd worked with a group of Cuban expatriates to achieve this goal. Some you met at my home that night. Many were living in countries in Central and South America.

He'd been raising money by shipping cocaine to Europe that was hidden inside the banana boxes and packed into refrigerated containers. It was perfect. The Colombians got the product directly into Banana Bay by small planes. From there it was packed into banana boxes and shipped off in refrigerated containers to France, Germany, the UK, three shipments a year and millions in profits. No questions, ever.

His goal was to raise fifty million and invade Cuba. That was the problem with the Bay of Pigs, he always said. If the U.S. government hadn't been involved, it wouldn't have turned out so badly. He was convinced it could be handled a different way, and be successful.

Then Julian Quintero, the overseer on Finca 8, got suspicious. He accused the Colombians of dealing drugs; he didn't know the whole story, of course. But the Colombians got nervous. They wanted a bigger cut of the action, that's what Papi told me. We spoke a few days before his disappearance. They were blackmailing him. Said if he didn't come up with a million in cash, they'd make it difficult for him. Frutas Tropicales was in trouble financially. Bananas imported from Central and South America were still being discriminated against. The WTO had allowed the quotas to stand. The market was being strangled.

Papi was desperate. He couldn't risk alienating the Columbians and he needed those shipments to keep going out. He would never use the funds he'd raised to invade Cuba to keep his business afloat. A Castro-free Cuba was his life's goal.

It was I who reminded him of the insurance, the K&R policy. He arranged for the Colombians to "kidnap" him. They could collect two million dollars against the policy, and then split it 50/50. After the ransom was paid, he could be "found" again. That was our plan. It seemed flawless.

But after they had Papi, the Colombians got greedy. They were connected to FARC and wanted to turn Papi over for a bigger cut of the cocaine action to Europe. Time dragged on and I was worried sick. They finally called to tell me FARC wasn't interested in a sick, old man and the original deal was on. Papi was still alive and they wanted the whole ransom—or else.

I found Gerry Velásquez on an Internet website. He flew to Boston, we met, and I hired him. Told him his payment would be two million dollars. He only needed to find Papi and keep him alive. The ransom—which the Colombians were sure to get from Ramón and which was guaranteed by Atlas—would be their fee. As mercenaries-for-hire they were happy to agree.

Velásquez and his partner found my beloved adopted father, got him into a private clinic somewhere in Panamá City and said his health was "stable". They had fulfilled their end of the bargain and were going to be flying out immediately. I even talked to Papi briefly on the phone.

Then Dolores called me with the news. Papi dead. All because of an insurance policy I sold him and a scheme to help make his dreams come true.

Well. The rest you'll know soon enough. My attorney will contact you regarding payout to La Familia Cubana, beneficiary of my own life insurance policy. La Familia Cubana is a group of Cuban exiles whose members are scattered throughout the world who assist other cubanos in getting resettled. It is a worthy cause, Matti—the only true one I've ever had. Please don't let me down.

Richard

Matti sat holding the letter, staring at the lilies, then read it again. Outside, the autumn sky was turning to dusk.

She reached for the phone and called Sam. He had to be there. Sam would know the truth by now, wouldn't he?

Muriel was away from her desk because it bypassed her extension and she was just about to give up, when Sam picked up himself. Flesh and blood and real voice, really there, finally.

"Sam," she said. "Is it true? Is Richard dead?" Somehow the normal courtesies no longer seemed to apply.

"Where are you?" So close now she wanted to pull him to her through the phone. "How did you know?"

"He sent me a letter. I'm in Hull. I just walked through the door."

"Yes. Yes, Matti, it's true. Can I come? Are you going to be there?"

"I'm here," she said. "I'll be waiting."

"I'm coming as soon as I can. The police are here. He's left notes for all of us. I'll be there as soon as I can." He was about to hang up.

"Sam," she told him with urgency. "Sam."

"What?"

"Drive carefully. For the love of God."

"I will," he said, and hung up the phone.

Matti walked into the bathroom, and looked at herself in the mirror, too stunned to cry. It was all such a waste, a sad pitiful waste of human life. The façade he'd worked so hard to fabricate could not be sustained. It had been his only defense—that and his deeply-held belief that Papi favored him over Ramón. Richard's suggestion that Papi "cash in" his K&R policy was the very thing that led to his demise, however. And how could Richard live with that? Knowing that he was in large part responsible for Papi's death?

She wandered through her condo tweaking dead leaves from plants, running her finger down the condensation on the big windows, but not seeing the view. She went to the bathroom, peeled off her clothes, had a long shower, and changed into a soft cotton sweat suit. She put on some lipstick, and sat down again on the sofa. The tears were lodged in her throat, and would not come.

At last she heard the quick blitz of the downstairs buzzer and Sam came through the door. He'd forgotten to take off his reading glasses, which were still perched on the end of his nose. He looked at her, his blue eyes electric. His strong arms came around her, and she buried her head into his neck, and smelled the faded scent of Armani.

They sat on the sofa. "This is getting to be a regular thing. Me and my crying jags, and you comforting me."

He rubbed her cheek with the back of his hand. "Do you have the letter?" He got up and walked to the window with it and read it shaking his head.

"I had no idea," Sam said.

"Me either."

"So, you went to dinner at his house, and met the insured's son?" She'd been preparing for this, but everything she'd wanted to say now sounded so lame. She nodded.

"I've been very, very worried about you," Sam said. There was also something in his voice that set off an alarm, a tiny bell that was a warning. It was the same sound she'd heard when she talked to him from Panamá.

"Is there something *you* want to tell *me?*" she asked.

"No," he said. But his voice was uncertain. She went over to him, and he gave her a hug that was a kind of buddy squeeze.

"Did he kill Carol Ann, as well?"

"He did. And the two dogs."

Matti felt her shoulders slump remembering the bubbly woman who'd been so proud of showing off the home she'd renovated and decorated herself. "I still can't believe Richard was capable of murder. Having Papi's kidnapping go wrong was one thing. But killing his wife in cold blood?"

"Apparently he believed she was having an on-going affair with the insured's son, what's his name?"

"Ramón," Matti said. *Jesus.* Now Ramón would also feel the weight of culpability. If he and Carol Ann had never become involved than maybe Richard would never had gone to such an extreme.

"Richard left a note spelling out his reasons, and that was the main one he gave," Sam said.

They went and sat back on the sofa. "Beautiful flowers," he said. "You had time to stop at the florist on your way home?"

"No, those are from my admirers."

"Plural?" he asked. He picked up the card and read it. "To a heart-massaging princess" he said. "Our undying gratitude. I'll have to meet Patrick and Brian, tell them the competition has arrived."

"Alright," Matti said. All of her sadness had transmuted into desire. She wanted to run away from all the hurt, let something else take its place.

"Matti?" Sam made her look at him. "I love you."

She looked into his eyes. "Prove it," she said, and they submerged into one another so they could both be set free.

***

It was over too soon. Night had fallen, the windows were dark. She lit the candles feeling lighter and happier than she had in days. The boulder of sadness that was going to roll off the cliff and crush her earlier, had been stopped at its edge .

"God, Matti. Why can't I ever stop with you?" He rolled off the sofa, went into the bathroom.

She lay back, arm over her head, and considered this. Sam sounded like a man who was trying to discipline himself against his feelings for her. Why?

He came back, and sat on the edge of the sofa, stroking her hair while looking distant and somewhat disturbed.

"What is it?" she asked him.

"I didn't move into the condo," Sam began. "I've decided to stay in Milton. At least until Devon is in high school. Judith has her own life, her own...agenda. She's ready to divorce me. She told me she's in love with someone else. But we both think it will be better for the kids if we wait two more years." He looked at her with fresh grief, willing her to understand.

She thought fleetingly of Adrian, the lies they had both told in order to keep his love addiction a secret. Was this better or worse? Knowing the truth, or not?

She thought of Ramón, how close she'd come to sleeping with him. Could she honestly say she was ready for another committed monogamous relationship herself?

"It will work out," Matti said, not knowing if it would or not. The news hurt her. She felt disappointed, but in light of everything else she'd faced in the last forty-eight hours, it was hard to see it as cataclysmic. "I'm not going anywhere."

He squeezed her tightly. "I don't want a relationship based on lies—and Judith knows how I feel. I can't kid myself about my love for you."

"I'm not sure if that makes it easier—but the truth is better." She smiled at him, and found it wasn't hard to do. "It will be hard sometimes."

"I know. And I promise I'll do my best to be straight with you."

"And I'll do the same," Matti promised him.

"And because I also refuse to sneak around, I'd like to take you to Saporito's for dinner."

She hugged him close. "Oh Sam, life is so complicated sometimes, isn't it?"

"And sanity is definitely the higher road." He held her under the chin and kissed her. "We may have a crazy side, but at least we're not homicidal."

She smiled at him. "Let's get in the shower."

"May I escort you?" he asked, proffering his arm.

EPILOGUE

R amón Cardozo, line one," Ashley told her on the intercom at nearly five o'clock on a chill November evening.

Matti looked through the plate glass window where the new claims manager, a woman named Jean Goring, was still pacing between the claims adjusters' desks with glossy dark hair and red lipstick that made her look like a tough broad—which she was. In Matti's book she was an improvement over Richard. She said what she meant, she owned only three suits, and she was alive. A big plus.

She picked up the phone. "Ramón, what a surprise."

"Matti. How wonderful to hear that strong American voice. I've missed you!"

Ramón—her almost Latin lover. It all seemed a little silly now her attraction to him. But it was a case closed, albeit after many days of paperwork, more committee meetings than she cared to think about, a surfeit of details to be recorded and kept for ten years in the archives in the basement. Not to mention dealing with Richard Paredes/Parker's post-mortem legacy.

Ramón Cardozo had found ten million dollars in a numbered account with instructions from his father on how he wanted the money spent. If he died before Castro did, they should donate all the money to *La Familia Cubana* who, in addition to their resettlement activities, should start a scholarship fund for students of Cuban descent.

Matti had also managed to convince Brandon of a reward to Louise Sands. He'd fought her on it, at first; the funds hadn't been Atlas funds but belonged to the family. It wasn't Atlas's two million she'd recovered, but the Cardozo family's money. Matti argued it would have *become* Atlas's money if Louise hadn't recovered it. They settled on a $25,000 reward instead of the full fifty.

And Ramón. He had his father's life insurance payout—also a negotiated settlement. Had Papi's death been accidental? The autopsy listed cause of death as myocardial infarction. This was not accidental in Brandon's book. This had to do with a "pre-existing condition", double bypass surgery and warranted a normal life payout of one million, he said, not a double indemnity payout of two for accidental death. Ramón's new lawyer stepped up and reminded Atlas's counsel of the mitigating circumstances, a kidnapping wherein his client had been drugged and held hostage in life-threatening circumstances. A client who had a Kidnap & Ransom rider on his life insurance policy. They'd settled on $1.5 million.

Now Ramón was calling two months later. He was in Boston he said. Was she free for dinner?

"Hmmm," Matti said, thinking about it. It was nearly Thanksgiving. Sam was busy with Judith and the kids. Lillian was inviting Ralph, and Bob was flying in from the west coast without Connie. Patrick and Brian were going to Maureen's.

"What are you doing in Boston?" she asked him, stalling for time while she made up her mind.

"Well, you're probably not going to believe this, but I've come to pay a visit to Worldwide Produce."

"You mean the Worldwide Produce extortionists who kidnapped your father?"

"Very funny."

"I thought you had a family tradition of hating that entire corporation."

"As it turns out, no, we didn't. It seems that some of transmissions we found on the fax machine in my father's study were *his* communication with *them*. It's uncanny, I know. But according to Bob Corcoran, the lawyer who's negotiating for them, my father had agreed in principal to a buy-out; he's even got the faxes to prove it. I guess Papi was tired of going it alone. Frutas Tropicales was having more problems than I knew."

"That must have been strange. Imagine being in the middle of negotiating a buy-out and the seller disappears. I guess your father thought he could still continue his special shipments to Europe either way."

"I think you're right. And I was right about something, too. It's the port they really wanted—not the plantation. I still have trouble believing my father never confided in me, but let's face it, there's a lot he never shared with me." They both paused and considered this. "Anyway, after his death 27% of his shares reverted to me. I now have 51% of FT shares; if Worldwide makes me a decent offer, I'm going to accept it."

"So why do they want Frutas Tropicales if they are having such problems in Europe?" Matti asked, genuinely curious.

"Like I said, it's principally the port they're interested in. The Frutas Tropicales deep-water port at Platanillo is something rare, and it's very centralized for them. They want to consolidate shipments from Panamá and Costa Rica, plan to construct railways linking all their farms, and build new superships to get their product to Europe. The whole area is exploding, and they can charge for the other ship traffic coming and going."

"Sounds like a plan," Matti said, laughing at the magnitude of such an undertaking.

"I'm glad I still have the power to *amuse* you," Ramón said, laughing his familiar light-hearted laugh, and Matti felt herself liking its sound.

"And Gerry and Larry?" she asked.

"Last I heard, they were still at La Joya Penitentiary learning some serious lessons in humility."

"I wonder how far Gerry's machismo will get him now." Matti said. "And Larry. I'm not sure if he had both oars in the water to begin with."

"You Americans and your analogies," Ramón laughed. "Now, Matti, stop stalling. You know I can protect you from the Gerrys and Larrys of this world. I proved it already, didn't I?"

"We can protect each other," Matti said, smiling. She took the suit jacket off the back of her chair and put it on.

*Cindy Cody is also the author of **Hubba Hubba**, a romantic comedy about one man's search for paradise, and **I Could Have Danced All Night**, a memoir about growing up in the fifties.*

***Banana Bay**, published in hardcover in 2004, hit the bestseller list south of Boston the same year.*

She lives in the Chiriqui highlands of Panama with her husband Paul and two dogs Elvis and Lucy.

For more information visit her website on www.cindycody.com

Made in the USA
Lexington, KY
08 December 2009